FOREST OF SHADOWS

WHISTLER IN THE WOODS

FOREST OF SHADOWS

WHISTLER IN THE WOODS

HOLLY KNIGHTLEY

Paperback: ISBN: 978-1-958761-58-8

eBook: ISBN: 9781958761571

For JD and the Leeds family

CONTENTS

CHAPTER ONE
A Victim of Fate

Pleasant Mills, New Jersey: Present Day

Uriah Leeds stood in front of his wife's grave as he did every day since he buried her nearly four months ago. It was twilight and an autumnal wind rushed in from the Atlantic, a storm was heading their way. The few leaves still left on the trees chattered nervously from high above him, his dark hair falling in wisps over his light blue eyes.

Uriah's fingertips traced Lilly's name over and over again on her headstone, not noticing the rain drops pitter-pattering on his shoulders. He went on tracing her name as if he divined something in doing so, the smooth granite headstone cold and unyielding under his touch. It served as the perfect metaphor for death. It wouldn't be long now, soon the reconstruction of Pleasant Mills Church would be complete, and he would no longer have to make up an excuse to visit Lilly where she lay buried six feet under the ground at Pleasant Mills Cemetery.

It seemed so long ago now, when he first came to Pleasant Mills as the new pastor right out of seminary school. He was so full of hope then, wanting to enrich the lives of his congregation. But his path was paved in death and that stain followed him. He was there as a replacement after the untimely deaths of two pastors, and after he took his place in the community more death would follow.

Then, as the wide-eyed, innocent pastor, looking to make his dent in the world, the thought of lying never would have crossed his mind, let alone to Trudy—his pregnant girlfriend. But he had, many times since then, lied to her with an ease that was as natural as breathing.

As innocent as it seemed to tell Trudy he was checking on the construction progress at the church, his excuses were lies. They were tears in his moral fabric, and the seam continued to fray with every day he came to the cemetery. He was a patchwork of lies. Lies he told others and lies he told himself.

Uriah had told Trudy when they buried Lilly, his past was over, that with the lowering of her casket, the covering of it with earth and tears, that he was in-kind burying the past and his connection to it. But he knew that was a lie. The past would never be over. He, the man she loved, was a shadow of the past—of a past she could never understand and a past he just came to comprehend.

Just a few months earlier, he'd been piecing together his shattered memories, to only find holes and gaps in every turn. But that had changed. His metamorphosis was complete, and he was a different man.

Uriah realized for the first time he wasn't a victim of some unlucky accident but a cog in the wheel. He was as much a part of the wrong in Pleasant Mills as Japhet Dean Leeds. He couldn't blame JD for his past crimes.

Uriah wasn't who he always believed himself to be. With each of the thirteen murders he'd consented to hundreds of years ago when he first sealed his contract with the Leeds devil, he got a little piece of himself back, and still believed himself innately good: a victim of a ruthless demon, a victim of impossible choices, a victim of fate. He had felt that in the beginning and clung to it. Even though Uriah knew he would've made the same deal with JD to save his son Joseph, none of it was really his fault. It was someone else's—his father's, his mother's, God's, for making him disfigured.

After Pleasant Mills Church burned to the ground, after Deborah was killed, after Tammy Handover died, after the bodies of all the murdered were put to rest in the ground, Uriah had a vision in the form of the dream that went on and on, filling all the nooks and crannies in his memory, plugging all the holes, connecting all the dots.

He remembered everything now. He remembered being a boy growing up disfigured and hated, his mother being whispered about as a witch. He remembered what it was like being poor living on the outskirts of town and how he sought solace in the words of Pastor Baker and God. He recalled with fondness how Lilly Baker was the only one besides his mother who was kind to him, the only one that didn't mock or shun him for having a cleft lip and a limp. Uriah recalled the faithless day he accidentally pushed Lilly into the lake when he lost his footing, and how she got cut. He recalled her on her death bed, a small child with hair like golden wheat and a face as white as snow. He recalled the Hanson brothers beating him up by the covered bridge, all the aches and pains he suffered at their rough hands. With vivid recollection, he remembered the smell of JD's cigarette as he offered him a chance to save Lilly and restore his health. Uriah felt renewed pride when he was the hero of the town for saving Lilly and was rewarded by being Pastor Baker's understudy. He recalled all of the bad things in his life: JD coming to collect Joseph, the deal he made with him to trade Joseph's life for thirteen lives for all of eternity, Lilly's death, Joseph's death, his mother's death, the Hanson brothers' deaths. All these memories he had pieces of, tiny segments of his past chopped up in his head, but now all of his memories were complete, and things didn't happen quite as he had thought they did in lieu of the absent puzzle pieces.

Uriah now saw things weren't so black and white. Good versus evil wasn't really a thing. The world was gray, and the new gray Uriah could lie, even kill. He had before and he knew he would again. That, he knew, was not his fault. It was in his blood. It was in his past. It was given to him by the God who he held so high in his heart.

Pleasant Mills, New Jersey: 1769

By the side of Batsto Lake a scuffle ensued. Uriah climbed on to Rupert Hanson, his penknife in his clenched fist. His son lay nearby, dead. His mother, also dead. The Hanson brothers bound his mother and son with rope and drowned them in the lake as witches. They wanted Uriah's confession. Wanted him to say he was a witch, and it was by that craft he infiltrated their town, beguiling everyone but them.

The storm picked up, whipping around the lake in a persistent howl. "Mercy," Rupert Hanson begged from under Uriah Leeds, Uriah's knife to his neck.

Jeffrey Hanson, ladened with injury, screamed in anguish trying to make it to his brother in time. "No! Don't!"

It was too late. Uriah dragged his blade across Rupert Hanson's neck, blood splattering across his face in a shower of red.

"No mercy for you, your family or this town. I have given enough. Leave it to the wrath of God, for it is written: *Vengeance is mine, I will repay, says the Lord.*"

Jeffrey now stood in front of Uriah, his brother's pistol pointed at him, much like Rupert had done moments ago. "You killed my brother."

Incredulously, Uriah looked down at the knife he still clenched in his hands covered in fresh, bright blood as if this nightmare was on repeat. Rupert had just said those very words to him.

"Jeff I . . . I am sorry." He glanced at Joseph and then back at Rupert's corpse. "Joseph is dead."

"He was never meant to get hurt," Jeffrey said, swaying on his feet. "He was only here to force a confession out of you. He was never supposed to be thrown in the lake," Jeffrey said, regret unmistakable in his voice.

"And my mother, what about her?!" Uriah shouted, grief consuming him.

Jeffrey shook his head. "I have to finish what Rupert started. I like you Pastor Leeds, I do, but something dark has clung to you and your family. I'm ending this tonight before anyone else gets hurt."

Jeffrey heard a voice in his ear, a woman's voice, sweet and kind as if her words were a lullaby.

"Come now, Jeffrey. Put the pistol down. You don't want to hurt anyone. You're a good boy. Remember what I told you when you were a baby."

"I'm a good boy," Jeffrey said robotically, answering the voice Uriah couldn't hear. "I must always be a good boy. Cross my heart and hope to die. For the moment my darkness grows, I will die."

The voice went on in the same soothing tone. "That's right, now put the gun down."

"I'm confused," Jeffrey admitted, thick, dark blood trickling down his nose, mingling with his blood covered face.

As Jeffrey lowered the gun, Uriah felt his contempt and hatred for Jeffrey and all of the Hansons grow inside of him like a hurricane building momentum over open water. It mattered not that Jeffrey was adopted. The Hanson family had taken everything he had left—His mother and his only son.

Uriah spoke to Jeffrey now as he did when he was at the church pulpit, with an unyielding confidence that made people stop and listen, that seemed to hypnotize. "*He will wipe away every tear from their eyes, and death shall be no more, neither shall there be mourning, nor crying, nor pain anymore, for the former things have passed away. For the wages of sin is death, but the free gift of God is eternal life in Christ Jesus our Lord. So it is not the will of my Father who is in heaven that one of these little ones should perish but 'mine'. Jesus said to 'me', I am the way, and the truth, and the life. No one comes to the Father except through me.* Now Jeffrey, turn your pistol on yourself and may you never know peace."

Jeffrey turned his brother's pistol on himself, placing the barrel of the gun in his mouth and pulled the trigger.

As Jeffrey took his last breath, Uriah heard the sound of gasping coming from behind him. He whipped his head to see his young son Joseph expelling water from his lungs.

Uriah itched the inside of his elbow where his bug bite from the summer still itched and oozed. He read his wife's name on her headstone, the sound of JD's cutlery on his wedding china as he carved up his wife's heart into bite size pieces, echoed in his ears with every breath. The past could never be buried for him.

JD may have preserved Lilly's body as a demented reminder of what he lost, but that was better than nothing and he was grateful. He needed her with him for always. Dead or alive, he needed her. Knowing his angel was entombed under his feet was torture. He wished she was back in her bedroom where he pretended, she was sleeping. He longed to touch her warm hand; her absence of a pulse didn't matter. He longed to kiss her soft lips; the absence of breath didn't matter. Nothing mattered but being with her and making good by her.

He had a score to settle before he could marry Trudy and start a new life. He knew then, if he was ever going to build a future with Trudy, he had to make right what was in his power to make right.

"Lilly, my sleeping darling, I've realized to beat evil, one has to be willing to perform evil acts." He knew now, he had murdered twice—Rupert Hanson and Jeffrey Hanson. Although Jeffrey Hanson didn't exactly die. He was his friend in this life as Jeffrey Lopez, the town mayor and loving family man, but Uriah, like Jeffrey, had a dark secret.

"Don't worry about my soul, it's already damned. I sold it to the Leeds devil a long time ago. But I feel purpose in doing God's work, and that will reinvigorate me. Besides, is an evil act really evil if it's done in the Lord's name?"

CHAPTER TWO
A Dream within a Dream

Jeffrey Lopez walked into his home office on autopilot, looking through the stack of mail in his hands, his eyes glancing over junk mail, when he suddenly stopped at a letter from his lawyer. He glanced over it as a nervous pit knotted up in his stomach. His lawyer hadn't mentioned he was sending him a letter.

Approaching his desk to get his letter opener, he became aware of a man sitting in his executive seat, which was pushed slightly away from the rich mahogany desk. Blood trickled down the side of the man's face in thick droplets like red syrup. His blond hair was encrusted with it and on the rug a gelatinous puddle of old blood amalgamated with each new red drop falling from the man's wound.

Jeffrey ran to him, dropping the mail on the floor. "Are you alright?!" he exclaimed, gripping his shoulders to turn him around. Jeffrey took a step back, sucking air as he did, his heartbeat moving into his head where it echoed. A large portion of the man's cheekbone had been blown away, by what he knew had to be a bullet. He scanned the room for a gun, finding nothing. However, he noticed the side of the man's face, not destroyed by the impact of the bullet, was also marred. Coagulated blood sat in an empty eye socket, the eye removed and missing. Jeffrey steadied himself on his desk, the surface slick with blood. "Oh God," he muttered, franticly wiping the blood on his pants. With trembling hands, he pulled out his cell and made the call to the one person he knew could help—Pearl Steele, Chief of Police and his close friend.

"Pearl it's me, I need you. Um, there's a dead man in my office. I think he was shot, but maybe more. I, uh, don't know who he is—I've never seen him before." Jeffrey's eyes went to the large window behind his desk to his Koi pond. Watching the large, graceful fish always calmed him down when he was anxious—and he was anxious, a million questions running through his head. There was something in the water amongst the large, brightly colored fish. "Pearl, call an ambulance, someone's face down in my Koi pond."

Hanging up, Jeffrey ran his hands down his thighs as if they were covered in blood again, his eyes glued to the man in his pond, his blond hair darkened by the water—another man he didn't know. Sirens wailed; the ambulance was in the driveway. "That was quick," he said gratefully, hurrying to the door. The doorway was darkened by a figure—by Japhet Dean Leeds. Little red rims encircled his irises, hinting at the demon hidden under his handsome face—the face they shared as twin brothers. "What's in the letter, Jeffrey?" JD asked.

Jeffrey's eyes darted to the floor where he'd dropped the mail, including the letter from his lawyer. "I don't know."

"Don't you think you should open it?"

"I can't now! Someone's in the pond, they may still be alive."

Jeffrey pushed past JD and out the front door. The ambulance's flashing red lights painted everything in the same scarlet hue. There was no sign of paramedics, yet there was a gurney and on it was a zipped body bag. Confused, Jeffrey went to it. "How did they get him out of the pond already," he muttered, unzipping it with trembling fingers. His eyes widened at the sight of blood seeping from the closed eyelids and mouth of Aiden Hanson— the little boy Zac's mother had adopted, and Uriah and Trudy had taken in after her murder. This wasn't right. Aiden was a little boy with dark hair, he wasn't the blond-haired man he saw floating face down in his Koi Pond from his office window.

"Do you know who did that to him?" Pearl asked from behind him. "Poor thing, someone cut out his eyes, tongue, and ears."

Jeffrey turned on his heels to the sound of Pearl's voice. Before he could react, detective Wes Weston spoke. "Oh he knows, Pearl. "Come on it's obvious, he did it. This is all his fault. Born bad. You can really pick 'em, Chief."

Normally Jeffrey would've lashed out at Weston, but he noticed a small red dot on his shirt that began to spread. "Wes," he said, pointing to his chest, "you're bleeding."

Wes ran a fingertip over the ever-growing stain and put his finger in his mouth. "So I am."

"Pearl, what's going on?" Jeffrey asked, in a hushed voice, pulling down the collar of her blazer at the sight of the purplish-blue bruise on her neck. "Who did this to you?!" She cocked her head, pushing her long, dark hair away from her shoulders, to reveal a bone protruding from her neck, distorting it but not breaking skin. "Oh God, no Pearl." Jeffrey ran his hands up and down Pearl's neck trying to smooth out the bulge. Her skin was cold under his touch. "I can fix this," Jeffrey said, his hands chafing her neck to no effect.

"Daddy."

Jeffrey looked down to see his twin girls, Alba and Maria. "Daddy, we don't want to die," Maria whimpered.

"You're not going to die," Jeffrey said, his arms wrapping around his daughters. "You have a cold, that's all."

Alba coughed. Blood dripped from the commissures of her small, pink lips onto the stuffed wolf she held to her chest. Scooping up the twins, Jeffrey shouted for the EMTs. "Some help here! My daughters need help." He went to the back of the ambulance, shifting the girls in his arms to pull open the door. Sammy was sitting in the back with an angry gash across his neck. His face was drained of color, highlighting his blood drenched torso.

"Sammy!" Jeffrey yelled.

"I told you Abby wanted to kill me."

That was right, Sammy had told his father his grandmother would try to kill him now that he came into his magic, like she had done with her own son who Sammy was named for and her brother, but Jeffery never thought Anita would actually hurt him.

Putting the twins down, Jeffrey leaped into the ambulance. Much like he did when he saw Pearl, he put his hands to his son's neck to no aid. He couldn't stop the bleeding. In fact, it had the opposite effect, blood gushed through his fingers. "Stop! Stop! Stop!"

Waking, his heart pounding in his chest like a drum, Jeffrey jumped out of bed and ran to Sammy's room and switched the light on. He rushed to his son's bedside; Sammy was safe and sound and asleep.

Fear and relief made Jeffrey unsteady. He put his hands on his knees, counting down from ten as his therapist had directed him to do when he was feeling out of control. He did this exercise three times before he was able to function. He checked his son again, to make sure he wasn't hurt. There was no sign of the cut on Sammy's neck, no sign of blood. He was fine. Shutting off the lights, Jeffrey went back to his own room.

He looked at his watch, it was almost midnight. He didn't mean to fall asleep, he meant to read for a little bit before going to his home office for some late-night number crunching. He stared at his cellphone on the nightstand for a few minutes, mulling over his dream, before he dialed Lindsey. He couldn't let it go. He had to check on the twins.

Life had been turned upside down since the church fire that landed Sammy in the hospital. While there, Sammy had a vivid nightmare. It was like Sammy's nightmare had played out in his own. Sammy had dreamed Anita, his grandmother, who since childhood he had lovingly called Abby when he couldn't pronounce abuela, came to murder him while he was defenseless.

Jeffrey had seen Sammy distressed over the last two years, but nothing could compare to his fear of Anita. Jeffrey had originally thought it was the morphine talking when his son begged him to keep Anita away from him, but Sammy had remained frightened after the drugs wore off. Sammy was convinced she would try to kill him for the magic that had recently awoken in him, like she had done to her brother, Enzo Serrano and had tried to do with Lindsey's younger brother, Samuel Cameron, before he darted into the woods to never be heard from again.

When it was time for Sammy to come home from the hospital, Jeffrey made the hard decision and told his mother-in-law she was no longer welcome in their home. He had made a promise to his son to keep him safe and he meant to keep it. Jeffrey wasn't completely unkind; he had offered to pay for an apartment for Anita or a flight ticket back to Spain. Anita was insulted and hurt, as was his wife, refusing anything from him. Jeffrey had not expected Lindsey to move out with her mother, taking the twins and Hugo with them to her sister Fran's house a few towns over. Even Zac and Mona abandoned ship. Mona, giving up on haunting Jesse Richards, had found a new purpose in protecting the twins and went where they went. Then there was the small business of Zac having a colossal crush on Mona. His heart compelled him to leave with Mona and the rest of the family, leaving Jeffrey and Sammy in the big house with the cat and dog.

"Jeffrey, it's late, is everything okay?" Lindsey asked, groggily.

"I'm just calling to check on the twins."

"They're fine. After you called, I tucked them into bed."

Jeffrey did his best to control his voice, but there was a hitch to it, he was sure Lindsey noticed. "How are they feeling?" How's Alba's fever?"

"It spiked again, but the Tylenol brought it down. Jeffrey, I already told you this."

"I know. I'm just making sure they're safe."

"They are. Like I said, they're asleep."

"Can you check?"

Lindsey took on a frustrated tone. "Jeffrey, you can't call me every night in the middle of the night. I need sleep. You're the reason the twins aren't at the house."

Anger spiked his pulse. "You know that's not true."

She sucked air.

He wasn't going to let it go. "You're not going to put this on me. Your son is petrified of your mother."

Lindsey raised her voice. "My mother loves Sammy. Why is it that you're not worried she'll hurt Alba and Maria?! My mother's right, you fed into Sammy's delusions and made things worse. If you sit him down and tell him everything is okay, he'll believe you, but you won't."

Jeffrey clenched his phone. "I'm not saying your mother would hurt him, but right now Sammy believes she would, and that's good enough for me. And as far as worrying about the twins, that's why I'm calling. You're the one who divided our family. You chose your mother over us. Why can't your mother just live with Fran, she's there already, and the kids and you come home?"

"Jeffrey, it's late, I'm tired. I'm going to bed."

"We have to talk about this eventually. This has been going on for too long."

"We finally agree on something. Good night, Jeffrey."

Jeffrey closed his eyes and counted down from ten again, focusing on his breaths. If only counting could solve his problems. He'd had the same conversation with Lindsey over a dozen times now and they all ended with her hanging up on him and him concentrating on his breathing like he was a yoga master. Counting wasn't going to cut it tonight. Jeffrey made his way downstairs, making a beeline for his office. In the top drawer of his desk, he kept a pack of cigarettes for emergencies. He grabbed them and went outside to the front porch.

He had sneaked a few cigarettes when the 'old Jesse' kidnapped Sammy but hadn't needed them since. Not even when his strange boyhood dream returned to him, the dream he now knew was a memory of his past, a past where he put a gun in his mouth and pulled the trigger, did he feel the need to light up. But tonight, he felt on edge, like he was on the brink of something—something bad.

He leaned against the house, sending hot air into the cold night sky in the shape of perfect, little clouds.

"You've had those in your desk for over a year. Better take one of mine," JD said, stepping out of the shadows.

Jeffrey raised his eyes to JD's voice. "I quit back in college. I just want to hold them."

"Suit yourself," JD said, taking a hand-rolled cigarette out from his cigarette case and lighting it. He stepped onto the porch, leaning on the house next to his brother.

Jeffrey glanced at him from the corner of his eye, taking in the sweet smell of his cigarette. "How did you know I'd be out here, right now at this very moment?"

"I didn't, not for sure, yet I do sense certain things." JD exhaled, turning to examine his brother's face. It was mostly in shadows but a faint light from inside the house highlighted the features of his nose and chin, the same features of his own attractive face. "You feel it don't you, that bond between us?" JD flicked the ash from his cigarette waiting for Jeffrey to say something. When nothing came, he went on. "I would describe it as belonging. I think you're what I've been missing my whole life. I thought it was Uriah, but it wasn't, it's you. I feel whole when I'm near you."

"Oh geez JD, knock it off with the creepy meant to be crap." Jeffrey said, running his hand down his face. "I'm gonna need that cigarette."

JD handed Jeffrey his case. He took one, letting JD light it for him.

"I just meant that we were separated all our lives and being back together feels right."

"Still f'n creepy," Jeffrey said, taking a drag. He hated that he felt it too. It was like a magnetic force was pulling them together. It had always been there. Jeffrey had felt it the day he went jogging at Batsto Village and first met JD face to face. It was this unseen energy between them, and he hated it—hated that he had no control over it—hated feeling helpless to the sense of belonging which JD had just mentioned. Worse than that, he felt indebted to JD for saving Sammy from the church fire. He'd never say it to him or to anyone, but Jeffrey was indebted to JD in a way he'd never been beholden to someone before.

He feared JD in an all-new way. Feared what this connection meant. When Jeffrey had emptied his blood pressure pills into his stomach as a means of suicide to free his magic from the Midwife's spell, he'd heard a voice in the cold, dark world he'd opened his eyes to. 'I am your father. Now join your brother and do wonderful, horrible things, for that is your destiny.' That voice was the only thing keeping his brotherly feelings for JD at bay. He didn't want to do wonderful, horrible things.

Jeffrey exhaled, pulling the cigarette out of his mouth to look at it. "That's pretty good. I see why you smoke these all the time."

JD nodded, examining his brother with keen interest. "Did you have the same dream again?"

Jeffrey took a quick drag, letting out a mouthful of smoke. "Almost the same. You were in it this time."

"What part did I play?"

"You asked me if I was going to open a letter."

JD stood perfectly still, letting his cigarette turn to gray ash as he thought. "What do you think it means?"

"Nothing, it's a nightmare."

They both took an exaggerated drag, looking like mirrored images of each other. "Maybe," JD said, thoughtfully.

Jeffrey crushed his cigarette under the heel of his sneaker. "I'm going in, it's freezing."

"Should I come in?"

"Your call. Sammy's asleep, so be quiet."

"Would it be so bad if Sammy knew we were friends."

"Friends is a strong word. We're brothers. Friendship is earned and you did kill a bunch of people I cared about. Not to mention, you took advantage of my wife and had my family kidnapped and were planning on murdering them. I don't think they'd take to kindly to us being friends."

"That's the past. I thought we were building our future?"

"Call it what you want JD, but I wouldn't expect an invite to Christmas."

JD put out his cigarette. "I said I was sorry."

"Actions speak louder than words. Sorry is not going to cut it."

"I'll show my loyalty then."

Jeffrey sighed. "Fine, show it by not killing anyone I know."

"I can do that," JD said, pointing to a small package and a stack of mail on the rocking chair near the front door.

"I didn't see this earlier. They must've delivered it late," Jeffrey said, picking up the mail and bringing it inside. He left the package in the foyer, it was for Sammy, and shuffled through the mail as they made their way to his office. Jeffrey stopped, recognizing the letter from his lawyer, the same letter from his nightmare. He flashed it to JD. "This was the letter I saw in my dream. The one you asked me if I was going to open."

"Hmm . . .," JD said, "that's strange."

Jeffrey went to his desk, happy to see no one was waiting for him dead in his chair. He pulled out his desk draw with too much gusto, giving away his anxiety. The sound of the letter opener slicing through paper filled his office. Jeffrey's face went slack, his entire body shrinking as he read the letter.

CHAPTER THREE
Lucifer and Ezekiel

Pleasant Mills, New Jersey: 1734

By candlelight a young woman of natural beauty sat in front of an oval mirror brushing her long hair. The lambent light danced over the red mane that traveled down her back like liquid fire. She wore a simple nightdress of eyelet lace that hung loosely around her delicate shoulders.

The candle flickered as if a breeze from an open window raced into the room attacking the flame, but the one window in the room remained closed, the shutters bolted from the inside. The candle succumbed to the vagrant wind leaving the woman in a darkness so complete in its infinity that not the faintest shadow was visible.

The woman didn't stir from her perch in front of the mirror adorned with hand carved dandelions, painted in soft gold tones. She continued to brush her hair, the rhythmic brushing evoking a grating noise that seemed to grow louder in the dark, boarded up room.

Suddenly and without provocation the candle lit, the flame a steady light in the dark. An amber glow highlighted the silhouettes of two cloaked men. They stood an arm's length behind the young woman. In unison, as if acting on cue, both men pulled back their hoods, their faces a bright spot in the gloom so often associated in Quaker life.

The taller of the two men, had raven-colored eyes with inky black hair. His hair fell in wisps like downy feathers, encircling a face as white as freshly fallen snow and as beautiful. The man's companion was just as handsome, but he had a golden complexion warmed by the sun to a coppery brown. His skin was as flawless as a Greek statue and so were the creamy yellow ringlets that curled down his back where two wings made from the purest white feathers sprawled out from his shoulder blades. On each plume there was a pale-blue eye, the same that warmed his countenance with celestial magnificence. The eyes of the men, and the ones peering out from each feather of the angel's wings, watched the woman brush her hair with a nervous excitement, their eyes raking over every minuscule gesture of her hand as the brush met her hair.

The woman, realizing she wasn't alone, smiled at her visitors through the looking glass before turning around.

"Deborah," the man with wings said. "You have called, and I have come." His voice was one of reverence and servitude. His eyes, all of them, darting to the grimoire opened on her vanity.

Deborah wasn't shaken to be in the presence of an angel, rather she was exalted by his visit. Her eyes fixated on only him as if the man with the raven eyes wasn't there. "I am ready to receive a true child of God."

"And I am bound to comply to one request and one request only," the angel said, closing the distance between them. Effortlessly, the angel pulled loose the tie keeping her nightgown closed. "A child of God, you shall receive.

The angel rose from Deborah's mattress, donning his robe he'd tossed to the bedside. The other man approached, his cloven hooves tapping the hardwood in an ominous rhythm.

The angel's wings fluttered, a sound like spring ringing from them. "I have done what you asked. I have inspired this woman to write a spell that would allow her to summon me and have complied to her wish. Let this be my last favor to you Lucifer."

"Ezekiel, remember our dream. We are close now. It had to be this way. To protect our progeny, this vessel has to think she is carrying a child of God and that she wanted this. Her power mixed with ours will create a new race of man. A race we alone will have dominion over."

Ezekiel nodded obediently.

Lucifer threw off his robe and took the form of the angel, his dark hair turning into sunny tendrils. His cloven hooves transformed to human feet with fleshy soles and perfect digits. Wings with eyes that twinkled in the candlelight stretched out behind him. He went to Deborah where she slept and kissed her awake. "We are not done here."

Sammy Lopez woke up panting, cold sweat dripping from his hair line in icy beads. He glanced around his dark room, making sure he was alone. He was. Just then, an uncontrollable desire not to be alone, to be with someone, anyone, washed over him. He wished Zac was there.

"You're not a child," he mumbled. Taking a deep breath, he closed his eyes and attempted to clear his mind. A sound indistinctly musical, something between a children's lullaby and a bird's song sounded in his ears. He knew it was the sound of the angel's wings fluttering. Then came the dragging thud of cloven feet.

He knew all too well what he saw in his nightmare—Deborah Smith Leeds conceiving her thirteenth child. And that child was the infamous Leeds Devil, a seemingly humanlike demon he had come to know as JD, the Jersey Devil. But there was more, somehow his father fit into this. His father was JD's twin brother. This nightmare was just as much about him and his family as it was about JD.

But was it just a nightmare or something more? Could this be how it really happened? How his family got tangled up with a demon. Were they themselves more than human too? Were they like him? Sammy grabbed the side of his head, attempting to stop his brain from reeling.

Normally the past can't hurt you, but Sammy knew in Pleasant Mills it could. In the small river town surrounded by ancient pines, protected by state law and haunted by the Jersey Devil, the past was alive and well and a supernatural pain in the butt. At this point, he convinced himself his nightmare was more than a nightmare; it was somehow a window into the past. Everything about it was too palpable, too detailed, too real not to be real.

Getting out of bed, Sammy headed across the hall to his father's room. There was no way he was going to be able to silence his mind and he didn't want to be alone. He wasn't sure if he was going to tell his father about the nightmare. The idea of being some half demon-angel combo scared him too much to say out loud.

His father's door was open; the room was empty. Sammy made his way downstairs to his father's office. If he wasn't in his bedroom, Sammy knew he could find him there. The door was shut, which in the Lopez house meant: 'Do not disturb, I'm working and if you do, it better be important'. This was important, so Sammy was going to knock. Just before his knuckles hit the door, he heard a voice he knew wasn't his father's. It sounded like it, but the draw was slower, more controlled. He knew who it was. Carefully, Sammy pressed his ear to the door and listened.

"You have to do something Jeffrey. You can't let this stand."

"What can I do? Maybe this is all for the best."

"It's not. You have to do something, or I will."

Sammy's heart raced he could hear it thumping in his ears like the bass of one of those rock songs Ivy liked so much.

"JD, I think—"

"Shh, we're not alone," JD said in a whisper that Sammy barely made out.

Sammy, as quickly and quietly as he could, raced down the hall. He had just made it into the foyer when he heard the door to his father's office open.

"Sammy, that you?"

Silence.

After a few moments the office door shut.

Sammy ran up the staircase to his room and locked the door. He pulled his phone off the charger where it had been charging on top of his nightstand. Slumping to the floor, he scanned his contacts for Ivy's number. He paused. "You can't call her," he whispered to himself. "You can't trust her."

Ivy's betrayal cut through him as his finger hovered over the call icon. Unfortunately for Sammy, the past was just as unavoidable as the present troubles. Since he made a deal with JD in Pleasant Mills Church, he had changed. His deal with JD, at the time, seemed an easy one. JD would save him from his injuries and the burning church and all he had to do was break up with his girlfriend.

Sammy and Ivy had had a rocky relationship, but he loved her and would die to protect her from any scheme JD was planning. But when JD showed Sammy Ivy's bracelet, a bracelet he'd given her for her birthday, and told him Ivy trapped his soul in it and gave it to him, dying to protect Ivy seemed like a stupid thing to do, especially when the deal JD offered him not only saved him, but it also protected his family.

JD had fulfilled his end of their contract. Sammy was miraculously rescued from the burning church and despite all odds survived his injuries. Sammy had also held up his end of the bargain. He had broken up with Ivy Teller.

Still, Sammy felt conflicted. His deal with JD seemed to have no negative side effects, no backlash, no epic sacrifice. With Ivy proven to be a liar, their breakup seemed like the only thing to do—not a sacrifice. JD had told Sammy he wanted to save him since they were family. Could it be true, did JD really care about him now that he knew they shared the same blood? Did he really have his and his father's best interest at heart, or was he playing at something? —Something bigger.

Sammy's mind went back to the conversation he just overheard. *'You have to do something, or I will.'* No—Sammy didn't trust JD. He didn't care if they shared the same blood, the same curse. He would never trust him. And he didn't like the idea of JD pressuring his father. He needed help. His father needed help. But it couldn't be from Ivy—not her.

He wished Zac was there again. Not that Zac was particularly good at giving advice, but he always cheered him up. Zac, along with Mona, were at his Aunt Fran's with the rest of his family, and you couldn't exactly call a ghost on the phone.

Sammy scrolled down his contacts, his finger stopping on Mike Handover. Mike was his best friend, he had always been, but with his younger sister Tammy passing away during what the Pleasant Herald called the Pleasant Church Tragedy, Sammy couldn't bog him down with his problems.

Tammy lost her life the day of the church fire and it was his fault. He was the one who wanted to put the jarred heart Ivy and he found in Pastor Leeds's attic in the enchanted, forever sleeping, heartless body of Lilly Leeds. They knew the heart, in life, belonged to JD's mother who was a witch. Sammy knew there would be risks but he coaxed his friends into going along with Ivy's plan from the Midwife, a plan that was supposed to put JD into an endless sleep and save the town. Sammy had used his influence and his confidence as he saw his father, the mayor, do with constituents. Tammy had opposed the plan from the beginning, only giving in to his will at the last moment and it had cost her everything.

Guilt and Sammy were close friends over recent years. Sometimes he wondered what he would do without it weighing him down. But Tammy's death was different. With the deaths of his other friends, Zac, Tyrone, Louie, Tim, and even Megan, he had failed to save them, with Tammy, he put her in the line of fire. He was just as guilty as JD. Making a deal to save his life proved that to him. He always knew he would do anything to save his friends, but he learned he would also do anything to save himself.

Thinking, Sammy let out a loud sigh. He couldn't call Jesse for the same reasons he couldn't call Mike. Jesse was still mourning Tammy, and he was pretty sure a part of Jesse blamed him for her death, although he never said it and put the lion's share of the blame on Issac Smith, the emergency doctor that had accompanied Pastor Joe Baker to the Church for the Henry sisters' funerals. Even with Jesse's hatred focused on Issac, Sammy wasn't sure if Jesse would pick up for him. That only left Elsa Tilton.

CHAPTER FOUR
Some Kind of Trouble

A knock more closely resembling a tap than a bang, sounded on Mary Teller's front door. It was so soft Mary didn't hear it from the kitchen where she sat at the kitchen table methodically using miniature tongs to add sugar cubes to her coffee. Another tapping knock sounded. This one was a little louder than the one before. Mary, knowing her hearing wasn't the best and thinking she heard something, looked toward the front door to see a crown of blonde hair. She glanced down at her watch, tapping the face. It was 9 a.m. on Saturday.

Mary hurriedly got up thinking it was Lindsey Lopez. Knowing how sick the twins were, Mary feared it was back to the hospital with them. She opened the door; relieved—it was only Elsa Tilton.

Elsa nervously knotted her hands in front of her. "Hi Mrs. Teller. Is Ivy home?"

Mary's brows furrowed. It wasn't every day Elsa knocked on her door. She wondered, in fact, if she ever had. "She is. But she's sleeping." Elsa nibbled on the bottom of her lip, tears forming in the corners of her blue eyes.

Before a tear could drop, Mary invited her in, in a Teller kind of way. "Hurry up, you're letting the heat out of the house."

Quickly, Elsa scooted inside. For an awkward moment they stared at each other before Elsa's pointer finger gyrated around the cramped foyer. "Which way to Ivy's room?"

Mary smiled. She was right, Elsa had never come to see Ivy before. "Back staircase. Her room's the only door at the top of the stairs. And when you're up there tell her to straighten up that pigsty."

"I'll tell her. Thank you, Mrs. Teller," Elsa said politely, before making her way down the hall.

Elsa took a deep breath and walked up the narrow staircase to the attic. She let her hand drag on the railing, feeling the smooth lacquered finish on her already cold palm. When she got to the top tread, she knocked on the closed door. She waited a few seconds for a reply. When none came, she let herself in, quietly closing the door behind her.

Ivy was asleep. Her covers and pillows were strewn on the floor as if she had gotten into a fight with her bed and lost. Elsa's eyes curiously darted around Ivy's attic bedroom, to the cobwebs hanging from the rafters, to the posters that adorned the walls, to the small photo of Sammy and Ivy on her nightstand.

Elsa leaned toward Ivy and whispered her name. Ivy's body twitched like an electric current pulsed through it before going rigid again. "Ivy," Elsa said, this time a little louder. Ivy didn't stir. Frustrated, Elsa picked up a pillow off the floor and bopped her on the head with it.

"Grams, it's Saturday. Leave me alone. I told you I'm not going to youth group anymore." With a groan resembling a dying animal, Ivy used the back of her hand to wipe drool from her chin.

"Ivy, get up. I need you. Please."

Ivy opened her one eye like a sleeping dragon ready to devour who or whatever disturbed her. Elsa Tilton came into focus—her long blonde hair bone-straight, her makeup flawless, her winter jacket fitted on her small waist. Ivy's other eye flew open. "Um, Elsa, what are you doing in my room?"

Elsa knotted her hands in front of her again. It almost looked like she was praying. "Your grandmother let me in."

"Uh yeah, but why? Shouldn't you be at youth group saving small animals from littered Dunkin Donut cups?"

"I should be," Elsa admitted. The grand reopening of Pleasant Mills Church was weeks away and the youth group had been busy with fundraisers. She would be missed today.

Ivy sat up on one elbow. "And you're here and not there because you wanted to be my alarm clock?"

Elsa picked at her nails, avoiding eye contact with Ivy. "I know we haven't been the best of friends . . . "

Ivy inclined her head in agreement. She and Elsa had never been friends. Elsa was the closest thing she had to an arch nemesis.

Elsa mustered her strength. "I have no one else to turn to."

"What are you talking about?" Ivy asked, now sitting up, worried something happened to Sammy.

"I need your help."

"I got that much," Ivy said, wishing she would just spit it out already. "What exactly do you need my help with?"

Elsa took a seat at the end of Ivy's bed. Ivy replied by swinging her legs to the side to sit next to her. Ivy was glad she was wearing the pajama set she got last Christmas from Sammy's mom and not one of her stained nightshirts.

"Do you remember Cameron Franklin from Poor Richard's Community Pool?"

Ivy smiled. "Yes, I'm sleepy, not senile."

"I'm worried something bad happened to him."

Casually, Ivy leaned back on her bed, relieved Elsa's problem had nothing to do with Sammy. "Maybe you should call the police then."

Elsa's eyes met Ivy's, a seriousness plaguing her beautiful face. "It's not the kind of problem the police can help with. It's like a supernatural kind of problem. And since that seems to be your thing, I thought you could help."

Ivy's interest piqued; her eyebrows corked. "Why do you think something supernatural happened to him?"

"He stood me up."

Ivy laughed out loud. She couldn't help herself. "Oh my God, Elsa, your ego is bigger than Sammy's. Maybe he's just not that into you. I know that must be a first, but there's a first for everything."

Elsa's complexion instantly reddened to that of an overripe tomato. With tears streaming down her face, she hopped to her feet. "I knew coming to you was a mistake!"

"Hey," Ivy said, also jumping to her feet, "wait, I didn't mean to make you cry. I'm sorry."

Ivy had never liked Elsa, but since Tammy's death, she'd felt bad for her. With her best friend gone, Elsa socially regressed. She talked to no one at school except Sammy and Mike. She had changed.

Facing away from Ivy, Elsa frantically wiped her eyes, embarrassed she cried. "It's fine. I can fix this myself. I know if I just kiss him again, he'll remember me."

"Remember you?" Ivy asked puzzled, taking a seat back on her bed. "You're saying Cam doesn't remember you?"

Elsa took up her seat next to Ivy. "That's what I've been trying to tell you. Someone has messed with his head. He remembers my name and where I work and that's about it. He doesn't remember kissing me." Elsa rolled her bloodshot eyes. "I know this may be my ego talking but no guy forgets kissing me."

Ivy handed Elsa the box of tissues off her nightstand. Taking one, Elsa went to Ivy's vanity mirror and carefully removed her smudged eyeliner.

Ivy watched her from the bed. Elsa was beautiful even when she cried. She didn't doubt a kiss from her would be remembered by any boy and particularly a nerdy one like Cameron Franklin. She wondered if Sammy had ever kissed Elsa.

"I'll help," Ivy finally said. "It'll get me out of cleaning my room."

Elsa turned away from the mirror, feverishly grabbing Ivy's hand. "Thank you so much!" She tugged Ivy off the bed. "I'll tell you everything that happened during the summer on the way."

"On the way?"

"Yeah, I have a tutoring appointment with Cam this afternoon. I didn't want to skip youth group with the church reopening around the corner, but it was the only day he had available. I hope you don't have plans."

"No. Why would I have plans on a Saturday?"

Before Ivy could say another sarcastic word, Elsa had her bedroom door open.

Ivy pulled her back into the room. "Give me five minutes to get dressed."

"Oh yeah, sorry," she said, grasping for the first time Ivy was still in her pajamas.

It didn't take long for Ivy to get dressed. She threw on a black T-shirt, jeans, and hoodie. She grabbed the Leeds grimoire from under her bed just in case she needed it and tossed it in her oversized satchel. Before 9:30 a.m. they were on the road heading toward Princeton University.

"So," Ivy said, fiddling with the radio. "How did Cam lose his memory?"

Elsa pushed Ivy's hand aside, turning the radio back to the classical listening station before turning it off. "My mom hates it when people mess with her radio. The only rule I have to follow when I borrow her car is don't change her station. And I don't know how he lost his memory. One second, he was the greatest guy that ever lived, the next it's like he never existed."

Elsa pulled onto the Expressway merging with oncoming traffic. "I don't want to bore you with my love life, but I've had a crush on Cam for years. I never thought I had a chance. With him being so much older than me, and being an intellectual, I thought he viewed me as a little girl."

"So, you didn't think the fact that you look like Barbie would impress him?"

Elsa shook her head, keeping her eyes on the road. "Cam's not like other guys."

Ivy smirked.

"Sure, he likes pretty girls. Everyone does, but that's not what's important to him."

"I'll have to take your word on that," Ivy said, resting her head on the headrest and looking out her window. She was trying to keep her focus on Elsa, but she had a strange dream last night about Deborah Smith Leeds being visited by two cloaked men. She needed time to sort that out in her head. She was used to her dreams not being merely dreams, and that was never a good thing.

"I gave up hope on Cam after he didn't seem to reciprocate my flirting when I went to the pool, but when Tammy got me the job there . . ." Elsa paused to wipe a tear at the mention of her deceased best friend. Elsa wasn't there the day of the church fire. Fate had left her out of that fight, having to work that morning at Poor Richard's Community Pool.

Regaining her emotions, Elsa continued. "Once I started working at the pool, Cam was so nice to me. Not nicer to me than he was to anyone else, but he really listened to me when I talked. I thought maybe there was a chance. I worked as much as I could and was the best employee Poor Richard's ever had."

Ivy yawned, not meaning to, but she was still tired.

"Long story short," Elsa said, "I got up the nerve to ask him to come watch me cheer."

"How fun for him."

Elsa rolled her eyes. "Anyway, he came. It was in the middle of all the craziness last summer and he had just been questioned by the police over the murders of Trudy's mother and grandmother, but he still came. We went out to lunch, and I told him I liked him. He couldn't believe it."

"I can see why," Ivy muttered, thinking of the dorky pool landlord.

"What?"

Ivy waved her hand dismissively. "Nothing. Go on."

"It was just like a fairy tale. He told me how much he liked me, but never thought someone like me could like him."

"Cam always seemed reasonable," Ivy said, her line of vision on the cars in the lane next to them.

"My mom wasn't thrilled he was older than me but was okay with us dating once I turned eighteen. Cam was supposed to come to my birthday party and make us official. But he never showed."

"I wouldn't know, I wasn't invited," Ivy said, her voice laced with loathing. Just another reason why they were never friends.

Elsa's blue eyes flickered toward Ivy. "Sorry about that. Sammy said he wouldn't come if I invited you. He's still really mad at you for some reason. I'm sure you two will work it out. He loves you, you know?"

Ivy longingly sighed.

"But, uh, don't sweat it. You didn't miss anything. It wasn't much of a party. I didn't even want to have it after what happened to Tammy. But Mike insisted she would be mad if I did nothing for my eighteenth birthday. It was just Mike and Sammy and me. Jesse and Rosa didn't come. After everyone left, I called Cam to rip his face off, but he seemed so surprised I called, it threw me off. When I told him he missed my party, he apologized then asked what party."

Ivy held back her judgment, pressing her lips together firmly, like she just sucked on a lemon.

Glancing at Ivy, "I know you think I'm being crazy but when I mentioned our date, he had no idea what I was talking about. He actually asked if he was speaking to Elsa Tilton from Poor Richard's Community Pool. When I said yes. He said: *This is Cam Franklin. I think you called me by mistake.*"

"I admit that part is strange," Ivy said, trying to piece together Elsa's story in her head. "A lot of time has passed since your birthday, why all of a sudden do you feel spurred on to bring me here?"

"I couldn't let it go," Elsa said. "I didn't think Cam's memory loss was just some lie to get rid of me. He was genuinely confused on the phone. I thought maybe it was a post-traumatic episode and he repressed everything. After all, he was accused of murdering Trudy's mom and grandmother. Even though he didn't, something like that has to affect you. I wasn't going to give up on him. With Tammy gone, Cam was my only other close friend. Of course, Sammy and Mike are my friends too, it's just different. I can't talk to them like I did Tammy or Cam. I decided I was just going to be supportive until he was his old self again. I started going to him for help with English once every two weeks or whenever he can fit me in."

"How do you get tutored in English?" Ivy asked, genuinely curious.

"We talk about themes, but the point is over the last several months I've seen a change in him. A physical change. It first happened during the summer. His eyes changed color. They went from brown to blue. He'd thought his face looked different too and I admit it looked thinner, but now his face looks so different. His eyes are brown again and he's all puffy like he had an allergic reaction."

"Maybe he did have one," Ivy suggested. "Or, with summer over, maybe he hasn't hit the gym lately and just gained weight. And they make a thing called contacts. I hear they work great changing eye color. You can even get contacts that look like cat eyes."

"I'm not stupid, Ivy. I know what contacts are. And it's not that. I've asked him about his allergies, he has seasonal allergies like everyone else and that's it. His body is the same and he goes to the gym every day, it's all in his face." Elsa changed lanes, cutting off an SUV with a soccer mom sticker on the bumper. Ivy impulsively shut her eyes. Elsa seemed unphased and continued speaking as the soccer mom she cut off beeped at her and threw up the middle finger. "Last week, I brought the summer up again. This time, Cam remembered even less. Soon nothing will be left of him. It's like he's disappearing right in front of my eyes."

Ivy opened hers, looking around like she was surprised to be alive. She should be used to aggressive driving with her grandmother, but she reasoned there are some things one just can't get used to.

"It was hard for me, but I brought up Tammy. He hardly recalls her. He doesn't remember they were friends. We have to help him, not just for me but for himself. Whatever is happening to him isn't right. Talking about the past hasn't helped. If anything, it's made it worse. I don't know what to do. I would've asked Sammy to come with me today, but he has so much going on with his mom moving out and his little sisters being sick. And now his dad is being wacky."

Elsa took the exit.

"Mr. Lopez is being wacky? What does that mean exactly?"

Ivy knew the twins had been sick. All fall, Alba and Maria had been in and out of the hospital—first a bad cold, then a virus, now the flu. They had missed so much school, Jeffrey hired a private tutor so his girls wouldn't fall behind. Grams kept her posted on things like that, but she never mentioned Mr. Lopez to her.

"Sammy wouldn't elaborate. I tried to get him to, but the more I asked the more he didn't want to talk about it. So, I dropped it. He just said his dad's acting wacky, and he's worried about him. You know how he is, but it's so bad he's thinking of asking his father to tell his grandmother to come home."

"Really?!" Ivy asked shocked. "Even after the warning from that ghost that haunts his grandmother, what was his name . . ."

"Enzo Serrano," Elsa said. "I was there. I heard the warning when he talked through Tammy telling Sammy his grandmother would kill him for his magic. The way his eyes and mouth were stitched up, still gives me the heebie-jeebies. I think Sammy's still really freaked out over that too, but things with his dad must be that bad that it doesn't matter."

"Oh, that sucks," Ivy said, trying to play off her anxiety. She had known the Midwife had locked Jeffrey's powers away for a reason. A reason she couldn't remember. He had absorbed even more power when he helped JD crush their mother's heart into dust. She should have checked on him, but he seemed so Jeffrey Lopez at Tammy's funeral she thought he was fine and hadn't given much thought to him.

Ivy felt stupid and reckless, she hadn't gone to check on him. The Midwife obviously knew something she didn't. Although she was the Midwife that helped bring Jeffrey and Japhet Dean Leeds into the world nearly three hundred years ago, she didn't have all of her memories, just bits and pieces of a past she knew she had lived. The Midwife not only bound Jeffrey's power as a baby, she had a built-in failsafe if he should come into it. The Midwife would rather have Jeffrey dead than have his power loose. But now, the power she sought to lock away was free, unchecked and inside Sammy's dad, and like most of the bad things that happened in Pleasant Mills, it was her fault. Ivy resolved to visit Mr. Lopez as soon as she was done helping Elsa.

Elsa coasted into a vacant parking spot on the street and turned off the car. "That reminds me," she said, putting the keys in her purse, "Cam told me in the summer he was getting these strange feelings. I promised him I wouldn't say anything. But at this point, I have to."

"Strange feelings about what?" Ivy asked with an inquisitive brow.

"It's hard to explain. I wasn't sure if I understood it when he told me, but that's how he found Trudy's mom and grandmother dead.

Something told him to go look in the tent."

"He was hearing voices?"

"I don't think it was that," Elsa said thoughtfully. "He said he felt it. Something was definitely up with him." Elsa turned to Ivy, her eyes burning with intensity. "I'm just worried he got himself into some sort of trouble. If you think nothing is wrong with him when you see him, I'll drop it. But if I'm right and something strange is going on, promise me you'll help."

"I'm here, aren't I?" Ivy said, unbuckling her seatbelt.

Elsa nodded. "Do me a fav, hand me my makeup bag in the glove compartment. I need to spruce up real quick."

Ivy complied.

Elsa reapplied liquid eyeliner to her top lid and mascara. She rubbed lip gloss infused with glitter on her lips. "Ready."

CHAPTER FIVE
An Unexpected Call

Mike wiped the sweat from his forehead with the back of his hand before reaching for his cell. He hated how even in the late fall landscaping made him sweat. His hands suddenly became shaky as Joe Baker's name flashed across his cell phone screen. Too eager, he answered it on the first ring. He attempted to recover with a casual, "Hey what's up?" But the tremble in his hands had already reached his voice box.

How could simple words have so much emotion, mean so much more. Joe calling was a literal dream come true. How many times Mike had wished, and even prayed Joe would call him. But after nearly four months he never did, and every day that passed, Mike gave up hope he ever would.

Mike hadn't seen or spoken to Joe after he returned his car keys to him at the hospital—the day his little sister died. He had sped to the hospital in Joe's sticker-covered Honda after his truck was used as a battering ram to create an escape from Pleasant Mills church, but he was too late. Tammy died in the back of Joe's car on the way to the hospital.

"Joe?" he said, into the silence of the phone. He peeled his sweaty face from the screen to make sure he didn't accidentally put the phone on mute or worse hangup.

"Hi Mike," a voice intoned in a crisp British accent.

Disappointment washed over Mike, culminating in slouched shoulders and a stooped posture. He knew the voice.

"Isaac, what can I do for you?" Mike asked, addressing him how his father addressed landscaping clients. It was the tone Big Mike used when he knew a complaint about a missed blade of grass in a senior's yard was coming, a tone of indifference, a business tone—a guarded tone.

Isaac was a hated man in Pleasant Mills. Jesse openly blamed Isaac for Tammy's death. Or more accurately, the hope that Tammy would survive her injury. Isaac had treated Tammy's neck wound that faithless day the victims of Deborah Leeds, under the guise of the newly awakened Lilly, rose. Jesse had believed Tammy would recover as Isaac was an emergency room doctor. He felt Issac had the power to save her. But he didn't save her. She died and Jesse couldn't forgive him or himself.

Mike didn't blame Isaac for Tammy's death. His dislike for him was simple and selfish. Isaac had come to Pleasant Mills with Joe—his Joe. The day after their ugly breakup, Joe had already replaced him, replaced him with Isaac Smith, a good-looking doctor with a sexy accent. He hated everything about Isaac. Isaac, not saving his sister, was just the icing on the cake. And Mike hated cake.

"It's Joseph. I need your help."

Mike groaned into the phone, his professionalism gone. The last thing he wanted to do was give Isaac dating advice. "I don't think you should be asking me. We were only together for a week." Mike hung up, heat rushing to his face. Every time he thought about Joe Baker and their firefly relationship, it was as if someone was turning a knife in his stomach to a metronome. It was true, their relationship had only lasted about a week, but it was the best week of his life. Mike felt idiotic giving it that mantle, but there it sat, the best time in his life, beneath going to Disney World and beneath the Eagles winning the Super Bowl.

Mike's phone rang, Joe Baker flashing over it again.

Mike put his phone on silent and was about to slip it back into his pocket when he decided to answer it. Maybe Joe had broken up with him.

Maybe an upset Issac would make him happy.

Mike took the call.

"Mike don't hang up. Joe's in trouble."

Mike froze, attempting to speak. "Tro—"

"I apologize for the call, but there was no one else. I can't take him to the hospital, and it's become too much for me."

Mike's tongue felt like jelly. "Is he okay? What happened?" Escaped his mouth, his voice sounding funny to his ears.

"For the moment. Are you busy? Can you come to Philly?"

Mike looked around the Henry sister's yard. He had just finished raking the front yard but needed to do the back. He had always done fall cleanup for the Henry sisters and after their untimely deaths their only living relative from California decided to move into their house and keep him on as the landscaper.

"Yeah, I just finished a job," he said into the receiver, deciding that he could skip raking out the flower bed in the backyard and hit it with a blower next week. The new Ms. Henry wasn't as detail oriented as her late cousins and would most likely never notice. "I need to shower. I smell."

He groaned. He hated when he overshared.

"That's fine, shower. He lives above Ray's Noodles. I'll text you the address. I'll meet you inside the restaurant."

At a small two-seater table in the back of Ray's Noodles, Mike anxiously sipped on Mountain Dew while he waited on Issac. He'd texted Issac over fifteen minutes ago he was there. Mike was going to give it another five minutes and then he was going to knock on the apartment above the Chinese restaurant.

Mike occupied his mind by trying to name the dishes pictured in the Chinese cuisines plastered over the walls. His family didn't eat a lot of Chinese food, his father was a meat and potato kind of man, so this guessing game was a good distraction.

The bell on the door chimed, signaling a patron walking in. Mike's eyes shifted to Isaac. Isaac flashed a brilliant smile, all his teeth perfectly aligned. He obviously had braces, a thing the Handovers couldn't afford. Isaac's chestnut brown, curly hair fell just past his shoulders. Each curl was a work of art falling in a perfect, tight spiral. He had on a fitted t-shirt and jeans, looking like he'd just stepped out of a Gap ad. Mike, feeling inadequate, blushed. He quickly glanced down at his shirt. It read: Handover Your Lawn. He hadn't thought about what he was wearing when he put it on. He'd grabbed the first shirt off the stack of clean clothes. The hate for Isaac burned in his chest. With all the time he waited, he could have put on a better shirt and spent more time on his hair. He knew his curls looked greasy. He rushed in the shower, and despite Tammy's warning sounding in his head not to put too much product in his hair, he did. He was going to rewash it but didn't want to waste the time.

Isaac took the seat across from Mike. His warm brown skin looked flawless in the fluorescent lights overhead. There was not one blemish or freckle on his face. Mike smiled to himself recalling that Joe liked freckles and Isaac had none.

"Thanks for meeting me," Isaac said.

"No problem. Where's Joe?" Mike asked, his eyes going to the door. "Is he meeting us?"

"Joe's in his apartment."

Mike got up, anxious to see him. "Okay, well, let's go."

Isaac didn't budge. "I didn't tell him I called you or that you were in the city."

"Oh," Mike said, sitting down awkwardly, almost knocking over his soda. His eyebrows furrowed into one thick red line. "I thought Joe asked you to call me?"

"I took liberty with his phone. I know it's all very garish and he'd kill me if he knew I'd called you."

Mike's spirit sank with his words. On the drive to Ray's Noodles, he felt guilty at being happy Joe was in trouble and asked for his help. Now he just felt stupid, and he was sure it showed on his face. He felt the heat on his cheeks and knew they were as red as his hair.

Mike, wanting to retreat to his bed, pulled the keys to his new, used pickup from his jean pockets.

"Wait, don't go," Isaac pleaded. Mike waited for him to continue. "It's his nightmare," Isaac said, pausing to look up at the drop ceiling. "It's getting worse."

"Joe said he was used to it," Mike said. "That it had been the same nightmare every night since he was a kid." Mike recalled Joe's nightmare about drowning. The way he told him how the cold water filled his mouth as it stung his eyes, the pain in his chest as he tried to breathe, unable to move his hands and feet to save himself.

"It's still the same nightmare," Isaac said, turning his attention back to Mike. "But the intensity of it has changed. He told me when you were together it had stopped."

Mike's blush deepened. "That's what he said. I don't know if it's true."

Isaac pushed his hair away from his face. For the first time, Mike could see fine red webs in his eyes, and he wondered how old Issac was. "This is going to sound like a crazy request, but could you stay over tonight. See if the nightmare stops. Just to give him a break."

"Um . . . you said Joe doesn't know I'm here. I'm pretty sure he wouldn't be cool if I slept over. We haven't talked in months."

Isaac grinned. "He won't mind. In fact, I think he'll be very happy to see you."

Mike's heart fluttered, hoping there was some truth to that. After the horrible things he'd had said to Joe, even if it was to protect him, he wouldn't be surprised if he never wanted to see him again. *You, disgust me. Everything you are makes me feel sick. I don't want you to stay in this town. I want you to leave and go so far away, I'll never have to see your face again.* Mike had used what Joe's first church had thought of him against him. It worked, Joe accepted their breakup and left town, but it also killed their friendship.

Isaac shook his head at himself. "I should have told you to pack an overnight bag. I'll have Stevie bring you something. We're about the same size."

"Stevie?"

"My boyfriend."

"You have a boyfriend?" Mike asked, his voice louder than he intended. The cashier looked their way.

Isaac seemed surprised. "Yes, Stevie and I will be celebrating two years of bliss next month."

"I thought you and Joe were a—"

Isaac interrupted Mike with a laugh. "Oh no no no. I'm sorry if you got that impression when I showed up in your hometown with him." He tapped on his chin, "I suppose that's how it looked, but I was merely on babysitting duty after you broke up with him. Joseph was really having a bad go of it."

Mike's heart fluttered again. He felt a great weight lift from it. Issac wasn't his enemy.

"But to be transparent, Joseph and I do have a past. I couldn't handle his obsession with Wendy and his nightmare."

Like his nightmare, Joe had also told Mike about Wendy. She was, after all, the reason why Joe was first interested in talking to him. Wendy was Joe's childhood best friend that went missing in Pleasant Mills. A friend he was still searching for when he came to Pleasant Mills to investigate Pastor Uriah Leeds's questionable conduct with his girlfriend. A friend he thought was in some way linked to the teens who were murdered the previous summer. The teens who were Mike's friends.

Isaac confided in Mike. "I wanted Joseph to get professional help and he did for a time, but that was short lived. He couldn't take my constant nagging and he broke up with me." Isaac steepled his hands on the table. "We remained friends. Probably because I went on loving him for a long time after we broke up. I find myself still looking out for Joseph, not able to turn my back on him." Isaac exhaled loudly. "Stevie is my soulmate, and he has been more than understanding. I don't know how much more understanding he has in him. We've been staying with Joseph every night. I work late hours at the hospital, so Stevie and I have been taking shifts. Taking care of Joseph has become a full-time job in itself. I know I have no right to dump this on you . . ." He drummed his fingers on the table. "I would take him to the hospital if I could, but whatever is going on with him is not normal. I thought if you really could silence his nightmare, we all could get a little rest and—"

"I'll stay the night," Mike said, cutting him off. "If I can help, I will."

Mike hurriedly made his way up the metal staircase in the alley leading to the apartment above Ray's Noodles. He pushed the key given to him from Isaac inside the lock, turning and pushing with one motion.

Mike's eyes danced around the cluttered apartment strewn with papers and empty beer bottles, finding Joe sprawled on the couch, his face toward the gray suede cushion. Mike stood silently in the doorway as Joe rolled onto his back, his eyes becoming alive with a blue flame when they perceived him. Joe, abruptly sitting up, brushed his uncomely blond hair with his fingers and did his best to smooth out his wrinkled gray t-shirt.

"Come in," Joe finally said, noticing Mike hadn't stepped over the threshold. "Sorry the place is a mess. Isaac's boyfriend likes to play housemaid, so I make sure I always have something for him to clean up. And uh . . . he hasn't come by yet today." Joe tucked his hair behind his ears. "But never mind that." Joe signaled with his hands for Mike to come into the living room. "I didn't know you knew where I lived. This is such a surprise. Um . . . how have you been?"

"I didn't," Mike said, taking a seat on the opposite side of the couch, clutching his Mountain Dew. "That is, I didn't know where you lived until Isaac called me."

Joe's smile faded. "Sorry he dragged you up here. Isaac has a flair for overreacting. He insists on babysitting me," he said using air quotes. "He has a messiah complex if you haven't picked that up yet."

"I'm not sorry he called," Mike said, pausing to evaluate Joe. "You look . . . well you look like . . ."

"Like hell," Joe said, finishing his sentence.

"I was going to say like you're dying."

Joe smiled; the cool smile Mike had fallen in love with. "We're all dying darling," he said, with a flair of his hand.

Joe was every bit as beautiful as when Mike first saw him, but there was a frailness to him now. Dark hollows encircled his light blue eyes. His pale skin was as white and placid as bone china. He looked like he was slowly dying but the Grim Reaper hadn't reaped his beauty. He looked more angelic now than human and that frightened Mike.

"You know what I mean."

"Yeah, I know I've lost some weight. And yes, I've been having a hard time keeping food down and sleeping. I'm just taking it one day at a time."

"Isaac said your nightmare is more intense now. I'm going to stay over tonight. Let's see if that helps."

With a dismissive shrug of his shoulders, "Mike it's nothing." He regained his old bravado. "Like I told you, Isaac worries too much. It's the same nightmare I always have. It's all in my head. Now that I know why I have the nightmare, I think it's just messing with me. In time, I'm sure I will get over it and things will go on as they always have."

Mike nodded. He couldn't imagine what it would feel like to learn you were murdered as a child—tied up and thrown in a lake, water filling your lungs until you drowned. To know this, and to know that you were somehow reborn, made to suffer your death every night seemed impossible to endure. Joe was cursed, and Mike wasn't surprised that he was having a hard time dealing with it.

"That may be so," Mike said, reaching to right a beer can on the antique trunk that served as a coffee table, "but Isaac thought it was a good idea I spend the night. See if I can't give you a break. Who knows, you may still have the nightmare, or you may not."

A flush passed over Joe's cheeks, a vulnerability breaking through his mask. It was gone as quickly as it came. "You don't have to."

"It's Saturday, so it's not like I have school tomorrow."

"What about your job? I thought weekends were a big deal in the world of landscapers."

"They are," Mike admitted. "My dad's gonna be pissed but December is our slow month. The rush to put up Christmas decorations is over."

Joe blinked away tears. "Ok, it's settled then," Joe said, pointing to Mike's shirt. "I *Handover my lawn* to you. —I want one of those."

"Done," Mike said, his cheeks burning.

Joe noticed and smiled softly. "I wish Isaac would've called you months ago. I had wanted to reach out to you. I almost dialed your number a handful of times, but I couldn't."

"You could have," Mike said in a low voice.

Joe hung his head, avoiding eye contact with Mike. "I talk to Uriah once a week and always ask about you."

"I didn't know you kept in touch with him."

Joe elevated his eyes to Mike's, holding him in the frame of his dark lashes. "What can I say, we hit it off. Sure, it's awkward knowing somehow he's my father and we're trapped in this strange time warp together, but I thought dealing with the truth would help me deal with my nightmare."

"Has it?"

Joe shook his head, his bangs falling into his eyes. "No. —I know it's all true—Lilly, Deborah, Uriah. The rational part of me still can't believe it, even though I lived it. It seems more like a nightmare than my nightmare. My nightmare was always real to me, but I had gotten used to it. But now it's more real than anything else in my life. Like my life is the dream and the truth is the cold, dark, stinging water." Joe exhaled loudly. "Maybe Isaac is right, and I should get a therapist."

"He is a doctor," Mike said with a playful grin.

Joe returned the grin. "Well, enough about me. How have you been?"

Mike didn't want to talk about Tammy, he hoped that wasn't what Joe was getting at. "I'm okay."

"I should've gone up to you at Tammy's funeral. I regret that I didn't. I think about it all the time. You were so upset. I wasn't sure if you'd want to see me, and I didn't want to make matters worse . . . but I wish I would've gone up to you."

Mike straightened up. "You were there? I thought you didn't come."

"Of course I was there." Joe reached his hand toward Mike's, thinking better of it, he retracted it, placing his hands in his lap. "I thought you saw me and, well ignored me so I never approached you. The last thing I wanted to do was make you feel worse."

"I didn't see you. I definitely didn't ignore you purposely. I had no idea you came. I thought you headed back to Philly."

"I did but drove back for the funeral. I stood in the back. I couldn't get into a pew comfortably on my crutches." As Pleasant Mills Church burned, the resurrected Henry sisters pursued Issac and Joe into Pleasant Mills Cemetery and Joe broke his leg after tripping over a small headstone.

Mike thought back to Tammy's funeral. With Pleasant Mills Church in ruins, her funeral was held at Port Republic Church in the next town over. The layout was different from the Quaker church he was used to. Port Republic Church had numerous concavities with statues and two levels. It would be easy to miss someone.

Mike smiled. He was happy for the first time since Tammy passed, the happiness warming his chest as if he swallowed the sun. It was the same sensation he got the first night he shared with Joe.

Joe, not attending his sister's funeral, had spoken volumes about his feelings for him. It was the proverbial nail in the coffin. But he had come. Maybe there was still hope for them.

CHAPTER SIX
Lost and Found

"The Royal Suites Apartments aren't very royal," Ivy said, sticking her nose up at the aged stucco apartment building. The old stucco, soiled to a ruddy brown, fit the monochromatic landscape. The leaves left on the trees had turned brown and shriveled, casting everything in a depressing mood.

"It's not the nicest neighborhood," Elsa had to admit, "but he has his place decorated nice and it's close to campus."

Elsa walked behind a wooden staircase that led to the second-floor apartments, cutting through what Ivy assumed was considered green space, to a first-floor apartment with a Fourth of July wreath still adorning it.

"He's a little late taking down the decorations," Ivy said with a raised eyebrow.

"Yeah, I told him."

"Um, Elsa . . .," Ivy said as they stood face to face with a sun-bleached Uncle Sam, "are you going to knock?"

"Yeah, doing that," she said, visibly taking in a deep breath. Elsa lightly tapped with her knuckles.

With a huff, Ivy moved her out of the way and knocked harder.

"What?!" Elsa exclaimed.

"With a knock like that we'll be standing in the cold all day." Ivy shoved her hands into her hoodie. "I should've grabbed a winter coat."

They didn't have to wait long; Cam opened the door right away with a smile. "Hi Elsa." His warm-brown eyes flickered to Ivy. "You brought a friend, great. Come in, come in."

"Hi Cam, hope you don't mind," Elsa said.

"No, of course not," he said, extending his hand to Ivy once they were inside. "Hi, I'm Cameron Franklin, everyone calls me Cam."

Ivy shook his hand. "Um, Ivy Teller. We've met before."

Cam gave her a curious look, an eyebrow going up in surprise. "We have? When?" He ushered them into the small kitchen where he had books laid out on the kitchen island that extended from the kitchen into the living room in an elbow shape. "Your name's familiar."

"We met at the pool. You were thrilled to meet me."

Elsa crossed her hands over her chest. "I wouldn't say thrilled."

Cam leaned on the island from the kitchen, so the girls could have the stools. "Sorry. I'm not good with faces."

"See," Elsa hissed.

Ivy plopped down on a stool, reaching over the small countertop island to poke Cam's cheek.

He rubbed it. "Is everything okay with your friend?" he asked, glancing to Elsa.

Not satisfied with her poke, Ivy got up and went over to Cam. She grabbed him by his shoulder, forcing him to turn around so she could get a good look at him. "He doesn't look like he's gained weight."

Cam chuckled nervously. "Maybe we should get started on English. I highlighted some key parts in *MacBeth* I think your teacher will quiz you on."

Ivy, still standing in Cam's personal bubble, "You really don't remember me?"

He took a step back to give himself a little space. "I'm sorry about that. I see tons of people at the pool."

"What about that stupid club you were the landlord of? What was it called . . ."

"Poor Richard's Society," Elsa said, finishing Ivy's thought.

"Yeah, what about that?"

He smiled nervously. "I'm not familiar with that."

Elsa gave Ivy a knowing look.

"And Elsa," Ivy asked, "what do you know about her?"

His eyes darted to Elsa who was nibbling on her bottom lip.

"I know Elsa from the pool. We worked together during the summer and um . . . I'm helping her with English," Cam said, not sure what Ivy was expecting him to say, yet surmising there was a right and wrong answer to her question.

"Anything else?"

Again, he glanced at Elsa, looking for a hint at the desired response. He watched her unzipper her winter coat and place it on the stool, a headache forming at the base of his skull.

"Umm . . ."

"What about Uriah Leeds?" Ivy asked. "What do you know about him?"

"He's the pastor of Pleasant Mills Church. The one that burnt down in the summer. I haven't met him. I . . . I uh, don't attend church. It's not my thing, but I heard he's very nice."

Ivy's eyes narrowed. "Have you ever been in his home?"

An awkward smile turned up the corners of Cam's lips. "No, why would I visit the home of a man I never met? I mean the guy's a stranger. That sounds crazy."

Ivy's dark eyes were like slits now, as if looking at him through tunnel vision worked as a lie detector. "You don't remember being there? You don't remember watching me shove a heart into a corpse?"

He laughed nervously as he continuously glanced at Elsa. "Your friend's very interesting . . . I think she's on drugs."

Ivy plopped back down on a stool. "As much as it pains me to say this, Elsa you're right. Cam's been bewitched, spell cast, or whatever you want to call it."

"What?! What are you talking about?" Cam asked.

Ivy and Elsa ignored him, talking amongst themselves.

"Can you help him?"

"I'm going to try," Ivy said. "Whatever spell was used on him is super specific. It's like you said, not all his memories are affected and for whatever reason his face is tied up in it." Ivy couldn't really remember what Cam looked like, besides to say he was indistinctive but there was something about his face that rubbed her wrong.

Ivy pulled out the Leeds grimoire and put it on the island counter, sliding the English books to the side.

"Wow, is that a real grimoire?!" Cam asked, reaching for it, noticing the crest of the Leeds family carved into the leather bounding. He marveled at the three wyverns sitting proudly on a shield.

Ivy pulled it out of his grasp. "It is."

"Can I see it? I'm an occult historian. Well, on my way to being one."

"Not now," Ivy said. "After I'm done helping you."

"Helping me?"

"Yes. If you haven't put it together yet, we're not here for Shakespeare. But all the same, I would like to know the quiz material. You can email me that later." Elsa may not have needed help in English, but Ivy could use a good quiz score.

Ivy thumbed through the musty book.

"What are we looking for?" Elsa asked, examining the strange drawings that accompanied the spells. She had never seen Ivy's spell book before, though she heard all about it from Sammy. Something about it captivated her, there was something in the swirling penmanship that marked each tattered, yellow page.

"A counter spell. Something to reverse what was done." Ivy had only used the spell book a handful of times and that was with Sammy, she didn't really know what she was looking for. She was hoping whatever it was would just jump off the page to her. She didn't think she could write a spell without Sammy.

"What about this one?" Elsa said, pointing. "*Lost and Found.*"

Silently, Cam read it the best he could from the opposite side of the kitchen island as Elsa read it out loud:

"What was lost now be found, put it back where it should be, safe and sound."

Elsa glanced at Ivy. "Is it really that easy?"

"No, not that easy. This is a generic spell. This would be perfect if you were looking for a missing sock. We're going to have to rework it for memory. But it's a good start. And for his face we can try a protection charm and see if that cancels out whatever was done to him. I ended up making a whole bunch of them as a supernatural bug spray. They didn't work against the particular brand of pest I was trying to get rid of, but this may be just what we need."

Ivy pulled a piece of string from the middle of the grimoire. Attached to it was a small opaque stone. "Bonus: They make great bookmarkers." She handed it to Cam. "Tie this around your neck."

"Um . . ."

"Do it," Ivy said. "And then lie on the couch."

He tied the suede string around his neck.

"Lie on the couch," Ivy said again, sensing his hesitation. She sat on the armrest of the red, velvet couch. It was very rockstar vampire, she liked it.

"Do what she says," Elsa said firmly.

Cam lay on the couch, his feet pointing toward Ivy. "Do you know what you're doing? That spell book looks real."

Ivy got up, taking a seat on the armrest at the other end of the couch by his head. "It's real. And no, I don't know what I'm doing. So, stay still, this may hurt."

"What?!" Cam shrieked, going to get up.

"She's kidding," Elsa said, giving Ivy an annoyed look.

"Yeah, kidding," Ivy parroted.

"I don't think this is a good idea," Cam worriedly intoned. "I study the occult and I believe grimoires can hold real magic. I don't like the idea of you guys reading spells that are meant to mess with my head. I know you both think something happened to me, but I feel fine."

"Please, you're going to have to trust us," Elsa pleaded.

"Like Elsa said, you're going to have to trust us. Forgetting who you are is not fine. And when you finally do remember how you know Elsa, you'll be eternally grateful."

Elsa smiled at Ivy as if to say thank you.

"Okay," Cam said," lying back down. "It's like a field study, that's all," he told himself. "I can draw on this experience for a future book."

His line of vision fell to Elsa, a slight blush graced his full cheeks. "I don't know if I trust you guys, but I'm strangely intrigued."

"Good thing for small favors," Ivy said, glancing at the classic horror movie posters in black frames around his apartment. She was surprised Elsa's idea of a nicely decorated apartment was horror posters.

Elsa grabbed her coat from the island stool and rolled it up for Cam to use as a pillow. He took a deep breath in, filling his head with the scent of Elsa's flowery perfume.

"Close your eyes," Ivy ordered.

He did as he was told.

Ivy placed the open grimoire on Cam's chest and knocked rhythmically on his forehead.

"What was lost now be found, put it back where it should be, safe and sound."

Ivy closed her eyes and did her best to focus on the Cam she knew from the pool, from Uriah's house, from Elsa's stories.

"That's it? I just read that," Elsa spluttered.

With her eyes still closed as she concentrated, "I gave the spell a location by knocking on his forehead. And this time *I* read it. There's a big difference in that." Ivy continued:

"What was lost now be found, put it back where it should be, safe and sound."

"Spell, I command you to do it now."

They heard a loud pop as the light bulb in the fixture overhead shattered. Elsa jumped. Cam didn't move, he remained on his couch with his eyes closed. The room became dark as if the windows were blacked out. Like a scared child, Elsa got down on her knees and clung to Ivy. The air in the room became thick, moist, like it was about to rain indoors. All the little noises normally heard from neighbors in an apartment complex were silenced. There were no echoes of televisions, no children playing, no dogs barking. The only thing audible was Elsa's heavy breathing.

Ivy repeated the spell.

"What was lost now be found, put it back where it should be, safe and sound."

"Spell, I command you to do it now."

Ivy opened her eyes shaking her arms out to rid herself of the pins and needles that prickled them. The room gradually lit as if a storm had just passed.

Elsa moved closer to Cam. They could see his pupils moving under his closed eyelids. "Did it work?"

"Yeah, I really think so," Ivy said. "He's sleeping while his brain is on overtime downloading his lost memories." She had never had a physical reaction to a spell like she had with the one she just read, it had to be a sign it worked. She hoped that was all it was. There was the possibility that the spell didn't work, and she made things worse, but she wasn't going to tell Elsa that.

Elsa took a seat at the edge of the couch next to Cam's legs. "How long is it going to take?"

Ivy closed the grimoire and put it on the coffee table. "No clue. It could take a while. We have no idea how much of his memory is missing. And I'm not sure if he's going to remember everything all at once or if he's going to get things back gradually. We're just going to have to wait and see."

"Who do you think would do this to him?" Elsa asked, gently putting her hand on his.

Ivy sat on the floor with her back to the couch. "That's a good question. I'm not sure. Maybe Deborah Leeds did it when she was in Lilly's body. She was only killing women but maybe he knew too much. Maybe finding Trudy's mom and grandmom like he did, messed up her plans and she wanted him out of the way."

"Wow, you think?!" Elsa said, grateful he hadn't been killed.

Ivy shrugged. "Cam seems pretty harmless. I can't imagine who would want to hurt him."

CHAPTER SEVEN
Memory Lane

It was dusk when Cam opened his eyes. The last of the sun filtered in through the narrow windows in the living room in oranges and gold, the only blue left in the room coming from Elsa's eyes. His head pounded with a relentless heartbeat that struck his temples, blurring his vision. Everything was washed out like he had opened his eyes under water.

The scent of Elsa's flowery perfume on his makeshift pillow brought him back to where he was, and what had happened to him. Memories bounced around his skull, filling in the nooks and crannies in his mind like melted butter on an English Muffin.

There was another smell. This one sugary and sweet—cookies. Cam propped himself up on the couch, turning to see Elsa in the kitchen pulling out a tray of chocolate chip cookies. Seeing Cam awake, she left the cookies on the counter and ran over to him.

"You're up," she said, throwing her arms around him. "You've been asleep for so long I started to think we made things worse."

Cam hugged her back, his arms encircling her as he pulled her closer to him. Close was not close enough. He sniffed in the sweet smell of cookies in her hair. He noticed Ivy where she sat on the floor in front of the coffee table with the spell book open.

"How do you feel?" Ivy asked, softly closing the grimoire. She was as relieved as Elsa, he was awake. Once it started getting dark, Ivy got really worried, wondering how long they should wait and at what point they should call an ambulance.

"I remember everything," he replied in a low voice. "I wish I didn't."

Elsa pulled away from him.

"No, not about you," he said, enveloping her in his arms again, his grip tighter than before. "Ivy's right. I'm eternally grateful. Elsa, I'm so sorry I missed your birthday, and for how I treated you. I'm sorry I wasn't there for you after what happened to Tammy. I want to make it up to you, if you'll let me."

Elsa buried her head in his chest.

"You remember everything?" Ivy asked. "So, what happened? How did you lose your memories in the first place?"

Elsa sat up, wiping her tears with her thumbs. Standing, Cam untied the protection charm Ivy had given him and handed it back to her. "That won't help." He walked over to the mirror that hung on the wall by the front door. He examined his face for a long while.

"What is he doing?" Elsa whispered.

Ivy shrugged, honestly confused.

Elsa moved to go to him. Ivy grabbed her hand to stop her. "Wait," she whispered.

The change had already begun, beginning where it had in the summer. His eyes were blue, a dark caerulean tone. He closed his eyes and put his hands over his face. His features blurred and reshaped under his touch before becoming solid again. Lowering his hands, Cam reexamined himself in the mirror. His dark eyes were now a pale blue that rivaled the sky on a summer's day. Where a more than slightly bulbous nose had been was now a perfect sloping one. His full cheeks had thinned out. On his neck was a scar that ran across the face of it. It was raised in shades of dull red and purple.

"Cam," Elsa said softly.

He hesitated to turn around; it had been so long since he had seen his own face. His face seemed like a mask now.

Bracing himself, Cam turned to face his friends with his delicate features highlighted by high cheek bones.

In shock, Elsa covered her mouth with two hands.

"Holy shit," Ivy blurted out. She couldn't help it. She had seen that face before, or at least its likeness.

"This is my true face. My real name is Samuel Cameron Gomez."

"You're Lindsey's long-lost brother . . . Sammy's uncle, the magical prodigy," Ivy said astounded. "Everyone thinks you're dead."

Cam grabbed his head.

Elsa rushed to him, breaking free of Ivy, who still held her arm. "Cam, are you okay?"

"Yeah, It's just my head. I uh, I'm feeling a little lightheaded."

She took his hand and led him back to the couch. She picked up her purse that rested by Ivy's feet and took out a pill bottle. "Take these," she said, handing Cam two extra strength Tylenol Migraine pills. "They work great, but you should take them with water. One minute," she said, hopping up to get him a glass of water.

Ivy watched Cam intently. It was uncanny how much he looked like Sammy's mom. He was just as pretty as she was. He was shorter than her and his hair wasn't blonde but a light brown, and yet it took nothing away from his attractiveness. In no time, Elsa was back with a glass of water and a plate of cookies.

Graciously, he took the glass and swallowed the pills.

"Eat something," Elsa insisted. "You haven't eaten anything all day."

He took a bite of a cookie. "Wow, these are awesome. I didn't know I had stuff to make cookies."

"I made them from scratch."

"Impressive," he said, taking another bite.

Elsa handed Ivy the plate of cookies for her to try one. It may have been Cam who looked more like Lindsey Lopez now, but it was Elsa that embodied her. That had always bothered Ivy. But at this moment, not so much. She was warming up to Elsa. "These are really good."

Elsa smiled approvingly, taking a cookie.

"We ordered a pizza," Elsa told Cam. "I can heat you up a slice when you're ready."

"Thank you," he said, putting his glass of water down next to the spell book on the coffee table.

Ivy scooted closer. "So, what happened Cam? You're killing me with the suspense."

"I guess I have to start at the beginning."

"Good place to start," Elsa teased, squeezing his bicep, and keeping her eyes on his face, getting used to it.

He smiled at her before beginning. "We'd just moved to Pleasant Mills. It didn't take long for Lindsey to get a boyfriend and she started sneaking out at night to see him." Cam chuckled to himself. "It's strange to remember my past knowing I kept living in the same town as my sister and didn't realize who she was." He shook his head at himself, "But anyways, she'd sneak out to see Jeffrey or, as I know him now, Mr. Lopez. We lived in a small trailer; Lindsey and I shared a room and my older sister Fran shared one with my mom. I hated it when Lindsey snuck out of the house. I was worried my mom would find out and we'd both be in trouble, so I covered for her. After Lindsey would leave for the night, I'd take her pillow and mine and pull the covers over them to make it look like she was asleep in bed. One night, my mom came in just after Lindsey left . . . She saw me placing the pillows on her bed."

Cam's hand trembled. Elsa took it, turning it over in hers.

"My mother sat down on my bed and told me to sit next to her. She looked really upset. And so was I. I never wanted to disappoint my mom. She was a great mother. She was raising the three of us by herself. She taught me everything I know. I always thought I was her favorite. She always told me how special I was."

Ivy was unnerved. Cam talking about Anita could have been Sammy talking about her. "I'd say," Ivy interrupted. "It's impressive how you removed that spell from your face. I would've had no clue how to do that. I guess you really are a magical prodigy."

He smiled, but his smile looked sad. "I believed her when she said I was special, that she loved me. That's why I can't make sense out of what happened next." With his free hand he rubbed the back of his neck. "My mother hugged me and told me she wasn't mad. In the reflection of the mirror in the bedroom, I noticed something glistening. It was a knife. As she pulled it from her bathrobe, I scrambled to get away. I was too slow, she'd cut me." He put his hand to his neck, feeling his raised scar. "I darted out of the trailer into the woods. I ran as fast and far as I could. I was so scared I didn't feel pain. But I got tired, so tired, probably from the blood loss, that I had to close my eyes. That's when I felt the pain."

Ivy and Elsa glanced at each other. They knew this story. The ghost of Enzo Serrano had told them Anita Gomez had attacked her only son. Everyone believed him dead, but here he was.

"I collapsed in the woods. I felt pressure being applied to my neck as someone tried to help me. I opened my eyes to see Benny Franklin. I barely had strength to speak but I was able to tell him my mother tried to kill me and asked him to hide me. He said he could help, but it would cost me my past. The next thing I knew, I was home, or what I thought was home with my father Benny and my older brother William. I had this fake past implanted in my head including a mother who died in a fire with all our family pictures. And that was that. I never knew any better. Not even last summer, when I started to feel different, could I have guessed at the truth."

He turned to Elsa. "My father's the one who took away my memories and changed my face to protect me from Anita, but there was something else. I think there's more to it than that." Cam recalled the dampness of the basement in his father's workshop, the pictures of his friends tacked to the wall.

"Big Benny's a witch too?" Elsa asked, making sure she understood.

Ivy groaned. She hated that everyone called Big Benny, Big Benny. It wasn't like there was a little Benny. Yes, the man was a big man but adding the word to his name just seemed superfluous.

"Yeah," Cam said, "he is. He's pretty powerful too. But he can't do that to me again. Not anymore. In the summer I just started to remember who I was. Now I know."

Cam rose urgently. "I need to call Lindsey. All these years she thought I was dead. She must've blamed herself when she came home, and I was missing."

"I don't think that's a good idea," Ivy said, also getting to her feet.

"Why not?" Cam asked, scanning the room for his phone.

"Because it's like you said. She thinks you're dead and Anita probably does to. Calling Lindsey could put your life in danger. You'll be back on your mother's radar, and she may try to finish what she started."

"What about Sammy?" Elsa questioned. "We should at least tell him the truth that his grandmother tried to kill Cam. Sammy could be in real danger. Remember, I told you his grandmother may move back in with him."

Ivy shot daggers at Elsa. "Trust me, no one cares more about Sammy than me and he's not in immediate danger."

"How do you know?" Elsa asked.

"I know Abby. She's smart. She's not going to do anything when Mr. Lopez is not himself. That makes him a wild card. She won't move when his behavior is unpredictable. She won't take that kind of risk. She missed her opportunity with Cam; she won't miss when she comes for Sammy."

"I'm confused," said Cam. "Why would Sammy be in danger?"

Elsa answered: "Because your mom tried to kill you for your powers, and she's been waiting on Sammy to come into his, which he recently did."

"That doesn't make any sense," Cam said, sitting back down. He drummed his fingers on his leg. "I came into my power when I was a toddler. If she was planning on killing me to somehow take it, why wait until I was old enough to run away?"

Elsa looked to Ivy for answers.

"I don't know," Ivy admitted. "Enzo said she killed him for power and you too."

"Who's Enzo?"

"Your mother's brother. So that would make him your uncle," Ivy answered.

"You never heard of him?" Elsa asked shocked. Ivy wasn't shocked, Sammy had told her his grandmother denied having a brother.

Cam furrowed his eyebrows. "No. My mother never mentioned having a brother."

Ivy spoke up. "I can see why she didn't tell you about him. It would be hard to explain what happened to him. But in the end, it doesn't matter who Enzo is. What matters are the facts, them being: Abby tried to kill Cam and Benny tried to hide Cam from her. Cam needs to stay as far away from Abby as possible. Who Cam really is does not leave this apartment. Like I said, if anyone finds out, he can be in danger."

Ivy turned to Cam, narrowing her eyes to slits. "So that means you stay out of Pleasant Mills and avoid people you know. We don't need Benny messing with your head again."

"I agree," Elsa said.

Cam looked unsure, biting his lip in thought.

"Cam . . .," Ivy said sternly.

"I don't know," he replied. "I think I should do something."

"You are. You're protecting yourself and everyone else. If Enzo was telling the truth and your mother kills for power, killing you would make her unstoppable. The best thing you can do is stay here and act as normal as possible."

"She's right," Elsa said.

"Okay, I'll stay put. I stay in Trenton most of the fall anyway. My dad only calls once in a while, so I should be able to play it off."

Ivy was satisfied. "Good. When we get back tomorrow, I'll stop by and see Sammy and assess the situation." Ivy's heart fluttered at having an excuse to see Sammy. This was even better than checking on Mr. Lopez. Her heart wasn't the only thing stirred to life, the butterflies turned wasps in her belly were buzzing, she couldn't wait till tomorrow.

"I hope you don't mind if we stay here tonight?" Elsa asked Cam.

"It better be okay," Ivy barked, sounding harsher than she meant to. "While we waited on your Lazarushian rising, we already texted we're sleeping at each other's houses as a coverup." Ivy would kill Cam herself if he got her in trouble with her grandmother, preventing her from seeing Sammy tomorrow.

Cam shook his head. "Not a problem. I have plenty of blankets."

Elsa smiled gratefully, a soft smile of just lips. "It's getting late, I'd better heat up your dinner." Before he could say thank you, Elsa was in the kitchen.

Ivy sat back down in front of the coffee table and flipped through the grimoire, her mind on Sammy.

"You ever unlock it?" Cam asked.

"Unlock it?" Ivy asked confused.

"The grimoire."

"Uh . . ."

"May I?" he said, reaching for it.

"Sure."

Cam ran his hand over the spine before thumbing through it. "Yep, it's locked. These spells are just superficial spells. Spells to do when you're bored or to impress non-magics. Once you unlock it, you'll be able to see the real spells. You must be pretty powerful Ivy, for anyone of these parlor tricks to have worked on me."

Ivy bit the inside of her lip nervously; she knew she was powerful. She'd had moments when she felt it, but her magic didn't come naturally. She couldn't call on it. In the past she knew it had been just the opposite, she and her magic were one harmonious being. Ivy wondered if that's how it had been for the Midwife in the beginning or if she was like Cam and was a child prodigy. "So uh, how do I unlock it?"

"Most grimoires use a blood key." Cam could tell by Ivy's twisted features she had no idea what he was talking about. "A drop of blood will unlock it. It's your grimoire, right?"

"Yeah, kind of. It sorta ended up with me."

"It will only open if the grimoire belongs to your blood line. In one way or another, most people in South Jersey can trace their lineage to a Leeds. Could be worth a try."

Elsa sat down next to Cam handing him two slices of white pizza with garlic and oil. He took a bite. With his hand covering his mouth as he chewed, "My breath is going to stink."

"Don't worry, I have breath mints in my purse."

"You have anything sharp in there?" Ivy asked, eyeing Elsa's bedazzled handbag.

"Yep. You want scissors, a safety pin, or a needle?" she asked, unzipping her bag on her lap."

"Needle."

"You carry scissors in your purse?!" Cam said surprised, his eyebrows arching.

"Not a full-size pair but enough to get the job done."

"What else do you have in there?" he asked.

"Tylenol for headaches," she said, poking the side of his head playfully. "I also have Band-Aids, mace, clear nail polish, and condoms."

Cam's face reddened. Elsa didn't notice, she was busy rummaging through her bag, but Ivy did and grinned at his awkwardness.

"Here it is," Elsa said, taking a needle out of a metal case that also housed string, and handed it to Ivy.

Ivy jabbed her thumb with the needle, blood instantly welling on the tip of her finger.

"What are you doing?!" Elsa exclaimed.

"Unlocking my book," she said, surprised she took ownership of it. That had never happened before.

Ivy turned her hand over, letting blood drip onto the open page of the grimoire. Nothing happened. "I guess I'm not family," Ivy said, partially relieved. Deborah had called her a sister in Pleasant Mills Church when she had tried to kill her friends and she had the vision from the past where she was to marry Titan Leeds. She wasn't sure if being married into a family would grant her access to the spell book, but that didn't matter. It was nice to know she wasn't connected to the Leeds, to JD, to any of it by blood.

Cam smiled, pointing. "You spoke too soon."

The pages of the book undulated as if they were being blown by wind. Before their eyes, the letters rearranged themselves, revealing the hidden spell in each page.

"Wow," Elsa said, "that's crazy!"

Astonished, Ivy turned to Cam, hopeful that in these unlocked pages she could find something to finally protect Sammy and his family once and for all from JD and now from Anita. "Thank you. I owe you."

"No. I owe you," he said, glancing at Elsa.

Ivy never understood Elsa's preoccupation with Cam, but they both seemed so happy to be sitting next to each other it made her heart ache all the more for Sammy. With Cam, she could see Elsa getting everything she ever wanted—her large family filled with blue-eyed, blonde-haired babies.

"Looks like you have a lot of reading to do tonight, Ivy."

"Yeah, I do," she replied to Elsa, snapping out of her musing.

"Well, it's almost midnight," Cam said, glancing at the clock on the wall. "I guess I should go get you guys some blankets. The temperature's dropping tonight and this apartment's drafty. Unless you guys want the bedroom?"

"Couch," Ivy said, not looking up from the grimoire.

"Kay, be right back. I keep the extra blankets in my bedroom." Cam deposited his empty paper plate in the trash can before making his way down the hall to his room.

Elsa went to follow him.

"You should take your purse with you," Ivy whispered.

"You're so right, thanks Ivy," she said, reaching for her open bag on the couch before going off after Cam.

Cam's bedroom door was open. His room was decorated in the same vein as the rest of the apartment—classic horror posters. His bed was neatly made. His sheets and pillows were stark white. The bedding made Elsa think of a hotel room.

"Let me help," Elsa said, taking a blanket from Cam who had his hands full of them.

Shutting the linen closet with his hip, "Oh, thanks Elsa. You didn't have to. I could've managed."

Elsa noticed a newspaper clipping on his nightstand next to his reading glasses sitting in The Three Monkeys glasses holder in which one monkey covered its eyes, one covered its ears, and one covered its mouth. The clipping wasn't framed, it was just casually resting on a book she assumed to be his diary. Elsa put the blanket she was holding down at the end of the bed and picked up the clipping. She recognized it. She had the same one tacked to her vanity mirror. It was from the Pleasant Mills Herald. She was featured in an article about the Jersey Devil Football team's winning streak. As head cheerleader, she was interviewed.

"Okay, that's really embarrassing," Cam said into his chest, wishing he could disappear.

"I don't get it," Elsa said. "I thought you didn't remember us, so why cut out this article."

Prickly heat traveled down his neck. "I didn't remember our date but that didn't stop me from liking you."

Elsa put the newspaper clipping back where she found it. "But when

I told you about us you acted like you didn't care."

"No, that wasn't it," Cam said, placing the folded blankets in his arms on the bed with Elsa's. "I thought you were playing a prank on me."

Her face scrunched up. "Why would I do that? Why would I make up us going on a date?"

The conversation was turning in a direction Cam would rather avoid, but now couldn't. "It was easier to believe you were playing a joke on me than for me to believe you could like a guy like me."

Elsa took a step closer to Cam. "Why wouldn't I like a guy like you?"

"Elsa," he said, inhaling sharply as if it was hard to breathe. "You're so smart and beautiful and I'm . . . well dorky and ugly."

"True, you're a little dorky, but so am I. But you're not ugly," she said, taking his hand. "Don't say that."

"Well, maybe not anymore, but I was."

"You look different now but not really." She ran her free hand over his cheek. "It's strange, you have all the same features, but they're just slightly moved around and thinner. It's really weird looking at you. I can't believe I never noticed how much you look like Sammy's mom."

"Yeah, that's definitely weird for me too. When we were kids, we didn't look that much alike."

Elsa let her hand fall to her side. "Cam you were never ugly and I always liked you."

"I wanted to believe you when you called to tell me that before, but I couldn't. I kept waiting to hear your friends laughing at me on the other line. Then, when you asked me to tutor you, I was confused. I didn't see why you would continue with the prank. I never expected you to show up, but you did, and you came again." He shrugged, rolling his shoulders. "I enjoyed being with you, even if it was only to help you with English. Which now I deduce you don't actually need help with."

She shook her head.

Cam could still feel the touch of Elsa's hand on his flushed cheek. His embarrassment was too great to handle; he looked down to avoid her gaze. He wished he didn't turn the lights on when he entered his bedroom.

"When Ivy said I would be eternally grateful, what you said about us going on a date crossed my mind. I hoped it was all true. I actually wished someone messed with my head. That was the only reason I let you two practice magic on me. I don't think any sane person would've let Ivy do that, but I was desperate for what you said to be true."

Elsa's lips softly touched Cam's, his face lifting to hers. "It's true," she said in a murmur, "and I fully intend on letting you make it up to me." He pressed her to him and kissed her back. It was as perfect as the first time they kissed in his car.

"Do I need a breath mint?" Cam asked sheepishly.

"No, but we're definitely going to need the condoms."

Ivy turned the pages of the grimoire, not sure what she was looking for. Her mind was racing. She wished she would've remembered to grab her earbuds before Elsa dragged her out of her house. She was worried about Sammy and his dad and could use a little bit of a distraction in the form of rock 'n' roll. She wished she could go over there now, but what could she do? She was stuck at Cam's till the morning. She would use this time to read the unlocked grimoire, hoping in doing so its knowledge would come to her when she needed it and finally be able to call on her magic like the Midwife of old.

Cam was right about the grimoire. Before the spells were generally superficial—innocent, consisting of mainly recipes and remedies. Now that the grimoire was unlocked, the spells were dark. There were curses, hexes, and poisons. There was one spell that seemed out of place to her, it didn't fit the destructive theme of the others. It was a spell to summon an angel. She was recalled to the strange dream she had about Deborah and the two cloaked men. Ivy ran her finger over a drawing of an angel, tracing the eyes on its wings. Under the drawing, penned in what looked like blood read: the Angel Ezekiel. Anita had told Sammy and Ivy over and over ad nauseum, every spell no matter how innocent it may seem, came with a cost. Ivy wondered what the cost of summoning an angel was.

She closed her eyes, humming the song she had stuck in her head from yesterday. It was a new song by a new band, and she didn't recall any of the words, but she remembered the beat.

Tap . . . Tap . . . Tap.

Leeds Point, New Jersey: 1734

Ivy opened her eyes to find herself in a familiar room. She had seen it before, had been there in the past. The smell of fresh blood stung her nose. In the corner of the room amongst broken furniture, a sheet covered a body, blood soaking through the white shroud. Ivy knew the person under the crimson sheet was Deborah Smith Leeds. By the door another figure was covered with a sheet. Blood dappled the surface where the heart should have been.

The Midwife had watched JD murder his mother and rip out his father's heart and devour it, leaving him in a slump. She'd had the nightmare of Japhet Dean Leeds's birth over and over again, knowing it was she who had brought him back from death as a monster.

Guilt bubbled up inside of Ivy. Not for Deborah. She was more wicked than JD, but for Japhet Dean Leeds and his twin brother. Suddenly, she realized she was holding the grimoire in her hands, the book still open to the spell for summoning an angel.

Ivy heard whispers and turned to see two men in black robes. She wondered if they were the same men from her dream. Something shimmered in the dark around them. She stepped closer to get a better look, the men unaware of her presence. The scanty light from a candle reflected off tiny eyes. She realized the eyes were attached to wings, angel wings. Ivy glanced down at the drawing in the grimoire. She was certain she was seeing the Angel Ezekiel, the same angel from her dream last night.

He spoke. His deep voice as smooth as velvet. "My dark prince, your plan has failed. Demon and angel blood cannot mix. In place of the intended child, we have two. I have fathered a child and you have fathered a child. And they both have died. Despite our failure, it appears paternal instinct brought us each here at a witch's beseeching. But I fear we have made another miscalculation. I have saved your son and you have saved mine."

The other man took off his hood, exposing hair darker than a moonless night. He walked over to Deborah's corpse and pulled back the sheet from her face. Ivy noticed the peculiar sound of his gate. Seeing his cloven feet, she instinctively took a step back.

The man smiled at Ezekiel. "Not a miscalculation brother, but intentional. I made it here first, and I chose to resurrect your son. I have integrated demon blood into him and have thus corrupted him."

"I see," Ezekiel said with a smile that rivaled his brothers, "and I have resurrected your son by integrating angel blood into him and have thus blessed him."

Lucifer recovered Deborah's face with the sheet. "Yes. Now we wait and see what good this can bring."

"Oh brother," Ezekiel said, flicking back a loose curl that had fallen onto his face, "it is true we have eternity to play games with mortals, but I bore of this. Humans can be so meddlesome, the pagans worse. Even now the witch who summoned us here acts to bind your influence on your son. She is in God's house asking him to protect the child from his father."

Ivy knew he was talking about her and Jeffrey. She had locked away Jeffrey's power and his darkness the night he was born. Jeffrey was born evil but had been blessed. With the evil locked away, he could live a normal life. JD was born good, but was corrupted by demon blood, and would live the life of a monster. Deborah had been right, she had been made to deliver evil into the world, but she had made a mistake. The evil she sensed wasn't JD, but Jeffrey.

"Let her try. Like you said, we have eternity. And I do not tire easily."

"Let it be your task to watch over our children."

"I will take this on. I will be their guardian angel." Lucifer turned in Ivy's direction, his dark eyes like pits fixating on her as if he could see her. "I will always be watching."

In a panic, Ivy shut the grimoire breaking the vision. She was back in Cam's living room sitting on the floor in front of the coffee table, the grimoire closed. The sound of Lucifer's voice echoed in her head, '*I will always be watching*.'

CHAPTER EIGHT
The Heartbreaker

In Joe's cramped kitchen, Stevie popped open a bottle of Pinot Noir. He poured the wine into four long stem glasses that he brought, dispersed them, and proposed a toast. "To Mike, for finally getting Joe to shower."

Mike held back a smile as Joe rolled his eyes. Mike liked Stevie. He was vibrant and outgoing in all the ways he wished he was. He could see why Isaac liked him. Besides him being handsome in a boyish way, with a slender frame and his long dark hair to the middle of his back, expressive gray eyes, and full lips, he was funny. Stevie was the perfect balance to Isaac, the more serious of the two.

Mike hesitantly took his glass, not sure how to hold it.

Joe took a sip. "I shower every day."

"My nose tells me otherwise," Stevie said, topping off his glass and making himself comfortable on the countertop next to the sink. He turned to Mike who was next to him in the galley style kitchen. "He's been afraid to go near water, or even drink it," Stevie said, pointing to the recycling bin filled with empty beer cans. "You came just in time, heartbreaker. My orange citrus Lysol was losing its magic."

"I'll drink to that. To the heartbreaker," Issac jested, tilting his glass to his lips.

"Can we please stop calling him that," Joe said, taking another sip of his wine, preferring beer.

Stevie smiled at Mike mischievously. "Give the heartbreaker credit where credit is deserved."

"Isaac, tell him to stop," Joe whined.

"Sorry," Stevie said coolly, twirling the red liquid in his glass, "once you're nick named, that's your name."

"What's yours?" Mike asked.

"Stevie, I thought that was obvious."

"Oh," he said, blushing from embarrassment and the wine. "I thought that was your name. Like short for Steven or Stephen. Like Michael to Mike."

"Stands to reason," Stevie mused.

"I wanted to nickname him uptight asshole," Joe laughed, but I was met with resistance from Isaac.

"I'm sorry Joe if I don't like stepping into your apartment and tripping over crushed beer cans."

"Key word, *my* apartment."

"What's Joe's nickname?" Mike asked, interrupting Joe and Stevie's squabble.

Joe smirked, leaning one arm on the counter. "It's a secret."

"This is what I'm talking about!" Stevie said excitedly. "You two and your secrets!"

"Please don't have one of your breakdowns. I'll tell you what it is. It's Big Dick Joe. Issac didn't want to tell you because before you got the nickname Stevie, he called you Thin Mint."

"Joseph," Isaac said sternly.

"You know what, I'm glad you're feeling better for Isaac's sake but it's time for me to go," Stevie said, hopping off the kitchen counter.

"Don't go," Mike said anxiously. He too felt uncomfortable with Isaac and Joe's closeness. "It won't be fun if you go."

That seemed to settle Stevie. "I *am* fun," he said, tilting his head for everyone to admire his profile.

Mike added with a wink in Joe's direction, "And there's no way Joe's nickname is Big Dick, trust me on that."

"Well," Stevie said primly, settling back on top of the countertop, "I will drink to that."

"That was nice of you to make Stevie feel big," Joe said, throwing himself on his bed once they finished off the last of the wine and determined to tuck in for the evening. "Even if it was at my expense."

"I didn't want him to leave," Mike stated honestly.

"He wouldn't have. Well, not for long. He would have made a dramatic exit and came back in an hour with dessert for everyone."

"Oh," Mike said, rubbing his arm nervously from the doorway where he still stood. "He seemed really upset when you called him Thin Mint."

"It was below the belt," Joe admitted. "I shouldn't have said that."

"Oh, so, um . . . you've been with Stevie? Is that how Issac met him?"

"Oh geez, no. Nothing like that. Thin Mint wasn't about his size. He has an eating disorder. That's *how* Issac and Stevie met. Stevie was hospitalized after he'd fainted in the street or something like that," Joe said indifferently, gesturing for Mike to come into the room. "Like I said, Issac has a messiah complex. Stevie needed saving and he saved him. When they met, Stevie only drank sugar water. That's how he got his nick name. He would add packs of Stevia to his water, to stop himself from passing out. Stevia became the only slightly more masculine Stevie."

"Oh," Mike said, feeling like a parrot on repeat as he thought about Stevie. He didn't notice if he ate any of the Chinese food from Ray's Noodles they had for dinner. He only saw him drink the wine. Stevie was thin, really thin, but he'd known people that skinny in the past and didn't think anything of it.

Joe looked off into space. "I should apologize to him. But I won't. Stevie just gets under my skin. He always thinks I'm out to steal Isaac."

"You can't blame him," Mike said, taking a seat on the side of the bed, his back to Joe. "You and Issac are really close. I'd imagine any boyfriend of either of yours would feel the same."

Mike could feel heat rushing to his cheeks again and was grateful Joe didn't turn on the lights to his bedroom when they'd entered. The only light in the room was a faint glow from the lights of the shops across the street that filtered in through slatted blinds.

Still facing away from Joe, "So is your nickname really a secret?"

"No. Isaac nicknames everyone we know, but he's never nicknamed me. He thinks it will make Stevie mad to know that."

"Madder than a secret?" Mike asked, mulling over it.

"Yes. Because it'll prove our relationship is different then there's."

Mike felt every bit as jealous of Joe and Issac's relationship as Stevie did. In fact, he disliked Issac more than ever now. "Why break up with Issac, if you guys were so great together?" Mike asked, his tone a little rough.

Joe sat up. "I never said that. I never said we were great."

Mike crossed his arms over his chest childishly. "You implied it. Implied you were better with Issac than Stevie is."

Joe tucked his hair behind his ears. "Issac and I are just friends. Best friends. Stevie knew that when he met Isaac. He needs to get over it and move on. I broke up with Issac, not the other way around, so Stevie has nothing to fear."

"Maybe he fears you made a mistake and fears Issac still loves you," Mike said, self-projecting. Issac did confess to him that he went on loving Joe for a long time after they broke up.

Joe laughed. "I think that *is* what he fears. Which is a good thing. I guess he fears it because he loves Issac. That was my problem when I dated Issac, the caring was usually one sided. With Stevie it's different, he cares just as much for Issac, if not more."

Joe playfully hit Mike in the back with a pillow. "Relax, you don't have to worry about Stevie. He has nothing to fear from me, I'm still not over my last breakup."

Mike tilted his head in Joe's direction. Joe had resumed his original repose on his bed, his arm folded under his head.

Joe tried to read Mikes face in the dark. "You know if this is too awkward for you, you can stay in the living room. The sofa pulls out to a bed."

"Do you want me to stay in the living room?" Mike asked, a lump in his throat.

"No. I want you to stay in here. You came all the way to Philly for Isaac's little experiment, we might as well give it our best."

Mike nodded, lying down in the bed next to Joe. He kept his arms and hands tight to his sides, keeping his eyes on the ceiling where little brown water stains spread like lily pads on water.

"Night," Joe said, pulling the chain to the blinds.

Mike turned on his side. "Joe, I need to tell you something."

Joe was already asleep.

Mike hugged Joe goodbye. It was nice to have him in his arms again, even if it was only for a platonic hug. Through Joe's long sleeve shirt, Mike felt his vertebrae protruding down his back. Joe had lost more weight than he had thought.

Mike would have hugged Joe forever if he could have, but they both felt Issac's and Stevie's eyes burrowing holes in them from the couch. Pushing apart, "Um, well, I'm, glad Issac's experiment worked, and you got a good night's sleep."

"Seriously Michael Handover, you're the best kind of medicine."

Mike knew his sister had special abilities, abilities that allowed her to see ghosts and for them to talk through her, like the ghost of Enzo Serrano had. Maybe he was a giant dreamcatcher or something. Whatever the reason, Joe stopped having nightmares around him, he was beyond grateful. He did something for him that Issac couldn't.

"I wish I could stay longer," Mike said, his voice faltering. "But I have a big exam tomorrow. But uh, maybe I could come back this weekend?" Mike lowered his head, his eyes in shadows. "That is if you think you'll need me."

Joe awkwardly put his hands in his pockets. "Yeah, that would be perfect. As you can see," he said, glancing back at Isaac and Stevie on the couch," they're not giving me a moment to myself. I'm sure they'd like the idea of the entire weekend off."

"Okay," Mike said, happily, "I'll be here Friday night."

Mike had just gotten on the Expressway heading home when his phone rang. He didn't recognize the number, but it was a Pennsylvania area code, so he decided to answer it.

"Mike, you have to come back! We need you!" Stevie said frantically into the phone.

Mike shifted into the right lane to get off at the next exit. "What happened?!"

"He won't stop throwing up. There's so much water, it's not humanly possible. It's like he swallowed a lake. You have to come back!"

Mike ran up the stairs to Joe's apartment. Stevie opened the door before he could knock. Mike rushed to the bathroom where Issac sat by the side of the toilet with Joe.

"We knew you were back because it stopped," Issac said.

"What happened?" Mike asked, crouching next to Joe.

"What can I say, I wanted to see you again," Joe said, his voice hoarse.

Mike looked at him pitifully. From the coughing, he had broken a blood vessel in his right eye, red now spilling over the white of his eye in a grotesque blight. "Crap," Mike said, wanting to do something but not knowing what to do.

Issac spoke. "A couple minutes after you left, it happened. He started to choke, and water began to spill from his mouth and wouldn't stop."

Mike rubbed Joe's back. "I don't understand, I thought this happened when you fell asleep and started dreaming."

"Normally that's how it went," Joe said, evidently exhausted, his head sagging.

"I made it worse," Mike said, his upset visible in his flushed face and shaky tone.

"No," Joe told him. "You couldn't make anything worse."

"What does this all mean?" Stevie asked, leaning in the doorway. "At least at night we could make sure someone was with him. But if this could happen at any moment on any day, for no reason, what can we do?"

Issac and Mike exchanged worried glances. "I'm staying," Mike said. "I won't leave."

Joe lifted his head away from the toilet bowl. "I'm fine now. Honestly, I am, and you have to go to school."

"He can't go," Stevie said, blocking the door as if Mike was going to make a run for it. "You almost died not even five minutes ago!"

"He can't stay with me every second of the day."

"He can't," Isaac agreed, "but what are our choices? If we can somehow find out what it is about Mike that makes whatever this is go away, then we can replicate it. It's not like I can take him to the hospital. Mistreating his symptoms will make him worse."

"I said I'll stay," Mike said. "I just have to make it to last period tomorrow. I'm failing math. If I don't pass this exam, I may not graduate."

"Thank you," Issac said relieved. Although Joe and Stevie butted heads, Mike could tell Stevie was also relieved, sighing deeply from the doorway.

CHAPTER NINE
Mr. Lopez

Ivy let out a sigh of relief. The iron gates to the Lopez estate were open. There would be no uncomfortable conversation with Sammy or Mr. Lopez through the gate speaker.

"Stop! Don't go down the driveway," Ivy said, almost grabbing the steering wheel, and stopping herself at the last moment. Crashing Elsa's mother's car into the front gate would be worse than any awkward conversation she could conjure up in her head. "Let me out here," insisted Ivy. "I'll walk the rest of the way."

Elsa let her mother's sedan idle between the open gate. "You sure? I can go with you."

Ivy shook her head while she unbuckled her seatbelt. "No, if you come with me Sammy will put on a song and dance for you."

Elsa flicked her hair off her shoulders as Ivy had seen her do many times. "I thought I'd act as a buffer between you two. You know," she said, with another toss of her hair, "the neutral friend."

"I'll be fine." Ivy opened the car door, feeling a hand on her shoulder.

"Ivy . . ."

"Yeah?" she said, turning to look at Elsa.

"Thanks for helping with Cam. You're a good friend."

This surprised Ivy. Twice now, Elsa had called herself a friend and in less than a minute span. Ivy had helped Elsa, mainly because she wouldn't take no for an answer, and it got her out of her chores. She didn't realize this made them friends. Ivy only had one friend and that was Rosa Littleton, the old Chief of Police Devan Rainier's granddaughter. The idea of having two friends seemed a feat of magic. Now only if that magic could carry over to Sammy, and repair their relationship, she could die a happy girl. She chuckled to herself, that would be her luck. She'd finally get back together with Sammy and be struck dead by a bolt of cosmic justice. Happy, but dead.

The sound of Elsa's voice snapped Ivy out of her ill-fated reverie. "Call me and let me know how you make out with Sammy and Mr. Lopez."

"I will," Ivy said, meaning it.

"Kay. Well, I'm going to go home and call Cam."

Ivy smiled. "Have fun."

Ivy watched as Elsa put her mother's sedan in reverse and sped away down the street. With Elsa gone, she made her way up the winding driveway to the front door, attempting to formulate her words. "I'm here to help—no, that's too superhero. I heard there's trouble—no, to policeish."

Time was up. In her anxiety, she nearly ran to the front door. She rang the doorbell with the last of her resolve, her mind as blank as a fresh canvas.

Sammy opened the door. Seeing him, Ivy's jaw dropped. She knew Sammy's mom had moved out with the twins and Hugo to live with his aunt Fran and grandmother but in her head, she'd still imagined Lindsey Lopez answering the door, wearing a tight fitting sweaterdress, her hair and makeup perfect, like it always was.

Speechless, Ivy took in Sammy's face. It had been months since she'd been that close to him. She could see the dark gray speckles in his light blue eyes sparkle, like crests on rolling ocean waves. His dark hair curled around his temples, framing a face she knew had to be from Heaven. His lips seemed too perfect to be real, she wanted to lean in and kiss him and see if she was dreaming.

That thought, however, was squashed when the door shut in her face. Ivy reasoned she deserved that for the number of times Grams and she had done the same to him.

Ivy quickly reached for the doorbell and pushed it. Then, pushed it again. She had to see him. Forget Jeffrey Lopez, she would sit there and push the doorbell all day just to have Sammy shut the door in her face—to see his blue eyes look at her—to see the curl of his dark hair spiral down the sides of his temples. Pushing a doorbell for eternity seemed a small price to pay to see her Spanish god. Though his tan had faded with the coming of fall, his skin retained its youthful glow of light, summer, and boyhood, bringing her back to the first time she saw him. It was hard to believe he just turned eighteen a few days ago. At the same time, she would've believed that he was as old as the mountains and lakes.

Sammy opened the door a crack, avoiding eye contact with Ivy, the majority of his face in shadow. "Are you going to do that all day?"

"If I have to," Ivy said, standing tall as if to retain some dignity.

In a whisper, "What do you want?"

"I'm here to see your dad not you."

Sammy's head jerked up, the sun highlighting the hollows under his eyes. Ivy could tell he hadn't been sleeping well.

Sammy opened the door. "What do you want with my dad?" Hot air rushed out into the cold morning as his black cat Catchup curled around his legs like a furry snake. If there was a sexy warlock calendar, Sammy would be on the cover. Ivy drank him in greedily. Faded blue jeans and a black Nike hoodie never looked so good. She tried not to dislocate her jaw like a python about to eat a plump dinner of rat. She noticed he was different than the Sammy who had left her slumped in the grass in front of a demolished Pleasant Mills Church, discarded and hated, only a few months ago. Not physically different but something else. It was the same feeling she experienced in the presence of Cam when the spell blocking his memories degraded. Ivy could feel Sammy's magic and it had nothing to do with those supernatural blue eyes of his. He had not only awakened his magic, but he was also getting stronger.

"So, uh, can I see your dad or what?" Ivy asked.

Sammy, lost for words, looked at Ivy as if through her, while he formulated his thoughts.

"How did you know something was up with my dad? Did *he* tell you?"

"*He*?" Ivy asked genuinely confused.

"JD."

"JD?!" Ivy repeated in a near shout.

Sammy covered Ivy's mouth with his hand. "Shh, don't say his name so loud, he could be listening." He removed his hand. "You better come in." Sammy didn't give Ivy a chance to speak. "I know he told you. Maybe you can do something about it. Tell him to leave my father alone."

Once inside the house, Ivy rubbed her hands together grateful for the warmth. Catchup brushed against her legs. She knelt, petting the silky feline on the top of the head. Ivy caught a glimpse of herself in the mirror in the Lopez foyer. She looked rumpled from sleeping on Cam's couch. She wished she would've had Elsa drive her home for a change of clothes before dropping her off at Sammy's.

"Sammy, you need to start at the beginning."

He looked at her puzzled. "You said you were here to help my dad."

"I am. But I don't know what's wrong. A little birdy said he was wacked out."

"And that birdy wasn't JD?"

"No," Ivy said. She could see the disappointment and the relief on his face, his emotions flashing in his eyes. "It was Elsa."

"Elsa," he repeated a little surprised. "I guess I freaked her out the other night."

"I think a little," Ivy agreed with a nod. "I said I'd check things out. Since I'm here, you might as well tell me what's up with your dad."

Sammy shrugged, leaning against the closed front door. "Nothing. Which is the scary part. I mean he finds out his brother is a demon, meaning he is one too or possibly is one and is cool with it. Let's not forget he killed himself to release his magic then helped kill his psychopathic mother and absorbed even more power. He should be freaking out. But he's not."

"Your dad is really good at being well-adjusted."

"Come on Teller, that's not normal."

Her heart fluttered at him calling her by her pet name. She'd had dreams of him whispering that in her ear. Her longing for him became unbearable. She was so close to him now, but she never felt further apart.

"But maybe . . .," Sammy said tapping on his chin like a detective on TV, "maybe he's not as well-adjusted as I thought. That could explain it."

"Um, explain what? You gonna clue me in?"

"It could explain why I heard JD and my dad talking the other night. Maybe he went to JD for help, because he felt he had no one else to turn to."

"That would be out of character for your dad. I didn't think he ever asked for help. You sure it was JD he was talking to?"

"I'm sure," Sammy said, his eyes narrowing to slits.

"Okay, well, what did he say?"

Sammy clenched his fists, his whole demeanor stiffening. "I don't know. I had to hide before I was discovered. But I think JD's trying to talk my dad into something bad. Normally, my dad never would have let JD step foot in the house and now they're having a late-night secret meeting. JD must've seen his window and took it."

"I don't think your dad would be that gullible. But I agree, something strange is up," Ivy said, picking up Catchup who kept meowing.

"She missed you," Sammy said, petting the cat on the side of her face, a fury of purrs rumbling through the small cat.

Ivy smiled. "I missed her too and missed . . ." Ivy stopped herself before she added 'you too'. Things were going well. She didn't want to make it awkward by confessing her undying love to him. Not yet at least.

Sammy waited for her to finish her thought with inquisitive eyes.

"Uh . . . so uh . . . how can I help?" Ivy managed to get out, wondering if he wanted her to admit she missed him. He must know that, or maybe not. He did block her on all social media platforms, not to mention her phone number. It was the same thing he did the last time they broke up—wipe her from his social footprint.

"Maybe you can see what JD wants with my dad and squash it. I'm sure for a kiss or two he'd leave my dad alone."

Ivy glared at him. "I'm not some witchy prostitute."

Sammy put his hands up in defense as if she was going to throw

Catchup at him claws out. Red spider webs creeped over the whites of his eyes. "I didn't mean it like that. I'm sorry. I just meant I have no leverage over him, but you still do. He loves you."

The words hurt Ivy. As if in saying JD loved her meant he didn't.

"I'll do what I can," Ivy said, putting the cat down unweaponized, as the family dog, Hotdog, came to her for pets. "I haven't seen JD in a long time and don't know if and when I will again. But uh, since I'm here, why don't we talk to your dad together? Oh, and what did your dad say when you asked him about his late-night visitor?"

Sammy brushed his hair away from his face. "He acted like it never happened. Said I must have dreamed it. My dad's an excellent liar. I almost believed him and would've if it weren't for the pit in my stomach telling me it wasn't a dream."

"I believe you," Ivy said.

He nodded, pointing down the hall. "My dad's in his office."

Ivy followed Sammy, walking a step behind him. "I guess I should say congratulations."

"For what?" Sammy said, abruptly stopping. Ivy almost walked into him, stopping herself at the last second before they collided.

"You're finally all hocus-pocused out."

Sammy furrowed his eyebrows, cocking his head in thought. "What do you mean?"

"You tapped into your magic."

He looked her over incredulously as if she'd just played a cruel joke on him. "Yeah, it happened after the church fire. You knew that."

"I knew it awoken in you, but now it's like bam. You're a pretty strong witch Sammy Lopez."

He smiled, but there was a mix of emotions in it, the smile never quite reaching his eyes.

Ivy wanted to be happy for him, this was what he wanted, and a small part of her was but the rest of her was terrified. He had wanted to come into his magic since she met him, but with doing so Enzo's warning divided his family. She couldn't get the scar on Cam's neck out of her head—couldn't stop seeing the same scar marring Sammy's neck. She hoped Anita hadn't come back to live with the Lopez's yet and that she could make it so she never did. With this much magic at Anita's fingertips, Ivy imagined it would be hard to resist killing Sammy.

"Really?" Sammy said, his rough demeanor softening. "You think I'm stronger now."

With her hands, Ivy made the shape of clouds around Sammy's shoulders. "It's surrounding you like a cloud."

"A storm cloud," he said, not pleased.

"Uh no, like a happy cloud with a rainbow," Ivy said, wishing she said anything but cloud. *Maybe a sunburst or exoskeleton would have seemed less ominous.*

Sammy's eyes shifted again in thought before turning on his heel and continuing down the hall to his father's office. He wasted no time knocking.

"I'm busy," Jeffrey said from behind the closed door.

"It's Sammy. I'm here with Ivy."

They heard muffled voices. "Come in," Jeffrey finally said.

Ivy walked into what looked more like a library than an office, with books encircling the large room from floor to ceiling. By the window stood Jeffrey, his long hair, now touching his shoulders, was tucked behind his ears. She had never seen him with his hair so long, it made him look younger as if Sammy and him could've been brothers. But they weren't, Jeffrey's real brother stood on the other side of the window, a smile playing on his lips when he saw her.

"Hello Ms. Teller," JD said, in a singsong voice that made Ivy want to throw a chair at him.

Ivy remaining composed, ignored JD. "Mr. Lopez, I want to help," she said, feeling a little bit like Supergirl and regretting saying it as soon as her words hit her ears.

"Help with what exactly?" he asked, turning to face her. He seemed perfectly collected if it wasn't for his insatiable need to play with his hair.

"With whatever you need help with. I guess, start by telling me how you feel."

"You're a shrink now?" he said, his tone close to nasty.

Irritated, Ivy got mouthy. It was one of those Teller traits she could never reign in. "Let me tell you how I think you're feeling, Mr. Lopez—desperate if you're letting JD in your house. And maybe a little crazy if you think taking his advice can help you."

Jeffrey sat down at his desk. "Thank you for your concern Ivy, but I don't need help and JD's my brother."

Ivy scoffed. "Yeah, he's also the same brother who murdered all of Sammy's friends. How's Zac? Still dead, I'm guessing."

Jeffrey and JD weren't amused. It freaked her out how their faces mirrored each other with their scowls.

"Dad, what are you doing with JD? Him, being here in your office right now is proof that the other night did happen. You keep meeting with him, why?"

Sammy couldn't look at JD. He felt like if he did, everyone would know what he'd done to save himself in the burning church—know how weak he was—know he was afraid to die.

Jeffrey didn't answer.

"Mr. Lopez, with all due respect, your situation is far from normal. This whole time you thought you were a non-magic and now you're JD's magical twin brother."

"Non-magic?" Sammy asked.

"A term I picked up," she whispered.

Her attention was back on Sammy's dad. "Naturally, you're dealing with stuff. Magic can make you feel off kilter. I know. I was in your shoes when I first moved to Pleasant Mills."

Jeffrey evaluated Ivy. They were in the same shoes. More than anyone in the room, she *could* relate to what he was feeling. Both of their pasts were shadows to them. Both had to deal with the discovery of who they really were and what that meant.

"JD was born with magic and learned to use it as a child learns to ride a bike. It was thrown on you and you don't know how to walk yet. Let Sammy and I help you. You know you can trust *us*," she said, shooting daggers at JD with her dark pupils.

"You're right, Ivy," Jeffrey said steadily. "You know how I feel, so you understand I can trust myself." He raked his fingers through his hair. "I admit I had some adjusting to do to having magic. If I can call it that. I can't pull a rabbit out of a hat or clear a storm. In fact, I can't do anything I couldn't do before, but I do feel different. At first, I felt great, better than I ever felt. Then I didn't anymore. The greatness wore away and I felt . . . emotional, for lack of a better word. My emotions are heightened. When I'm happy, I'm ecstatic and when I'm angry . . . well, I'm very angry. But I'm handling it. I avoid all the triggers my therapist helped me to identify. So, there's no reason for you kids to worry about me. And as far as JD, I thought with him being my brother and having the same kind of magic as me, he could help," Jeffrey said, fueling Sammy and Ivy's suspicion JD was there as some sort of magical advisor.

"He doesn't have the same magic as you, Dad."

Jeffrey and JD both looked at him fascinated.

"What would make you think that Sammy, we're twins of course we do."

"No," Sammy said, "it's not like that. You're brothers because you share the same mother and fathers, kind of. Deborah was pregnant with twins, but they were fathered by different people. Dad, your father was a demon and JD's was an angel. When you both died the Midwife called for help and the same demon and angel resurrected each other's child, mixing their blood with the both of yours, making you and JD some weird demon angel hybrids."

Ivy looked at Sammy shocked. Could Sammy have had the same vision she had. And if so, how was it possible? Were they linked or was this a glimpse into Sammy's unlocked magic?

Sammy continued, elaborating. "When Deborah smothered JD and the Midwife cast a spell for help, the demon saved the half angel, introducing demon blood into him and corrupted JD—essentially cursing him into a monster."

JD involuntarily twitched at the word monster.

"And Dad, you were the evil one, but you were saved by an angel and God's grace was bestowed on you making you conflicted. Ivy, or rather the Midwife, tried to bind the thing that made you a demon when you were a baby. You unleashed that part of you in the church to help defeat Deborah."

Jeffrey struggled hearing this, his hands compulsively raking back his hair. "I was the evil one?" He looked to JD for answers. JD didn't stir. He was so still; he seemed like a statue of flesh and bone.

"The evil Deborah sensed in her womb was not JD, but you. The evil she meant to snuff out was you. She didn't know she was pregnant with twins."

JD finally spoke. "How did you come to learn this, Sammy?" His eyes flickered to Ivy then back to Sammy.

"I saw it in a dream. More than once. I know it's real. I came into my magic. Ivy can confirm that or maybe you can sense it yourself, but what I saw was true. I know it."

Jeffrey was speechless, his words coming out in clicking sounds. "It's true," Jeffrey got out. "Anita sensed the darkness in me from the beginning. I was destined to be evil."

"No Mr. Lopez, you were destined for more. You're not evil. Nature vs nurture. You don't have to give into your nature." Ivy glanced at JD. "And neither do you. You don't have to be a monster, JD."

"Promise me Dad," Sammy said, "promise me you will never take any advice from JD. Promise me no more meetings with him. Ivy may believe nurture can beat out nature, but I don't. JD is evil. He may have been born half-angel, but he was resurrected as a demon. He can't be trusted. I heard him say, if you don't do something about it I will."

"Sammy, you don't have to worry about JD, there will be no more meetings." Jeffrey looked to JD.

JD nodded.

Jeffrey opened the drawer to his desk and pulled out a letter. "I guess you're going to find out sooner than later, and you should hear it from me." He got up and handed the letter to Sammy.

He opened it. "What am I looking at?" Sammy asked.

"Your mother filed for divorce. JD was telling me I had to do something about it, or he was. He wanted to go talk to your mother and I told him no."

"What?!" Sammy said, his eyes as smooth as glass as they darted between his father and JD.

"This is because of me. Because I don't trust Abby."

Jeffrey put a hand on his son's shoulder. "Sammy, I want you to listen to me. None of this is your fault." Tears stood in Sammy's eyes. "It's been coming for a while. We tried to push it off as long as we could."

"Tell Abby to move back in," Sammy said excitably. "I was wrong. There's nothing on Enzo Serrano. You're right Dad, Abby didn't have a brother. As far as I can tell, he never existed. Why should I believe a ghost I met once over my grandmother I've known my entire life?!"

Jeffrey leaned on the edge of his desk. "I don't think it will help Sammy. Your mother's not happy with me and to be honest I understand."

"You have to try. You and Mom being apart for so long isn't good. Or is this about Pearl? Maybe you don't want to try," Sammy said, tears falling down his cheeks.

At the mention of Pearl, Jeffrey took a deep breath. Ivy watched his lips silently count down from ten.

Calmly, Jeffrey spoke. "Pearl has nothing to do with this. I have never cheated on your mother."

"Not physically," Sammy said, "but you talk to her all the time."

"She's my friend. Just like Elsa is yours. I don't appreciate you bringing this up again. We've had this conversation before and it hurts your mother, Pearl, and me."

"Then you're going to talk to mom and have her move back in?"

"I promise to talk to your mother," Jeffrey said, taking the letter from Sammy and putting it back in the envelope. "But now I think it's time for you to take Ivy home and for me to let JD go about his day."

"Do you think your dad told us the truth?" Ivy asked on the car ride to her house.

Sammy looked at her puzzled. "About Pearl?"

"No, not that, about why JD was there? I believe JD would maybe be okay with magical advice, but relationship advice seems a little bit out of his scope of understanding. I lie—a lot out of his scope—toxic relationship material all the way."

Sammy nibbled his bottom lip in thought. "It does seem unlikely he was there for relationship support. My dad would probably call a girl for that. And since he has Pearl on speed dial, he'd call her. Which means JD was there for another reason." Sammy sighed, gripping the steering wheel with both hands. "Like I said, my dad's an excellent liar. And like always, I fell for it. I guess it's one of the perks of being the spawn of Lucifer."

"About that," Ivy said, putting her numb fingers up to the heat vents, "I had the same dream vision."

"You did?" Sammy said, relieved. "I wasn't sure that was what it was. I thought I was going crazy, especially when I kept having it over and over again." Sammy's eyes darted to her, where she now had her fingertips wedged in the heater vents. He turned the heat up. "You think it's *the* Lucifer?"

"I don't know and don't think it really matters. A demon is a demon in my book. I'm just glad you didn't tell your dad its name. Your mother would never come home if she heard that one."

"No way," Sammy said, his eyes going off the road for a second. "I didn't want to freak my dad out. I'm still freaking out myself, I don't need mass hysteria at the house. And I don't want to give my dad any excuse to consult JD."

"Agreed," Ivy said thoughtfully. "The Midwife locked your dad's magic away for a reason. We have to find out what that reason is before JD does."

"It has to be a very big reason. Colossal. The reason of all reasons, I reason," he said with a smile. "It's so big, she'd rather have my father dead than let his magic loose."

Ivy scanned the leafless tree line. "And whatever JD's up to, we can count on him to keep his promise and not visit your dad at the house."

"Shoot," Sammy said, realizing Ivy was right. "I shouldn't have said anything. Now we can't spy on them."

Ivy liked the sound of 'we'.

Sammy pulled into Ivy's driveway, letting his car idle.

"It's not your fault, Sammy."

"I'm hearing that a lot lately."

"It's not. We know your dad. No matter what's up, he would never hurt you or your family. I believe that," she said, not really believing it. There was a time not that long ago when Jeffrey did hurt Sammy, a time when he couldn't control his anger and that anger found an outlet in hitting his son.

"You just don't know who else he would hurt."

"We'll figure this out." Ivy said, not really sure what else she could say. She had no idea what JD was up to. The fact she hadn't seen him since Sammy broke up with her had her worried. She assumed he was laying low because he was plotting something. She just didn't think that something involved Jeffrey Lopez.

"Abby can help," Sammy said, filling the awkward silence that came over the car.

Ivy felt guilty. She rather Sammy's parents get divorced than Sammy live under the same roof as Anita Gomez. She avoided eye contact, looking down at her seatbelt. "You have every reason not to trust me Sammy, but I hope you know that I love you and I'll do anything for you. So, you have to believe me when I say, you can't trust your grandmother."

She wanted to tell him about Cam, but that would put Cam in danger. Ivy knew Sammy couldn't keep a thing like his long-lost uncle being found alive and well a secret for long, making Cam a target along with Sammy, now that Sammy had come into his magic.

Sammy's lips sagged into a frown. His mind went to the same warning given to him from the 'old Jesse' on the side of Pleasant Mills Church before his friend Timothy Chen's funeral. He had doubted his grandmother then, though she proved to only be protecting him from getting involved with his mother's deal with JD to cure her cancer. All of his doubts were proven to be unfounded, and Enzo's warning appeared to be the same.

Sammy mulled over Ivy's words in his head before he spoke. "*Do anything for me,* including handing my soul over to a demon."

Ivy's eyes remained glued to Sammy's. She didn't blink. She wanted him to know she meant business. "Yes Sammy, even that. I know you don't believe me that I did it for you, but I did."

"I may not have found anything on Enzo but that doesn't mean I fully trust my grandmother and I think you should know I don't trust you either."

Sammy looked away, avoiding Ivy's eyes. Her heart sank. A heavy weight compressed her shoulders. Things had been going so well today.

"Not entirely," Sammy added, his eye's flickering to her, his thick eyelashes as beautiful as butterfly wings.

"You didn't tell Sammy the truth," JD stated plainly, looking out toward Jeffrey's Koi pond.

"I don't need him or Ivy to worry. Recurring or not, the nightmare is just a nightmare."

"It's so easy for you to lie," JD said, turning to his brother. His eyes ran over him, fixating on Jeffrey's lips. He examined them from where he stood as if the ability to lie came from them. "I can't do that. I've tried but nothing comes out. How different we are, and yet how similar."

Jeffrey nodded, happy to hear the part about them being different. They were brothers, twin brothers. There was no denying that, but that didn't absolve JD from all the terrible things he'd done to his family. Jeffrey found himself in a difficult, yet strange place. Family was everything to him and now JD was family.

"We have to respect Sammy's wishes. You can't come to the house anymore."

"Where will we meet?" JD asked, running his hand over his cigarette case tucked in his jacket, fighting the urge to pull a cigarette out and light it.

"Is there a need to meet again?"

JD let Jeffrey's words sink in slowly, not letting it show how much they hurt him. "Well," he said, walking around to the front of Jeffrey's desk, "if you should find yourself in need of me, you can find me near Uriah's. I usually linger around those parts."

"That works," Jeffrey nonchalantly said, accompanying JD out of his office. "If I need to get in touch with you, I'll meet you at the rectory."

CHAPTER TEN
Corruption

"*Turning him into a monster*," JD said on repeat under his breath. He walked in a trance through the woods. The fallen leaves crunched under his feet as a cold wind whipped around him. He felt nothing, not the sting of the wind or the clawing nail-like projections on the shrubbery he walked past. He was numb. The idea that he was meant to be good, innately good—an angel, burned through his consciousness making him sick. He had been good but had been corrupted. First by the demon the Midwife summoned for help, next by the man who called himself a friend.

Batsto Village, New Jersey: 1735

JD felt a nudge on his shoulder. He turned around to see a young man dressed in finery. The metallic tip of his cane glared at him in the morning sun which broke through the last of the clouds left from the previous night's storm.

"I say boy, are you okay?"

On alert, JD sat up, pushing his mother's heart behind his back, burying it under the pine needles that had served as his bed, completely naive to the awkwardness of him being naked.

"What happened to you. Let me guess," the man said, not waiting for a response. "Thugs. There is a new breed of roughies in these parts. They quite literally took the clothes right off your back. Barbarians!"

The man briskly unbuttoned his long wool jacket and handed it to JD. "Here boy, put this on. This will do until we can make it to my lodging. It's only a hundred paces that way," the man articulated with his cane, which was a thing of status, not necessity, pointing with it in the direction JD had fled from. "I will see to it you are well clothed and fed before I see you off."

JD donned the coat. It was too large, nevertheless the softness of the material pleased him. He buttoned it closed.

"Now then, let's go. Be quick about it or you'll be sure to catch your death in this damp."

JD followed, but not before kicking more pine needles over his mother's heart to make sure it was fully hidden. The dandelion Ivy had given him from her hair at their parting was still clenched in his fist. She had saved him, after his mother had smothered him with a pillow. She had saved him, and she had named him: Japhet Dean. They had made love, and she had given him a token of that love in the small flower. *'When a dandelion dies it leaves you a wish. Don't be afraid to make yours . . . I've made mine Japhet Dean. I wish to be with you forever.'* His heart soared. He loved her and would cherish the flower forever.

The gentleman and JD made their way down a narrow dirt road, passing no one in the early dawn. Soon they came to a humble cabin clad in pine board. Two small windows, facing the road they ventured in from, peered out from the facade like lonely eyes.

BEN'S CABIN

As the man opened the front door, he spoke to JD. "This is where I stay when I'm in town on business. It's easy to get where I need to go and comes with plenty of privacy."

JD ducked through the squat opening into the sparsely furnished room. The man motioned for JD to take a seat. He complied, pulling out a stool and making himself comfortable at the table.

"Tea? The man asked, already busy at the hearth where a kettle hung over a fire that had recently been snuffed out.

JD nodded, as he looked around the room. The room consisted of a large table with several chairs haphazardly tucked under it. The table was littered with knickknacks, gadgets, and books that puzzled JD. He picked up a skeleton of a kite off the table to examine it closer.

"Don't mind the mess," the man said, placing a teacup on a saucer in front of him and taking a seat across from JD with his own cup. "I have a girl come once a week to clean up after me." He smiled. "She hasn't come yet. Mark my word, when she does, she will right all." He raised his teacup to his lips. "Not sweet enough," he said, placing his teacup back on the saucer before pushing stacks of clutter away to gain purchase on a tin canister. He opened the lid and pulled out dried apple slices. Adding two slices to his tea, he gestured for JD to take some. JD followed his example and let the apple slices seep in his tea.

"Milk shortage this winter, apples give it a tang," the man said, stirring the tea with his index finger. "Now that we're settled in, what's your story? What's your name?" He laughed at himself, "How impertinent. I should have introduced myself on the path." He extended his hand to JD over the table. "My name is Benjamin Franklin. I'm pleased to make your acquaintance."

JD shook his hand saying nothing.

"Well out with it boy, what's your name?"

In a soft voice, "Japhet Dean."

Benjamin rubbed his chin, running his hand over the stubble that grew there. "Now that's a name you don't hear every day. I take it it's a family name?"

JD's eyes flickered to his tea.

"I knew a man by that name just yesterday. He was the brother of my dearest friend. He was murdered last night along with his wife. Their child is missing, presumed dead . . . How intriguing it is you bear his name."

JD's heart raced. He glanced at the door.

Benjamin smiled a large grin. "Fear not, Japhet Dean. I am not set on hurting you but helping you. I know who and what you are and want us to be bosom friends."

JD's eyes shifted to the man across the table.

"That's right, there's nothing to fear from me. I am a man of science, as well as the metaphysical. I have heard of beings like yourself. Shifters. You can change to and from a beast at will."

"How do you know that?" JD asked, intrigued.

"Your hands," Benjamin said, nonchalantly taking another sip of tea as if this was a perfectly normal conversation to have with guests.

JD glanced at his hands on the table. His fingernails had grown out to resemble claws. He quickly hid them in his lap.

"When you're anxious, you cause cracks in your human appearance. Your true self shines through. When I found you under the tree, I noticed the same thing but with your eyes. They changed from brown to red when you felt threatened. When you perceived that I wasn't a threat your eyes returned to their warm brown."

JD glanced at his hands in his lap, his nails again a normal length. Benjamin wasn't a threat.

"I can help you learn to control your power and summon it. With my help you will be able to hide in plain sight amongst your fellow man."

"I would like that," JD said.

"You are new to this world . . . And I presume there is no one to guide you or you wouldn't have been sleeping under a tree where anyone could have come upon you, many not as friendly as me. With the state of you, stark naked and covered in what must be blood, you would've been seen as a danger to any learned man or simpleton."

JD's pulse spiked, his heart thudding away in his chest again. He'd forgotten about the blood. He had just assumed the rain from the storm had cleansed him.

"It's a lucky thing I was the one to find you, my boy. Lucky indeed. It will be my duty to help you. And for you to help me with whatever gifts you have been endowed with. Do we have a deal?"

"Yes," JD said.

Benjamin smiled, a wide grin that consumed his face until his eyes became half-moons. "That's good Japhet Dean. That's very good."

CHAPTER ELEVEN
Boneyard

Jesse sat in his room working on a charcoal sketch of Tammy. This was how he spent every night once the sun went down since he moved in with his boss. He would get done with his shift at Titan Tires and go straight into Danny Leeds's old farmhouse, into the room that used to be his son's and draw. He liked living with Danny. He never pressured him.

Before Jesse moved in with Danny, Uriah and Mary nagged him every day for one reason or the next. First, it was because he didn't return to high school in September for senior year. He opted to get his GED certificate instead. He was never crazy about going to high school, but he had friends and then there was Tammy. With her gone, it seemed silly to pretend he was a normal teenager.

Working helped to keep his mind off Tammy. While he worked on cars and trucks with Danny, his mind was set to learning the job. Tammy only slipped through after the workday ended and he went to work on Tessa, the vintage Volvo Tammy had picked out for Jesse to restore—the car he was to drive her to school in. After hours, he would apply what he learned from

Danny on Tessa and when it became too dark to work, which was getting earlier and earlier with winter around the corner, he went to his room to draw.

A loud knock sounded on Jesse's bedroom door. Expecting it to be Danny letting him know the pizza and wings were there as it had become a tradition to order in every Sunday, he answered the knock with his usual: "Coming Boss."

Jesse lifted his head from his drawing when he heard his door open. That wasn't like Danny. "Ivy," he said surprised.

"Hi Jesse. Can I come in?"

Jesse put down his sketch pad. "Um, yeah, sure."

Ivy's eyes darted around the room to the sketches of Tammy all over his walls. He had done a few that hung in his old room at the rectory while they dated, but now his room was a shrine to her.

"Danny invited Grams and me for pizza night."

That wasn't surprising to Jesse. Grams was dating Danny and was always there on Sunday, what was surprising was that this time Ivy accompanied her.

Ivy hovered by Jesse's bed. "I feel like I haven't seen you forever." She covertly scanned Jesse. She hadn't seen him since the summer. He no longer came to the house to play dominoes with her grandmother. He'd had a growth spurt. He closely resembled the Jesse she'd first met in Pleasant Mills. His light brown hair had grown out to his chin which he kept tucked behind his ears. It looked good on him. Ivy thought he seemed thinner or maybe that was from the growth spurt, his already angular face looked sharp. The biggest change was in his amber eyes. They were sad, like a caged animal begging to be released back into the wild.

"Before you ask, I haven't talked to Sammy. I don't talk to anyone anymore. Not even him. Well, no one besides Rosa." There was no snap in his tone. He was just relaying the truth.

A blush rose on Ivy's cheeks. She was glad Jesse was busy examining the drawing he put on the bed next to him. Ivy had tagged along with her grandmother for one reason and that was to see if Sammy had talked to Jesse about her after she made her surprise visit to the Lopez house earlier that day. How well Jesse knew her.

Ivy scanned the room thinking of another reason why she'd come to pizza night and why she would invite herself into his room when they hadn't talked in months. Nothing was coming to mind. She noticed a stuffed rabbit with a carrot in his mouth sitting atop Jesse's pillow. "I didn't take you for a stuffed animal guy."

"It was Tammy's. It was her favorite."

"That was nice of Mike to give it to you."

"He didn't."

Ivy's eyebrows furrowed.

"I stole it."

Ivy wasn't sure what to say to that and decided to play with the strings on her hoodie in response.

Jesse continued arbitrarily. "I broke into her house and took it off her bed, along with some other things."

It was a challenge, but Ivy tried not to let her face twist up in one of those disapproving looks her grandmother always gave her.

"Don't look at me like that," Jesse said. "Come on, does it really surprise you? Remember, I'm a kidnapper and an accomplice to murder. I thought being a burglar was a step in the right direction."

Ivy's disapproving face smiled kindly. She'd forgotten how funny he was. "I think it is."

He smirked at that. "I take it Sammy's still not talking to you?"

"No," she said, rubbing her elbow nervously. "Maybe, not exactly. We talked today. At first, he gave me the ol' shut the door in my face routine but he did drop me off at my house."

"Progress," Jesse said, leaning on one elbow.

"I hope so."

They heard Mary yell from downstairs. "Pizza's getting cold!"

"We better get down there before Grams sends a search party after us. And maybe after dinner you can show me that car Grams keeps telling me about."

It was pitch black as Jesse and Ivy made their way to Jesse's project car. The thin slice of moon was blacked out by thick clouds. The only light came from a pole mounted floodlight on the side of Titan Tires. The light reflected off the chrome bumpers and mirrors casting shadows over the dark junkyard.

"Where cars come to die," Jesse said, as he opened the gate. "Danny calls it the Boneyard. It's a little dramatic but he's right. We take parts from here all the time."

Ivy looked out over the Boneyard, visualizing each car part as a vital organ to a machine. "How did he get them all?"

"Usually, cars end up here because the work they need costs more than they're worth. Danny pays the scrap price for them, and they come here, so we can have access to the parts. We have some really nice new models here that insurances have totaled out. You can talk to Danny about picking out one."

Ivy stuck her hands into her hoodie as a breeze whipped around the junk cars making a whistling noise that set her on edge. For a second, she thought it was JD, before she saw a piece of metal scrap attached to a car antenna spin around in the wind like a weathervane.

"I will," she said, liking the idea of not having to rely on her grandmother and Danny for rides, now that she didn't have Sammy. "Which car's yours?"

"This way," he said, pulling out his phone and flashing it in front of them. Jesse had on a long-sleeved T-shirt with the Titan Tire's logo on it. The cold didn't seem to bother him.

Ivy knew very little about cars. She either liked them or she didn't. She decided before she saw Jesse's car she was going to like it, but when she saw it, hints of pearly white peeking through rust on its sleek body, thrown amongst bulky cars and trucks, she genuinely smiled.

"Wow, that's really nice."

"Yeah, Tammy picked it out."

"She had good taste."

He smiled, opening the passenger side door for her. Ivy hopped in and shut the door, hoping it would be warmer in the car. It wasn't. Jesse left his phone on flashlight and put it on the dashboard before pulling out the car key and putting it in the ignition. "Got the engine going last week." He let the engine purr for a few minutes before shutting it off. "Tessa's coming along."

"Tessa?"

"That's the name Tammy gave the car."

"Oh cool. That's a nice name. It's different; I like it."

Ivy jumped up, hitting her head on the ceiling. "I don't even want to know what type of bug just bit me."

"This time of year, I'd say a rat."

Ivy looked at him mortified.

"I'm kidding," he said with a chuckle.

Ivy wasn't amused; she didn't like rats or anything creepy crawly. She turned around and examined the seat before sitting down on the edge of it. She noticed a spring wedged at the base of the seat cushion. She tugged at it. "False alarm. Not a rat, just a notebook. She took Jesse's phone off the dashboard to illuminate the cover.

It looked like any notebook you would buy at the drug store, but the cover was heavily worn. Scotch tape had carefully been placed over the cover in neat strips to protect it. Ivy flipped open the book to read: "Property of Tessa McCarthy."

"What'd you say?!" Jesse asked, taking the notebook from her.

"Do you know who that is?" Ivy asked as Jesse thumbed through the notebook. Ivy inched closer to see what was in it. "Funny coincidence your car's name is Tessa."

"No . . .," Jesse said in thought, "it's no coincidence. Tessa McCarthy is Tammy's mother."

"I don't think that's right," Ivy said, closing her eyes to clear her mind. "Her mom's name is Sarah."

"Yes, Sarah is her mother, but Tessa McCarthy is her *biological* mother."

Ivy opened her eyes. "I didn't know that. Sammy never said. I just figured with them all being red heads, well, that they were just one big happy family of red heads."

"I don't think anyone knows, or at least talks about it. Big Mike remarried right after Tammy was born."

"So how is it that *you* know all of this? I thought you don't remember things once you're reborn." That's what Jesse had told everyone, told them when he dies, he returns to Pleasant Mills as a sixteen-year-old, the age he was when he made his deal with JD. Reborn at sixteen, he would only have the memory of his first life and nothing more.

Jesse had died a young man when Ivy had accidently pushed him down a hill and he struck his head on a tree. Only JD and Anita knew that was not entirely true. Anita had been in the woods that day and helped send Jesse tumbling to his death. He died and came back a teenager not remembering what he did just the day before.

Jesse shook his head wearily. "I don't remember. Danny told me. Tessa was a friend of his. Don't say anything. Like I said, I don't think Mike knows about Sarah."

"I won't say anything. I hardly see Mike, but I mean Tammy had to know. She did name your car after her."

"I don't think so."

"Then why would she put her mother's notebook in the car?"

"She didn't. Tammy named the car before we ever got into it. I had thought this was her mother's car from Danny talking about it. He said she always brought her little white Volvo in. But, I wasn't sure and I couldn't ask. I didn't want to bring up Tammy with Danny and get the lecture about finding peace Uriah and Mary have been giving me since Tammy passed. This though," he said, waving the notebook, "proves it. Tammy was drawn to the car. As far as I know, she didn't know about Tessa."

"Very weird," Ivy said, "even for this town." A chill ran through her. Ivy wrapped her arms around herself in a hug. "How about we go back to your room and check out the notebook before I freeze to dea—" She stopped herself. She didn't want to bring up death and dying with Jesse. "Come on Jesse, let's get inside."

Ivy and Jesse sat side by side at the foot of Jesse's bed with Tessa's notebook open on their laps. "I feel horrible for having read this. It reads too much like a diary. And poor Tessa was terrified."

Ignoring Ivy, Jesse read the last passage out loud again: "I heard the voice again. I didn't tell Mike; I can't tell him. He agrees with the doctors. He thinks the voice is in my head. Mike believes my new medicine is working, but it's not. The voice is getting louder. I can't block it out. I hear it the loudest in Tammy's room. I'm so scared. I think something is after her. God, please help me and my daughter. I'm going to the pastor for help. Pastor Baker will have to believe me."

Ivy shook off a chill, she couldn't seem to get warm. "Tessa must've had the same gift Tammy had. Talk about a misdiagnosis."

"It does look that way," Jesse admitted. "She was hearing ghosts and thought she was going crazy."

"What happened to her?" Ivy asked, closing the notebook. "Was Pastor Baker able to help?"

"She's an inmate at Pleasant Asylum."

"She's alive?!" Ivy said shocked.

"As far as I know, Danny said Big Mike had her put in Pleasant Asylum after Tammy was born. He said she lost her mind."

"Oh my God."

"I don't think God had anything to do with it, or maybe he did. Do you believe in fate?"

Ivy looked to the ceiling as she thought. "In a way, I guess. Why?"

Jesse tossed Tessa's notebook on his nightstand and got up. "Tammy picked out Tessa's Volvo out of all the cars in the Boneyard and you found her notebook."

"What are you getting at?"

"I need to see Tessa."

"Do you think that's a good idea? News of Tammy's passing is not going to help her situation."

"I won't tell her. I just need to see her."

"I want to know what the voice said. The voice that scared her."

"Nowhere in there," he said, pointing to the notebook, "did she write down what it said, just that she heard it."

"Hmm, you're right. Maybe she didn't write it down in case someone found her journal. Maybe she didn't want anyone to know."

"Or, she was afraid what they would do if they found out. I have to know what the voice told her."

"Jesse, what good will it do?" We both know no one was after Tammy. It's not going to . . ."

"I know it won't bring her back, Ivy," he said sharply, pacing his room. "Even if Tessa won't tell me what the voice said, she has a right to know that her children didn't know about her, and that Tammy was the best."

Ivy grabbed Jesse's arm. "If you do that, she'll want to see her children. And she can't. Think of the problems you'll cause between Mike and his parents."

"Funny, I thought you more than anyone would know being lied to ruins your life. Look what JD did to you and what he did to me. Lies are not the answer Ivy. And if Tessa is locked away for hearing voices that are really ghosts, we can help her. I'll be able to see the ghosts," he said, flicking the charm necklace around his neck. "Remember seeing ghosts is my specialty. If I see ghosts, it proves she's not crazy and we can't leave her in there if she's not actually crazy. I owe it to Tammy to help her mom if I can."

His amber eyes were alive with a fire she'd never seen burn there before. "Please help, this is important to me."

Ivy sighed; she knew he wasn't going to take no for an answer. "Okay fine, we'll visit Tessa.

Jesse sat back down next to Ivy. "Can you help me look the place up. Does it have a number? I'm still working on my phone skills. It will take me forever to find it."

Ivy pulled out her phone typing in Pleasant Asylum. "I never knew Pleasant Mills had a mental hospital," she said, trying to be politically correct. "Pretty sure Pleasant Asylum should get with the times and change their name."

Ivy came to what she was looking for. "Problem Jesse. Visitors must be 18 or older or accompanied by an adult."

"What's the big deal? I'm seventeen, but you're eighteen, aren't you?"

"I am, but when I said we'd visit Tessa, I didn't think that would mean I have to go in to see her."

Jesse shook his head in frustration. Pulling out his phone, he made a call.

"Who are you calling?"

"Sammy. He's eighteen."

Ivy felt a hiccup travel up her throat. She inched in so she could hear his voice.

Sammy answered on the second ring. "Hey Jesse. How are you?"

"I'm okay," he said, knowing he hadn't returned any of Sammy's calls over the last month. "I need your help."

"Anything," Sammy said.

CHAPTER TWELVE
Experiments

Being forsworn from the Lopez house and with Uriah and Ivy not at home, JD found himself outside Pearl's apartment complex. He knew it well—knew the aged brick and the sad small windows that repeated in uniform patterns across the complex like office suites. Unobserved, he had watched Jeffrey go to Pearl's first floor apartment—watched them talk on her dull gray couch through the window that faced the woods. He was as familiar with Pearl as Jeffrey was, and in his lonely state was happy to see her familiar face.

He watched Pearl as she sat on the couch watching TV. She had lost the suit jacket and let her hair down but was still dressed for work.

JD thought about what Jeffrey had said the night he opened the divorce letter, that maybe it was for the best. He found that hard to believe. Less than two years ago, Lindsey was the most important thing in his brother's life, then something shifted. A shift he caused. He had seduced Lindsey and had Devan kidnap the twins and her. He couldn't have stopped what Devan did, but what he did was just as horrible. It started the crack that was now a cavern in his brother's marriage. As he watched Pearl channel surf, he wondered if there was anything he could do to repair the damage.

He couldn't deny the appeal of Pearl. Devan had loved her and so did Jeffrey. He wondered if part of him loved her too. Or was it the need to corrupt others that made him knock on her door?

"Uh . . . Jeffrey's brother," Pearl said, opening the door to her apartment.

He extended his hand. "JD, nice to officially meet you." Pearl shook his hand, glancing at her watch.

"Um, is everything okay with Jeffrey? Did I miss a call from him?" She reached into her pants pocket pulling out her phone. There were no missed messages.

"Everything is fine. I was in the neighborhood and saw your light was on."

"Uh, you know where I live? That's . . . that's strange. Jeffrey warned me to stay away from you. I'm seeing why."

JD smiled, knowing he looked just like his twin, and knowing how much Pearl loved his brother. "He said the same thing about you to me."

"Jeffrey is a consistent man, if nothing else," she said with an awkward smile. "Well, if that's' all, I should be getting to bed." She went to close the door. JD stopped her, putting his hand between the door and the opening.

"I came to ask you to dinner tomorrow."

"Oh," Pearl said abashed.

"Now that my brother has promised Sammy to talk to Lindsey about coming home, I don't see why I should stay away from you."

At this, Pearl's ears, that were poking out of her hair, burned red. "He didn't tell me that. We've been keeping our distance since Lindsey moved out, trying to squash town gossip."

JD ran his hand down the cold brick exterior of the building. "I imagine going into a new relationship as the homewrecker would be unsavory, and then there's your image as the Chief of Police to protect."

She scoffed. "Well, I guess that doesn't matter anymore. His little experiment has obviously given him clarity of mind."

"His loss," JD said with a grin. "I'll be here at eight tomorrow night to pick you up. Wear something short."

"I'm really seeing why Jeffrey said to stay away from you."

A charming smile spread across his face. "That wasn't a no."

"No, it wasn't a no."

JD walked home, mulling over Pearl's words. '*His little experiment has obviously given him clarity of mind'.* He was no stranger to experiments gone wrong.

Pleasant Mills, New Jersey: Ben's Cabin: 1735

"How much longer are you going to carry on with this experiment?" Titan Leeds asked as he rubbed his fisted hand at Ben's table. His hawk-like eyes watched JD where he read in the corner of the cabin. His knuckles had long ago turned red with irritation from the continuous friction, but Titan couldn't stop himself. This slight distraction of mind was the only thing keeping him from revenging the murder of his brother and sister-in-law, right there in his lover's cabin. It didn't help that he could see his sister-in-law in the seemingly innocent boy, in the way his lips curled into a smile, how his soft, dark hair fell around his face, there was no doubt he was kin.

Benjamin covered Titan's fist with his hand. "The experiment goes on as long as it takes."

Titan spoke through clenched teeth. "It doesn't deserve to be babied by you like some pet. It deserves death after what it did to my brother."

"You misunderstand what I'm doing here. This is for us, not to torture you. We could kill *him* now, but that will benefit no one. Your brother is dead, not even this being's magic can bring him back, we've tried.

He can't resurrect a fly. He can never bring back your brother, but I believe he can give us immortality. I'm so close to understanding his power, I just ask for your patience."

"Why can't you just make him? Wild animals respond to brute force."

Japhet Dean is not a wild animal. He's highly intelligent. He, along with me, do not know the limitations of his power. It would be unwise to force anything on him. We have come a long way in only a few months, it won't be long now." Benjamin got up. "But if seeing him unnerves you, I will make sure he's outside when you come."

"Don't call him by my brother's name."

Laying a hand on Titan's shoulder, "Of course, my apologies, JD. Sometimes I forget what he is. He has a kind heart. Don't look at me like that, he does. It surprises me to this day, that he could have killed your brother and his wife so brutally. I know I'm fooling myself, I know it was him. He was covered in their blood when I found him by the side of the road. But so often he seems so in touch with nature, it's as if he can talk to the trees."

"That's just great, Ben," Titan snickered. "How does that bring us immortality?"

Ben grabbed the tea kettle from the hearth. "It doesn't'. It's the other side of his nature I'm trying to tap into. The side of him that comes from the Beast."

"If fresh air doesn't work, try the opposite. Cage him. Try pain."

"We must be careful, Titan. JD is new to the world. I want to establish a moral foundation before I expose him to pain and punishment."

"Oh Ben," Titan said with a light laugh before leaning in to plant a kiss on his cheek. "You really are the best person I know. I still feel we should destroy it before it destroys us but go on with your experiment. Just be quick about it."

Titan threw opened the door to Ben's cabin, "I came as soon as I got your letter. What have you found out?!"

Benjamin collected Titan's hat and coat from him. "A good deal. JD cannot leave his native soil."

"How so," Titan said, looking around for JD and not seeing him.

"Let me explain, "Ben said excitably, his hands moving as quickly as his mouth. "I was going home to Philadelphia to see my wife and children as it's called to do sometimes. I decided it was high time to test JD in public and resolved to take him with me. We traveled very amiably, the weather was good, and JD was thrilled to be in a carriage. As we approached the road that would take us to Philadelphia, he grew dreadfully ill, doubling over in pain. And when we crossed over the New Jersey, Pennsylvania line he vanished from the carriage.

Titan took a seat at the familiar oak table. "Vanished? Do you mean to say he's gone?!"

Ben took a seat next to him, drawing it close to Titan. "Vanished, yes, but not lost. I had the coachman stop at once. Behind us, in the middle of the road curled up in pain, was the boy. It took him two days to recover from the bulk of it, and he's still not well."

Titan leaned in on his elbows. "That's interesting."

"Agreed. And that's the least of it. After the ordeal, I noticed his fingers were fused together and so were his toes. Whether this was because he crossed over the New Jersey line or from the energy exerted from doing such a thing, I cannot tell. But his hands and feet continue to morph. His disfigurement is so great, he can no longer pick up a fork to feed himself. His deformities seemed to cause him great pain, mentally and physically."

"By God, what does this mean?"

Ben rubbed his meaty chin. "It means we are getting to see the monster who destroyed your brother. It was not the man, but the beast hiding inside of him."

Titan promptly stood up reaching for the hunting rifle by the door. Benjamin clutched Titan by the arm to stop him.

"Ben, your experiment has gone far enough. I can't allow this metamorphosis to continue. What if resorting back to a beast makes his mind that of a beast. He will kill you like he did my brother and think nothing of your kindness."

"I believe I know how to stop the change. But the idea is so dark, I can't entertain it. On the other hand, I'm so close to learning all of his secrets." Ben took the rifle from Titan and placed it back in its place by the door. "Can you imagine the two of us living forever. Can you imagine a time when we don't have to hide behind late night meetings and marriages. Immortality will give that to us."

In a soft voice, "It's for nought if you're dead," Titan said.

"JD relies on me for his welfare. Killing me would be the death of him. I am sure he will know that in any form."

In submission, Titan leaned into Ben. He had a way of getting what he wanted from him. It was a mixture of Ben's passion and confidence that always thawed Titan's heart. "Against my better judgment, I trust your instincts. Tell me how you propose to stop the change."

"Your brother and his wife were not only killed but their hearts were missing. This leads me to think he ate them. The heart is the core of the human body, it stands to reason he needs it to retain *his* human form."

Titan's hands instinctively balled into fists. "So he has to eat people."

Ben brought each of his fists to his lips and kissed his knuckles. "It's only a hypothesis."

"Fine, we'll test your hypothesis, then this experiment comes to an end."

CHAPTER THIRTEEN
An Important Night

JD found himself on the sidewalk in front of Ivy's house again. Dark clouds moved overhead in thick clusters blocking out all traces of the moon. He took out his cigarette case and carefully plucked out a cigarette. Lighting it and taking a long drag, he looked up to the attic, hoping to catch a glimpse of Ivy through the sheer curtains.

A light went on in Ivy's room. He exhaled slowly, waiting for her silhouette to pass in front of the window. In a few moments, her darkened shape stood in front of the curtain. The sound of the sash opening filled the still night, like nails on a chalkboard.

Ivy, not looking pleased, called to JD in a whisper. "I need to talk to you. Be quiet, don't wake my grandmother."

With a nod, he placed his cigarette under the toe of his shoe, extinguishing the amber glow as a few raindrops hit his cheek. He walked up the steps of the Teller porch, kneeling to take from a flowerpot a fake rock designed to hold keys. He smirked at the 'Happy Whatever Holiday You Celebrate' sign staked in the flowerpot as he took from the fake rock the key to the front door. JD unlocked the door, returning the key to its place before letting himself in.

JD made it to the top of the old stairs with not so much as one floor creak. The attic door was open a crack, a thin ribbon of light zigzagging down the stairs like a lightning bolt. He gave the door a light knock and pushed it open.

Ivy was at her vanity. She had on an oversize long-sleeved tee and fleece pants featuring a goofy moose with Christmas lights strung between its antlers.

He took care to shut the door softly.

"What's wrong with you?" Ivy asked, evaluating him with slit eyes.

With arched eyebrows, "Me? You're the one in Christmas pants."

"You're not your usual cocky self. Since when do you knock?"

He grinned. "I beg your pardon for my politeness."

"I will have you know my moose pants are freaking adorable."

JD skirted past her and went to the window, sliding it open. He perched on the sill and watched rain drops trickling down from the starless sky while Ivy intently scrutinized him; this was not the first time he sat on her windowsill like that. There was something so natural about him being there with her.

"May I smoke?" he asked, his eyes still fixated outside.

"Go ahead. You're going to anyway."

He took his time lighting another cigarette. The smell of the sweet smoke overcame the room. A smell Ivy came to hate, partly because it was so familiar.

"You wanted to talk to me."

"Yes, about a couple of things," Ivy said, her fingers out as if she was about to count to five.

"First off, what are you up to with Mr. Lopez? We both know you weren't there for relationship counseling."

JD flicked the accumulation of ash off his cigarette. "You don't have to worry about Jeffrey Lopez. He's well-adjusted. What's your next talking point, Ms. Teller?"

"Wait, you heard me say that?!" Ivy sputtered, remembering her earlier conversation with Sammy and how she said Mr. Lopez was well-adjusted.

He inclined his head slightly. "Yes."

"Is there anything you don't hear?"

A smile played on his lips. He looked every bit as evil as he was, the shadows in the room accenting his handsome face to suspicion. "Many things. Many things I wish I did hear."

"Fine, keep your secrets. I really don't care. Mr. Lopez isn't as gullible as—"

"Sammy," JD said, finishing her sentence.

Ivy's face burned. "You make it so easy to hate you."

"Yes, I believe I do," JD said, not looking at her. "You're right, Ms. Teller, Jeffrey doesn't need me and has asked me not to come to the house, as you yourself heard. I will respect his wishes."

"Oh, so that's why you're sulky."

"I didn't realize I was."

"It sucks not being wanted, doesn't it?"

JD's dark eyes flickered toward her. "A fate worse than death, Ms. Teller."

She hated it when he looked at her like that. Like she'd just kicked a puppy. He was the bad guy, not her. She crossed her arms over her chest. "Next question, did you know the Leeds grimoire had a blood lock?"

"I did."

"Why didn't you tell me?!"

"Oh yes, tell you, and help you find a way to hurt me," JD said, imitating Ivy's voice.

She hated it when he did that too. "You admit it then! There *is* something that can hurt you, and it's in the spell book?!"

"Not permanently," JD said, taking a long drag. He exhaled out the window, letting the smoke waft out to the street. "I wouldn't waste your time."

"Okay, um, did you know that I could open it? I mean did you know specifically my blood could open it? Oh, please tell me we're not related," Ivy rambled to herself. "That would be very bad. Deborah called us sisters in the church. Please, tell me it's not true."

"Because that would mean you and Sammy are related," JD said, crossing his legs. "And that is very taboo in this century."

"Yes, that. It would really mess up my life." She brought her fingers to her mouth in anticipation of his answer, biting at her cuticles.

"Disaster avoided then; you're not related. You can sleep well tonight my darling."

"I'm not your darling, I'm not your anything."

"Not yet," he said into his cigarette.

"If what you said is true, how can I open the book if I'm not a Leeds?"

"It's not typical genealogy. You're not genetically related, so ease your mind, Ms. Teller. But you do share blood with the Leeds."

"What does that mean?! Cut the crap JD and just answer me plainly. I don't want you in my room any longer than you have to be."

He went to get up. "I could leave now."

"No," Ivy said, also standing. She put her hands on his chest to stop him. "Not yet. Please, just answer the question."

"You made a blood pact with Deborah Leeds. Thus, you share Leeds blood. It's that simple. The grimoire in question works off the Leeds blood line, thus you can open it."

She withdrew her hands. "A blood pact . . . how do you know?"

"You told me," JD said.

"You mean the Midwife told you," she corrected, making sure he knew there was a difference between herself and the Midwife."

"Yes, the Midwife told me."

Ivy chewed on the inside of her cheek. "Did I—I mean, did she tell you why?"

JD sat back down on the windowsill. "I found out."

"Well tell me," Ivy said impatiently, continuing to stand.

"You were to marry a man you disliked immensely. I think you hated him more than you hate me."

"As if that's possible," she mumbled under her breath.

JD heard her; nonetheless, he continued as if he hadn't. "This man was kin to Deborah's husband. That's how you became friendly with her and why she chose you to be her midwife when she was pregnant for the thirteenth time. Deborah was a well-practiced witch when she met you. You had no clue what you really were. She offered to help you get power, by sharing hers as a way for you to circumvent your marriage to this man. You and she performed the blood pact ritual allowing both of you to tap into each other's magic."

"We're linked through magic?" Ivy said, considering what that meant as a knot twisted in her stomach. "So that means when you and Mr. Lopez crushed Deborah's heart, she's not really gone, she's linked to me?"

"As I am linked to you. Destroying you in the church fire within the Seal of Solomon created by her victims would have destroyed all three of us."

"That's heavy," Ivy said sitting on her bed.

"Deborah's reasons for helping you were selfish ones. You were unaware what you signed up for. You had all this power but no idea how to tap into it and she wasn't about to show you, but you learned, and you learned quick. But now, Deborah could share in your power, and she did so to summon an angel."

"Ezekiel," Ivy said, more to herself in thought than to JD. "You knew about Ezekiel when Sammy mentioned the angel in Mr. Lopez's office?"

"I did, you had told me. You told me it was your motivation to save me . . .You said when I was born that I was good. Born perfect in God's image." He smiled, but it was burdened with sadness. "After all these years, I still find it hard to believe you didn't want to remember me. To recall what we shared even if it did mean you have to remember what I did to our son." He inclined his head toward the street, watching a car wiz by. "I didn't know about the demon. It all makes sense now. That's why she smothered me. She thought I was evil, but it was really Jeffrey. She knew she was tricked and set out to get the last laugh."

Ivy rubbed her shoulders. She wasn't sure if it was from the cold draft from the window or the truth. Ivy had felt the Midwife's feelings firsthand through her dreams. The Midwife's love and desire for JD had coursed through her veins. She had seen beauty and grace in him too perfect to be of this world and now she knew he was. JD was half angel. He was truly born perfect in God's image; the Midwife was right about that.

JD's face was in shadows, his eyes were in complete darkness. In the dim light of the room his cheekbones were sharp. In that moment, he truly looked immortal. "But I *was* good. I was half angel."

"You *were*," Ivy agreed.

"Now I am a contorted, twisted thing. A monster." He looked to her for absolution. He needed to hear from her he wasn't.

It didn't come. She avoided his glance.

"I have a question for *you* Ms. Teller. Do you know the name of the demon my mother summoned. The one who made me into this?" he asked, glancing at his hands.

"No," Ivy lied. She wanted JD to believe he was capable of redemption. Because if he was, she was. She spoke in a whisper. "I meant it when I said you weren't a monster."

He smiled. There it was, the spark of the old flame between them. "Nice of you to say that, Ms. Teller."

"JD?"

"Yes . . ."

"Did I—I mean did the Midwife still have to marry Titan."

"You remember him?" JD asked, knowing he hadn't mentioned the loathed man she was to marry as Titan Leeds.

Ivy felt a chill run down her spine. "A little. I know I was afraid of him." She recalled Titan pinning her to the wall and threatening her when she came home soaked the night JD and Jeffrey were born.

JD put his spent cigarette out on the sill and shut the window. Facing Ivy, "You, nor I, couldn't have prevented it."

He walked toward her bedroom door. His hand was on the knob when Ivy spoke up. "One more question . . ."

"Yes," he said, craning his neck to look at her, his dark eyes glinting like coal.

"What are you planning?"

"Planning?"

"You've been too quiet. I haven't seen you since the day Sammy broke up with me."

"Did you want to see me?" he asked earnestly, taking his hand off the doorknob.

"No," she said, with a shake of her head. "I didn't, the radio silence just got me worried. I feel like I'm just waiting around for more people to die."

"People die every day, Ms. Teller. Your God is cruel."

It's not *my God* I'm worried about. When are you going to kill the rest of the thirteen people? You know, the ones you need to fulfill Uriah's contract?"

JD let his hand fall to his waist side, turning around fully to face Ivy. "I don't typically discuss my contracts with others, but that particular contract is satisfied. I won't reap again until Uriah dies and is reborn and this whole thing starts over again."

"Wait what?!" Ivy said, more than a little surprised. "Zac, Tyrone, Louie, Timothy that's not thirteen."

"You're forgetting Megan and her aunt, Trudy's mother and grandmother, and the Henry sisters. Sammy, though, as you know, I gave that one back . . ." He hesitated to name Rosa, not wanting Ivy to know where her loyalty really lied.

"You didn't! You killed them. Oh my God?!" Ivy said in a near shout. "You killed Megan?!" She hoped she didn't wake up her grandmother.

"No Ms. Teller, I didn't kill them, that was the work of Deborah Smith Leeds, but Deborah is a Leeds, and her victims were church members. The deaths were because of me and thus for me. It fulfilled the contract, without my hands getting dirty. It's over."

Ivy's heart raced. "So that means Pastor Leeds has all of his memories back? He didn't say anything."

"I imagine he's busy with the rebuilding of his church, caring for his ward, and there is baby Lilly on the way."

"Still, you think he'd say something."

JD opened the attic door. "I know it pains you to hear this Ms. Teller, but it's not always all about you."

He walked down the stairs, careful not to let the treads croak under his weight as he spoke in a whisper meant for Ivy not to hear. "It's not always all about you, to anyone but me."

JD made his way into the cold night. His mind on his past, a past he shared with Ivy.

"Remember JD, tonight is an important night for me," Ben said, donning a black robe. I'm presenting you to the Hell's Fire Club. Membership is awarded to an elite group of free thinkers. Tonight, we have prepared three sacrifices."

JD nodded; his eyes fixed to Ben as he helped him into a matching robe. JD knelt and Ben tied a simple black mask around his face. The mask covered only the upper half of his aspect, leaving his lips and chin visible. The forehead sloped lifelessly to a near shapeless nose. The mask was smooth and took on the appearance of porcelain, dulling the features of human anatomy.

Ben secured his own mask, an exact replica of the one he just helped JD with. "You will be fine. It will be just like we practiced in the cabin. A sacrifice will be made and in return you will grant a request. We are no longer able to test the limits of your power in theory anymore. If you can grant the requests asked of you tonight, grant them. If not, we learn the boundaries of your power. You have nothing to fear from them or me. Do you understand?"

Another silent nod.

It had been two months since Titan Leeds had brought a shackled man to Ben's cabin and demanded JD devour him in order to stop his metamorphosis. Ben had theorized it was JD's consumption of his parent's hearts that allowed him to take on a human form and Titan was willing to test this theory.

JD remembered all too well the night he came into existence. Ben was almost right about him. He did murder his parents, consuming his father's heart, but he'd kept his mother's as a memento. But that seemed so long ago, like it was a different life. That wasn't him any longer. Now he was human, or at least he felt like it, despite the fusing of his digits. Benjamin had treated him like a friend and that made JD feel like a human being. He was no longer the monster who tore apart his mother and father and had no desire to do that to anyone. Especially a bound man he didn't know.

Titan had explained, the man was a horse thief and was to hang the next morning. He told JD the man's death didn't have to be meaningless that he could give it purpose by preserving his human form, a form his dear friend Ben said was impossible to keep without the aid of this horse thief.

Something was wrong with Titan's request. Not in a moral sense, JD knew murder was wrong, but there was something else. He hungered for something, and he could sense it, whatever it was, in this horse thief and also in Ben and Titan, but he knew he just couldn't give this man's death purpose without giving something in return.

"What do you want in return for me giving this man's death purpose?" JD had asked, putting his thoughts to words. The question rolled off his tongue like liquid. It felt necessary. It felt right.

Titan's smile had turned into a calculated grin. "Tell me how to gain immortality from you."

"Offer me a deal, I can't refuse."

The time for experimenting was over. With that one sentence Ben and Titan had learned how to tap into JD's power.

Benjamin put his hands on JD's shoulders waking him from his reverie. "Look at your hands. Look at your fingers. Do you want to be a man or a beast?"

With his head hung low, he looked at his hands. JD's left middle and index finger were fused together. The horse thief's heart had not sustained him as long as his father's had. "A man. But there has to be another way."

"Perhaps," Ben said, squeezing his shoulder, "but until we find it, we have to make do. If you want to be able to walk amongst mankind this partnership with the Hell's Fire Club is necessary. Ensure that you keep your hood up and mask on. We don't want anyone guessing at who you are and complicating our work."

"I won't let you down, Ben."

"I know you won't," he said, patting the shoulder he had moments ago squeezed.

Under the cover of the night, Ben and JD traveled to Pleasant Mills Church. Owing to the fact JD couldn't leave the state, and Ben being worried about untoward side effects from leaving town, the Hell's Fire meeting was being held at the church. It was far enough away from the village to ensure privacy and the pastor, a member of the Hell's Fire Club, was known to entertain special guests at his private home attached to the church.

It was a hot and humid night. The clouds hung low in the sky, the moon cresting over a sea of gray haze. JD continuously adjusted his ill-fitting mask, his peripheral vision hindered by the small eye holes. He had not been this close to the town since the night of his birth and felt a crushing yearning to go there and look for the young girl who had helped him. "Ivy Teller," he said in a soft whisper to himself. Ben didn't seem to hear. He walked on at a brisk pace, JD two paces behind him.

The church doors were open for Benjamin and JD by a cloaked man who had been awaiting their arrival at midnight. They had hardly put a foot on the church steps when the doors were thrown open.

Benjamin hurriedly made his way up the few steps and shook hands with the man.

The man extended his hand to JD. "It's an honor to meet you my Dark Lord."

JD lifted his head to see blue eyes beaming from a black mask. He said nothing, ignoring the hand that was still extended to him.

Ben ushered JD further into the church. Candles glowed from their stations at the small windows. On the floor, candles were clustered together in a ball of fire, the flame dancing in the drafty church throwing exaggerated shadows on the wall. The pews had been cleared from the center of the floor and in their place was a dark ring of cloaked men.

JD and Ben, followed by the man who let them in, walked toward the circle. The circle perceiving them, opened to receive JD and Ben into the center of it as if they had just been swallowed. The man with the blue eyes who had first greeted them disappeared into the human perimeter encircling them.

JD anxiously eyed the men surrounding him. All of them wore the same robe and mask. The exposed lower halves of their faces blended into the androgynous masks. Only the whites of their eyes were visible in the candlelight. JD's line of vision came to rest on the tall crucifix behind the cloaked men. Christ's eyes, like the eyes of the men, were blank and cold. Candles lit under the crucifix emitted their radiance on it. The blood from the crown of thorns piercing Christ's forehead seemed to undulate under the power of the flames as if the blood were dripping. JD wondered if it was.

"Let the first ask," Benjamin said, returning JD's attention to the circle of men where a cloaked figure stepped forward. The man now stood a few feet from JD and Ben. JD could see the pigment in the man's irises. He recognized the bright blue eyes; it was the man who'd let them in.

The man let down his hood and untied his mask, showing his face to his brethren. "My name is Pastor David Baker and I ask for immortality."

JD looked to Ben, not sure if he should speak. He had been given very few details into how tonight was going to go. He just knew there would be three sacrifices. Ben had not indicated what would be asked of him.

"What do you offer the Dark Lord?" Ben asked.

There was that title again. JD cringed at it. Ben had never called him that before.

The Pastor spoke up, his voice confident. "I offer you my wife."

From the back of the church two men, clothed and masked like the others, ushered forth a woman. She was dressed in the same dark robes as the members. Her hands were bound, and her mouth gagged with what looked like her own handkerchief. She had light blue eyes like her husband and long blonde hair that fell over her shoulders in loose curls. She struggled against the two men, but to no avail, they pushed her into the circle. Seeing her husband, she clung to him for protection. "It's going to be okay," he said, untying her hands. When her hands were free, he untied her robe, letting it fall to the floor. Her naked body shivered. Without removing the gag, the pastor pushed his wife toward JD. She fell to her knees, sobbing.

JD moved toward her, helping her to her feet and removed the gag. She looked back toward her husband and the cloaked men behind them before whispering to JD: "Help me. I have a newborn. Please help me."

JD again glanced at Ben for guidance.

Ben approached, putting a hand on his shoulder as he did in the cabin. "What's wrong, friend?"

"She's an innocent," he whispered to Ben. He had no doubt she could hear him despite his whispering. She clung to his robe like a scared child. "The man in the cabin was a thief. This woman is honorable and good."

"How can you be sure?" Ben asked intrigued.

"I see it in her eyes. I can see her soul and it's beautiful."

"I think extinguishing that soul is a fair price for immortality, don't you?"

It was. He knew it, but he didn't like the idea that she, herself, was not offering it to him, but her husband.

"I need more, may I ask it of him?"

"Of course," Ben said, "ask what you need to make the contract binding."

"Pastor David Baker, immortality will be granted along with your servitude to me," JD said. "That is my price."

All of the masked faces turned to Ben but before he could say anything the pastor spoke. "I agree."

The woman, understanding what was about to happen, ran from JD. She tried to break through the circle of men but was pushed back. JD grabbed her by the shoulders, turning her around to face him. She was powerless against his force. His hands wrapped around her slender neck. "I know," he said to her in a calm croon as tears streamed down her beautiful face. "You don't deserve this. Neither of us do, but it is necessary. I will make it up to you and watch over your daughter, Lilly."

"How do you know her name?" she asked, barely audible.

His nose rubbed against hers, "I see it in your eyes."

He snapped her neck with one fluid motion. Limp in his arms, and conscious of the many eyes focused on him, JD sunk his pointed teeth into her bosom.

JD wiped the blood from his face with the sleeve of his cloak. He had lost himself in the moment—lost awareness of his onlookers and indulged. He now looked down at the dead woman in his arms ashamed. He handed the corpse to the pastor. "This belongs to you."

Benjamin whispered into JD's ear. "Very good. An impressive show of power."

JD scanned the Hell's Fire Club members. He felt powerful, felt that power pulse through him, making him feel alive in a way only death could provide. Everything was in focus now, despite the dim light provided by the candles. He saw fear in their eyes and liked it.

"Titan's next. Do what he asks with no strings attached. Nothing about servitude. Do this for me, you know how much I adore him."

JD nodded, feeling better than he had in months. The pastor's young wife reinvigorated him more than the horse thief. He flexed his fingers. They were free now—human.

"Bring on the next," JD said, drunk on blood.

Titan, like the pastor, stepped into the circle, lowering his hood and untying his mask. "I am Titan Leeds and I too seek immortality. And with it fame and good fortune with my father's almanac."

"What do you offer your Dark Lord," JD said, imitating Ben from earlier, before Ben had a chance to say it. JD was a quick study. He looked into Titan's eyes. There was no fear there, just hatred, hatred for him.

"I offer my Dark Lord my fiancé."

Like before, two men dragged forth a cloaked woman. This woman was gagged like the last, but she also had on a black mask. She fought against the men dragging her by her arms, with more fury than the pastor's wife, kicking at them from all angles. The result was the same, they pushed her into the circle, where she was restrained by Titan.

JD, at once, recognized the dark eyes peering out from the mask and was seized by a fear greater than the sum of all the men in the church.

Titan went to untie his fiancé's robe.

JD stumbled forward. "No stop! I refuse." Ben rushed to JD's side, whispering in his ear. "Do not embarrass Titan in front of the club."

As if not hearing him, "I refuse." JD broke through the circle of men, it was easy, they stepped aside for him. No one wanted to challenge his power and end up like the pastor's wife.

JD ran for the church doors, knocking over the candles as he made his escape. Fire spread down the church floor to the altar. The screams of men as they attempted to clear the church filled the small space, spilling out into the night.

JD's way home was lit by the burning church blazing behind him. He refused to turn around and look, he couldn't. Before he knew it, he was at Ben's cabin. He wasted no time getting inside. He slumped down in the chair by the chimney and cried.

Titan stormed through Ben's door dragging his fiancée behind him by the rope still tied around her wrists. Ben followed.

"What was that about?!" Titan yelled at JD.

JD still wearing his ceremonial black robe, cradled his masked face in his hands, refusing to look at Titan.

"He got frightened," Ben said, going to JD and patting him on the back. "We pushed him too far tonight. We should've started with one sacrifice to make sure things ran smoothly. It was just too much."

"Things were running smoothly," Titan said, loathingly fixated on JD. "It even seemed exulted after murdering Faye Baker." Titan shook his head in disgust. "This is your fault, Ben. He's your pet, put him on a leash and make him obey."

Ben's face turned scarlet. He smoothed his hand over JD's back. "It's okay. There's still time to set things right with Titan."

"She's innocent," JD said through splayed fingers.

Titan scoffed. "Faye Baker was innocent, my fiancé is like the horse thief, whether you claim her life for yourself or not, she will die."

JD sat up, his eyes darting to Ivy. She was still gagged and wore the Hell's Fire Club mask, but that didn't matter. He knew her. He would know those eyes anywhere. Tears stood in her dark orbs along with love. Love for him. She didn't know the man of her heart, stood before her, she couldn't see the real him through his mask. "She's convicted of a crime?" JD asked.

Titan ran his hand over the bump of his fiancé's stomach. "This is the crime. She's pregnant with another man's child. She has disgraced me and as her future husband it is up to me how I deal out her punishment."

JD was on his feet now. "I can still offer you immortality," JD said, "but let me propose a different contract."

"Servitude to you. I don't think so," Titan snickered.

"Hear him out, Titan," Ben pleaded. "You are always so impatient." Ben turned to JD, "What do you propose? And please do remember I have been a good friend to you these many months."

JD untied his mask, so the Midwife could see his face. "I will give you immortality, fame, and fortune as you requested in exchange for you marrying this woman and taking care of her and the child. No harm is to come to either of them by your hand or the contract is void."

"You do this to embarrass me!" Titan said, pointing at JD.

"See sense, Titan," Ben said. "This is a very reasonable contract. Refusing this deal and killing your fiancé solves nothing. She will be marked and hung as an adulteress and that *will* embarrass you. You will a have a firefly life and will have to find another woman to marry. It will be hard to find someone as understanding of our situation as Ivy Teller." Ben put a hand on Titan's arm. "I strongly suggest you accept the offer. We will have you married to Ms. Teller by the end of the week and say the baby came early. It's a simple enough fix, and you will then have a child to consummate your marriage."

CHAPTER FOURTEEN
Pleasant Asylum

"**Y**ou should've borrowed a pair of Mike's pants and just wore a belt," Zac said to Jesse, pointing out that his ankles were showing in the full-length mirror in his room.

Jesse would've regretted Sammy inviting Zac if he hadn't missed him so much. He hadn't realized how much that was until he came through the door with Mona. Mona and he were on okay terms, but it still hurt him to see her. She was a reminder of everything wrong with him. He had loved her, and he had killed her for JD. He may have only remembered his first life, which he referred to as his true life, but in that one lifetime he learned so much. He knew he could never do something like that again. He had been scared and had acted out of fear. He would never hurt someone he loved now. He could never have hurt Tammy.

Jesse was happy, Mona seemed happy, despite being a ghost because of him. It eased some of his guilt. She looked completely different now. She traded in her bloody wedding gown for jeans and a hoodie, her sneakers like Zac's were dirty and untied. It seemed almost miraculous she didn't have on a matching Pleasant Mills Jersey Devil Football hoodie. It somehow suited her, like trading in haunting Jesse for protecting the Lopez twins, had changed her. He was sure a large part of that change was Zac; you couldn't help but smile in his presence.

"You had to bring Zac with you," Jesse said playfully to Sammy. He was happy to see them, all of them, even Mona.

"You missed me," Zac said.

The bridge of Jesse's nose and cheeks flushed, he played it off. "Yep, that's me, I love being annoyed."

"It's not that bad," Sammy said, looking at Jesse's reflection in the mirror. "With the black socks, it all blends in."

"That's because you're looking through a cracked mirror," Ivy said, her eyes darting from Jesse's fragmented appearance to his person. It always frustrated her how every mirror in Danny's house was cracked. On several occasions her grandmother had urged him to replace them, but because they were family heirlooms, he refused to throw them out.

Jesse definitely looked like he borrowed his outfit. Regardless of what Sammy was wearing, he always looked like he'd stepped out of a magazine. Today, Ivy thought a cologne advertisement. He looked extra slick in his black dress pants and dress shirt, his shirt unbuttoned just enough to make you want more. Then there was the dark dress jacket and blue scarf he had draped over his shoulder that matched his eyes perfectly.

"You look presentable," Mona said, "Even if you can tell you borrowed someone else's clothes."

Jesse nodded. He didn't care that his pants were too short, and his shirt was loose in the chest, he just wanted to get to the asylum. Presentable was good enough. He pushed Sammy and Ivy toward the bedroom door then out the front door.

"Um, what did you tell Danny?" Ivy asked Jesse as Danny waved from the garage as they made their way to Sammy's Hummer.

"Senior Skip Day."

"I'm sure that's gonna get back to Grams," she mumbled under her breath, already coming up with something more plausible than a Senior Skip Day in December.

"You look nice, Ivy," Mona said.

Ivy ran her hand over her skirt. "I didn't think jeans were gonna cut it for this. No offense," she added, realizing that's what Mona was wearing.

Mona smiled. "You're right." Her image blurred in smoke for a few seconds, rematerializing with her wearing an outfit identical to Ivy's.

"Well, not that anyone can see you Mona, but you look very professional."

"She just likes to show off," Zac said, "I still can't do that."

Mona nudged Zac lovingly, a thing they all noticed and didn't say anything about.

Jesse got in the passenger seat, forcing Ivy to sit in the back. "Come on, it's getting late."

PLEASANT MILLS ASYLUM

Sammy and Jesse walked in through the front door. Sammy led the way as if he had been there before. Ivy was a few paces behind them with Zac and Mona at her heels. Sammy casually leaned on the reception counter attempting to get the attention of the middle-aged woman sitting behind the computer monitor playing on her phone. Her hair was pulled up in a tight bun as if the bun was supposed to be a natural eyelift.

Ivy cleared her throat.

"Oh, hello," the embarrassed receptionist said. "We don't get many visitors, you all caught me by surprise."

"I'm sorry to have startled you," Sammy said, his charm turned all the way up.

The woman put her hand over her heart and blushed. "I needed something to stir the blood. A little scare is good sometimes. I was just checking emails, the computer runs so slow sometimes I have to use my phone," she offered as an excuse for being caught on her phone during the workday. Who are you here to see?"

"Our aunt."

She looked at the three of them. "My aunt," Sammy clarified with a kind smile.

"Do you have a parent or guardian with you?"

Sammy pulled out his license and handed it to her. "I'm a legal adult," he said with a tone that implied something more.

She studied his license, before handing it back. "You're Jeffrey Lopez's son. I knew I knew that smile from somewhere. Oh, you look so young, or maybe I'm getting old."

"You, old? No way," Sammy said, with a toothy smile.

Ivy felt sick to her stomach. "When did Sammy get so slimy?" she whispered to Mona who seemed not to notice or care.

"Sign in please." The receptionist pointed to the clipboard in front of her with a pen before popping it into her mouth and nibbling on the lid.

Sammy wrote down his name, hesitating what to right under 'Guest Visiting.' He decided to go with Tessa McCarthy over Tessa Handover. If Big Mike wanted to keep Mike's and Tammy's mom a secret, he figured he'd start by erasing the last name Handover.

"Tessa McCarthy," the receptionist said, looking up from the clipboard, "she hasn't had a visitor in years. I guess it was overdue with her being so chatty now. I'd better make sure she's allowed to have visitors."

Sammy politely smiled as the receptionist disappeared behind the double doors located directly behind her desk.

Jesse looked to Ivy. "What do you think that means?"

Ivy didn't have a chance to respond, the receptionist, looking anxious, came back through the doors with a loud swoosh.

"I'm sorry kids," she said, focusing on Sammy. "It's recommended, she have no visitors."

"Lenore," Sammy said, reading her name tag as he hung on the counter, twisting toward her. "That's why we're here. She's been so chatty," he said, using her own words against her, "because she wants to see us. I'm sure seeing me will be a good thing. She's always been my favorite aunt."

"You must've been a baby when she was admitted. Tessa's been here as long as I have."

"It's true, but my mother always told me how wonderful she was before her problems started."

"It's a shame to have such a pretty little thing be comatose for all those years, and now that's she's up, she's denied visitors."

Sammy nodded in full agreement, spurring her on.

"Let me see what I can do. I don't think it could hurt to drop your father's name."

"Please do. I'll let him know how helpful you've been."

She smiled and hurried away.

"You're good," Zac said.

"Good at lying," Ivy followed up.

"I'm not lying. Lenore's not that old compared to others. And I'm sure if Tessa would've raised Mike and Tammy, she would've been a favorite aunt. It's all perspective."

"You sound like JD," Ivy said. It was a slip of the tongue; she couldn't believe she said that out loud even if it was true.

Sammy's eyes became slits. "Jesse wants to get in to see Tessa and I'm getting him in. I thought you'd understand since you'd do anything to protect your friends."

Ivy's cheeks burned. She deserved that.

Lenore came into the waiting room with an elderly gentleman wearing a white lab coat over dress clothes. He adjusted his thick brim glasses, pinching the center. "Good to see you, Sammy."

"You too, Dr. Lemmen," Sammy said, shaking his hand.

As Sammy's cool façade cracked, Ivy wondered if Sammy had indeed been in this hospital before. It was only a little crack, it was in his eyes, she doubted anyone else noticed the little spider veins webbing across them.

"I didn't know Tessa McCarthy is your aunt," Dr. Lemmen went on to say evaluating Jesse and Ivy.

Luckily, Sammy had an answer for everything. "Well not genetically speaking, but that's not what makes someone family. You know I've always been best friends with Mike Handover."

The doctor glanced passed him again, no doubt checking for Mike. Sammy guessing at that, "Mike's not with me. He wants me to visit his mother first."

The doctor nodded, validating everything Danny had told Jesse. Tessa was Mike and Tammy's mother, and the older generation seemed to know it.

"That's understandable," Dr. Lemmen said, in a tone he used with his patients. "I'm going to allow you to visit Sammy, but only for a few minutes. She's in a highly irritated state."

"If she calms down, do you think my friend Jesse can also see her."

"We'll see," he said, already turning his back on Sammy. "This way."

Before Sammy followed him, he put his hand on Jesse's arm as if to console him and whispered a thank you to Lenore.

"You kids better take a seat," Lenore said, pointing to the chairs surrounding the perimeter of the room with her pen. The chairs had black metal frames with faded burgundy cushions that reminded Ivy of dried blood. Boy did she hate the color red and all shades of it. She took a seat facing away from the laboratory that looked out to the hall, so she could see people coming and going. There seemed not to be much activity. Ivy could see why Lenore was on her phone, but she did have a nice view of plants on a shelf marking the end of the waiting room.

"I'm going with Sammy," Zac said, running to catch up.

"I should go too," Mona said, "in the event there's another ghost in the room."

Jesse nodded in agreement, careful not to speak because Lenore was thoroughly examining him where he sat next to Ivy. He hung his head, letting his hair fall in his face. He didn't want to chance her recognizing him as his older self.

Sammy followed Dr. Lemmen down a stark white corridor with countless identical doors lining the walls.

"I was sorry to hear from your father you wanted to end your sessions."

"They ended, but what we've talked about has stayed with me," Sammy said respectfully. "I feel like because of them, I was able to move on."

"That's good to hear from your father but better to hear from you in person."

Sammy nodded even though Dr. Lemmen didn't take notice. He looked straight forward as he walked as if it was physically impossible for him to turn his head. Dr. Lemmen had always been dry, a trait Sammy liked as he tended to be emotional, but he never noticed how stiff he was during their sessions at his office outside of town, but maybe that was because he was always sitting on a couch.

"I want to prepare you for what you're about to see, Sammy. Tessa has been restrained so she doesn't hurt herself. I normally wouldn't let visitors see a patient in a perturbed state such as the one Tessa finds herself in, but as I know you and your family, I'm making an exception."

Sammy read between the lines. It was because his father had given Dr. Lemmen a very large check for helping Sammy through his mental crisis after being kidnapped. Dr. Lemmen played a large part in Sammy's bounce back and Jeffrey let Dr. Lemmen know that with a check that added a wing to the hospital. Sammy couldn't help but notice that wing was named after his family. As far as Sammy knew, Dr. Lemmen was on the list of yearly donations from the Lopez family thanks to his role in Sammy's recovery and the few sessions Dr. Lemmen had with his father on how to control his temper. Either way, Sammy was grateful Dr. Lemmen was making an exception on the basis of 'knowing' his family. Sometimes being the spoiled brat, everyone took him for, worked in his favor.

"I understand," Sammy said. "I'll be quick." He looked at Zac and Mona as if to say try to find out what you can as fast as you can.

Dr. Lemmen led Sammy past a room where the walls were constructed of glass. He could see patients, all wearing the same long, white gowns, sitting quietly. Some of the patients were reading, while others painted. "The Rec Room," Dr. Lemmen said, to satisfy Sammy's curiosity.

They turned down a hall, and as they went, he saw less and less people. They stopped in front of a door with a small window punched out near the top. It looked like all the other doors in that hall, but this door had the metal numbers 215 on it.

Sammy peeked through the window as Dr. Lemmen pulled out a skeleton key and unlocked the door. He knocked, then let himself in. "Tessa, you have a visitor."

The woman sitting on the bed in a straitjacket, who he had seen through the closed door, lifted her head, her hair a knot of red curls streaked with white. Her pupils dilated. "Sammy!"

"Hi Tessa," he said pensively, assuming ghosts were telling her his name, but all the same he was happy she knew it. It helped sell to Dr. Lemmen she was a beloved aunt. And how beloved he must have been for her to recognize him after all those years.

Tessa struggled against her restraints, wiggling her body. "Thank God it's you! Please get me out of here!"

"Be calm Tessa," the doctor warned.

Sammy wished Dr. Lemmen would leave the room but knew he wouldn't. He also knew in Tessa's agitated state he didn't have much time, even less than he thought he would have.

"Tessa, I wanted to come see you about your journal. I found it in your car."

Dr. Lemmen glanced at Sammy, trying to ascertain what he meant.

"Why does everyone keep calling me Tessa?!"

"What should I call you then?" Sammy innocently asked.

"Please don't play into her delusions, Sammy."

"It's me Tammy! Tammy Handover!"

At that, Sammy's heart raced. He was in a near swoon.

"Zac tell him!" she cried, seeing Zac who had inched into the room.

"Is it really you?" Zac asked, sitting on the side of Tessa. Mona followed him into the room, sitting on the other side of her.

Tessa nodded her head, tears running down her cheeks like rapids. "Yes, it's me. Who else would it be?" She fixed her gaze on Sammy. "What's going on? Where's Jesse? And Mike, where is he?" she sobbed into her chest. "Why would my mom and dad leave me here?"

Sammy stood frozen in place, trying to figure out if it was really Tammy or some kind of trick.

Tessa turned her head to Zac. "Please tell Jesse to save me."

"Tessa there's no one sitting next to you," Dr. Lemmen told her in a calm voice.

Tessa glared at the doctor. "I'm talking to a ghost. He's my good friend. I don't care that you don't see him. It doesn't mean he's not real."

"You can see for yourself, she's dealing with a lot," Dr. Lemmen said, putting a hand on Sammy's shoulder and snapping him out of his trance. "I know in time, she'll make a full recovery. We better go now; I fear she's putting on a show for your benefit and that does her no justice."

"Goodbye," Sammy said.

Tessa fought to her feet. "Sammy don't go. Please! Why don't you believe me?!"

"I'll be back," he said, trying to hold in his tears. Tessa was undeniably Tammy's mother, they looked so much alike it was uncanny. Tessa was just older, worn, broken.

Dr. Lemmen ushered Sammy out.

"I'll stay with Tammy," Mona said to Zac. "You go with Sammy." Without a word, Zac ran through the wall after Sammy.

When they returned to the waiting room Jesse stood up. "Can I see her now?"

"Not today," Dr. Lemmen said.

"Tomorrow?"

"If she's up to it, but I'm sure Sammy will tell you that's not likely."

Dr. Lemmen shook Sammy's hand warmly. "It was good seeing you today."

"Thank you, Dr. Lemmen. I'll let my dad know how great everyone treated me today."

"Not a problem, Sammy. You kids have a nice day."

Sammy stopped by the front desk to thank Lenore again as everyone else made their way outside.

"This is bullshit. Why can't I see her? What did she say? And where's Mona?" Jesse demanded of Zac as they waited for Sammy in front of Pleasant Asylum.

"I think Sammy should tell you. He's better at that kind of thing," Zac said, just as the door swung open.

Sammy rushed over to Jesse, placing his arm around his shoulder and pulling him to the Hummer. "We have a big problem."

"What problem?" Jesse asked.

"Tessa is no longer comatose because Tessa is not in the driver's seat. Tammy is."

"What?! Jesse and Ivy said in unison.

"Tammy's trapped inside Tessa," Sammy said, hoping that made things clearer. "Let's get in the car, I don't want anyone overhearing us."

He unlocked the Hummer and they all piled in.

"You're sure?" Jesse asked, leaning forward from the back seat as Ivy hopped in the front passenger seat.

"Very sure. She knew me and knew Zac. And asked for you and Mike. It wasn't a trick. I believed her." Answering Jesse's earlier question, "Mona stayed behind with her. They have her in a straitjacket, the kind you see in the movies. We have to get her out."

Ivy tried to put the brakes on. "Sammy, I think we should call your dad and ask for his help. Dr. Lemmen seems to know your family pretty well, maybe your dad can pull a few strings."

"Not on this. Tammy told him she's talking to a ghost. He thinks she's clinically insane, no amount of money from my dad will get the hospital to release her. Dr. Lemmen likes money, like everyone else, but he's ethical.

He's a good doctor. He won't release her if he thinks she's a danger to herself, which he does."

"We have to break her out then," Jesse said.

"Agreed," Sammy nodded. Zac nodded too from where he sat next to Jesse, his hands on his hips, ready for action.

"Stop!" Ivy said, putting her hands up. "You can't break her out. They'll know who did it. The police will have her back in the asylum in a couple of hours and cart you off to jail." Ivy nervously tugged on her hair. "You're a legal adult now Sammy, you can't be reckless."

"What else can we do?" Zac asked. "You didn't see her Ivy. It's bad."

"If a bribe won't work, we're going to have to do this the right way, through the right legal channels. Mr. Lopez knows them; it's just going to take time."

Jesse clenched his fists. "We don't have time. If that's really Tammy in there, she's been trapped in that hospital for months thinking we abandoned her—thinking I abandoned her!"

"There's something more," Sammy said gravely, his eyes like oceans. "I don't think she knows she died. I definitely don't think she knows she's in someone else's body."

He looked to Zac for collaboration. "I got that impression too."

"We'll deal with that once we get her out of there. We'll work everything out," Jesse stated confidently.

"Jesse," Ivy said, not unkindly, "Tammy's dead, what's there to work out."

"Everything that makes Tammy, Tammy, is in that hospital waiting on us to help her. Everything else can be worked out." He turned to Sammy, "What's the plan?"

Sammy walked into Pleasant Asylum with an Edible Arrangement. He talked to Zac in a whisper as he approached the front desk. "Quickly, tell Mona the plan, then meet Jesse in the bathroom and show him where Tessa's room is."

"Got it," he replied, running ahead of Sammy.

Lenore lit up when she saw Sammy. He put the basket of chocolate covered fruit on the reception counter. "After I dropped my friends off, I began to think how nice it was of you to help me and thought I'd bring you a little thank you." He tugged on the clear wrapping surrounding the basket. "I didn't know what you liked so I told them to put a little of everything in it and make sure everything was dipped in chocolate."

"I love chocolate covered strawberries," she said, untying the bow with a smile. "This is so thoughtful for such a young man."

"I'm glad to hear you're not referring to me as a kid any longer," Sammy said flirtatiously, plucking out a chocolate covered strawberry and handing it to her as Jesse sneaked in to wait in the bathroom.

Lenore took a bite. "Very good," she said, shielding her mouth with her hand as she chewed.

"I like the bananas myself." He took off a chocolate covered banana and took a bite. He offered the rest of it to Lenore, holding his hand under it while she took it with her lips.

The fire alarm sounded overhead.

Lenore in a panic, and still with the chocolate covered banana in her mouth, "What on Earth could that be?"

"I think it's the fire alarm."

They heard footsteps in the hall. Lenore slapped her hands on the fronts of her thighs "You're right! Oh Sammy, you better get outside. The patients are going to be moved into the courtyard." She squeezed his hand before running off through the doors behind her desk.

Sammy made his way outside to the courtyard. A crucial part of the plan was to be seen by Lenore and Dr. Lemmen during the evacuation and remain there until the patients were returned to their rooms. When the commotion calmed down and they realized Tessa was missing, he'd have two airtight alibis.

"It's done," Zac said, snapping his knuckles as he appeared through the door in the bathroom. He was talking a mile a minute, not stopping to take a breather, not that he needed air. "Fire alarms on both sides of the hospital have been pulled. Mona thought it be better if there was a real fire. Nothing crazy, just a fire in a trash can near a smoke detector. She's going to wait for it to burn a little before she puts it out. She said this way the hospital won't think the fire alarms were pulled intentionally. Mona thought it would help make sure Sammy doesn't get in trouble."

"That's good thinking," Jesse said.

Zac smiled as if the compliment was paid to him. "Follow me, it's not too far."

Zac and Jesse ran out of the bathroom and down the hall. They saw a nurse hurrying down the corridor and ducked into a room. They found themselves in a breakroom. Jesse, seeing a lab coat hanging on a hook on the wall, put it on.

"Clever, Dr. Jesse."

"Come on," Jesse said, "let's get going before I'm spotted."

Zac stuck his head through the wall, before tucking it back into the room. "Clear."

They ran past the Rec Room which had already been evacuated and turned down the hall. "This one," Zac said, standing in front of Tessa's room, as the fire alarm continued to boom overhead.

"It's locked," Jesse said exasperated, his entire body drooping like a flower caught by frost. "Sammy never said the door was locked, but I should've known. Of course it's locked!"

Zac struck his forehead with his hand. "It was. I remember now, the doctor took a key out of his lab coat.

Jesse felt his lab coat for pockets, they were empty. He looked into Tessa's room through the small window. All he could see was a mob of hair.

"Locked doors are not a problem for an experienced ghost," Mona said, appearing behind them.

Without a word, Jesse and Zac moved aside. Mona dematerialized into what looked like gray particles of sand. The sand turned in a funnel resembling a mini tornado before diving through the doorknob.

Jesse smiled as the doorknob clambered to the floor. "Thank you, Mona."

Rematerializing, she smiled back. "It's nice to be on the same side as you again Jesse Richards."

"It is," he agreed with a knowing smile that made Zac visibly jealous.

Jesse wasted no time pulling Tessa's door open.

The woman who looked up at him looked so much like Tammy, Jesse took a step back. Tessa and Tammy shared the same delicate nose and sharp chin. Her skin was also fair and adorned in freckles. Danny had mentioned Tessa had black hair, but she must have dyed it. He could still see the dark tips, but her hair was mainly white now. Only a few traces of red still clung to the curls.

"Jesse!"

He ran to her, scooping her up in his arms. "Tammy, I love you. I love you so much."

All Tammy could do was sob.

"We need to move," Mona said, seeming a little uncomfortable about Jesse's declaration of love. Her image fluctuated between her blood-soaked wedding gown and Ivy's outfit.

Jesse pulled himself from Tammy, trying to unfasten the buckles that kept her restrained.

"I got it," Mona said, when Jesse's nervous hands fumbled.

Tessa's arms were free, she stretched them out, wiggling her fingers. "Thank you," she said to Mona.

"Guys," Zac called to his friends, "we need to move now, they're starting to evacuate this hall."

Jesse gave Tessa the lab coat to wear and they ran out into the hall toward the fire escape.

They made it to the stairwell, but they could hear voices traveling their way from above them.

"What do we do?" Zac asked. "This is the only way out from here.

We can't go back into the hall we'll be spotted."

"Clear the stairs!" Jesse yelled as Tammy clung to him as if she was a child. "The fire is coming this way. Quick, clear the stairs!"

"Thank you," a man with a deep voice yelled back.

"That was too easy," Zac said," but I'll take easy."

"We're not out of this yet," Mona said, looking up.

Once the stairwell was silent, they climbed them.

"On the top floor there's a fire escape. It's obsolete, so we won't run into anyone using it and it takes us within running distance to the car," Jesse told Tammy, who had been quiet since they left her hospital room.

They made it to the third story of the hospital without being seen and down an old wing currently being used for storage. Jesse spun around trying to get his bearing. He looked out a window, "Access to the fire escape should be from one of these windows."

"Found it!" Zac called, and they rushed to him.

The window had been painted shut and wasn't going to budge without a fight. Jesse used both hands, straining his biceps to throw the sash. The window buckled under his force, sliding up just enough to give them room to escape.

From the exterior of the window, a small metal platform was attached to the roof giving way to a ladder that traveled down the body of the building.

"Jesse, this doesn't look safe," Tammy said, clinging closer to him.

He spoke to her in the soft voice he reserved only for her. "It will hold you. You're so light. You go first and once you're on the ground, I'll follow."

"I don't know if I can."

Jesse hugged her, talking into her hair. "You can. This is the only way out. You have to. And you have to do it now before we're discovered." He separated from her, but not before kissing her softly on the lips.

She crouched through the window. "Zac and Mona will be with you." Just concentrate on your footing and don't look down." She made it onto the platform. It shook under her weight. She glanced at Jesse, who was nodding encouragingly. "You got this," he whispered.

Jesse watched Tammy's descent, his chest tightening with every squeak of the old fire escape. He sighed in relief only when she made it to the ground. It was his turn. He climbed out to the platform doubting if the rickety ladder could hold his weight since his growth spirt. He decided to climb down as quick as he could, two steps at a time, if that was possible.

He was nearly a story from the ground when the metal staircase let out a loud groan. It seemed to float against the building as the fetters anchoring the ladder to the wall broke. Jesse jumped before the whole thing came down on him.

He hit the ground hard, the air knocked out of his chest. Tammy, Zac, and Mona were by his side. Tammy offered him her hand. He grabbed it and without a moment to spare, pulled her toward Sammy's Hummer where Ivy was waiting to drive them to safety just as the fire escape crumpled to the ground. He glanced back at the hospital as he ran, he could see the patients in the courtyard. Sammy was there, he stuck out in his dark clothing amongst a sea of white gowns.

Ivy drove Sammy's car around the block, parking in the small parking lot of Pleasant Asylum just as the fire engines arrived on site. She crawled into the passenger seat, letting the seat down so a passerby couldn't see her.

"I'll let Sammy know we're in the parking lot," Zac said, hopping through the car in a leap.

Mona, not saying a word, accompanied him. She lost the dress shirt and skirt and was back in jeans and a hoodie.

Ivy had never felt more like a third wheel as Jesse continued to tell Tammy how much he loved her. She felt like their conversation was private, and she shouldn't get a front row seat to their reunion. She wondered if she should sneak out, but knew she had to stay put. As soon as Sammy got back, they had to leave. Things had run smoothly so far; Ivy wasn't going to muddle Sammy's plan at the last moment.

"What happened? Why was I in that place?" Tammy asked into

Jesse's chest as he embraced her in a bearhug.

Ivy's vision darted to the rearview mirror, she couldn't help herself. She watched Jesse's eyebrows furrow into an Oscar the Grouch unibrow.

"What's the last thing you remember before you woke up in that place?"

"Um . . . it wasn't a real thing I remember but a nightmare. We were all in the church and were trapped. Everyone was there but Elsa. It was crazy, Megan was there and Zac's mom, and those mean Henry sisters. They were like zombies but not real zombies, they were being controlled by Pastor Leeds's wife and they were trying to hurt us."

Jesse squeezed her, his fingers tensing around her back. "Tammy, it wasn't a dream. We were trapped in the church, and you got hurt."

Her hand went involuntarily to her neck.

"You didn't make it."

She pushed Jesse off of her. "What do you mean?"

Tears stood in Jesse's golden eyes. "Everything's going to be okay."

"What do you mean I didn't make it?" she asked again this time in a louder voice.

Jesse couldn't answer.

"Ivy, what does he mean?"

Ivy didn't answer either.

"I know you're still there. Ivy, tell me!"

"You died," Jesse said in a soft whisper, the tears rolling down his cheeks one after another. He'd held them in for so long, he couldn't hold them in any longer. "You died." He wrapped his muscled arms around her, hugging her to him.

"I don't understand."

"The body you're in is not your own."

She struggled against him, trying to get free, but Jesse maintained his grip. "What do you mean?! Tessa . . .," she said to herself, realizing the implication. "That's why everyone keeps calling me that!! Oh my God! Oh my God!"

He wrangled her in closer, forcing her head against his chest. "It's going to be okay. We're going to get your body back."

Ivy let out an audible groan.

Jesse, hearing it, got frustrated. "Why not?!" he said to Ivy, his tone venomous. "Why can't we?"

Ivy didn't want to get in a fight with Jesse—not now. She knew emotions were high and it was hard for him to see Tammy crying and scared. She chose to say nothing. Anything she said would set him off.

"I'm going to ask JD for help."

Ivy let out another groan. She had to say something now. "That's not a good idea and you know it."

"You're wrong, it's a great idea. I have nothing to lose. He already has my soul. I'll give him anything else he wants or do anything for him to help Tammy."

Tammy settled down. She wiped her tears with the sleeve of the lab coat as Jesse kept her close to his chest. Ivy wasn't sure if Tammy's calm was because she believed Jesse would fix everything or because she didn't want Jesse to go to JD.

"What about the girl I'm in? What happened to her?"

"You didn't hurt her," Jesse said. "She was gone, her mind was at least. I think you were able to jump inside Tessa's body because she's your mother."

"What?!" Tammy said, giving herself just enough separation from Jesse to look him in the face, his eyes alive with tears. "My mom's Sarah Handover."

Ivy thought Jesse should have eased into the whole Tessa-is-your-mother thing but was glad it was out even if that meant Tammy was agitated again.

"Yes, she is, but Tessa is your biological mother. Your father never told you about her."

"That's crazy! Why would he do that?!" She freed herself from Jesse and reached for the rearview mirror. "Get down," Jesse warned. "Someone could see you." He pulled her back.

Tammy got what she wanted, she glimpsed herself in the mirror, having done so, she let herself fall back into his arms. "It's all true . . . I died."

CHAPTER FIFTEEN
Bishop Baker

"I don't think this is a good idea," Joe said to Mike as Mike parked on the street outside his grandfather's house. Joe had made a promise to himself to never see his grandfather again. They only corresponded through email and that was for work related things only. Joe blamed his grandfather for his childhood best friend Wendy's disappearance and hated him for it.

Mike looked around. They were in a wealthy suburb just outside of Philadelphia. The homes were two-times the size of his house. He couldn't help but notice all the lawns and landscaping were perfectly kept. There was not one stray leaf littering a yard.

"It's the only idea," Stevie reminded them from the back, pushing his long locks off his shoulders. "We've waited long enough; you had all night to recover from heaving up your lungs. Isaac and I would like to have a normal life and Mike would like to graduate high school."

"Don't you have something you have to do today, like work?" Joe asked.

"That's the beauty of being an author, I can write from anywhere."

"You're an author? Cool," Mike said.

"Yes, our Stevie is the fine author of fart books for children."

Stevie rolled his eyes, "I write to market. If the market wants fart books, then I shall deliver the highest quality fart books they've ever read."

"Ignore Joe, we're both glad you're here," Mike said, turning off the engine.

Joe looked at him incredulously. "Speak for yourself."

"Fine, I'm happy Stevie is here," Mike said, getting out of Joe's car. "That means you're outnumbered two to one. We're talking to your grandfather. We have to assume he knows what's going on with you. He's Lilly's father after all. Pastor Leeds confirmed that much when I forwarded him the pictures you had of your grandfather. That means that when he sent you to Pleasant Mills to investigate Pastor Leeds's conduct, he knew what he was sending you into and that means he may have an idea how to stop the effects of your nightmare before it kills you."

"Not a moment to spare," Stevie said, not truly understanding what Mike was talking about. He got out of the back seat and stretched. "Joe your car is so cramped, I think I would've rather squeezed into Mike's truck." Joe ignored him, reluctantly getting out of the car. Together they walked up the pavers to a beautifully manicured brick home. It had all of the storybook appeal of the movies with English Ivy sprawling on the façade and up the chimney.

Joe inclined his head to the Audi in the driveway. "We're in luck; he's home. He must just have his phone on silent." Joe rang the doorbell. They waited a few minutes. When no one answered, Joe used a key on his key chain to open the door.

"Pops," Joe said, walking in. "It's Joe, I need to talk to you."

A small Pomeranian trotted into the foyer. Joe knelt to pet the dog. "Hey Prince Charles."

"What a cutie," Stevie said, scooping up the Pomeranian.

"Uh Joe," Mike said, tapping him on the shoulder and pointing to the red paw prints on the light gray rug. "I think Prince Charles stepped in something."

Joe, becoming aware of the ruddy paw prints at the same time Mike pointed them out, ran in the direction of the prints. Mike and Stevie with the dog still in his arms, followed close behind.

"Pops!"

Joe ran into his grandfather's study, abruptly stopping. Mike and Stevie collided with him. In his fragile state, Joe almost fell over. Mike steadied him.

"Holy blood Batman," Stevie said. "Is he. . . is he dead?"

Leaning over his executive desk was Bishop Baker, his arms hanging lifelessly at his sides. His blood pooled over the mahogany surface, spilling onto the floor in a dark puddle.

"We should make sure," Mike said.

"You do it," Stevie said squeamishly. "I'm not good with blood. I'll call an ambulance." He held the small dog close to his chest with one arm and with his free hand reached for his cellphone in his pocket.

Joe silently nodded, agreeing with their delegation.

Mike entered the study careful not to step on the bloody footprints left by the dog. The room had a stillness to it that made him look back at Joe and Stevie. Mike hesitated. He was sure with that much blood Bishop Baker was dead. But what if he wasn't, what if he could spring to life like the Grindhouses had, like Megan and Zac's mom had, like the Henry sisters had. A vision of Tammy bleeding from the wound on her neck flashed in his mind. He felt lightheaded but moved on. He couldn't let Joe be the one to check on his grandfather and Stevie was occupied, excitably speaking to the dispatch agent on the phone. On guard, Mike slowly made his way to the side of the desk, making sure not to step too close to the gun that lay near it.

Mike lightly pushed on Bishop Baker's shoulder. His head lolled to the side. Mike jumped back. Blood covered his face, coagulating at his eyes and mouth like red pits.

CHAPTER SIXTEEN
Help Needed

Mike had never been in Danny Leeds's house before. The pleasant aroma of coffee beans was in distinct contrast to his growing anxiety. With every door he'd flung open and consequently every empty room he passed, Mike became fearful. While being questioned by the Philadelphia Police Department, he'd missed a call from Sammy. The voicemail was cryptic. 'Mike, as soon as you get this head to Danny Leeds's house. It's the old farmhouse behind Titan Tires. Hurry, it's an emergency.'

The voicemail went unchecked for a lengthy period of time as Mike, Joe, and Stevie were each questioned about Bishop Baker. When Mike finally got a free moment to listen to the voicemails, as now he had several from Sammy and saw countless texts to hurry, Sammy didn't answer his phone. Sammy's phone went to voicemail along with Jesse's, Elsa's and Ivy's.

As soon as the police finished with them, it was a quick trip back to Joe's to get his truck. He flew down the Expressway as he flew down the hallway now, opening the last door down the hall, ready to scream if he didn't find Sammy. It took his brain a few moments to realize what he was seeing. His eyes danced around the room, not hiding the shock of seeing the Tammy shrine as well as Ivy had in seeing it. All the eyes in the drawings seemed to be staring back at him. He couldn't take it, his eyes fell to the stuffed rabbit on Jesse's bed, but more so to the woman holding Tammy's favorite stuffed animal.

"Tammy?" Mike said shakily.

The woman looked like his sister, but could it really be her? She had died. He had held her dead body in his arms.

Thanks to Elsa dying Tessa's hair Tammy's fiery red, she was a dead ringer for her daughter, minus the small difference of age.

Elsa, who sat on one side of Tessa, while Ivy sat on the other, nodded with a smile. She was never happier to cut class.

"Tammy!" he said again, this time with the vigor of life. He barreled into the room and wrapped his arms around his sister, squeezing her as tightly as he could for all the times he couldn't hug her.

Mike didn't attempt to cover up the fact he was crying; he wouldn't be able to even if he tried. Seeing his sister alive and being able to feel her embrace was beyond his most fervent prayer. "I thought you were dead."

Tammy patted her brother's back, trying to console him the way their mother would have. "It's okay Mike, I'm okay. I've missed you too."

To Sammy, who he assumed was in the room somewhere, "You should have left this in the voicemails." Mike released his sister from his hug, wiped his tears, and took her hand, refusing to lose purchase on her. He took the seat on the bed that Ivy had occupied moments ago. He realized something was off, something he hadn't noticed from the doorway. He spied Sammy where he stood with Jesse and Ivy. "Why is she so old?"

Tammy pulled her hand from his. He jerked his head in shock by her reaction, clueless to her sensitivity to being older now. Elsa threw her arms around her best friend to shield her from the insult. "What are you talking about, she looks great!"

Mike tripped on his words. "Yeah but . . . yes, she does . . . but—"

"Is this a bad time to put my opinion in?" Stevie said, from the doorway, the Pomeranian in his arms.

"Who are you?" Sammy asked, realizing for the first time they weren't alone. He noticed Pastor Joe Baker was with him and eased up.

"Pardon me," Stevie went on to say, "Mike's being rude, so I will introduce myself. I'm Stevie and this cutie in my arms is the newly ordained King Charles." He gestured to Joe. "I believe most of you know Joe." At his mention, Joe waved. Confidently, Stevie took the hand Tammy pulled away from Mike, jostling the Pomeranian onto his hip to kiss Tessa's hand with pomp and circumstance. "It's an honor to meet you." Turning to Mike, "It's such a pity your sister got all of the good looks in the family."

Tammy, who had been on the verge of tears, smiled. Jesse noticed this and instantly liked Stevie. He shook his hand. Sammy followed suit.

"Sorry," Mike said, recovering from his blunder, "everyone this is Stevie. He's Issac's boyfriend."

Stevie went to shake hands with Zac. "Nice to meet you. What's your name?"

"Um Zac. I'm a germaphobe," he said, sticking his hands into his hoodie. "I don't shake hands, sorry."

"Me too," Mona said. "And it's Mona."

Ivy exchanged glances with Sammy. Before Joe could ask who Stevie was talking to, Ivy mumbled the spell to let Joe see them both.

Stevie shook Ivy's hand before making himself comfortable next to Elsa who wanted to hold King Charles.

"No Issac?" Jesse asked, looking toward the hall.

Making himself comfortable, Stevie crossed his legs. "I know you don't like my boyfriend very much and blame him for the death of the beautiful young woman I'm sitting with. I hope since she is indeed alive, we can bury the hatchet. Issac was the biggest baby after you broke his nose," Stevie said, poking fun at Issac by pinching his own nose and talking with a muffled voice. "He couldn't sleep properly for a month, something about something or other being swollen, and all he did was whine. So, for my sake, please, if you happen to cross paths with him again don't break his nose or any other part of him. I'm particularly fond of his face."

Jesse smiled. He had never met anyone who sounded like Stevie. "For your sake, I promise not to hurt Issac."

"Good," Tammy said, surprised Jesse did that.

Seeing Jesse disarmed, Joe shook his hand. "Good to see you again." He shook Sammy's "How are you?"

"Hanging in there, Pastor Baker."

"Please, just Joe."

Sammy couldn't wait for the update from Mike about Joe. Mike had texted him Joe had been having trouble sleeping but Sammy hoped he was going to be okay. He didn't look so good, especially with his eye the way it was.

Ivy's mind was whirling, Baker was the name of the pastor Tessa wrote she was going to see for help, but it couldn't have been Joe, he would've been just a baby. Ivy and Jesse exchanged glances as if they had the same thought. *Joe's grandfather.*

Jesse's eyes landed on Tammy; she was playing with the dog as Elsa attempted to put a bow in its hair. It was a good time to sneak away. "Let's talk in the hall," Jesse whispered to Mike.

Jesse moved into the hallway with Mike and Sammy. Zac followed, while Mona stayed. She too seemed enthralled with the dog. Ivy and Joe locked eyes, before she went into the hall, closing the door behind her. She knew Joe was Uriah's son and in turn her grandson, but she couldn't handle that. Not now, probably never. Denial could be a wonderful thing. She felt like dismissing her ancient past. That was the Midwife's life not hers. She owed Joe nothing.

"Don't call Tammy old," Jesse said, reprimanding Mike as soon as the door closed behind Ivy. "She's very sensitive about that."

"I'm sorry," Mike said, feeling horrible. "I knew as soon as I said it, I shouldn't have. I was just surprised. It doesn't matter of course. I'm so happy she's okay." His eyes went to Ivy, "I can't believe you didn't tell me you were going to bring her back."

"It wasn't me or any of us," Ivy said, amazed Mike thought she could even attempt something like bringing a person back from the dead.

Mike was visibly confused, his eyebrows knitting together. "What do you mean?"

"She body hopped," Jesse said.

Jesse told Mike everything: Tammy naming his Volvo Tessa, Tessa's notebook, his mother's troubled past, the asylum, the breakout.

Mike rested against the wall of the hallway overwhelmed as he digested everything Jesse had just told him. "You really think JD could get

Tammy's body back? . . . It's been months, won't it be decayed?" His mind went to his friend Megan Hanson, to the gash on her neck, the muted color of her cadaver skin, causing him to shiver.

"I'm not sure," Jesse admitted, "but Lilly's body was frozen in time for hundreds of years and still is. Uriah buried her like that."

It was true, Lilly's unmaimed body was recovered from the rubble of Pleasant Mills Church. It survived Deborah's heart being torn from it and crushed, the church collapsing and the fire.

"Maybe JD can do something like that for Tammy. It's worth a try."

"You're okay with this?" Ivy asked Sammy.

"I am," Zac said, not that he was asked.

"Yeah, I am too," Sammy replied without hesitation. "I feel responsible for what happened to her. If there's a chance to get Tammy back to her old self, we have to try. We should make a deal with him if we can." Sammy warded off Ivy's concern. "He's family now," he said plainly. "I think he would help for an invite to Sunday dinner."

Jesse nodded. "It's settled then. I'll go ask JD for help."

"I'm going with you," Sammy said, his tone not leaving it up for discussion. "You might need me."

"That goes for me too," Ivy said.

"Fine," Jesse consented. "We leave now."

Mike spoke up. "Can you ask him for something else?"

CHAPTER SEVENTEEN
Flying Kites

Stevie and Joe along with Elsa, Tammy, Zac, and Mona sat in Sammy's Hummer in front of Pleasant Mills High School waiting for Mike to take the math test that would decide his high school fate while Jesse, Sammy, and Ivy went to JD for help.

Stevie rolled down the driver side window so King Charles could get some fresh air. From the front passenger seat, "it's freezing can you roll the window up," Joe barked.

"Look," Stevie said, with a nudge, "look how happy the fresh air makes him. King likes the window open."

Joe rolled his eyes and pointed across the street to the recreational fields. "Why don't you take him for a walk. Mike's going to be at least an hour taking his test."

"What if you start hacking up a lake again? I promised Issac not to let you out of my sight."

"I'll be fine," Joe said, glancing at his watch. "If anything was going to happen, it would've happened. Mike's already been in there for fifteen minutes. We parked close enough to him. All is well.”

“We’ll watch over him if you want to take King Charles for a walk,” Elsa said, from the back seat. “Right Tammy?”

“Yeah, we both had to learn CPR last summer when we worked at Poor Richard’s.”

“That’s the community pool,” Elsa told Stevie, knowing he was from out of town.

Stevie shook out his shoulders like he had fleas. “You’re dolls,” he said, rolling up the window.

“What the heck is that guy doing?” Joe asked, watching a heavy man stake kites to the center of the football field.

Stevie leaned over Joe to get a better look.

“What *is* he doing?” Joe mused again, captivated.

“Capturing energy,” Stevie replied on autopilot.

“With a kite?” Joe asked incredulously.

“With a kite. He ties a key to it before he stakes it. When lightning hits the kite, it will travel down the tail of the kite to the key and charge it with electricity.”

Joe looked at him like he had ten heads.

“Really Joseph, don’t you know your history? It’s how man discovered electricity.”

“No, I didn’t know and honestly I’m surprised you did.”

“Big Benny does it for every storm,” Tammy told them. “When school lets out, I bet you everyone stays to watch the kites get zapped. He always attracts a big crowd. Mike and I love to watch.”

“Yeah, I always watched it with my Mom,” Zac said with a hint of sadness. “You’re gonna love it Mona, sometimes the tails of the kites sizzle up. I think everyone is waiting for one of them to catch on fire.”

“What a wierdo,” Joe said. “What’s he do with all the keys once they’re charged?”

“Come on King Charles,” Stevie said, ignoring Joe’s question and opening the car door. “Let’s take a walk before the storm hits.”

Stevie, with King Charles trotting by his side, made their way onto the football field approaching Big Benny.

“Still collecting energy?” Stevie asked as Big Benny staked another kite to the grassy floor. The wind had whipped his gray, shoulder length hair over his eyes. Benny pushed it back with his inner arm, slicking it over his large forehead with cool sweat.

"Well, well, if it isn't the prodigal son. What brings you back to Pleasant Mills?"

"Visiting a friend."

"You should come by the house."

"I'm not staying long."

Benny grunted in disapproval, pulling yet another stake from his pocket. He took a kite from the pile he had stacked nearby and threw it up into the air, letting the wind lift it high above their heads. "You talk to your brother?"

"No, I haven't in a while. I should give him a call. Stevie lightly kicked the stake King Charles was sniffing at. "So, what do you do with all of them?" Joe's question to him was a simple one. One, he never asked his father, not even when he was a young boy helping his father stake kites while onlookers gawked. In his youth, he never wanted to talk about the kites or the keys. He just staked them as quickly as he could and pretended it never happened.

"Collecting God's energy for him."

Stevie shook his head. "Of course you are. Well Dad, take care of yourself."

"You too, William."

"It's Stevie now," he said walking away, King Charles, following.

"What did he say?" Joe wanted to know when Stevie and King Charles got back into the car.

"Nothing much, just the usual. Fine weather we're having for flying a kite, etcetera, etcetera, etcetera."

Stevie noticed Mike was in the car. "How'd you do on your math test?"

Mike nodded enthusiastically. "I think good. I'm pretty sure I passed."

"Perfect. I hate to think you flunked high school for Joe."

Joe, who was usually cool and collective, flushed. He quickly changed the subject back to the kites. "So ah Mike, Elsa and Tammy were saying the guy flying the kites owns the pool you work at."

Mike's eyes trailed off to the field. "Yep, that's Big Benny Franklin. He does that every time a storm's forecasted. Funny enough, his son's the author you wanted to meet."

"Cameron Franklin the author?"

It was true, Joe had wanted to talk to him about his book and ritualistic killings. He hoped Cam could shed new insight into the cold case he was investigating and help him to discover what happened to his childhood best friend, Wendy, who went missing.

"Yep, that's his dad."

"Geez, small world," Joe said. "I still would like to meet him. Maybe you can arrange it when I'm down here."

"He's back at school now. He's only in Pleasant Mills for the summers."

"That's too bad."

"Yeah," Mike said, "but to be honest, before he left to go back to school, he was acting really strange." Mike turned to Elsa. "Right Elsa? Didn't you think he was acting weird?"

Elsa fidgeted in her seat; she was afraid the conversation was going to take this turn. "Yeah, a little, but I don't think it's a big deal. I'm sure he'll work it out," she said, playing it off to the best of her ability. She had to keep everything Cam a secret to keep him safe.

"I hope so," Mike said. "I think he's on drugs or something. I know he has an older brother he's pretty close to, so hopefully he can help Cam work through whatever it is that's going on."

In the driver seat, Stevie nibbled on his bottom lip.

CHAPTER EIGHTEEN
Two Cases

Pearl waited for Jeffrey to open the gate to the Lopez estate. The iron bars and laurel leaves were not the only thing keeping her apart from Jeffrey. They had made a pact not to see each other alone. With Lindsey living with her sister, and them being seen constantly alone, rumors started to circulate around town. Jeffrey not only wanted to protect his image as a family man, an image vital to his existence, but Pearl's image and reputation. Jeffrey had carefully constructed the mask he wore and Pearl, not that long ago, had gotten promoted to Chief of Police. He didn't want to do anything to jeopardize that or give anyone any reason to scrutinize her. Pearl's job was hard enough.

But today they would be alone. Pearl couldn't spare Weston for another baby-sitting session. He was busy taking statements from the staff at Pleasant Asylum.

"Hey Pearl," cracked over the intercom. "Sorry I didn't realize I locked the gate, drive up."

Jeffrey was waiting with the front door open when Pearl got out of her Crown Victoria.

"No Weston today?" Jeffrey said, stepping aside so Pearl could get in out of the cold.

"Not today," she replied stiffly, feeling an explanation wasn't warranted. He, after all, had made his choice and it wasn't her.

Jeffrey shut the door behind her. "I'm glad. I need to talk to you and wanted to do it in person."

Pearl took the familiar path to the kitchen. "I'm here on official police business."

"Oh, is that so," Jeffrey said, pouring a cup of coffee for Pearl, a soft smile on his lips. He loved it when she acted tough.

Pearl greedily took the mug from Jeffrey. The warmth felt good on her cold hands, and it gave her something to do with them besides shoving them into her jacket like a brooding teenager. She looked up to meet his dark eyes, awkwardly she took a sip of coffee. "Where's Sammy?"

Jeffrey looked at his watch. "Getting ready to leave school I imagine. Why do you ask?" He took an anxious step toward her. "Official police business, you said. Is he okay? Did something happen? Where's Weston?"

"Relax Jeffrey, he's not hurt but he's in trouble. Did you hear about the mess down at Pleasant Asylum?"

His face twisted up. "I heard there was a fire."

"Yeah, there was a fire alright. One started in a trash can most likely by your son and his friends. He's eighteen Jeffrey, this is a big deal."

Jeffrey shook his head, taking a seat on the kitchen stool closest to Pearl. "That's not like him at all. Why would Sammy do something like that?"

It was agonizing to sit so close to Jeffrey. Pearl could smell his cologne, smell the coffee on his breath. All she had to do was turn her head and their lips would touch. Out of her control, her heart raced, but she acted cool. Working mostly with men at the police station, she had learned to hide her emotions. "That's what I want to know. This morning the asylum had three visitors, two boys and a girl. I know the one boy was Sammy. I believe the girl to be Ivy Teller as she along with Sammy skipped school today. The other boy fits the description of Jesse Leeds."

Carelessly, Jeffrey leaned against the kitchen island from his position on the stool. "Pearl, seniors skip school, we sure did." He flashed her a wide smile. "Didn't we, Pearly Girly?"

Pearl remained stony. She was not going to let him know what his smile did to her. She was going to remain professional.

"I'm telling you it wasn't Sammy and his friends. Sammy and Ivy aren't a thing anymore and Jesse doesn't talk to anyone. You can't assume someone did a crime Pearl, not even in this town."

"Sammy signed in as a visitor," she said bluntly.

Jeffrey was on the defensive, his cool demeanor becoming rigid. "Anyone could have signed his name."

"Dr. Lemmen, the head psychiatrist, confirmed Sammy was there."

"Shit," Jeffrey mumbled to himself while raking his fingers through his hair. He pulled out his cell phone and dialed Sammy.

They waited. Sammy didn't answer.

"Sammy, when you get this give me a call," Jeffrey said nonchalantly, leaving a message.

"Not the get-your-ass-home routine?" Pearl said, lacking a playful tone.

Jeffrey stared into his phone on the counter as if he expected it to ring any second. "No, if I go all alpha male on him, he won't come home." His dark eyes flickered to her, then back to the phone. "How much trouble is he in?"

Pearl took a sip of her coffee. It was a good cup of coffee; she could tell he had just made it. She savored Jeffrey's angst. She liked that he needed her to fix this for him.

"Do you know a Tessa McCarthy?"

"No," Jeffrey said anxiously, drumming his fingers on the quartz countertop. "Should I?"

"It's the woman Sammy went to see and the woman who's now missing. Sammy told Dr. Lemmen and the receptionist . . ." Pearl pulled her notebook out of her back pocket to check the name, "and Lenore Mcdermit that Tessa McCarthy was his aunt."

"I've never heard of her. I don't know why he would say that." On autopilot, Jeffrey raked his fingers through his hair again. "Level with me Pearl, how much trouble are we talking about here? Should I call my lawyer?"

She put her hand on his arm, comforting him cost her, but with Lindsey coming back into the picture, there wouldn't be many more moments like this.

"Sammy's not in direct trouble. He has two alibis. He was with Dr. Lemmen and Lenore Mcdermit when Tessa went missing." Jeffrey exhaled in relief, breaking a visual on his phone to lock eyes with Pearl. He was still on edge, there was something in her tone. "We both know Sammy's a smart kid. He made sure he was seen. That means Jesse and Ivy helped orchestrate Tessa's escape, and I want to know why. Dr. Lemmen said she's a threat to others and herself."

"Can Sammy be prosecuted?"

"As long as I'm the Chief of Police, no evidence will be brought against him."

Jeffrey swiveled on his stool. He took Pearl's hands that still encircled her mug. "Thank you."

"When you find out where Tessa McCarthy is, give me a call and I'll pick her up, and this whole thing will be like it never happened."

He ran his one hand over her knuckles and up her wrist, under her coat sleeve. "Pearl, I've been doing a lot of thinking. Staying apart has given me clarity."

Pearl pulled away from him, almost spilling her coffee. She couldn't hear it now. She couldn't have Jeffrey tell her he was going to try to reconcile with Lindsey. She had too much on her plate. First with Joe Baker landing back on her radar after the call from the Philadelphia Police Department and now Tessa McCarthy.

"I don't have a lot of time, Jeffrey," she said, heading toward the front door. "I'm split between two cases."

"Is there anything I can do to help?" Jeffrey asked, following her into the foyer.

"Yes, find Tessa McCarthy."

"I will. I promise." He placed his hand on the doorknob to stop her from opening it. "Can you spare five minutes."

"No," she said, biting back tears. "There was a murder in the outskirts of Philly that may be connected to this town. I got the call this morning. I have to head down there now, I'm already late."

"What's going on? How is it connected to Pleasant Mills?"

"I'm not sure, but when I got the call that our very own Michael Handover was one of three who found Joseph Baker's grandfather murdered, I had this gut feeling, it was going to come back on us."

"Joseph Baker . . ."

"Yeah, do you remember him? He was that young pastor with blond hair that spent time here in the summer. He was at the church fire with that British doctor."

"Yeah, of course I remember," Jeffrey said, opening the door for Pearl. "If Weston is busy, I can go with you to Philly."

"No, I want you to find Tessa McCarthy."

"I'll call you as soon as I do," Jeffrey promised.

She nodded. "Thanks, got to run," she said, avoiding eye contact with Jeffrey. Coffee mug still in hand, Pearl jogged to her car, "I'll return the mug later!"

CHAPTER NINETEEN
The Gift of Knowledge

Ivy was glad Jesse knew how to find JD. The woods seemed more twisted, the trees more gnarled, than the last time she ventured into them. Ivy had been able to find JD when she'd needed him in the past, but the path to him had always been cathartic, like walking through a dream. She just got where she needed to go, or he found her. It was a thing she couldn't explain to Sammy and Jesse and didn't want to.

Sammy's phone rang. It sounded like a shot firing in the eerily still woods. Quickly, Sammy silenced his phone. "It's my dad," he whispered to them. Ivy wasn't sure why he was whispering but felt at that moment it was imperative. "I'm sure he knows about the asylum by now. Urgh, I was hoping to talk to him before Pearl did."

"I don't want you to get in trouble with your dad," Jesse told him. "If you need to go home, go, I can go on alone."

"You wouldn't be alone," Ivy said annoyed. She'd had just about enough of Jesse's arrogance. She counted just as much as Sammy. She may not be related to JD and her abilities were sketchy on most days but the reputation as the Midwife, even if it was from a past life, should count for something.

Ivy was ignored. Sammy went on talking to Jesse as if she wasn't there. "No, I'm going with you. We planned it out too perfectly, I can't get in trouble. Pearl's going to tell him I was at the asylum, and he'll know I skipped school." He slid his phone into his pocket. "I don't think he'll be too mad about that. He probably just wants to make sure I'm okay."

Jesse acknowledged his words with a slight nod as he ducked under a fallen tree that was braced against two larger ones. It was as if those trees formed the entrance into another world. The sky, since ducking under the fallen tree plagued with tiny orange mushrooms and soft moss, was dark—too dark to be the middle of the afternoon. It was as if the trees leaned into each other creating a hallway of bark and branches.

Ivy instinctively rubbed her arms. She wasn't cold, not thanks to the coat she borrowed from Jesse before they left Danny's house. The chill she felt could mean only one thing—they were close.

She was right, they were very close. She spotted JD. He was perfectly still like an owl camouflaged into a tree. He was watching her.

"You're looking for me?"

JD's voice shook her. It had never done that before, and she wondered why it did now. There was something in the tenor tone, a fragileness she had never noticed before, but now couldn't help hearing.

Sammy and Jesse spun around.

"We are," Jesse said. "We need your help."

He stepped out of the canopy of the forest into the small clearing they stood in. What was left of the light bounced around them like fireflies at twilight. "All three of you?" JD asked, his eyes moving over each of them slowly.

"Yes," answered Sammy.

With a smile, "I am your mercenary for hire. Who do you want killed?"

"No one," Ivy stammered. JD had murdered too many people. The part she'd played in the bloodshed was in the past and she wanted it to stay there.

Seeing Ivy's face grow pale, JD anxiously reached for his cigarette case lighting it as quickly as he could and took a longer than usual drag. He was relieved to have something in his hands. "Pardon me. My joke sounded funnier in my head."

"This is not a joking matter," Jesse retorted. "We need you to preserve Tammy's body like you did Lilly's."

JD cocked his head in thought. "Why would you want this, Jesse? Lilly's body was meant to serve as an albatross for Uriah—an image of his guilt. You didn't kill Tammy, you shouldn't harbor any remorse."

"Nice of you to say that, but I don't care what you think. I just need you to do this for me." As if knowing JD was going to refuse to help, Jesse went on. "The one life you let me remember, I did everything you asked of me. I murdered Mona, led countless people astray, kidnapped countless kids, all to keep your *real* son safe. You can do this one thing for me."

"Your perception of the truth is skewed. You are also my son."

Jesse took a deep breath in, the sweet smell of smoke filling his lungs. "We both know Uriah's your only son."

JD flicked the ash from his cigarette, as his other hand tapped on his leg. "That's not true, Jesse."

Ivy recalled the look on JD's face after the 'old Jesse' had tumbled to his death. He looked so similar now. He seemed weighed down by sadness.

"I chose to adopt you when you were a baby."

Jesse raised his voice. "You should have left me alone."

"I couldn't do that. To do that would have meant your death."

"Yes, because lifetimes of serving you is so much better than the alternative."

JD shook his head. "You don't understand. Your unique ability to see ghosts made you a calling card for demons worse than myself. Demons with no moral compass."

Jesse sucked air. He was never sure if JD knew about his ability. He couldn't remember. It was never addressed in his first life, and that was the only one he could recall.

"When you were only a few days old, I found myself at your cradle. I was drawn to your power. Amazed by you, I visited every night. On the third night, I found myself in your nursery with another who was there to claim you. I only saw his shadow as he came out of your closet. He acknowledged I was there first, and conceded you to me. I claimed you then Jesse," he said, touching him on the chest, "in order to save you from a fate worse than death.

"My birthmark," Jesse said, more to himself than anyone else, recalling what Mona said about him being a man with two hearts, and Anita Gomez digging her nail into what she called the mark of the Beast.

JD nodded, confirming the presence of Jesse's unusual heart-shaped birthmark, a birthmark Uriah also had.

Sammy swallowed hard; he too bore it now. He had noticed it when he got home from the hospital. Not only did he have a scar on his stomach from where a piece of wood had impaled him, but next to it was a strange discoloration of skin that was in the shape of a heart, just like the one Jesse had on his chest.

"I claimed you to protect you and I have watched over you ever since. I made sure you gained your father's estate."

"And made sure I killed Mona. That was very fatherly of you."

JD glanced to the ground, he could feel Jesse's, Ivy's, and Sammy's eyes boring holes in him. "I am sorry for that Jesse. I have apologized countless times, I know you don't remember them. But I have, and I will continue to apologize. My jealousy has always been my undoing."

"None of that will matter if you do this for me now. Help me save Tammy and I will forgive you."

JD's dark lashes hooded his eyes. "I can't bring people back from the dead, you know that."

"You don't have to. That's not what I'm asking. You see, Tammy's soul is in another person. We just need her body preserved so she can return to it."

"In another person?" JD asked, genuinely surprised.

"Yes."

JD clutched the lapel of his dark wool overcoat. "That's wonderful. I felt so guilty over her death."

Ivy eyed JD suspiciously. He'd told her just the night before he had nothing to do with the deaths in the summer, but he'd withheld information from her before, turning Sammy against her and used Deborah to collect the thirteen souls owed to him by Uriah. She would never trust him again.

"You'll help then?" Sammy asked.

JD bit his lips, drawing blood, a red bloom growing on his bottom lip. "I'm more than willing to help, for there's nothing I desire more than the forgiveness of the three of you, but there's a problem."

"What's that?" Ivy asked, before anyone else could speak.

"For a small trade, like Sunday dinner at Sammy's, I could preserve Tammy's body . . ."

The color drained from Sammy's face to a vampiric hue.

"Dagnabbit!" Ivy shouted, sounding a little too much like her grandmother. "You were eavesdropping again! You knew we were looking for you and you made us trek through the woods for hours for nothing!"

"I wasn't eavesdropping but listening and you were only in the woods about fifteen minutes, Ms. Teller. I, in fact, did come to you."

"Fine, dinner at Sammy's on Sunday, it's done," Jesse rushed before JD could change his mind.

Inclining his head to Jesse, "I could preserve her body, but her body would be as it is now, and it has been in the earth for months. It's nothing she would want to return to."

With burning disdain, Sammy shook his head at JD.

"Let me explain," JD extended. "Lilly was preserved when she died because I had already made a deal with Uriah that he would always have her. I had no such contract with Tammy or anyone else upon her death. I cannot restore life in any way."

Jesse's complexion pinkened with disappointment. Ivy thought he was going to cry. She went to take his hand. He pushed it away. "You can't or won't?!"

"Jesse, if I could, I would."

"I don't believe you."

"It's true," Ivy said. "If he could've brought anyone back, he would have brought the Midwife back after she drowned."

JD looked at Ivy with sad eyes, the browns of his eyes picking up the little bit of light remaining in the sky. "More than anything, I would've done that."

"Can you help Joe at least? He's your grandson after all," Sammy said, remembering what Mike had asked of them after Ivy mentioned the Midwife drowning.

"Joe is proof you're a liar," Jesse accused. "Joe drowned and you brought him back."

JD took a quick drag, exhaling forcibly, without flourish. "It's true, I pulled Joseph from the lake, but I *did not* revive him in any way. Like Ms. Teller said, if I could've brought anyone back that day it would've been her."

"The Midwife," Ivy said, under her breath, feeling the need to make the distinction.

Jesse turned to leave. "Come on guys, coming to JD was a waste of time. He's not going to help us."

"Wait," JD said, gesturing in a panic, letting his cigarette fall to the ground. "I can't help you in the way you want, but I can give you something else."

"What's that?" Sammy asked, knowing Jesse wouldn't. His back was still turned to JD. He was ready to leave.

"I should tell Jesse in private."

At that Jesse turned around furious. "Same old JD, trying to pit us against each other with secrets and suspicion."

JD crushed his smoldering cigarette under his boot heel. "Have it your way, Jesse Richards. We will have this conversation in front of Sammy and Ms. Teller. —I know how Tammy died."

Jesse threw up his hands in pure frustration. "We all know that!"

"No, you only think you do."

"I'm biting," Ivy said, "tell us."

"Tammy died because of a laceration to her carotid artery but do you know who delivered the fatal wound?"

Jesse thought about it. He had often tried not to. The moment had come so quickly and there had been so much smoke. He'd only heard Tammy's scream, then saw the blood."

"It was one of the Henry sisters. I didn't know them well enough to be able to tell them apart," Jesse finally answered. Ivy and Sammy were on the other side of the church when Tammy got hurt. Their knowledge of what happened was second hand. They nodded at Jesse's response.

"No Jesse. It was Rosa. She used your knife to cut Tammy's throat."

FOREST: PLEASANT MILLS, NEW JERSEY

Ivy gasped, covering her mouth with her hands. Rosa was her best friend and only friend before Elsa. Rosa was kind and docile.

"That's not true!" Jesse said, stumbling back like a knife just struck his heart. "Rosa tried to help Tammy."

"Rosa's jealousy got the best of her. She wanted you all to herself. If you don't believe me, look in her black purse that's hanging on the back of her bedroom door. She kept the knife."

Jesse remembered handing his hunting knife to Mike to help cut down Trudy from the wooden cross Lilly had tied her to. In the tumult, he didn't get his knife back from Mike and thought it burned with the church.

Sammy put his hand on Jesse's shoulder. "We can't trust him. Rosa wouldn't do that. He's trying to manipulate us."

"Why do you think I took her eyes Jesse," JD said, speaking directly to him and ignoring Sammy. "I did that for you . . . to punish her. I made it so she could no longer see the object that she desired. I would have killed her, but I owed it to Devan not to. I understand Rosa, I too know the horrible things jealousy will drive you to in the name of love."

Jesse wiped tears from his eyes with the back of his arm before they could fall. "Rosa killed Tammy because of me . . . Why didn't you tell me?"

"Before, knowing wouldn't have done you any good. But now, maybe it can help."

"Help how?! Ivy said in disgust. "He doesn't need more guilt. You really are a monster JD."

"Come on," Ivy said, taking Jesse's hand, "let's go." This time he didn't refuse it.

CHAPTER TWENTY
Monster Love

JD sat on a nearby log watching Jesse, Sammy, and Ivy retreat as Ivy's words rang in his head like a siren. He felt the cold or thought he did. His need to wear a jacket was for the sole purpose of fitting in; yet he clenched his coat closed.

"As always, she's right," he said to himself in a reproachful manner. "Without me none of this would've happened. I am and will forever be their monster."

He lit another cigarette and blew a ring of smoke into the air, a simple thing he delighted in when he first picked up the habit. Things were so much simpler then. The line between good and evil wasn't so blurred. But everything changed the night Uriah was born.

Pleasant Mills: New Jersey: Ben's Cabin: 1736

"Checkmate," the young boy said, knocking over JD's queen.

"You beat me again."

The boy eyed JD suspiciously, then eyed the hand-carved queen made by his father. "You're letting me win. Father tells me you can't lie. So, what is it? Are you or are you not, letting me win?"

JD smiled.

The boy folded his arms over his chest, puffing it out to look stronger. "If you keep letting me win, I won't get any better. You have to test me."

"Let the test begin," JD said.

The boy had just finished setting up the chess board when a loud knock sounded on the cabin door.

"It's late," the boy said in a whisper, as if the knock startled him. "It must be for father."

They heard another knock.

Ben, in his night shirt, rushed to the door.

"Open up!" Titan yelled.

Ben threw back the latch, opening the door with a mighty pull. Titan pushed past Ben, making a beeline for JD. "This is because of you," he said, pushing a wrapped bundle toward him.

JD didn't react. By now, he was used to Titan's outbursts. His gaze remained fixed on the chessboard as if the game could start at any second and he wanted to be ready.

"Titan," Ben said still drowsy, "what is this all about? Please calm down." Ben tried to offer him a seat, but he refused. Instead, he paced the short distance from the door to the table like a caged animal.

"This is about your pet and his contract with me."

Ben turned to his son. "Go to my room."

"But father—"

"Now William."

William obeyed, getting up but not before whispering to JD he'll be back.

Ben took the seat he had intended for Titan. He rubbed the lens of his glasses clean with his night shirt. "Now tell me what has gotten you in such an uproar."

Titan stood still long enough to make his point. "He had me marry Ivy Teller and play father to her bastard, knowing the child would be hideously disformed. He did this to bring shame on me!"

Ben became aware of the bundle in Titan's arms. "Come now," Ben said, "there's no way he could know the future." Ben gestured to Titan to hand him the baby. "Let me see the child, it can't be all that bad."

JD remained in his seat across from Ben, his dark eyes moving from the chessboard to Benjamin, then to Titan.

Ben unwrapped the bundle as the door to the cabin pushed open. The Midwife stumbled in, slumping against the closed door, her white linen gown soaked in blood.

"My dear girl!" Ben said, shooting up. "You shouldn't be out of bed. Before he could ask JD to get her a chair, he moved his to the Midwife and helped her to sit down.

JD hadn't seen Ivy since the day Titan dragged her into Ben's cabin threatening to kill her. He had saved her life by proposing Titan marry her and take care of her unborn child. He had thought about that day, every day, wondering if he did the right thing tying Ivy to Titan. At the time, it was all JD could think of doing to save her, but he hated himself for it more than he disliked Titan. Titan was only a man after all and plagued with faults not unlike most of the men JD had encountered at the Hell's Fire Club.

JD often hoped on one of Titan's many trips to see Ben, Ivy would accompany him, but she never did. Seeing her now was a dream come true. Their separation had only made him love her more.

JD gently wiped the sweat beading at the Midwife's hair line.

"Japhet Dean," she said in a raspy voice. "You have to help me. Titan means to kill the baby."

"Be still. He cannot harm you or the baby, if he does, our contract is void, and I will not offer him immortality again, no matter how much Ben asks it of me." He made sure he said this so Titan and Ben could both hear.

Titan became enraged, wrestling for the baby. Ben turned his body away from him, preventing it. "The contract is already void! You brought me into this deal under false pretenses."

"I had no idea the baby would be born disfigured," JD said. "Like Ben told you, I can't see the future."

"I don't believe you. You had this planned out from the beginning. First, you murder my brother and his wife and now you're out to destroy the rest of the family. What will the town say when they look upon my son?! I'll tell you, they'll say the Leeds family is cursed by a devil! We'll be shunned as pariahs!"

The baby let out a weak cry. "Poor thing," Ben said, placing his finger in the baby's mouth, feeling a small hole on his palate. "This baby will never be able to suck. A cleft lip, although unsavory, is survivable but a cleft palate . . . that is a different matter. It will most likely die."

"And it shall, before any one in town can lay eyes on it." Titan cast his gaze on JD. "I would have done the deed the moment the baby was born, but I require permission."

The Midwife clutched JD's arm. "Please, do not condemn the baby."

"JD," Ben said in a low tone, as though it pained him to admit Titan was right, "death would be a mercy."

JD left the Midwife's side and went to Ben, taking the baby from him to get a good look at it. The baby had lulled itself to sleep. JD gently ran his index finger over the lower half of the baby's face as if to evaluate the extent of its deformity.

Seeing JD soften to Titan's cause, the Midwife pleaded again. "Please "Japhet Dean, the child is yours."

"What?!" Titan exclaimed, working himself up again.

"Is that true?" Ben asked.

The baby opened his eyes and smiled. JD did the same.

"Yes Ben, it's true. I read it in his eyes. Uriah Leeds is my son."

Titan threw his hands up. "There you go, Ben! I told you, you can't trust him. He orchestrated the whole contract with me so he could have someone raise his bastard son!”

“My stars,” Ben said, wiping the sweat from his brow with his nightshirt. “What are we to do?”

JD’s gaze fell on Titan. “You are right about one thing, the Leeds family is cursed. My son bears my sins.”

“I know it to be so,” Titan said. “I have to purge the family line. I need to do what should have been done months ago.” Titan pulled a small knife from his belt loop and struck out at JD. JD stepped back, the blade just clipping the inside of the baby’s arm. The baby burst into screams. William, who had been listening in the other room, peaked his head out of the bedroom door at the sound of the baby’s sobs.

“You have just voided our contract,” JD said, handing the baby to Ivy, “and with it my obligation not to harm you.”

“It was you, I was aiming for,” Titan said, a hint of fear in his eyes. “You moved, making me hit the baby! You wanted me to hit the baby.” As what was so often the case, Titan’s temper had gotten the best of him. He was no match for JD with a small paring knife. He looked to Ben to step in.

“Everyone calm down,” Ben said, examining the baby’s arm. “It’s just a little scratch. The baby will be fine.”

JD remained fixed on Titan, who had taken several steps back, backing himself into the closed cabin door. “*I’m going to do what I should have done* the day you drug Ivy Teller into this house,” JD said in a calm voice. “In trying to please Ben, I punished her. Punished her to a life of servitude under a man who’s more of a monster than I am. I will not do that again.”

JD turned to the Midwife and repeated the words she’d spoken the day she gave him the dandelion from her hair. “*When a dandelion dies it leaves you a wish. Don’t be afraid to make yours. I wish to be with you forever.*”

JD grasped Titan’s hand that still held the knife, not giving him a chance to strike out against him, and yanked Titan forward. Titan was powerless to move, JD had a superhuman strength he didn’t expect. “You want immortality Titan? Then I will give it to you. You will live forever between the world of the living and the dead. You will be there alone looking in on those you love and never be able to communicate with them.”

Ben was at Titan's side. "Please JD, spare him!"

"No Ben, not this time."

Ben pleaded. "When we met you made me a promise and I you. That promise is a binding contract. I've helped you in countless ways, given you a safe haven, and I now ask you to help me save Titan."

JD's eyes flickered red molten, the nails on his fingers digging into Titan's wrist as they extended into animal claws. "The whole time you were helping me in *countless ways* you were also using me, Ben. Although you were kind to me, for it is your way, you always had alternative motives."

Titan whimpered from the pain, blood now trickling from the wounds in his wrist. JD didn't seem to notice.

"The promise I made you when you first brought me to this cabin was to help you with whatever gifts I was endowed with. From my gifts you have known happiness, pleasure, and power but there is another side to what you call gifts. There is pain, suffering, and loneliness. You and Titan will know the extent of my many gifts and learn that anything given can be taken away."

JD returned his attention to Titan. Titan's hand that he clutched with his dagger-like nails blurred, becoming see-through as if Titan was fading away. The tiny drops of blood running down Titan's arm disappeared before they hit the floor.

"What . . . what's happening?!" Titan stammered.

"You are being banished from this world Titan Leeds, brother of my father who sought to slay me. Enjoy purgatory."

Ben tugged on JD's arm with all of his strength, attempting to get JD to release his grip. "Make another deal with me! I will do anything! Give you anything! Spare Titan!"

Tears stood in Titan's eyes as he spoke. "I'm sorry Ben. I lost my temper. This is not your fault, but my own. I love you."

His body continued to blur out of focus, piece by piece disappearing into the background as JD's grip held firm.

"Please," Ben said, falling to his knees. William ran to his father as the last of Titan vanished. He watched a dark swirl of smoke circle the room before clustering by the still screaming baby in a looming dark cloud. As if by suction, the smoke was drawn into the cut on the baby's arm before the skin stitched shut.

Ben's desperation emerged like a curse. "You will regret this JD. I will make sure your eternity is as lonely as mine."

CHAPTER TWENTY-ONE
Brotherly Love

"You think you can be left alone for a couple of hours?" Stevie asked Joe. Stevie was hoping Jesse, Sammy, and Ivy would've been back by now. After the girls, with Zac, went to Jesse's room for what they dubbed girl talk, Stevie felt like a third wheel stuck between Mike and Joe on Danny Leeds's couch. As comfortable as the couch was, he was ready to give them some space, and had his younger brother on his mind.

Joe reclined on the couch with a smile. "Going back to the city already? Good riddance."

"Play nice," Mike warned.

Stevie got off the couch, placing his arm behind his head and cracked his back. "Don't get to excited Joseph," Stevie said sounding a lot like Issac as he over pronounced his name. "I'm coming back. I promised Isaac I would watch over you, so I will. We're getting you healed, fixed, spiritually exercised, or whatever it takes for Issac and me to get back to our normal lives." Joe rolled his eyes. "I just need to grab a few things. Looks like I'm going to be in this Podunk town for longer than I thought."

Mike jumped at the chance to get some time alone with Joe. He handed Stevie the keys to his truck without him asking.

"Hey Willy!" Cam said, opening the front door to his apartment. "What a surprise! Cute dog. He yours?"

"Hey back, little bro. And it's Stevie. How many times do I have to tell you that," Stevie said in a clipped tone.

"I know that," Cam said, apologetically. "I'm sorry my brain's been fuzzy lately."

"That's why I'm stopping in," Stevie said, plopping down on the couch. "And to answer your question, yes, this little cutie pie is the new addition to the family. Say hello to King Charles."

Cam sat down next to his brother and petted the dog between the ears. King Charles was receptive to Cam's caresses, taking a seat on his lap.

"So Cam," Stevie said, narrowing in on his brother, "the rumor mill has it you're on drugs."

Cam laughed. "Me on drugs? Where did you hear that?"

The laughter upset King Charles. He opted for Stevie's lap. Stevie brought the pooch to his face and gave him a kiss before scrutinizing his brother. "From a very reliable source."

"Well," Cam said, seeing his brother was being serious, "your source is wrong. I'm not on drugs. In fact, I'm great."

"Yeah . . .," Stevie said, keeping his eyes on his brother, "you look great . . . really great." Stevie grabbed his brother by the chin.

"You're hurting me."

"What did you do to your face? Did you get work done? It hasn't been that long since I've seen you. When did you become such a little hottie?" Before Cam could respond—"Omg you got a nose job and didn't tell me! For shame Cameron Franklin. I wouldn't have talked you out of it. I always felt bad you got dad's nose."

"Funny you should bring up Dad. It's strange, I should have his nose when I was adopted."

Stevie's eyes grew large. "He finally told you, you were adopted?! It's about time, I guess. I just never thought he would."

"No, he didn't tell me. I remembered."

Stevie rested his head back, looking at the mildew stains on the ceiling while he stroked King Charles behind the ears. "I'm not going to lie, I was surprised when Dad brought you home. It's not like he told me he was thinking of adopting." Stevie's eyes flickered to Cam. "Dad said you came from a rough life and that you needed a fresh start. You always acted like you didn't know you were adopted, and I never wanted to burst your bubble. Dad made up this elaborate lie about Mom dying in some gruesome fire and with it all our family pictures. I thought you blocked out the truth, suffered from post-traumatic stress disorder or something over the whole adoption process."

"No that wasn't it. I was made to forget. Dad, he made me forget."

Stevie smiled. "That's his bravado. He can make you think anything sometimes."

"Is that why you left home?"

In a jerk reaction, Stevie sat up, the dog jumping to the ground. "Oh God, no. I didn't leave home because of you. I don't care if little green aliens dropped you off on our front door. You're my brother. You know that right?"

Cam nodded. "I know. I meant, did you leave home because of Dad?"

Stevie's gray eyes shifted to the ground, he didn't want to talk about dropping out of high school and running away to Philadelphia. "Dad was part of it, but I needed to get out of Pleasant Mills. *I* needed a fresh start. A kid can only be called Free Willy so many times before he snaps. You may have had a nose that look like Dad's but I got the body. It was torture working at the pool every year and being the size of a whale. I really hate that freaking family favorite movie. It was a waking nightmare."

Cam pulled on a loose string jutting out from the velvet couch cushion. "So, you never noticed anything weird about Dad?"

Stevie laughed, his laugh sounding like hiccups. "Define weird.

Everything's weird about that man. Sometimes I think he's really an alien and I should report him to the FBI. I may, if they start offering rewards."

Cam joined his brother in laughter. "Agreed."

Stevie tousled Cams' hair. "You sure you're okay, kid? You know you can talk to me."

"Have you ever been in Dad's workshop?"

Stevie furrowed his perfectly shaped eyebrows. "Yeah, I think once or twice. You know I'm allergic to manual labor."

"Not the one in the garage, the one *under* the garage."

The little hairs on Stevie's arms stiffened, a line of goose flesh traveling up his biceps. "What are you talking about?"

"There's this trapdoor that leads you down into the basement of the garage. He has all these pictures on the wall. Private pictures of my friends and girlfriend."

Stevie's face exploded with a smile. "You have a girlfriend and didn't tell me?! First the nose job and now this. Seriously Cam, what's up with you?!"

"I'm being serious Stevie."

With a big grin on his face, "So am I. What's her name?"

"Elsa."

"She sounds lovely, go on."

"She is," Cam said, showing him a picture of Elsa Tilton on his phone. "We just started dating. I was going to tell you when you called this week."

"Wow Cam, she's a knockout," Stevie said, taking the phone from his little brother. "This warranted a call to me before our weekly!"

He smiled, proudly. "She's really smart too."

"Yes, I can see that about her." Stevie handed his brother back his phone. "And I wouldn't worry about pictures Dad has hanging on the wall. He used to take pictures of my friends too. You know he's strange like that. But I would definitely keep Elsa away from Dad. She may stop his ticker."

"She works at the pool, well did, during the summer."

"There you go!" Stevie said with a clap, getting the attention of the dog who hopped back on his lap. "He has pictures of Elsa because she's an employee and you always say you work with friends."

"That's true," Cam said, thinking about it, "but the pictures don't look like they were taken at the pool," Cam said, almost positive he recalled pictures of Elsa in her bra and underwear. Cam couldn't tell his brother about their father wiping his memories; he would never believe it. "Maybe you're right, I didn't get a chance to look at them for that long, maybe I should."

"I'm sure they were," Stevie said with authority. "Promise me you won't go back to Pleasant Mills to check."

Cam's eyebrows furrowed. "Why?"

"Because Dad heard the rumor you're on drugs. Like I said, my pop in was because of that. I actually spoke to Dad earlier today. He wanted me to check in on you."

"Wow, you talked to Dad?! That's big."

Stevie waved his hand in dismissal. "Not so big. We talked about you. So, promise to stay up here until I tell you the coast is clear. Trust me when I say you don't want Dad poking around your life."

"I promise to stay put," Cam said. It was an easy promise to make. He had already promised Elsa and Ivy the same thing. "I'm not planning on going home anytime soon."

Stevie perused the premade sandwiches at Wawa convenient store. "Whatcha think?" he asked King Charles. "We need to pick something. Issac's going to call and ask what I ate, and I can't say nothing. And I won't lie to him."

Stevie already felt horrible about lying to Cam. Typically, he wouldn't have lied. He was very close to his brother, but when the workshop under the garage was mentioned, he got this funny feeling. Stevie had never been in the underground workshop, but that didn't stop a pit from forming in the middle of his stomach and it wasn't hunger pangs. This stabbing feeling that something was off stopped him from being honest with his brother about why he didn't want him to go home to visit their father, and from saying he had met his girlfriend and liked her. It was also the reason he was going to stop by his father's house on the way back to Joe.

"Fruit, nut, and cheese mix looks good." The dog barked in agreement. "Deal, I eat the fruit and nuts you get the cheese."

He grabbed two bottles of water, one for him and one for King Charles and headed to the checkout.

"You're all grown up," he heard a man say from behind him.

Stevie turned, not recognizing the man.

JD put his hand out. "I'm an old friend of your father's."

Stevie juggled the dog and shook hands. "Yes," he said combing over him. "I think I remember you, it's a little blurry, but I recall you were really good at chess, and you always let me win. JD—Japhet Dean, wasn't it?"

"Yes," JD said surprised.

"Very good to see you. I'll tell my father I ran into you."

"Very good to see you too, William. You did always promise to come back."

Stevie backed Mike's truck into his father's driveway. Hesitating for a few moments, he opened the driver side door and got out, King Charles following suit, trotting alongside him. It had been a long time since he laid eyes on the old house. It looked exactly how it did when he was a child: moss still clung to cedar shingles in emerald clumps, the knee-high iron fence was still flaking with rust, and off to the side of the house was the garage—the place where his father spent most of his free time.

Stevie made his way to the garage. It was dark in there, even with the lights on. He kicked at the floor in search of the trapped door Cam had mentioned.

"Looking for something?" Benny asked, coming from the back of the garage.

"You," Stevie replied coolly. "You said to stop by, so here I am."

"It's not like you to come to the garage."

THE FRANKLIN GARAGE PLEASANT MILLS, NJ

Stevie inclined his head to the dog. "King Charles was looking for a good place to pee."

"You talk to your brother yet?"

"Not yet, but I will."

Benny took a few steps closer to his son, leaning against the push lawnmower. "Why are you in Pleasant Mills after all these years William. I thought you never wanted to come back here."

Stevie yawned, bored with the conversation. "It's Stevie and I'm here with a friend. I'm only staying till the weekend."

"Does that friend happen to be Joseph Baker?"

"You know him?"

"I know everyone in this town and he's bad news. Be a good boy Willy and stay away from him."

"Stevie," he muttered under his breath, picking up King Charles, and heading toward Mike's truck.

"You're leaving?" Ben asked, following his son out of the garage.

"Yep. Nice chat, Dad."

Stevie yanked the passenger side door open and put King Charles in before closing the door. His father stood so closely behind him, Stevie found it hard to turn around without rubbing against his father's large frame.

"I'm serious William. Death follows that boy; he can't help it. I don't want you hurt."

"I can take care of myself, thank you very much," he said, sidestepping his father.

"Can you?" Ben asked, stopping him from opening the driver side door.

He pushed his father's arm away. "I can. Have been for years now."

"That's not what I heard."

"From whom?!" he said, furious.

"From that nice boy you're dating."

Incredulously, "You talked to Issac!?"

"I have. He called me the last time you were in the hospital. Said you relapsed and wouldn't eat."

"Oh that," Stevie dismissed with a flourish of his hand. Issac said he was legally obligated to call you since you were listed as my emergency contact. Don't worry, you've since been removed." Stevie's steel gray eyes cut to his father. "Funny, where was your fatherly concern then? I don't remember you caring or even visiting." Stevie put his finger to his chin and looked up at the cloudy sky. "Oh, that's right you couldn't make it to the hospital because a storm was coming, and you had to go fly your kites."

He hopped into the truck and slammed the door. "Well Dad, go fly a kite. Pun intended. And by the way, your old friend Japhet Dean said hi."

CHAPTER TWENTY-TWO
One of a Pair

"Jesse," Mrs. Littleton said, answering the knock on the front door to see him. "Rosa was getting worried when you missed lunch. Are you hungry?" Not giving him a chance to answer. "I left your sandwich in the microwave if you are."

"Sorry Mrs. Littleton. I should've called to say I wasn't going to make it." Jesse went to Rosa's every day on his lunch break, so he'd have the time to work on Tessa after work and had his evening to himself to draw. He hadn't expected the morning at Pleasant Asylum to go as it did and calling Rosa to say he wasn't making it for lunch never crossed his mind.

"Don't apologize," she said, closing the door behind him. "I was just gonna run up the street to Shoprite. Rosa asked for eggplant parmesan tonight, can you believe there's not one eggplant in the house?" Again, not giving him a chance to respond. "Is there anything special you want?"

He shook his head.

"Well don't let me keep you. Rosa's in her room."

Mrs. Littleton grabbed her handbag off the walnut bench next to the door and left hurriedly, as if worried the supermarket would be sold out of eggplants. Jesse reasoned this could be the case, since it was out of season.

Jesse walked the familiar picture-lined hallway to Rosa's room. He always liked to look at the faces staring back at him in black and white as he went. He felt like he was walking through a timeline and figured that was pretty accurate. It was the Littleton family line. If you looked closely, you would see that Rosa Littleton and her mother and father and her grandfather, Devan Rainier, appeared out of the sequence of time, appearing in different pictures among the expansive generations of Littletons.

Jesse stopped to stare at the portrait of JD he'd painted lifetimes ago and had sold to Rosa at the community yard sale in his last life as Cousin Jesse. Jesse couldn't believe there was someone he hated more than his adoptive father. Taking a deep breath, he knocked on the last door in the hall before entering.

Rosa, who was sitting at her vanity, turned around, knowing the sound of his gate. "Jesse!" she said, her face lighting up behind her blacked-out sunglasses, her hair done up in its usual two braids that flopped over her shoulders like rope. "Where were you this afternoon? I called a billion times. I even made my mom call Danny. He said you took the day off and went out with friends. Who were you with?"

Normally he thought Rosa's rattling was amusing, but not today. He didn't see how he ever did. "I was with Sammy."

"I didn't know you were talking to him again, but I'm glad you are. Where'd you go?"

Jesse looked around Rosa's room at the many drawings of flowers he'd drawn for her. The trust he had in her was broken. He wanted to take the drawings off the wall and tear them in half, a physical representation of their friendship.

Still, deep inside him, where he kept his feelings locked away, he clung to the hope that Rosa didn't do it, that she wouldn't hurt Tammy out of jealousy, hurt Tammy because he loved her.

Jesse needed more than JD's word; he needed proof. He located Rosa's purses hanging behind her door on metal hooks in the shape of birds sitting on a tree branch. JD said he'd find his knife in her black purse. But

Rosa had many black purses, even one that was in the shape of a cat's head.

He talked as he looked through her handbags, unzippering and unbuttoning as quietly as he could, hoping his voice would drown out the rustling.

"Yeah, I was with Sammy and Ivy Teller. I'm sure she'll tell you all about it, but I also saw Mike and that guy he likes Joe."

Jesse held his breath. He found what he was looking for, from a small black crossbody he pulled out his knife. He recognized it. It was one of a pair. One knife he'd used to stab Lindsey Lopez and was consequently lost and the other he thought he'd lost in the church fire.

Jesse's heart beat so loud, Rosa's chattering became static. He mulled over his knife. Blood was dried on the white handle that was supposed to resemble bone. He opened the blade to further examine it. A single piece of red hair was stuck to the knife-edge where dried blood crusted over it.

"I was glad Issac didn't come," Jesse said, not knowing if he talked over Rosa. "You remember him? The doctor who couldn't save Tammy?"

"I do," Rosa sympathetically replied. "Poor Tammy."

"Yeah, poor Tammy," Jesse said, his tone off. "I don't think I will ever love anyone like I love her."

Rosa's face pinkened under the shadows of her glasses.

"I keep running the day through my mind wondering what happened. You were right next to her, you sure you didn't see anything?" It was Jesse who now rambled on, not letting Rosa get a word in. "I always thought it was the Henry sisters. I thought one of them went around Mike and got to her . . . but that's not what happened, is it?"

Rosa, agitated, shifted her weight on her vanity stool. "It doesn't really matter which one killed her. It's not like it was really them, they were all part of Deborah, and part of a hive mind. I'm glad you talked to Sammy, Ivy, and Mike today, it was overdue, but you all have to let it go. Bringing it up doesn't help."

"I want you to tell me the truth, Rosa," Jesse said, taking a step closer to her with the knife still gripped in his hand, his knuckles now white. "I want to hear it from your lips."

Rosa took off her sunglasses and looked at him as if her brown eyes weren't made of glass. "He told you," she said in a whisper. "Jesse . . ." She reached out her hand for him, only clutching air.

"On the way here, I hoped JD was lying, somehow skewing the facts, and making it fit his needs. But the truth is plain and simple," he said in a low voice as he fixated on his knife.

"Jesse, I love you so much. I hated how you treated me when she was around. You're supposed to love me."

Jesse spoke with conviction, his tone authoritarian as was his demeanor. He stood tall, his eyes locked on Rosa. "I will never be yours Rosa. I don't love you. I've spent a lot of time thinking about you—about us—since you told me we were a thing. I could never figure out what it was about you that I supposedly loved. I couldn't find it. I could barely find things I liked about you." Rosa sucked air, a hissing noise filling the room. "I came to the conclusion, a long time ago, that I must've used you, because there's no way I could've ever had one genuine feeling for you, besides pity. That made me feel guilty and I've tried very hard to be your friend because of it."

"You don't mean that, you're just upset with me."

He went on as if he didn't hear her. "Why do you think I stopped talking to all my friends, but you? —Guilt. I visit you every day on my lunch break because I feel bad for you Rosa, because I used you and you lost your vision. Now I see, JD blinded you for me. He has a funny way of showing his loyalty, but I understand why he did what he did and don't blame him. For once I'm grateful to him."

"You say that now, but it won't always be that way," Rosa said through clenched teeth, knowing she wasn't going to be able to manipulate a way out of this. JD had ratted her out, there was no hiding from the truth. "I get the last laugh Jesse. When you die, because you will, you'll be reset, and you'll forget all about Tammy. It'll be like she never existed, and you will love *me*. I will make sure of it."

He shook his head, his hair falling into his eyes. "No Rosa, I won't."

"Because of your stupid journal?! I will make sure they're all destroyed. And with all your friends dead, you'll have no one but me. And you, you will love me," she said, pointing to her heart as if that made her prognostication true.

Jesse brought the blade of his knife to Rosa's neck, the edge grazing her soft skin. A thin line of red flowered on her throat.

She laughed. "We both know I can't die."

"You're right," he said, taking a step back and seizing control of his temper, his hands shaking. "If I kill you, you'll come back with your vision restored. You don't deserve that."

Jesse rushed to the door, before he changed his mind. Killing Rosa would make him feel better, if only for a moment. His golden eyes fell on her one last time. "Goodbye until we meet in the next life."

CHAPTER TWENTY-THREE
The Letter

Stevie chucked the rest of his meal out the window, he was too frustrated to eat. His father always did that to him, rankled his Zen. "Waste of time," he muttered to himself, clutching the steering wheel. He glanced down at King Charles who was sniffing the empty Wawa container. "You already ate all the cheese, you wouldn't have wanted the rest. Trust me, it didn't taste all that good." The handful of grapes he popped into his mouth on the ride to his father's house were enough to settle his shaky hands. He didn't need more than that and wouldn't eat more than that.

He pulled down the long driveway to Titan Tires, slowing to a stop in front of the mechanic shop on account of an old white station wagon blocking the way further down the driveway.

The tall man hanging on the window of the station wagon looked Stevie's way. Stevie recognized him as his father's friend Danny Leeds. It had been just as long since he'd seen him as his father, the difference being he always liked Danny. Often, Stevie had wished Danny was his father and not Big Benny Franklin.

It took a moment for Danny to realize he was looking at William Franklin but when he did, his blue eyes lit up and he waved. He gave the woman in the station wagon a peck on the cheek, sending her on her way before sashaying up to Mike's truck.

"I can't believe my eyes," Danny said, extending his hand to Stevie. "If it isn't Little Willy Franklin." Stevie's ears burned red with embarrassment, there was another one of his horrible nicknames. Little Willy, was coined because everyone always told Big Benny William should've been named after him, being they looked so much alike.

Stevie shook his hand, not bothering to tell him he'd changed his name. It was pointless, after things were taken care of with Joe, he was never coming back to Pleasant Mills.

"You sure look different," Danny said. "I almost didn't recognize you. Big Benny said you were as thin as a rail these days, but I guess you don't believe some things until you see them."

Stevie politely smiled.

"What brings you home? I thought a city slicker like you wouldn't be caught dead in Pleasant Mills."

"A friend."

"Mike Handover," he said, patting Mike's truck like it was a faithful dog. King Charles extended his head toward Danny for similar attention. Danny complied.

"Yes Mike."

"A good kid, shame about his younger sister."

"I thought she was older?" Stevie posed, thinking about the woman he had met earlier that day and wondering if he needed to get his contact prescription checked. At the very least, he thought she was a few years older than Mike.

"No, Tammy was only a baby when it happened—sixteen. It was a real shame."

"Yeah, I did hear about it from my boyfriend, his details were a little blurry."

"Boyfriend?" Danny asked. Stevie wasn't sure if he was asking about his boyfriend's name or questioning the fact that he had a boyfriend. He answered with his name instead of catching Danny Leeds up on his sexual orientation. "Yes, Issac Smith."

"Oh the doctor," Danny said. "My girlfriend, Mary Teller, told me all about him. I know he did his best to save little Tammy Handover but my Jesse, he didn't see it that way. He took her death really hard".

"I heard that too. But I think everything is going to be fine since she didn't actually die."

Danny laughed, play punching Stevie's cheek. "Faith is a powerful thing. You were always a bucket of sunshine."

"Yep, that's me, a big bucket of sunshine," he said confused. "Well, I better get Mike's truck back to him. I'm sure I'll be seeing you. Your house seems to be the place to hang."

A toothy smile flashed across Danny's face. He patted the truck again. "You kids have fun."

Stevie continued his drive down the dirt road to the old farmhouse. It looked like it always had when he'd visited with his father. It was pristine, like it could've been the featured house in one of those magazines that made you feel guilty your house could never look like that. The inside of Danny's home was the same, nothing had moved, and everything had a place, a thing very different from how his father kept house. But Danny still hadn't replaced the broken mirrors all over his home.

Stevie took solace in the fact that he no longer looked like his father and was a clean freak. He couldn't be less like him.

Stevie coasted to a stop, spotting Jesse walking out of the woods a few yards in front of him. He rolled down his window. "Want a lift stranger?" he said in a southern accent.

"It's right there," Jesse said, pointing at the house and avoiding looking at Stevie with his red rimmed eyes.

"Get in," Stevie said. "You look like you could use a break and King Charles needs some love."

As if on cue, the dog barked, getting Jesse to look his way. Jesse's resolve softened and he got into the truck. King Charles sat on his lap demanding attention, rubbing his head under Jesse's chin.

"You okay?" Stevie asked.

"I just found out one of my oldest and closest friends is the one who murdered Tammy."

Stevie sucked air. "I'm not trying to be insensitive, but I'm confused. I heard Tammy died from Issac, Mike, and just now Danny Leeds, but I met her this morning."

Jesse aimlessly petted the dog as he looked out the window. "I keep forgetting you're not from this town. Things are different here. You're probably not going to believe me, so I don't see the harm in telling you the truth. Tammy did die—well, her body did. Her soul was able to jump into her biological mother's body. We think it was possible because her mother was comatose, her body acting as an empty vessel for Tammy's spirit to latch onto. The Tammy you met is my Tammy, but she's in the wrong body."

Stevie blinked rapidly as if that would help him digest Jesse's story. "Yeah, you're right, I don't believe you," Stevie said, parking next to Sammy's Hummer. "But a while back I watched this documentary on group hysteria and learned it's contagious. So, I'm sure the longer I stay here, the more it will seem plausible. Be patient with me Jesse, I'm a stickler for common sense."

Jesse cracked a smile. He really liked Stevie.

Stevie, with King Charles in his arms, walked into the house with Jesse to see everyone gathered in the living room. Stevie had spotted Issac's car outside and was anxious to see him. However, his happiness was soured by Issac sitting impossibly close to Joe as if they were a couple. Stevie was no longer a bucket of sunshine, but a raging storm cloud.

Jesse, on the other hand, found his hatred for Issac greatly diminished; he had a new outlet for his hate—Rosa. He was glad he was going to be able to keep his promise to Stevie and not break Issac's nose again.

Issac got up and rushed to Stevie. Taking the dog from him, he placed King Charles on the floor, so he could hug Stevie hello properly. The dog made a bee line for Tammy and Elsa who'd squeezed onto the couch next to Mike, ignoring Ivy, Sammy, Zac, and Mona who sat on the floor.

"I've been trying to call you for hours," Issac wined.

After being released from his hug, Stevie checked his phone. "I hate this town. I've been in and out of service all day. Sorry I missed your calls, but you didn't have to drive down here to check on me."

"I came for Joe."

A blush streaked across Stevie's face. "I have everything under control here and Joe has lots of babysitters," he said, gesturing to the many faces in the living room and noticing the room was quiet besides the two of them speaking. He didn't want to have this conversation in front of an audience.

"We must have just missed each other."

Stevie scanned Issac's face for answers, not sure what he was talking about.

"Joe said you went to Philly to get a few things."

Stevie was so distressed at hearing Issac came to Pleasant Mills for Joe, he'd forgotten all about the little lie he told before he visited Cam.

Issac went on, taking a lock of Stevie's hair and playing with it as he spoke. "It's not that I didn't trust you. I received a letter for Joe and had to deliver it. I told the hospital I had an emergency, and I was able to take family leave."

Stevie's flush reached the tip of his ears. "Family leave, for Joe . . . "

"Relax Stevie, I'll be out of your way soon enough," Joe said from the couch.

Mike hissed at Joe. "Don't talk like that."

Jesse's amber gaze landed on Tammy. "I love you," she mouthed to him from across the room. His heart fluttered. Even after everything he cost her, she still loved him. He walked over to where she sat on the couch and planted a kiss on her lips, letting her know he didn't care about the age gap between them, and he didn't care what anyone thought about it. He loved her too. She scooted up so he could sit, finding her place on his lap, as she had often done before she died.

Jesse observed the room. He'd thought everyone was solemn over the news from JD, but gathered there was more to it than that. "So, what's in this letter that's so important?" Jesse asked, taking notice of Stevie's burning ears.

"You can read it if you want," Joe said, twirling it between his fingers like a magician. "Everyone else has."

"I will, thank you very much," Stevie said, plucking it from Joe's fingers.

"It's from his grandfather," Issac told Stevie and Jesse, getting them up to speed. "It was mailed to the apartment. His grandfather must still have it listed as Joe's." Stevie's pulse surged. He didn't like to be reminded that before he lived with Issac, Joe did. "Anyway, I was just opening the mail and didn't realize it wasn't for me until I started reading it."

"This must be the letter of all letters to make you take family leave," Stevie mumbled before reading it out loud so Jesse could hear it.

Dear Joseph,

If you're reading this letter, that means I'm dead. I'm dead and I'm not coming back. I gave my lawyer strict orders to mail this letter to you in the event of my death. I've been keeping a big secret from you all your life. I have no idea how much of the truth you've glimpsed or would care to know so I will keep this short.

I have taken care of you since you were a baby, this you know but what you don't know is that I have done this for several lifetimes. This would be hard for most people to believe but I gathered you've guessed at the truth. You were always a smart boy, too smart.

You died as a young boy January 19, 1769. You drowned and were brought back to life by unnatural means. There is a cost for something like this. The scales of balance were thrown off and need to be balanced. For you to live, each year a sacrifice has to be paid to Batsto Lake, the lake you drowned in.

The nightmare you had us a boy, and I imagine you still have, was more than a nightmare. It was a memory from when you drowned. If you want to live another year, you must drown someone in Batsto Lake before the anniversary of your death or you will die.

I am sorry to bring this burden on you.

Eternally your grandfather,
David Baker."

Stevie's steely eyes shifted to Joe. "Is this a joke? This can't be serious."

"It's not a joke," Mike answered for him.

Stevie looked to Issac bewildered. "You can't believe this, you're a doctor."

"You weren't there, Stevie. You didn't see those women trying to murder us in the church. They were already dead. I know this is crazy, but I believe the letter."

"You're saying we have to drown someone in a lake to save Joe?" Stevie asked, making sure he got it right.

"Pretty much," Ivy said, from her place on the floor next to Sammy.

"I'm sorry, but this is crazy," Stevie said, refusing to believe it.

"No one asked for your opinion," Joe grumbled.

"Hey, lay off of him," Issac said, jumping in front of Stevie as if he was a shield. "He's right, this is crazy. But the more important question is what are we going to do about it?"

"That group hysteria, still not kicking in, is it?" Jesse said to Stevie, getting up to take the letter from him to read it again. "Well Doc, this is an easy one. I can fix this. I'm going to drown someone in Batsto Lake."

CHAPTER TWENTY-FOUR
The Well

"**I** have to go home," Sammy whispered to Ivy, while everyone argued what to do about Joe. Jesse's willingness to drown someone had set the room in an uproar.

"Right now?" Ivy asked. "We're in the middle of a crisis. You can't actually let Jesse drown someone, not even to save Joe."

"Yes, now. My dad's called me close to ten times. If I don't go home, he'll come looking for me. And you heard him, his emotions are heightened. He could be having a mental breakdown right now. We both know he was lying when he said he was okay."

"You're right," Ivy said reluctantly, wanting to keep Sammy as close to her as she could for as long as she could. "You should go, I just don't want you to."

Sammy pulled Ivy away from the melee and into the kitchen. "How about I stop by your house tonight like old times and you can fill me in on what I missed."

She smiled, she couldn't help herself, she felt the swarming of the hive in her belly. Unattainable love never felt so good. "Like old times?"

He pressed Ivy to the wall, trapping her under him. She took in the smell of cologne, the smell of the forest that still clung to his clothes, and the smell of stupid boy. "Yeah, that wouldn't be so bad, would it? We don't have to worry about Grams. I've gotten really good at making it up that old staircase without making one peep."

Ivy stared into his blue eyes. They seemed as they always did, full of life and forgiveness. "I want things to be like old times."

"Me too. Today, hanging out with you again . . . was fun."

"It could be like old times. All you have to do is believe all I ever wanted was to help you." She put her finger to his lips to stop him from uttering a word. "And yes, even taking your soul was to help you. I had to, handing over your soul was the favor I owed to JD for saving your mom from Jesse's stab wound."

He brushed her hand away from his mouth. "I forgot all about you owing him for that. JD chose the one thing that would guarantee me breaking up with you. Talk about master manipulator and I fell for it."

"I've been trying to tell you, but you just wouldn't let me speak. If I didn't do that one thing for him—that one horrible thing, your mom's cancer was going to come back, and he was going to kill the twins, and I think he was seriously considering stealing your father's identity for good. I should've told you what was going on, but I was hoping to fix it before you found out. But before I could, he manipulated the situation to hurt me in the only way he could."

"By breaking us up, because he wants you for himself."

She averted his gaze. "I don't know if he wants me for himself, maybe he does, but he will never have me." Her eyes lifted to his. "My heart belongs to another. . . It belongs to you."

He leaned into her, she could feal his warm breath on her face. How she missed this closeness with him. "I always figured we'd find a way to end him, so it wouldn't matter. That has always been our goal." She searched his eyes, "Sammy, you have to know I love you."

He lowered his lips to meet hers; she raised her chin—the perfect kiss. The perfect crash of emotions and urgency as their lips glided over each other's to the beat of a love song only their lips could make. His light blue eyes sparkled like stars in the dim kitchen. "Ivy Teller, I love you. I can't help it. I don't want to help it." He kissed her again, with all the ardor of love, his need consuming him. He pressed his body against hers, his lips connecting with her neck just as the wall behind them gave way.

Ivy toppled to the ground, Sammy falling on top of her.

"You alright?" he asked, getting to his feet and pulling Ivy to hers.

"Yeah, just got a little scratch," she said, pulling up her sweatshirt sleeve to reveal a thin line of red highlighting her forearm. She craned her neck to kiss him again, but he was busy examining why they fell, the moment had passed. "This is awesome. It's a hidden door," he said, the excitement building in his eyes as he opened and closed the hidden door again. "Did you know about this?"

"No."

He took her hand. "Let's see where it leads!"

Ivy didn't budge. "Or, we could stay here and kiss some more."

He smiled sheepishly. "I would like that, but you know I have to explore the creepy passageway hidden between the walls," he said, pointing down the corridor with his free hand. He was gyrating like a toddler that needed to pee.

Ivy let out a loud sigh. "I know."

They were no longer between the walls of the kitchen and living room. They were deep in the house now, but she wasn't sure how deep. It all looked the same under the glow of Sammy's phone flashlight. They were surrounded by wood beams overhead, with wood lats lining the corridor. They could see the plaster spread between the lats holding up the walls. Ivy was relieved by the light up ahead and quickened her pace. She felt like a mouse in a maze, and desperately wanted to go back to the kitchen, but Sammy was in all his glory like he'd just discovered buried treasure.

They came to the source of the light. It was coming from a circle shaped room that had a well in the center. The ocular room was several stories high, culminating in a skylight that allowed what was left of the sunlight to filter into the center of the otherwise dark room. This room wasn't constructed of plaster and lath but of bog ore—the natural resource that put Batsto Village and the Richards family on the map. The natural light from overhead pulled out the ruddy brown hue of the bog ore giving the impression the room was under a giant red-light photographers use to develop negatives.

Ivy internally groaned. It had to be red. It was always red. Why couldn't they find a bright yellow room? Her hands ran down her arms. "This is . . ." Ivy said, searching for the right words to describe the dread building in her core.

"Awesome," Sammy said, finishing her sentence. "It's like a temple. It looks like the house was built around it."

"What makes you say that?"

"Um, because there's no way the house came first. This house is old, but not that old. Bog ore used to be used as a primary building material in the 1700s through the1800s in Pleasant Mills and even earlier but when Batsto Village financially collapsed it was hard to get. My dad has a little around his Koi pond and he paid a buttload for it."

Ivy smiled. She remembered his father's magnificent Koi pond. It's where they got the ingredients for their first spell together. "I meant the temple part."

"Oh," he said with a light laugh, "because of the shape. Circle motifs were used in a lot of ancient temples. It's supposed to represent the circle of life." He spun in place, taking in the roundness of the room, as what he assumed was leaves crunched under his feet. He pointed up. "And there's the odd window to the outside world over the well. It all feels very secret ceremony. Don't you think?"

Ivy approached the well in the center of the room. The well was also constructed of bog ore and came to her chest. "I don't know," Ivy said, blowing on the water that filled the well to the tippy top. In thought, she watched the ripples travel to the other side "It seems strange. Why would someone build a house around a temple?"

"To use it in secret silly," he said, hugging her from behind as if they'd never broken up.

"Yeah, and why would they need to do something like that?"

"Religious persecution."

Ivy had to smile. Sammy had an answer for everything. It felt just like old times. There was no awkwardness between them.

"Or," Sammy added, "because they were up to no good." He pressed a kiss to the side of her face. "I wonder if Danny ever found this place, or if we're the first ones to find it."

"I was wondering the same thing," she said, turning in his arms to face him, "either way we should go."

He pressed his lips to hers, pulling her closer to him. "I thought you wanted to kiss some more?"

It killed her to push him away. "I do, but not in here."

"Okay," he said, his lips falling into that sideways grin she loved so much, "but before we go, let me see if I can't find any markings on the walls or floor. It could clue us into what this room was actually used for."

Ivy crossed her arms over her chest. "You have five minutes. And don't forget you still have to check in with your dad."

He beamed. "Feels like old times already."

She smiled despite herself.

Sammy flashed his phone on the concave walls and then the floor. "What's that?" Ivy asked, watching Sammy pick something up off the floor.

"This whole time, I thought we were walking over leaves that fell in through the skylight, but it wasn't leaves but little scraps of paper." He walked to Ivy and showed her the piece of paper he'd picked up.

"What language is that?"

"Latin."

"You know Latin?"

He smiled awkwardly, "Uh, yeah, I take Latin in school, you know that. Remember, my father wouldn't let me take Spanish for an easy 'A'. He wanted me to take French, so I took Latin to piss him off."

"Oh yeah," Ivy said, not actually remembering that. "Well, if you can actually read that, I'll be happy you took an out-of-date language to get under your dad's skin."

"I can," he said with a smile. "It reads: When will my son come home?"

"That's weird."

"Yeah, what's even weirder is that from what I can tell, all the pieces of paper say the same thing.

Ivy picked up a scrap of paper by her foot and looked at it. She couldn't read it, but the letters looked the same.

"You have anything to write with?" Sammy asked.

"No why?"

"I think this well serves as an oracle. You ask a question, and it answers you. Why else would this room be filled with these papers?"

"This might be a tad gross," Ivy said, pulling up her sleeve, "but I have blood."

"Gross yes, but more than gross, it's resourceful. I like it."

She grinned, excited by the prospect of this well being a crystal ball of sorts. "What should we ask it?"

"Let's start with the basics to test it. How about: What's my name?"

Ivy agreed with a nod. "That's a good start."

Sammy dipped his index finger into the well then on to the cut on Ivy's arm making his own kind of paint. He wrote out the question in Latin on the flip side of a piece of used paper from the floor. He placed it in the center of the well, where it floated on top of the water like a lily pad.

"Well, so much for it being an oracle," Ivy said, not sure what she was expecting to happen, but was hoping for something.

"No wait!" Sammy said. "Look, the blood on the paper is moving around to spell Ivy Teller. This is so cool!"

Stricken by fear, Ivy watched as the blood slivered around like a snake spelling out the letters of her name. "That's, that's scary," Ivy stammered. "You wrote the question. It should've spelled out your name, not mine."

"But the blood, was yours."

"Yeah, exactly," Ivy said. "How did it know that?! I'm officially creeped out. We should go."

"You know what Teller, this must be what Danny uses for his almanac. I recall you telling me more than once how eerily accurate it is. What should we ask next?"

Ivy placed her hands on her hips. "Nothing," she said. "I was serious about going."

"Why?"

"For starters, I'm not opening a vein, and we don't know who's answering us."

He cocked his head to the side in thought. "What does it matter?"

"It matters Sammy. The well knew the blood was mine. Whatever is answering the questions is powerful and smart. I don't want to poke a powerful, smart bear. I'm not happy that bear got a taste of my blood as it is."

"I guess," he said disappointed, "but, I wouldn't worry about it."

Her eyebrows furrowed. "Why's that?"

"The paper's gone."

"Where did it go," Ivy said, grabbing Sammy's phone and looking around for it when she realized he was right, the paper was no longer floating on top of the water.

"The well, must've taken it."

"Sammy, I'm freaking out."

"Don't, it's probably what happens when it answers the question. That would make sense to why all the papers on the floor say the same thing. The well rejected the question and I don't know, spit it out," he said, shrugging his shoulders.

"You better be right."

Ivy's mind was spinning. She was sure Sammy was right and this was how Danny got his almanac as accurate as it was, but what did he mean by asking when his son was coming home? And why did he ask so many times?

She didn't think it was possible Titan could be the son of sweet, caring Danny. She regretted Grams and her decision to keep Danny in the dark on all things hocus-pocus.

"Let's not tell anyone about this room. I don't think Danny would be happy we found it."

Sammy wrapped his arms around her again. "My lips are sealed and don't worry, no big, scary well-dwelling bear is coming after you. I have magic now too; I can protect you."

"I'm sick of the need to protect people or needing to be protected. I would like for once to have a normal day. Take today for instance. Why did us kissing after months of torture have to lead us to a secret door, to a secret room, to a secret-exposing well? When will it end?"

He kissed her cheek trying to settle her down. "When we're dead, and we don't want that. And besides, I thought you liked being my guardian angel? I'm almost offended."

Ivy threw her hands in the air dismayed. "And that reminds me, Jesse is full blown homicidal in the living room. I know he's upset about Tammy and Rosa. I don't blame him. I'm upset too, but he's a loaded gun."

"Let me worry about Jesse, okay?"

"Yeah, he's your problem. I know he won't listen to reason. He never did, why would he start now?!"

Sammy took Ivy's hand. "Come on, I better get home so I can come by your place later for more kisses."

CHAPTER TWENTY-FIVE
A Handover Family Dinner

"Where have you been?" Big Mike asked, when Mike came in the front door. "I've been calling you for hours."

"Dad, do you remember Pastor Joe Baker?" Mike said, gesturing to Joe who stood next to him.

"I do," Big Mike said, his eyes boring holes into Joe. "Do you mind Pastor, I'd like to talk to my son for a few minutes alone."

"Of course not." Joe glanced to Mike, "I'll wait in the truck."

As soon as Joe was outside, "Dad why do you have to be so rude?"

"Sit down Michael, we need to talk."

Mike took a seat at the kitchen table. He could see his mother in the kitchen. She looked over her shoulder and gave a quiet wave and mouthed hello as not to disrupt her husband.

Big Mike took his seat at the head of the table. He was so tall, he looked like he was sitting at a table meant for a doll. With his large hands he hugged the corners of the table leaning over it like a medieval judge. In place of the white wig and gavel there was fiery red hair and a beard. He meant to intimidate Mike and it worked.

"Where were you this morning?" He put his hand up to stop Mike from answering. "Don't say school. Chief Steele came by looking for you. I called Pleasant Mills High. I'm glad you had enough good sense to go in for last period to take your math test, which you flunked by the way."

Mike's shoulder slouched, a blush blooming across his cheeks and the bridge of his nose.

"Your teachers are willing to work with you to get you graduated. They know you're under a lot of pressure and know you've been through a lot . . . We all have. But we all have to make ourselves okay with what happened to Tammy. She wouldn't want this, Mike. It's time for you to put the past behind you."

"Like you did with Mom," Mike said sharply.

Big Mike looked to his wife who was making dinner in the kitchen. "What's that supposed to mean?"

Mike bowed his head, not able to challenge his father. "Nothing. I'm sorry I skipped school this morning. It was the first time. It won't happen again. I'll do what I have to, to pass math, I promise."

"Sorry to interrupt but is Pastor Joe staying for dinner?" Mike's mom asked.

"Yes Mom."

"No," Big Mike said. "No, he's not."

Mike's head darted up. "He drove with me. He's in the truck, you heard him."

"Drop him off and come home," Big Mike said in a stern voice that normally would've silenced Mike.

Mike's face scrunched up, his freckles disappearing into his blush. "What's your problem with him?"

"My problem with him is that Pearl called me during the summer calling him your boyfriend. "Is there any truth to that?"

"Mike," his wife said from the kitchen, "I don't think you should do this so soon after Tammy."

"Well, is there any truth to that?" Big Mike asked again.

"There was truth to it. We were dating, but we broke up."

"Good," Big Mike said relieved, his hands relaxing on the tabletop.

"I knew if anything, it was just a phase. No son of mine could be gay."

Mike's face felt like it was on fire. This was his chance to tell his father and let his father find a way to be okay with it. "It's not a phase Dad. I'm gay and I love Joe." Saying he loved Joe out loud, shook his body. He wished he had the confidence to tell Joe how he truly felt about him. "I'm sorry if you can't handle that, Dad. I feel if you really loved me as your son, you would accept me." Mike bit back tears. "Tammy did. She knew and she accepted me."

His father remained silent. Mike got up from the table, making his way to the front door.

"Michael, please stay for dinner," his mother said.

He turned around, tears blurring his green eyes. He blinked them away. "I'm going to have to pass, Mom. I'll call Detective Steele and I'll be at school tomorrow."

Getting up, Big Mike put a hand on his son's shoulder. "Stay for dinner." Mike was surprised to see his father's eyes as glassy as his. "You, and Pastor Joe too."

Astonished, Mike stared at his father for a few moments, not able to speak. He had sunk low, using Tammy to guilt trip him, but he didn't think even that would soften his father. He was wrong and was never happier to be so.

Mike swallowed the lump in the back of his throat. "Okay, I'll tell Joe."

Mike and Joe came through the front door together. Big Mike shook Joe's hand and apologized for being rude. Mike looked around confused as if aliens had abducted his father. His father never apologized, and certainly not to clients. He always said apologies wasted time and money, and a Handover should do neither, although Mike found himself apologizing often, especially to his father.

"It's so nice to see you back in town," Sarah Handover said to Joe, putting dinner on the table.

"Thank you," Joe said, his eyes fixating on the plate of fried chicken she placed in front of him.

"Snap Mom! I should've said something. Joe's a vegetarian."

"Oh my goodness," she said embarrassed. She pushed the plate closer to Mike. "I'll make something else."

"It's fine," Joe said. "There's lots of sides for me to eat and they all look great."

"There's some of Tammy's veggie burgers still in the freezer."

"Mom it's fine," Mike said, knowing Joe wasn't going to eat much anyway.

"Yes, please don't," Joe added.

Sarah took a seat, clearly still upset. "I'm sorry," she said again to her husband's disproval which sounded like a grunt.

"I dropped by for dinner unannounced, it's me who should be sorry," Joe said, his charm all the way up.

She smiled.

Big Mike speared a piece of chicken onto his plate. "More for me and Michael."

"Joe," Sarah said, "I noticed your eye."

His hand instinctively went to the side of his face. "I broke a blood vessel."

"Where you in the same accident as your grandfather?" she asked.

"Hmm? Accident?"

"I guess I should've started with my condolences. Sorry to hear he passed. They were talking about it at the station." She leaned in his direction. "I work at the police station. I get all the news."

"And turn it into gossip," Big Mike said unapprovingly. "Sorry to hear about your grandfather," he added.

"Thank you. Both of you."

Sarah watched him intently, anxious to get the news firsthand.

"To answer your question, I wasn't with my grandfather when he had his accident." Joe didn't know how much she knew, but the details were not the kind of details someone talks about over dinner. "I have bad allergies and I broke the blood vessel during a coughing fit."

"I met your grandfather before. Years ago," Mike's mother went on to tell them. She turned to her husband. "Do you remember Pastor Baker?"

"Yeah," he said, focusing on his plate.

Mike and Joe said thank you for dinner and were about to head out the door when Big Mike placed a hand on his shoulder like he had done earlier. "We need to talk." Big Mike turned to Joe. "Pastor Joe—"

"Please just Joe."

"Joe, I need to talk shop with my son, if you would excuse us."

"Certainly," Joe said, thanking Mike's mother for dinner again before heading to Mike's truck to wait.

Mike followed his father to the pole barn in the backyard where they kept the landscaping equipment. "Michael, I need to talk to you about Tessa McCarthy."

Mike stiffened, not saying anything. He didn't want to steer the conversation; he wanted his father to tell him all he knew.

"I'm sure you heard about the fire at Pleasant Asylum and the missing patient. I wasn't dumb to your comment about me putting your mother behind me. I'm not sure how you found out, but that's not important. What is, is that you hear it from me. Tessa McCarthy is your biological mother." Big Mike leaned on his arm, hiding his face from his son. "Sorry . . . this is hard to talk about. Tessa and I got married right out of high school. She was the love of my life. I love your mother," he said, his hand gesturing toward the house. "But Tessa . . . she was, I can't even put it into words. She was a lot like Tammy. Look wise and personality wise. Tammy got all of her spunk from Tessa."

"What happened?" Mike asked, hanging on his father's every word.

"After Tammy was born or maybe it started before that, she started hearing voices. One more than the others. She was terrified by them and so was I, not that I heard them, because I never did. I took her to countless doctors and psychiatrists. She tried priests, even went to Joe's grandfather for help. Nothing helped."

"And that's why you locked her away?"

"Locked her away," Mike said, his eyes flashing to his son. "I could

never have done that. She left me."

"Left you? What do you mean? She divorced you?"

"It happened a few months after Tammy was born. We were at Titan Tires picking up her Volvo when she got a nosebleed. She went into Danny's house to clean up. His shop wasn't nice like it is now. There was no restroom for patrons. Tessa had been at Danny's loads of times. They were great friends; she even worked at Titan Tires for a bit before we got married. Anyways, she went inside while I paid the bill. It had to be twenty minutes, maybe longer, but she never came back outside. We decided to go check on her." Big Mike wiped tears with his thumbs before they could fall. "Mike, I never saw anything like it. She was standing in the foyer. Just standing there in front of the foyer mirror." Big Mike ran his hand over his mouth and beard. "Drool was dripping from her mouth. And her eyes, they were rolled back in her head. All you could see was the whites of them."

Mike covered his mouth, as a shiver went down his spine.

"I called an ambulance. They did all sorts of tests and scans. She was brain-dead. The doctors said it was an embolism. A vessel burst in her brain. She was gone, but her body was still there. But Tessa, my sweet Tessa, was gone forever."

Big Mike turned away from his son. "Dr. Lemmen, the head psychiatrist at Pleasant Asylum, had been treating her before the embolism and said they would take her. I had to let him. I couldn't care for her myself; she needed around-the-clock care. You were a baby and Tammy was still an infant. I was in over my head. Sarah had always had a crush on me, and she looked like she could be your mother, so I married Sarah.

"You married Mom, so we'd never have to know about Tessa . . ."

Big Mike's eyes lifted to his son. "No Michael. So you would never have to know the pain of losing her. There's not a day that goes by that I don't wish Tessa was here. I love her so much. Life can be so short for some people. If I would've only known Tessa had such a little bit of time in this world, I would have worked less. A lot less." He exhaled loudly, resting his back against the barn. "I know I told you to leave things in the past Mike, but I was never able to. I do love Sarah. It may not have started out that way, but I came to love her. She's been a good wife and a loving mother to Tammy and you. I don't want you to misunderstand that, but I don't want you to think I put Tessa in Pleasant Asylum to forget about her. I used to visit her, but I stopped years ago. I couldn't see her like that. It was too hard." He let out a deflating sigh, shifting on his shoulder. "I spoke to Dr. Lemmen today, he called to explain the situation. Tessa has been alert for months. Somehow, she went from being brain-dead to talking. He explained he didn't call me when she first woke up because Tessa was out of control and he knew if he'd called, I would come, and he thought it would make her worse. He said she's out of her mind, and even claimed to be Tammy." He wiped a tear. "I need to find her before she hurts herself. After you kids leave, I'm going to drive around and see if I can't spot her. I can't just sit around and do nothing. If something happens to her, I'll never be able to forgive myself. I already let Tammy down. To know Tessa was locked in her mind this whole time and I left her there, makes me sick to my stomach."

At the risk of not being manly, Mike hugged his father. "Dad, you did nothing wrong, you're going to have to trust me on that."

"Everything okay?" Joe asked as Mike got into his truck.

"My dad told me about Tessa. He said when she was placed in Pleasant Asylum, she was already gone. I'm glad to know that, but now he's beating himself up over leaving her in there when she wasn't really brain-dead."

"Too bad you can't tell him the truth," Joe said.

Mike sighed. "Yeah, I wish I could," He started the engine and backed out of the driveway. "I've never seen him that upset, well besides at Tammy's funeral." Mike took the turn to Danny's. "I don't know what we're going to do. We can't leave Tammy in Tessa's body, not with everyone looking for her."

"Jesse and Tammy could always move away."

"I don't want it to have to come to that, but maybe they should." Mike kept his eyes on the road, making sure not to look at Joe. "My father also got me thinking about you."

Joe pointed at himself. "About me? Did you tell him I want one of those T-shirts."

Mike smiled. "I'll grab you one, I promise."

"Don't forget, I only have a few weeks left to wear it. We should probably turn around and get it now."

"Don't talk like that," Mike snapped.

"It's okay. I'm okay with it. We all have to die. As long as I spend the rest of my time with you, whether it's at awkward family dinners or waiting outside your school while you take a test, I'll die happy."

Mike kept his eyes on the road, trying not to blink. He knew if he did, the tears would spill over. The thought of gaining Tammy to only lose Joe was unbearable.

"I probably shouldn't test my luck," Joe said, drumming his fingers on the tops of his thighs, "but I want to tell you something."

Mike's eyes flickered to him.

"Michael Handover, I love you. I never stopped loving you. There, I said it," Joe said his eyes red rimmed.

Mike pulled off onto the shoulder of the road.

Joe's eyes widened. "Seriously, you're tossing me out?! I got it. You're not gay. I'm sorry, I shouldn't have said anything."

"Tossing you out?!—No," Mike said, the salty tears beading on his lashes. "I just can't drive and talk about this kind of stuff." He locked eyes with Joe, his pulse racing, he could feel the blood under his skin pumping to his heart. His father's words replayed in his mind. *Life can be so short for some people. If I would've only known.* 'But Mike did know. He had to tell Joe how he felt about him. "Joe . . . I love you, so so so much." His words were spilling out of his mouth like a cyclone along with his tears. "All of those horrible things I said were lies to get you out of town to try to protect you. I was worried if you stayed in Pleasant Mills, you'd get hurt. I knew you were Pastor Leeds's son that drowned before you did. I'm sorry I didn't tell you. I only ever wanted to keep you safe and knew you wouldn't leave as long as I was here. I've been wanting to tell you, but the right moment never came up. We broke up, then you show up with Issac. Then I thought you didn't attend Tammy's funeral. And now, we're running out of time. And I just want to spend what's left together as a couple."

Joe heard all he needed to hear. He grabbed Mike's face and kissed him with all of the urgency of a dying man. "I seriously think we should drown Stevie in the lake and shag like rabbits for the next year."

Mike smiled through his tears before returning Joe's urgency with a flurry of kisses that made them ache for more time.

CHAPTER TWENTY-SIX
The Questioning

Pearl, along with Weston, knocked on Danny Leeds's front door. Danny was all smiles as if the Chief of Police and head detective knocking on your door was a good thing.

"Sorry to bother you Danny, but we're looking for Joe Baker. I just spoke to Big Mike, we just missed him at the house and he said Mike and Joe were heading here."

"You're at the right place," Danny said. "Come in. We got a full house." Pearl and Weston followed Danny into the kitchen. "Just ordered Chinese, help yourself."

Weston reached for a crab wonton. Pearl hissed. "Seriously Wes, we're on the job."

He popped it in his mouth. "And I need energy to do that job," he said, with his mouth full. "You're the one that made me head detective, so it's technically your fault. This new title requires more fuel."

She exhaled slowly, wishing there was someone else she could have made head detective. If only she could've cloned herself.

"Hello everyone," Pearl said, scanning the room. Danny did have a full house. Mary Teller was there with Ivy and the coveted Joe with Mike. She also recognized the doctor with the British accent she met during the summer. He sat next to a thin man with long hair she didn't know. She was hoping Sammy was there, but he wasn't. She was still waiting for the call from Jeffrey with Tessa's location. She wanted everything tied up before her date with JD tonight. "No Jesse?" Pearl asked, wondering if he was with Sammy.

"Jesse's in his room," Danny said. "He's not feeling well. Ivy made him a plate and took it to him." He beamed at Ivy proudly as if she was his daughter and she just saved someone's life.

Ivy nodded. She had made up a huge plate of food for Jesse, knowing the plate would be shared with Tammy and Elsa who were hiding out in Jesse's room. Ivy wished they could just tell Danny everything. Hiding Tessa in his house was going to be really hard, with them being old friends.

Pearl focused her attention on Joe Baker. "Joe, could we talk to you for a moment?"

"Uh, yeah," he said, glancing at Mike before getting up.

Danny took his seat next to Mary. "What's this all about?" she whispered to him. She glanced to her granddaughter who shrugged.

"I wouldn't worry about it Grams."

"Your granddaughter's one smart cookie. No point in worrying over things you can't control," he said, forking fried rice onto his plate. "Eat up now before it gets cold."

Joe took a seat in the chair across from the couch Pearl and Weston sat on in the living room.

"No offense Pastor," Pearl said, "but I was hoping to never see you again."

"I assure you the feeling is mutual."

Joe had been ruthlessly interrogated by Pearl when Uriah and he found the Henry sisters murdered, leaving a bad taste in his mouth for the Pleasant Mills Police Department. Not to mention, Pearl had marked him as a suspect. Then there was the mayhem at the church. If it weren't for Mike, Joe would never step foot in Pleasant Mills again. Mike had been right about that.

"Your leg's healed I see," Pearl said.

"Yep."

"Yet, you look sick, is everything okay?"

"Just getting over the flu. Bad flu season this year."

Pearl narrowed in. "You broke the vessel in your eye from the flu?"

"My doctor, Issac Smith, is in the kitchen if you'd like to speak to him."

"That's not necessary," Pearl said, changing the trajectory of the conversation. "I'm sorry to hear about your grandfather."

"Thank you."

"It's my understanding Mike Handover and you, along with one other . . ." She pulled out her notebook, "A William Franklin found him dead."

"I already talked to the cops in Philly. Pretty sure this is out of your jurisdiction," Joe said annoyed his time with Mike was being bogarted.

"Hold your tongue," Weston said.

Pearl didn't bat an eye. "We're working together on this case because of the strange manner of his death. The harvesting of body parts is similar to murders that happened in this town."

He looked at her confused. "What are you talking about? What body parts? I thought he shot himself."

"You tell me," Weston said, "you found the body."

"I didn't get that close. Mike checked to see if he was alive."

"His eyes, ears, and tongue were taken," Pearl said.

"That's . . ."

"That's fucked up," Weston said. "Talk about see no evil, hear no evil, speak no evil taken literally."

Pearl looked at Weston. Sometimes he was brilliant. She hadn't thought of that connection.

"What?" he said, noticing how Pearl was looking at him. "I got my daughter one of those three monkey figurines for her birthday. Ugly as shit, but she wanted it."

Without a word, Pearl returned her focus to Joe. "Did your grandfather have any enemies?"

"Like I told the other detective, no."

Pearl checked her notebook. "No enemies, but his only grandson hadn't spoken to him in over five years, is that right?"

Joe's cheeks flushed. "Yes, that's what I told the other detective. I haven't spoken to him since I turned eighteen."

"That's a heck of a coincidence that you hadn't spoken to your grandfather in half a decade and happened to show up the day he was murdered."

"You know what I call that," Weston said, not giving them a chance to answer, "a stupid criminal."

"I know it's a crazy coincidence, but it's just that."

"Tell me, Joe," Pearl said. "Why after all that time did you stop at your grandfather's today?"

"He's sick, terminal," Stevie said, from the doorway with King Charles in his arms. "Joe doesn't want anyone to know about his sickness. Isaac, as his doctor, can't break patient confidentiality, but I can."

"What are you doing?!" Joe hissed.

"Protecting Isaac," he said with sass. "I won't have him jeopardize his medical license for you. It's my duty as his boyfriend to protect him, not *you*."

Joe shot daggers at him with his eyes, his voice tight as where the muscles fanning from his neck. "Stevie, this doesn't involve you."

"On the contrary," Pearl said, "join us."

Stevie jostled King Charles to shake Pearl's hand. "Hi, I go by Stevie Frank, nice to meet you." He thought better than to shake Weston's hand and went for a head nod in his direction, taking a seat in the chair next to Joe. "Joe visited his grandfather today to ask him if there was anyone else in the family who has the same rare disease he suffers from and hopefully get some good news on how to treat it."

Pearl nodded. "What disease is he suffering from?"

"Not sure," Stevie said, stroking King Charles between the ears. "He's violently throwing up. That's how he broke the blood vessel in his eye. And there's no reason for it and seems to be no way to stop it. Next step feeding tubes, then death. It really was a coincidence we were there the same day. Joe didn't want to go, but Mike and I forced him, hoping for any way to beat this thing."

"Is this true?" Pearl asked Joe, evaluating him with new eyes. She knew he looked ill, really ill, but could he be terminally ill?

Joe nodded. "Yes, I'm dying. And as much as I didn't get along with my grandfather, I thought maybe he could help me."

Pearl glanced to Stevie, "Thank you for your help. We'll talk to Joe alone now."

"My pleasure," Stevie said, heading back into the kitchen with King Charles.

"Joe, level with me," Pearl said. "Is your grandfather's murder some supernatural shit like we saw in the church? We have Philly PD blaming us for their problems."

"I'm not sure. I don't see how it would be."

"Someone murdered your grandfather, right before you came to ask him an important question, one that could've possibly saved your life, and you don't think that's odd? Maybe he was murdered to keep his mouth shut."

Joe thought about that. He didn't think that was likely. Besides, it didn't matter that his grandfather died before they spoke, he had his grandfather's letter and that explained all. But he wasn't going to tell Pearl about the letter.

"I think it was all a coincidence detective Steele; who cares if I live or die?"

"He's got a point," Weston said.

Pearl let out an exaggerated sigh. "I guess we're done here."

"You don't want to talk to Mike or Jesse?" Weston asked.

She looked at her watch. "No, let's wait to hear from Jeffrey." She knew no one in that house would give Tessa up. Her best bet was Jeffrey.

CHAPTER TWENTY-SEVEN
Permission

"Can I talk to you," Issac said to Stevie as he sat on the front steps of Danny Leeds's house. Not waiting for a response, Issac sat down next to Stevie. "Are we okay?"

"We?" Stevie said, kicking at the dirt with his teal Pumas. I thought we were a trio: you, me, and Joe. But I think the arrangement is more like: you and Joe plus me."

"You know that's not true."

"I don't know what I know anymore," Stevie said, his eyes going to King Charles where he sniffed at a trunk of a tree. "I know that you love Joe. When it comes to me, I'm not sure. I think Joe's right about you."

Issac's eyebrow corked. "What do you mean? Of course I love you." He placed his arm around Stevie. He shrugged it off. "He's right about you having a messiah complex. You know I've a sickness that I will most likely never be able to shake. You think you can save me so in your mind you twist that into love. The difference between Joe and me is that I love you. I really love you Issac," Stevie said, his gray eyes flashing to him in pain before going back to King Charles. "And Joe could care less if he ever talked to you again."

Issac spoke in a calm manner. This was not the first time they'd had this conversation. "I can't speak on Joe's feelings for me, but I know how I feel about you. I thought after two years you'd know that."

Stevie held Issac in the frame of his lashes. "Here's what I know after two years. You've broken up with me over Joe once, not that long ago in fact, and I came crawling back to you begging for forgiveness. I know I've been hospitalized three times since we met, and you never took family leave to sit by my bedside. Maybe I wasn't sick enough," Stevie scoffed. "Maybe I should've had my father write a letter that I'm going to die unless you spend every waking second with me."

Issac shook his head. "That's not fair Stevie, you were hospitalized at the hospital I work at. I didn't have to take off. And if you think for one second, I want you to have to keep struggling with your eating disorder, you don't know me at all."

"Maybe I don't," Stevie said, getting up. He buttoned his coat and whistled for King Charles. "We're going for a walk."

Danny came out of the house to see Stevie heading into the woods with King Charles. "I still can't believe that's Little Willy."

"You know him?" Issac asked, surprised to hear Stevie being called by a variant of his legal name. He knew he was late getting to the farmhouse, but there was no way Stevie would have introduced himself as Willy and certainly not Little Willy.

"We go way back," Danny said, rubbing his hands together to keep them warm. "I'm friends with his father. I'm sure he's happy he's back in town."

"Back in town?"

"Sure, Little Willy grew up in Pleasant Mills."

Issac getting to his feet, looked at him incredulously. "This is Satan Mills?"

Danny smiled. "I don't think I've heard it called that, but Willy grew up here. His family home is only ten minutes down the road."

Issac's face lit up. "Does his father still live there?"

"Sure does."

"Can you give me the address? I'd love to stop by."

Issac knocked on Big Benny's front door. He scanned the old house. It would've looked abandoned if it weren't for the one outside light that was lit over the front door. The house was fraught with neglect, from an old roof to dirty windows. Trash and odds and ends littered the yard.

Benny opened the door. "I'm not interested," he said, taking a good look at Issac before going to close the door.

"Please, a moment of your time, Mr. Franklin. My name is Issac Smith. I'm William's boyfriend. We've spoken on the phone."

Ben smiled, his entire demeanor softening. He extended his hand for a handshake. "You should have said. Come in."

"I'm sorry to drop by like this but I was in town," Issac said, entering the house through a cramped foyer. The inside of the house was just as neglected as the outside, things piled everywhere, including near the front door.

"Not at all. I'm glad you came by. Willy's not with you?"

"No, just me." Issac realized his impulse to see Stevie's father was in fact impulsive. It was so non-British of him. He couldn't believe he drove there uninvited. "I should have called. I'm sorry, this is very rude of me. I was raised better."

"Not at all," Benny said, clearing away paper from the couch to make room for Issac to sit.

Issac smiled graciously, taking a seat. "I wanted to talk to you about your son."

"I knew it. He looked too thin." Benny shook his head "He was here a couple of hours ago, telling me he was fine. I should've known something was up. He never comes home."

"Oh, he didn't tell me he'd stopped by."

Benny sighed in aggravation. "No, he wouldn't have. We had some words. We always do when we're together. You're a good man for putting up with him. So how bad is it this time?"

"No, it's not that. He's constantly struggling with food as you know. We're working hard to get him to have a healthy relationship with eating. It's one day at a time."

"That's good. One day at a time is the way to go," Ben said.

Issac nodded his agreement.

"Being English, I assume you like tea?"

"Very much so."

"I make my own blend from my garden. Jasmine peach."

"Sounds delicious," Issac said.

"Where do you hail from?"

"Manchester."

"Lovely," Ben said from the kitchen.

Issac's eyes danced around the living room while Benny put the kettle on. The Franklin house was like a museum. The walls were surrounded by bookcases stuffed with books, knickknacks, and pictures.

Ben came back into the living room, his barreled belly sliding against the bookcase as he did. "Sorry for the state of this place. I'm not very good at keeping a tidy house."

"Stevie is." Issac blushed. "I mean no disrespect, I just meant he really enjoys cleaning and organizing."

Ben took a seat on a recliner chair. "He's been like that since he was a boy. I think the last time this place was dusted was the night before he ran away. Probably why he was in the garage today. Tidying up seems to be his nervous tick."

"Is that a picture of him?" Issac asked, pointing to a picture of a young overweight boy with short dark hair situated on a bookshelf. The boy's eyes were so squinty in the photo he couldn't make out Stevie's gray eyes, leaving him unsure.

"Yep, that's my boy. Looks a bit different now."

Issac had never seen a childhood picture of Stevie.

"I think he believes he burned them all," Ben said, making himself comfortable in his seat. "That's the last surviving one. Willy's childhood was rough. Working at the family pool and having a weight problem, I'm sure was part of the reason he ran away."

The kettle whistled. Benny rolled out of his seat. "Be right back."

Ben came back in with a tray. He placed it on the coffee table over a stack of old newspapers. "Sugar?"

"Yes please," Isaac said, adding two cubes to his tea.

"I didn't know Willy ran away."

"Afraid so. His senior year of high school. It was a crazy time for his brother and me. Have you met Cam?"

"Oh yes, a bunch of times. Stevie—Willy that is, is very fond of him, they talk at least once a week."

"Do they now?" Ben said, taking a sip of tea and recalling Stevie saying it had been a while since they talked.

"Yes. I'd say they're best friends. Cam comes to the city at least once a month and they go out to this vegan restaurant near our apartment."

"Glad to see they stay in touch."

"I wish he'd call me more," Ben said into his tea.

"It's nearly impossible to get him to do anything he doesn't want to do."

Ben chuckled. "Don't I know it."

"He doesn't know I'm here," Issac said, clutching his teacup. "But I'm old fashioned. I guess it's the Brit in me. I wanted to get your blessing."

A deep furrow set in between Benny's eyes. "Blessing?"

Issac set his teacup down. "Next month we have a big vacation planned. We're going to a series of islands in the Virgin Islands. I'm planning on proposing. I know you're not on the best terms with Willy, but I know you still matter to him, and I'd like to have your blessing."

Ben shook Issac's hand vigorously. "It warms my heart to know my Little Willy is in good hands."

CHAPTER TWENTY-EIGHT
A Family Outing

"You've had a busy day," Jeffrey said to Sammy as they ate pizza in front of the TV.

"Here it comes," Sammy mumbled under his breath. He had been waiting for it since he opened the front door. He expected to be scolded or at the very least lectured about not answering his phone. But instead, his father yelled from the kitchen: "The pizza's getting cold."

"Breaking a patient out of a mental hospital—now that should look good on your college resume."

"Dad, it's not what you think."

Jeffrey kept his eyes glued to Sammy, not giving him an inch. "It's exactly what I think. I promised Pearl to return the woman you broke out by tonight. So, where is she?"

Sammy put his pizza down.

Jeffrey took the moment to pause the football game. "There's no point lying to me Sammy; I know you and Ivy have something to do with it. And I'm guessing Mike too. Big Mike's called looking for him. I guess he also doesn't answer his phone for his father."

"Dad . . ."

"Tell me why you did it and where she is, and we can go back to eating pizza and watching the game."

"This is going to sound nuts."

"Well, in this family it would really have to be off the wall for me to think it's nuts, so go on."

"Tessa McCarthy, that's the woman we broke out, well, she's Tammy's biological mother. When Tammy died her soul jumped into her mother's body and we're trying to help Tammy by getting JD to freeze her body like he did Lilly's so we can return her to her real body, but he said he can't do it." Sammy breathed. "That was a major run on sentence."

Jeffrey let out an exaggerated sigh, brushing his hair back with both hands. "I wasn't expecting you to be so honest."

Sammy looked at his father with half lidded eyes. "Are you mad?"

Jeffrey waved his hand dismissively, as he reclined on the couch. "The thing I'm mad about is that you risk the rest of your life committing a felony instead of coming to me. I could've pulled some strings at Pleasant Asylum to help. We're just lucky Pearl is willing to forgive and forget."

Sammy looked down at his hands and nodded. "I'm sorry. I didn't want to bother you. I know you have a lot going on."

Anger spiked Jeffrey's tone. "That's what I'm here for. I'm your father, you can always come to me. And I told you, Ivy, and JD, I'm fine." He took a deep breath in as he counted down from ten. —"What exactly did JD say about helping Tammy? We need to do this switch-a-roo now and get Tessa back to the asylum. I promised Pearl by tonight."

The doorbell rang.

"That's probably Pearl now," Jeffrey said, getting up. Sammy followed. "This is going to be a hard one to explain to her. He opened the door to JD. "Oh, hi, I wasn't expecting you."

JD was dressed in black slacks with a black dress shirt. He left the top three buttons undone exposing the top of his chest. A long, dark wool dress coat went to his knees.

"Hello brother. I apologize for the surprise visit, but I was just thinking about the conversation I had with your son, Jesse, and Ivy this afternoon about Joseph Baker, and wanted to talk about it with the both of you."

"Joseph Baker?" Jeffrey asked, looking at Sammy. "You didn't say anything about him." But Pearl had. She told him Mike and Joe, along with one other, had found Bishop Baker murdered. His brain was working overtime to piece everything together.

Just hearing Joe's name sent a shiver down his spine. The wind from outside whipped around them. He felt the same cold he did the day he stood in front of Batsto Lake—the kind that seeps into your bones and freezes your heart. In his mind's eye he saw little Joseph Baker bound and dead as Uriah sobbed. He felt the weight of his brother Rupert's gun in his hand as he turned the gun pointed at Uriah on himself.

"He better come in Dad," Sammy said, breaking his father out of his musing.

"Thank you, Sammy," JD said, entering.

"Okay," Jeffrey said, leaning against the wall to steady himself. He could taste the barrel of the gun in his mouth, the metallic taste making him dizzy. "What's going on, JD?"

"As we all know, Joseph Baker drowned and was brought back."

"But not by you," Sammy said, clarifying.

"No, not by me. I can't bring people back from the dead, but maybe my twin can."

Jeffrey's eyes bulged. "Me?!"

"Why not?" JD said, examining his fingernails. "You were blessed by an angel. Resurrection is the work of God; death is the work of demons. You were the only other one there, that's besides Uriah. Uriah is of me; you are of something different. I think it's worth a try."

Jeffrey's eyebrows burrowed. "What are you saying?"

"I'm suggesting we exhume Tammy Handover and try to do what Jesse asked of me. Once we return Tammy's soul to her body, you can give Tessa McCarthy back to the authorities as Pearl asked of you."

"And if it doesn't work?" Jeffrey asked in a low voice.

"What is that they say? Oh yes, no harm, no foul. No one has to know about it. It will be a family secret. Just the four of us."

"Four?" Sammy asked.

"We should bring Uriah. He was there the day Joe was resurrected. He should be there today."

It was the warmest day of the week; however, it was still bitter cold. The ground was nearly frozen. They could see their breath rushing out of their noses and lips with every heave of their spades. The wind moved through the trees rustling the few leaves that clung to the branches. JD whistled. His song complemented the wind and the leaves in a melancholy symphony. When the wind stopped so did JD's whistling.

"This would go a lot faster if you helped," Jeffrey said to JD, tossing another dirt load over his shoulder.

"I would help, but I have somewhere I have to be tonight and can't get dirty."

"That's why he wanted to bring Pastor Leeds," Sammy said under his breath.

"I'm still not happy about this," Uriah said. "But if there's a way we can undo just a little of the trouble we caused the Handovers, we should try."

"That's why I'm here," Jeffrey said. "We owe that much to Tammy."

Uriah's shovel hit the top of the coffin. He crouched down to clear the rest of the dirt by hand as Sammy joined JD on the surface to make room for the opening of the coffin.

"Open it," JD demanded.

"You do it," Uriah said to Jeffrey, switching places with him. He anxiously itched the inside of his elbow through his coat as he waited for Jeffrey to take his place at the head of the coffin.

In position, Jeffrey's hand ran along the side of the coffin looking for a point of purchase. They heard the sound of a gun cock back. "Put the shovels down and your hands up!"

Sammy dropped his shovel, putting his hands high in the air. Uriah and Jeffrey stood up slowly with their hands up. JD didn't move.

"Oh this is epic," Weston said. "This *is* epic. I don't know if I should be freaking out or laughing. If someone told me some jerks were digging up a little girl's corpse in the graveyard, I never would have thought I'd find Jeffrey Lopez and his creepy doppelganger, Little Jeff and the beloved pastor Leeds. Oh, Pearl's going to love this."

Pearl sat at her kitchen island waiting on JD. She had given up on getting the call from Jeffrey with Tessa McCarthy's whereabouts and was now more than ever hoping JD would show up for their date to piss Jeffrey off. But it was getting late. She was watching the minutes go by on her cell phone when it rang. "Hey Chief, you're gonna wanna get down to Pleasant Mills cemetery right away."

Weston hung up, closing his flip phone with his chin.

"You can put the gun down," Jeffrey said, lowering his arms. "We're not going anywhere."

"You're right about that Jeffy Boy. The only place you're going is the slammer. You know what they do to pretty boys like you and your brother there? And you Pastor Leeds," Wes said, pointing his gun at him, "you're the cherry on top of a manwich." He focused his attention on Sammy. "Sammy, you're eighteen now, aren't you?" Sammy didn't answer. "Well, it looks like the county jail is going to have a welcoming party to talk about for years to come."

Jeffrey turned to his son. "He's just trying to scare you. He has no real authority."

"Don't look so smug," Weston said to Jeffrey. "You can't lie or buy your way out of this. You and the rest of them were caught red handed digging up this poor girl like a bunch of medieval grave robbers."

"I won't have to do either," Jeffrey said knowingly.

"Oh, because you think Pearl will look the other way on this? She won't, I know her."

JD took out his cigarette case. He rolled his hand over his cigarettes before choosing one. He offered his case to Sammy who declined with a shake of his head. Trading his cigarette case for his lighter, he lit up.

"Did I say you can smoke?!" Weston hollered.

JD blew a stream of smoke in Weston's direction. "I like you, Wesley Wilham Weston. It's the only reason you're still breathing. I don't take kindly to guns being pointed at my family and me."

Worried JD would hurt Weston, Sammy glanced at his father. "It's fine JD. He's not going to shoot anyone. He's just overcompensating. Some men feel powerful pointing guns at children."

Weston redirected his gun at JD. "Put the cigarette out," he said, trying to regain power over the situation.

"When I'm done, I will. I need to keep my hands busy. You see, it's either smoke or tear out your throat."

JD glanced down at Jeffrey, taking a long drag. "Brother, why don't we try our little experiment while we wait for Ms. Steele's arrival.

"Try what?" Weston asked, focusing his attention back on Jeffrey.

"We're going to resurrect Tammy Handover's body," Jeffrey said plainly.

Wes took a step closer to them from the other side of the hole they dug. His gun now pointed at Jeffrey's chest. "The hell you are! We don't need any more of those undead freaks running around town."

"It won't be like that Wes," Jeffrey said, not sure how it would actually be.

"If you move Jeffrey, I will shoot you."

"And if you shoot me Wes, my brother will kill you and there's nothing I can do about it."

JD flashed a smile.

"I don't want any trouble," Wes said. There was something about JD that made him think Jeffrey wasn't bluffing. He never went against what he called the police instinct.

"Good," Jeffrey said, bending down to open the coffin lid. "That makes two of us."

Jeffrey pulled on the lid, his nails bending under the pressure. A pop sounded into the night and with it the top half of the coffin opened. Jeffrey gasped, covering his mouth and nose with his hands. A waft of decay filled the air around the grave.

Uriah coughed. "Jeffrey, it's too late. This isn't right. Even if you can resurrect her body, it's just not right."

Jeffrey's eyes teared from the smell. Not even the cold could hide the effects of being in the ground for months. He glanced over Tammy's still body. In the dim light cast by the waning moon, he could tell Tammy was dead. The signs of decay were visible in small, dark patches on her otherwise pale skin. He worried Wes was right, if he tried to resurrect her now, she would be like Megan Hanson. But he knew he could in fact resurrect Tammy.

In the pit of his stomach, he felt something there, it was a small ball of fire. He'd first felt it that day long ago at Batsto Lake while Joseph Baker lay dead. Joseph was not supposed to get hurt, that was never part of his brother Rupert's plan. They were there to get Pastor Uriah Leeds to confess to murdering his wife. But when Rupert signaled for Bud and him to toss Joseph in the lake, they did it without thought. It wasn't until Uriah dived in after his son, did it hit Jeffrey, what they'd just done. The next thing Jeffrey remembered was waking up injured. His body felt like it was on fire, starting at the eye that was missing. When he saw little Joseph Baker dead, a fire in his stomach consumed him. He wanted nothing more than to reverse time and save the small boy.

Jeffrey had had the same burning sensation at the church after he was released from the Midwife's spell. His powers were no longer bound by the Midwife, he could use them if and when he wanted, and he realized that must have been the case the day young Joseph Baker died. Jeffrey had come into his power and killed himself at the same moment, the result being Joseph's resurrection and his death.

Jeffrey knew he could use his powers to resurrect Tammy Handover, the burning in his stomach to use his gift was almost a yearning that he suppressed. Anita, from the moment she first met Jeffrey, told him he had a darkness in him. He had known she spoke the truth, without understanding why and where the darkness came from. But now he knew it came from his demonic father. The idea of bringing Tammy back from the dead seemed like a good thing. He'd struggled to see the wrong in it, but as he stood over Tammy Handover's corpse, he understood.

It was strange to know he had the power to resurrect. As if the blueprint on how to do something so magnificent was part of his DNA. He just understood how it was done. A thing he must have realized without knowing it when he resurrected Joseph Baker after drowning. But the situation with Joe was different. He had been dead only a few minutes. His body was fully intact, Tammy's had been embalmed and was decaying. He knew that what he would be restoring to life would no longer be Tammy, but a creature worse than Megan Hanson or any of the women resurrected by his mother, Deborah Smith Leeds. He knew why the Midwife had stripped him of his power. Playing God was blasphemous, but the ability to raise an undead army was world ending.

He closed the casket top. "JD, Uriah's right. It's too late. She's too far gone."

JD put out his cigarette with the heel of his shoe. "Yes, she is. It was foolish for me to think she wasn't. I'm sorry, I asked this of you, brother," he said as if he somehow shared in Jeffrey's fears. "I wanted to please Jesse so badly. Please forgive me?" Sammy, still covering his nose, watched the tears bead on JD's lower eye lashes.

"It's nothing, JD," Jeffrey said kindly, feeling the magnetic pull to his brother, his tears almost bringing him to tears. "It was worth looking into. Now we know."

Sammy was surprised by his father's reaction to JD. He seemed genuinely upset JD was upset as if they somehow felt each other's pain.

"What's going on?!" Pearl asked, jogging in their direction. She stopped, covering her nose and mouth with the sleeve of her coat. She had on Ugg boots and a zipped winter jacket that fell above her knees. Her naked legs were covered in gooseflesh. "What the hell is going on?!"

"Found us some grave robbers," Weston informed her proudly.

"What are you doing here?!" Her eyes were like laser beams

directed at JD. A thing Wes and Jeffrey both noticed.

Jeffrey answered for him. "We wanted to make sure Tammy was really dead. We thought maybe she wasn't."

"Don't forget to tell her you were going to try to resurrect her Jeff," Weston scoffed.

Pearl lowered her hand trying not to breathe in the air. "Wes put down the gun. And you all," she said, waving her hand across Tammy's' grave, "cover her up now! Mark my word, if I see any of you in this graveyard again, including you Pastor Leeds, I don't care if you're presiding over a funeral, I will toss you in jail and throw away the key."

She stormed off in the direction of her car. Weston followed. "Please tell me you're not sleeping with Mr. Creepy. I thought Jeff was bad, but please anyone but Jeff's twin."

She turned to him sharply, "Wes, mind your own business and go help cover Tammy before anyone sees. DO NOT call me the rest of the night. That's an order!"

CHAPTER TWENTY-NINE
Moth to the Flame

Pearl answered her door expecting it to be Weston with an update. He was never good about following orders.

"You," she said with slitted eyes, feeling silly she still had on the black turtleneck dress she had planned to wear out that night with JD. She hadn't felt like changing when she got home and now, she was regretting it.

"Me," JD replied with a smile, eyeing her dress with an approving grin.

"You have some nerve showing up here after that stunt you and Jeffrey pulled at the cemetery. What were you thinking?!"

"I was trying to help my son," JD said with honest eyes, his lashes fluttering delicately, making him look like anything but the slime ball she knew he was. She was only going on a date with him, in hopes it would get back to Jeffrey and piss him off. Jeffrey was used to people doing what he said. His whole stay-away-from-my-brother order being ignored was sure to warrant attention her way.

Pearl shook her head in disbelief as the cool night air filled her house. "I'm not a parent and don't pretend to be, but if your idea of helping anyone is digging up the body of a teenager, you're mad. You and the rest of your archaeological dig should be in jail." Her anger morphed into paranoia. "What if the Handovers find out?!" She bit her nails distractively. "I don't think Wes will tell anyone."

"He won't."

Her eyes were back on him. Back on that face that looked so much like Jeffrey's. "And how do you know? He hates Jeffrey and you, by the way."

"Because he, like me, loves you."

Pearl moved to shut the door. "Good night."

JD stopped her. "Good night already? Aren't you going to invite me in?"

"You're already off the hook JD, there's no need to be over dramatic. We've spoken once, and you broke our date to dig up a corpse. I'm pretty sure love has nothing to do with it and there's definitely no respect. I should've figured as much since you tricked your twin brother's wife into sleeping with you. I'm sure that boils down to rape. Lindsey should press charges." She shook her head at herself. "I don't know why I said I would go out with you."

"I do," he replied, pushing the door open and strolling into her small apartment. Pearl shut the door behind him. "You wanted to make Jeffrey jealous. But there's more, you're attracted to me because I look like him." He grinned, looking every bit like Jeffrey Lopez. "Technically, he looks like me. I was born first."

Pearl leaned against her kitchen island casually. "I'm sure that has a lot to do with it. You're the spitting image of each other."

"And yet, you recognized me as myself at the church. You knew I wasn't Jeffrey. Amongst all the chaos, the screams, the fire, the death, you still noticed me."

"Don't flatter yourself. I told you apart because I know Jeffrey. And I know it was you who talked him into digging up a corpse and I want to know why. He never would've done that and never would've dragged Sammy into it. It's way out of character for him."

"It's like Wes told you, I was hoping Jeffrey could resurrect

Tammy.”

"Jeffrey?”

"Yes.”

Pearl threw her head back and laughed. JD resisted running his hand up its smooth surface and looked away. "So now Jeffrey Lopez moonlights as a god. It figures.”

A smile played on JD's lips, his face once more inclining toward her as if he was a flower and she was the sun. "I see he hasn't trusted you with a lot of his secrets.”

Pearl's cheeks burned. "Oh, he trusts me. But he doesn't trust you. Like I said, he's warned me to stay away from you.”

JD's smile grew, turning up the corners of his mouth mischievously. "I think he's afraid I'll tell you his secrets.”

"Will you?”

JD exhaled loudly, taking a step closer to her. "I think I might. Before tonight, I didn't think you had any feelings for me that were more than skin deep.”

"I don't.”

"That's not true, Pearl. We both know it." He took another step toward her, locking her against the kitchen island. "When you jogged up to Tammy's grave tonight, you looked at Jeffrey first then your eyes landed on me where they lingered. I heard your heart skip a beat as you drank me in. You were worried for me.”

Pearl looked down at the countertop and picked at a groove left by a knife cut. "I was worried for everyone. Everyone could have been arrested tonight. If a pedestrian would've seen, I would've had no choice but to arrest everyone, even Sammy.”

"It's more than that." He took her hand and placed it on her heart. She looked into his dark eyes, they seemed endless. "Your heart cannot lie to me Pearl Steele. You were concerned for me. It's been a long time, a very long time since anyone has been concerned for me.”

"Ok, I was concerned. That's not love. I was just as concerned for Jeffrey, more in fact.”

"I never said you loved me," JD said, his eyes beaming.

Pearl's flush deepened, traveling down her neck. "I was only concerned," she said breathlessly. JD leaned into her, forcing Pearl to arch her back to create distance between them. His hip bone rested against hers.

"It's hard to compare to my brother and maybe I never will, but concern could grow into love, don't you think?" He lightly pressed his lips to hers. She resisted a moment before parting them for him. He drew her closer, wrapping his arms around her waist. Pearl's hands reached into his hair twisting the locks around her fingers. He had become the sun and she the flower, desperate for sunshine.

Pearl stirred in bed, the knock on her apartment door arousing her. She slipped on her silk bathrobe, tying the belt around her waist to keep it closed. "I told Wes not to bother me," she muttered, stumbling to the door as another knock struck.

She opened her front door. "Jeffrey!"

"Hi Pearl, I'm sorry if I woke you up." He nervously rattled on. "I know it's late. I tried to get here as soon as I could, but Wes held us up forever and then I had to take Sammy home and then I had to shower. You see I was filthy and couldn't skip that. And I know it's late Pearl, but this couldn't wait. I had to talk to you tonight. Can I come in?"

Cold air pushed past Jeffrey into the apartment. Pearl rubbed her arms. "What time is it?'

He checked his watch. "It's a little past two."

"Where to start," he said, tugging on a button on his peacoat. "I'm sorry about tonight. I was out of line, we all were. I knew we shouldn't have done that and knew I should have left Sammy at home. It was crazy to dig Tammy up. I see that now." He ditched the button and grabbed Pearl's hand. "I want to tell you everything, I have to. Keeping you partially in the dark has made me look like a creep. And the idea of you thinking of me as some, how did Wes put it, medieval grave robber, has made me sick."

Still holding her hand, he pushed his way inside her apartment, closing the door with his foot. His hand ran up her arm to her slender neck.

He compulsively checked for the bruises he saw in his dream, relieved to find only smooth, beautiful skin. His hands cupped the back of her head as he pressed his lips to her cheek, his lips sliding to hers. He let them rest there for a moment before deepening the kiss with a long, gentle caress he and Pearl had been dreaming of. "Pearl," he said in a soft voice as their faces rested against each other. "I can't stay apart from you any longer. Being separated from Lindsey and you, has given me clarity. It's you I want, Pearl."

His confession shook her body. More so with realizing he'd tried to tell her that earlier when she came looking for Sammy and she wouldn't let him. He had chosen her. Pearl was uncertain how she still stood without aid. Sensing it, he held her closer.

"There are so many things I have to tell you about myself before we can be together. I've been afraid if you knew the truth you would reject me. But I need you to know everything. All of my secrets. No matter how crazy they are and then from there you can decide if you still want me."

He kissed her again. Pearl froze. Her lips resisted his touch with a quiver.

"What's wrong?"

"Oh Jeffrey, I've made a horrible mistake."

"Is everything okay?" JD asked, walking into the living room naked.

Jeffrey sucked air, taking a step back from Pearl. His eyes danced around the apartment noticing the clothing strewn about.

"Good God, get some clothes on!" she yelled at JD.

"You're with him?" Jeffrey managed to croak out, still in shock.

"It's not like that," Pearl said.

"You thought he was me?" he asked relieved. "This is the horrible mistake?"

Pearl's eyes watered.

"*It's* like that," JD told his brother. "She knew very well who she was sleeping with."

"Jeffrey, I'm sorry. He told me you were getting back with Lindsey. He said you made up your mind and chose her over me and didn't tell me yet."

"What I said was this," JD said in a concise tone. "Now that my brother has promised Sammy to talk to Lindsey about coming home, I don't see why I should stay away from you."

Pearl's head whipped toward JD. "You said he was getting back with her."

"No," JD corrected again, slipping on his pants, "I said talk to her about coming home. You filled in the blanks."

Jeffrey raked his fingers through his long hair, biting back tears. "How could you do this to me?! What happened to all of that brotherly love shit?!"

"Jeffrey don't be upset. I made things easy for you. Lindsey slept with me not knowing it was me and Pearl slept with me knowing I wasn't you. Lindsey's unknown infidelity started a crack in your relationship that became a chasm. But tonight, I shattered your relationship with Pearl. Go back to your wife, Jeffrey. You're meant to be with Lindsey not Pearl. You will thank me. Maybe not today but someday you will."

"You tricked me! You used me!" Pearl yelled at JD.

"No," JD said, "everything I told you was true. I can't lie. Again, I told you Jeffrey promised Sammy to talk to Lindsey about coming home, you interpreted what that meant on your own. It's just a bonus that tonight helped my brother realize you're not for him."

"I need time to think," Jeffrey said, reaching for the doorknob.

Pearl clung to his arm. She didn't want him to go. She had waited for this moment for what felt like a lifetime. He had finally come to her. He had finally chosen her, and she ruined it with one stupid moment of weakness. "I'm so sorry Jeffrey."

A solitary tear rolled down Jeffrey's face. "This isn't your fault. If I had trusted you with the truth, none of this would've happened. You asked me so many times to confide in you and I couldn't; and now I don't think I ever can. I'm sorry Pearl."

Jeffrey opened the door, and slipped out before Pearl could say another word.

"It's for the best," JD said, fully dressed from the couch.

She turned to him, her hands clenched in fists at her sides. "Why are you still here?!"

"Because I'm going to tell you what Jeffrey never did. My brother came here tonight planning on bearing his soul to you, but he wouldn't have.

Just as you know him, I also know him. He cannot come to terms with what he is and I have. To be fair, I've had more time to dwell on the situation."

"Well go on with it, then get out."

"I'm the Pleasant Mills Serial Killer you've been looking for."

"What?!" she gasped out of breath.

"Jeffrey didn't know that at first and, in fact, we didn't know we were brothers despite our mirrored faces. He was hunting me, and I was having a fun game of cat and mouse with him and his family. That's about the time I slept with Lindsey. As it turns out we're brothers. I never would have bedded Lindsey if I'd known that. I respect the sacrament of marriage. It's one of the few I do. You see, I love my brother and I will do anything to protect him and his family. That's where you come in. You have always protected Jeffrey. You did that tonight. You protected him and his son and my son Uriah."

"Wait, how can Uriah be your son?! You're about the same age."

"I'm older than I look and so is he."

Her face screwed up, her emotions about to spill over in salty tears.

"I'm sorry tonight's little episode hurt you, but you don't belong by Jeffrey's side, you belong by mine. I need someone like you Pearl. Someone who will protect my family and love them as I love them." His eyes darted to the floor before meeting her's. "And I hope one day you'll love me."

Pearl didn't react, she remained perfectly still as her mind spun like a cyclone.

"I won't keep anything from you, and I will always tell you the truth." He inhaled audibly. "You remind me so much of this woman I knew centuries ago, but you're so much more. She wanted to protect people from my brother and me. While you want to protect us from people."

Pearl tried to formulate a sentence but didn't know what to say or ask. "I . . . I . . . —"

JD ran his hands over his shirt to smooth the material. "Come take a seat next to me Pearl and I'll tell you anything you want to know."

Pearl didn't budge. "Are you really Pleasant Mills's serial killer? You killed Tim?"

JD's eyes remained fixed on Pearl. "Yes, it was I who murdered Timothy Chen, Louie Grindhouse, Tyrone Jones, and Zachary Lewis."

Pearl's hand covered her mouth to smother her sob as the image of her little cousin Tim's corpse flashed in her mind. Her words came out muffled. "Why? How could you? They were just children."

"I'm cursed, Pearl. Jeffrey and I are both cursed."

Pearl leaned against her closed front door, near collapse. "None of this makes sense. Wake up Pearl," she said, pinching herself. "Wake up!"

"You're not dreaming, Pearl. Jeffrey and I were damned by our vengeful mother and because of it are a mixture of angel and demon, us both having different powers and limitations. I'm hundreds of years old and my brother has lived many lives before he was known as Jeffrey Lopez."

In frustration, Pearl pushed her hair away from her face. "This can't be true."

"Can't it, Pearl? You saw with your own eyes the reanimated corpses at the church during the summer."

"It was you, you killed Megan and Zara?"

"No, I didn't kill them, or Trudy's mother and grandmother or the Henry sisters. But I have killed many, many people Pearl. I want to be perfectly candid about that. And before you ask, Jeffrey has not killed anyone to my knowledge."

"Why are you telling me this?"

He stood. "I thought I made that point."

Before she could react, he was standing in front of her, looking down at her with his coal dark eyes. She could feel his hot breath on her face. "I want you to join me." She pushed him away, reaching for her gun holster that hung on a kitchen island stool. Grasping it, she pulled her gun on him.

"This has been happening a lot lately," he sighed.

"Get out of my apartment!"

"I've told you a lot tonight, some things harder to digest than others. I will take my leave and give you time to think. You will no doubt have more questions for me, and I'm prepared to answer them all. But before I go Pearl, I want you to know I felt what you felt tonight."

"I felt nothing," she said, through clenched teeth, her gun aimed at his beautiful face.

"Don't lie to yourself. You thought as I lay next to you in your bed, that you'd finally found someone who understands you. And you're right, you did. Let me be that person to you and I will cherish you every waking moment of the radiant day and every second of the obscure night. You will be my moon and my sun, and I will love you always. Eternity will be but a blink of an eye for us."

Pearl fell to her knees, her gun still pointed at him. "You have the right to remain silent. Anything you say—"

"I've waited a long time for you, Pearl. I can wait as long as you need."

JD took the gun from her; she didn't put up a fight. "We both know you wouldn't shoot me." He kissed the side of her face as she sobbed. "I really do love you, Pearl." He left the gun on the kitchen island before letting himself out.

CHAPTER THIRTY
A Mirrored Dream

Ivy sat on her bed listening to music while she waited for Sammy. She'd strategically picked out an outfit that made it look like she didn't care, even though it took her an hour to find the right hoodie and sweatpants. She wanted to wear a cute pair of pajamas, but her only matching pair was the moose Christmas set from Sammy's mother that JD had made fun of.

Ivy sighed, free falling onto her pillow. She was just about to give up on Sammy and go to bed when her phone dinged. "About time," she said, taking out her earbuds. She'd already straightened up her room, her grandmother was going to be very happy about that, and less about Sammy Lopez coming up to her room in the middle of the night, but she wasn't going to find out.

Ivy took to the old staircase giddy, so light on her feet the steps didn't let out a single croak. It really was like old times, Sammy stood at the front door wearing his cocky grin that drove her crazy. "Don't wake my grandmother," Ivy said, for the sake of nostalgia, more than anything else. She wanted to take his hand, lead him to her room, and throw him on her bed but worried it would come off too aggressive. They'd kissed several times in Danny's kitchen and in the weird well room, but that felt like days ago. All of the anxiety was back. The butterflies turned wasps in her belly swarmed around making her feel a little woozy.

Sammy slipped off his sneakers and climbed the stairs with Ivy. "You're late," Ivy said, once they made it to her room. She closed the door behind her, taking care to shut it softly. "I was about to go to bed." Not that the swarming hive in her stomach would have let her sleep.

Sammy took off his winter jacket and tossed it on the end of the bed. "Sorry about that, my dad gave me the ninth degree over Tessa."

"That bad?"

He took a seat on Ivy's bed. "Yeah, and then we did a little family bonding."

"Anything good?"

"Nope, nothing worth mentioning. What did I miss? *Anything good.*"

"Actually," she said, sitting next to him, "*something* worth mentioning."

Ivy crossed her arms over her chest smugly.

"What, you're not going to tell me!"

"You didn't tell me anything," she bantered.

"There's nothing to tell. We watched football and ate pizza."

"Then you're going to have to give me something."

"You can have my coat."

Ivy's face scrunched up. "What am I going to do with your coat?"

"I don't have anything else to barter with," he said as a sly grin bloomed across his face. "Unless you would accept a kiss from a devoted boy?"

Heat rushed to Ivy's face. She was hoping he'd say something like that.

"I guess, if that's all you have, it'll have to do."

"Well, out with it," he said, leaning back on his elbows.

"Oh no, kiss first."

"No way," he said, sitting up. "If I kiss you first who's to say you'll still tell me. I know how you work, Teller. How about this, I'll give you one kiss now and a better kiss after you tell me."

"Deal."

He leaned in and quickly pressed a kiss to her lips. He smelled fresh, like he had just showered, his familiar cologne sending the wasps in her stomach into a tizzy.

"That's it?!" I've gotten better kisses from my grandmother," she said disappointed.

"That sounds really gross," he laughed. Ivy blushed, that didn't come out quite how she'd intended. "Like I said, there's a better kiss waiting with your name on it."

Feeling a little bit like her grandmother, she again crossed her arms over her chest. "There better be."

"There is."

"We figured out the Joe thing. It took all night, but we finally agreed."

"Wow really?! What's the solution?"

"Tomorrow afternoon Jesse's going to drown Rosa in Batsto Lake."

Sammy's dark lashes curtained his eyes for a few seconds before he opened them again. "What?"

"Yeah, Jesse and Rosa had a huge fight over her killing Tammy, so he called her and asked her to do this for him. She was more than willing to do anything to get back on his good side. She can't die, and actually dying gives her the bonus of being brought back with her eyes. It's a win, win," Ivy said, recalling JD had said the same thing to justify asking her for Sammy's soul.

Sammy exhaled slowly in relief, remembering JD's idea of a win, win when he offered to save him from the burning church and his injuries for breaking up with Ivy. "For a moment there, I was worried. I guess that's why JD told Jesse about Rosa. He knew she was the answer to fixing Joe's problem."

Ivy thought about that, remorse stifling the wasps for a moment. She'd called JD a monster for telling Jesse the truth about Tammy's death, but he wasn't, he saved Joe.

Sammy leaned in to kiss Ivy; she created separation with a hand to his chest. "There's more."

"Oh, okay, what?" Sammy asked surprised she refused his kiss.

"Jesse also figured out a way to help Tammy."

"Wow, I missed a lot! I can't believe he didn't text me."

"He wasn't sure if your phone got confiscated and didn't want to get you in more trouble with your dad. I told him I'd be seeing you."

"Good thinking. So, what is it? How do we help Tammy?"

Sammy had caught a glimpse of Tammy in her coffin and could still smell the decay as if it was trapped in his nose. It was another nightmarish image for Sammy to carry with him, one he could do without. He wished Jesse would've texted him, so he could've skipped out on the family bonding.

"After he drowns Rosa and before she comes back, Tammy is going to jump into her body. Jesse wants us there to signal the moment Tammy needs to make her jump and in case something goes wrong."

"What?!" Sammy said, sitting up, red webs forking over his eyes. "What happens to Rosa?"

Ivy shrugged.

"You're okay with this?"

"I mean yeah, I guess."

"Wow," Sammy said, leaning back on the bed. "This is heavy. I wished he would've just done it and didn't tell us about it . . .We're murdering Rosa." His eyebrows furrowed. "Tammy's okay with this?"

"Not at first, but you know how Jesse is. He was able to convince her it was for the best.

Sammy ran his fingers through his hair like his father. "Wow, this is dark, Teller. So dark . . . I don't know how I feel about it."

"It's a question of ethics, right? Think of it like this: Is it right to kill Rosa for killing Tammy?"

"And eye for an eye," Sammy said, leaning on one elbow. "I don't think it's right, but I suppose it's fair."

"I'm okay with fair," Ivy said. "Are you?"

"I am and that scares me. What happened to Tammy was at large my fault. I'll be there to help in any way I can."

"Good. How about that kiss now?" Ivy said, raising her eyebrows.

He smiled, thinking he should be more upset about murdering Rosa than he was, they both should be. He inched closer to Ivy. "I almost forgot."

"That's me, Ivy Teller witch and mood killer."

He put his hand on the side of her face, letting it slide to the back of her neck where he cradled her head. "I missed you, Teller."

"I missed you too."

"Is it too cliché to say let's never fight again."

She laughed, in a burst. "Yes, but let's say it anyway."

"Let's never fight again," he said, pressing his lips to hers. Her lips parted as he deepened his kiss, his body melting into hers. His free hand went to the other side of her face. She was trapped between his two hands, right where she wanted to be. His blue eyes never shone so clearly.

Pleasant Mills, New Jersey: 1736

"Where are we?" Sammy asked Ivy. She stood next to him holding his hand, but he couldn't feel it. He felt nothing. He knew he was dreaming, there was something about the way the periphery of his vision darkened as if to say this wasn't real.

"We're in the past," Ivy said, her eyes dancing around the pockets of light that bled through the trees.

"How do you know?"

She pointed to the woman dressed in white who danced through the trees to a song only she could hear. "I've been here before."

"Who's that? Do you know her?"

"It's me."

He looked at Ivy through downcast eyes, his eyelashes just grazing his cheek bones. "You?"

"The Midwife." Ivy tugged Sammy's hand, willing him to come with her. Together they followed the Midwife through the woods. The swaying pinecones in the tall trees were silent, their footfalls over the fallen pine needles were silent, their clothes as they passed through the understory were silent. It was as if the world was on mute. That was until they heard the sound of a crackling fire. It popped and sizzled, filling their heads with the feeling of déjà vu. Only Ivy had this dream before, but Sammy felt what she did. They were connected in this moment, in this dream, they were one.

"Stop here," she whispered to him when they came to the edge of a clearing. A tan-skinned boy, his head a crown of feathers, each plume alive with the color of the flames, placed straw on the fire. The fire smoldered around it, sending smoke into the ever-darkening sky.

"What's he doing?" Sammy asked, focusing on the Midwife. She looked so much like his Ivy, it scared him. He never liked the idea of Ivy being JD's before she was his, but to see the girl JD had loved in front of him and for her to look like *his* Ivy, made him frightened in a different way. Sammy tightened his grip on Ivy's hand, wishing he could feel it.

"This boy tried to help the Midwife with Uriah."

"Help how?" he whispered, not sure if the Lenape boy or the Midwife could hear him and not wanting to get their attention.

"By taking the evil out of him."

"The evil he inherited from JD?"

Ivy nodded.

Sammy bowed his head. He wondered what evil he'd inherited from his father, and he knew Ivy wondered the same thing.

The Lenape boy took the baby, swaddled in the same white of his mother's dress, and placed him on the hay smoldering under the fire as if it was a bed made just for him. Sammy went to intervene; Ivy held him back. "It's just a shadow of the past, you can't change it. I've tried."

He nodded. "We can't change the past, but we can learn from it."

She looked at him astonished. Ivy had never thought of her dreams as lessons to be learned from.

"Why's he doing that?" Sammy asked, his eyes going back to the Midwife who stood near the fire watching her son wail into the night.

"He's trying to drive the evil out."

"He'll kill him."

"No wait," Ivy said. Just like the last time she'd had this dream, rain fell, refreshing the crying baby. The Lenape boy took the whimpering baby from the smoldering fire and cut his arm with a handmade knife made from bone.

"He's making an exit wound for the evil," Ivy whispered.

A shadow seeped out of baby Uriah's arm, dark, inky and oozing, charring the ground before it escaped into the woods like a black bolt of lightning, shaking the woods as if the shadow had taken on human form.

"I hope that's not in me," Sammy said, his pulse racing under his skin until he felt itchy. He was wishing for the numbness he initially felt.

"I hope so too," Ivy intoned barely audible.

The Lenape boy swaddled the baby again and handed the whimpering infant to his mother.

"Thank you, Sky Wolff," the Midwife said, bringing the baby to her lips and kissing the child's forehead.

The boy blew a red powder into the fire, extinguishing it. Smoke billowed up from the fire, swirling upward toward the moon like an offering. "May it be enough."

Ivy repeated the words the Midwife had said to her the first time she'd had this dream. "It wasn't enough. You should've been more patient Ivy Belle Teller. You should have waited until every last drop of evil died. Small things left alone will fester. I see blood. Lots of blood. Blood of the Leeds: Japhet, Jeffrey, Uriah, and Samuel."

Sammy and Ivy woke up simultaneously, turning to face each other.

"Did you just have the same dream?" Sammy said, moving a stray piece of hair away from Ivy's face.

She swallowed hard. "Yes."

"What does this mean?" Sammy asked. "Are we connected? That's two dreams now that we've both had. The one about Ezekiel and Lucifer and this one. And in this one we were actually together."

"I don't know, but I've had that dream about Pastor Leeds before." She still couldn't call him Uriah, it felt too awkward. Knowing she was his mother in the past was beyond uncomfortable. No matter how many times

Uriah insisted she call him by his first name, she just couldn't. "I thought the dream was a warning to watch out for him, which I do anyway. I've been a little lazy about it now that he has Trudy, but I do worry about him." She turned away from Sammy, resting on her side.

"Hey, what is it?"

"I don't know why I worry about him. Is it because in the past I was his mother or is something going on with him? It's weird and gross and I don't like to think about it."

He kissed the side of her face. "I think you worry about him because you're a good person and you worry about everyone."

Ivy rolled on her back, so she could look into Sammy's blue eyes. "You really think the best of everyone."

"What can I say, I'm an optimist."

"No Sammy Lopez, you're stupid. You're a stupid boy."

He twisted a lock of her hair around his finger. "You forgot devilishly handsome."

Ivy groaned, resembling a dying animal. "Was that a pun?"

He flashed her that mischievous grin he used only when he was being playful. "Yes."

"Less of the Devil please."

"Angelically handsome then."

Her eyes narrowed. "Less angel."

"Dead sexy."

Her fisted hands struck the bed like bricks. "OMG less death!"

"Okay," he said, pressing a kiss to her lips. "Just handsome."

"That's better. I like simple."

He sat up.

"Where are you going?"

"It's late. I better get back to the house before my dad gets up and freaks out." He craned his neck to look at her. "This was nice Teller, sneaking back over here like old times."

"Yeah, it was," she said," taking his hand, their fingers interlocking like they had in their dream.

"Same time and place tomorrow?" Sammy asked.

"I'll be here."

CHAPTER THIRTY-ONE
Hidden Truths

Jeffrey stirred, rolling over in bed. Seeing Lindsey next to him, he smiled and sidled up to her to kiss the side of her face. With another kiss, this one planted firmly on her lips, he whispered to her: "I'm so glad your home." Her eyelids fluttered like the wings of a hummingbird before opening slowly to the sound of his voice. Something was wrong—her blue eyes were dark brown, her blonde hair—jet black. "Pearl," he exclaimed, pushing himself to his elbows. "Oh God, Pearl!" His fingers traced the dark bruises on her neck, stopping at the bulge in it. "What happened?"

"Jeffrey, I want to go home."

"Let her go home," Wes said from the door. Jeffrey jerked his head in his direction. From a small bullet hole in his chest, blood ran down his uniform in a stream of red.

"Why won't you let us go home?" Aiden said, appearing on the side of his bed. Blood trickled from his eyes, ears, and mouth. A pregnant Trudy took his hand, her neck bruised like Pearl's neck. "Please let us go home."

"I want all of you to go! Go home or go anywhere you want! Just get out of here!" he shouted, jumping out of his bed wearing only his underwear. I want all of you to go right now!"

Jeffrey knew he was dreaming. He'd had many others like this. He noticed his chest was bleeding, that was new, but then again, he was usually fully clothed in his dreams. He touched his chest; the blood came from a pinky-size hole right where his heart was located. He was glad he didn't feel it, nevertheless he wanted to wake up. He tried to wake up by focusing but couldn't, and pinches never did the trick. He would've run out of his bedroom, but Weston blocked his only route out. Or did he? Jeffrey ran to his bedroom window and pried it open.

"Daddy," he heard from behind him. It was the twins. Just as in his other nightmares, they had dark circles, like bruises under their blue eyes. "You're going to leave us?"

"No," he said, turning to them, "never." He picked them up and went to the window. Sammy was there, standing next to the open window, a cut in his neck opening up out of thin air. "Let me help, Dad."

Jeffrey swallowed hard, trying his best not to look at the gash in his son's neck. "Okay, we're going to climb out the window with the twins."

"Let me help," Weston said, appearing next to Sammy.

"Me too," Pearl joined in. She was out of bed and dressed for work in her go-to-outfit, a black blazer and dress pants. The bruises on her neck were still visible, and her brown eyes were cloudy and distant.

"This isn't real! You can't help me!"

"But I can," a hooded man in a dark robe said, his figure now blacking out the doorway where moments ago Weston had been standing.

"Okay, then help!"

The man snapped his fingers, and everyone disappeared. It was just Jeffrey and the man now. "Now, that's better."

"Thank you," Jeffrey said, looking around his empty bedroom.

The man let down his hood, leaving the rest of his dark cloak closed.

Curiously, Jeffrey's eyes raked over the man. He looked so much like himself. At first, he thought the cloaked figure was JD, but this man's features were sharper, from his nose to his chin everything was more angular. He looked severe, yet with his dark hair and marble-like skin he was beautiful.

"You, Jeffrey, can do amazing things. Why didn't you bring back that little girl last night?"

"Because it wouldn't have been her."

"No," he said, taking Jeffrey by his chin to examine his face. "She would have been yours."

Jeffrey suddenly became embarrassed to be in his boxer briefs. He was no longer sure if he was dreaming or if the man was really in his room. His touch felt real. His hot breath on his face—real. Jeffrey viewed him in perfect detail from the softness of his wispy hair to the little flecks of gold shimmering in his dark eyes, to the texture of his cloak. It all seemed too real to just be a dream.

"Next time, don't be afraid to use the gifts Ezekiel has given you. Never before has a demon possessed such power. Do not waste your gifts my son."

Jeffrey recognized the man's voice. He had heard it before. After emptying his blood pressure pills into his stomach, he found himself in that strange place where everything was gray. Before he opened his eyes in the burning church, free of the Midwife's spell, he heard the voice say: '*I am your father. Now join your brother and do wonderful, horrible things, for that is your destiny.*'

Jeffrey shot up in bed, panting. Lindsey put her arm around him. "Are you alright?" He grabbed her by her shoulders, combing over her feverishly for bruises. He ran his hand up her neck, planting a kiss on her cheek. "I missed you." She grew emaciated in his arms, shrinking to skin and bones. Her cheek bones, along with her bulging eyes, protruded from her skull like lumpy tumors. He tried to pull away from her, but her skeleton-like hands clutched his arm. "I know everything about you Jeffrey Lopez. I know your deepest, darkest secrets and have always accepted you. I knew who you were before you did and loved you for it. I have been a good wife to you and bore you beautiful children. Would she do the same? We both know she wouldn't. You can't tell her the truth because you fear she wouldn't be another Lindsey."

"This isn't real!" Jeffrey said, pulling at her skeleton hands.

"No, it's not, but that doesn't make any of the truths less true," the man said, appearing in the doorway again. "This is one of your many gifts Jeffrey. Your dreams hold many truths, but it's up to you to see them. Open your eyes."

Jeffrey knocked on Fran's front door frantically. Fran came to the door. Her long, dark hair was disheveled, hanging half out of a loose ponytail. Her blue eyes were bloodshot. "Jeffrey, what are you doing here this early? Is everything okay?"

"I need to see Lindsey."

"Alright, come in. She's in her room."

He rushed past Fran into the spare room. Lindsey was still in her nightgown, making the bed. He enveloped her in a bear hug.

"Jeffrey," she said surprised. At Jeffrey's miraculous appearance, Lindsey glanced over her shoulder at her older sister. Fran shrugged. Lindsey hadn't spoken to Jeffrey or seen him since she sent him the divorce papers. He hadn't even called to talk to the twins.

Jeffrey kissed her hard, pressing their bodies together until it hurt.

"That's my cue to leave. I don't want to bear witness to baby number five," Fran said, stumbling back into her bedroom.

"Lindsey, I made a terrible mistake."

Pearl's words echoed in his ears. *I made a terrible mistake.'* He knew it was wrong of him to bring Pearl into a world she could never understand and would most likely never accept. His dream was right. Lindsey and he were from the same world. She, like him, was not happy to be part of this darker world but that didn't change the fact she's a witch and he's a demon. He had no business corrupting Pearl. He loved her too much to let her be part of his world.

He also loved Lindsey. She had always been there for him, and he knew she always would. They belonged with each other, were meant to be together, just like JD had said. He couldn't believe he ever entertained letting her go. Like his dream told him, he would never find another Lindsey.

"Come home right now. I want you home with me where you belong—you, the girls, Hugo, and your crazy mother. I want all of you forever and ever. Please come home with me?! I promise to never take you for granted again. I love you so much Lindsey. I need you with me."

Lindsey's eyes swelled with tears. She delicately slipped her hand out of his embrace to wipe them. "I thought for a moment you signed the divorce papers. I kept waiting to hear from your lawyer when you didn't call me. I only sent them to try to force you to bring us home. I just wanted our family back together. I never thought you would give us up, but when I didn't hear from you . . ."

He kissed her tears. "I'm so stupid. So very stupid. Please forgive me Lindsey. As soon as we get home, I'll tear them up." Not giving her a chance to answer, he kissed her again.

"Yuck," Maria said, peeking through her fingers where she stood in the doorway.

Jeffrey smiled at her. He released Lindsey from his bearhug, but not before planting another chaste kiss on her cheek. He knelt to the height of his daughter. "Come here, you." Maria ran to her father and hugged him. "Where's your sister?"

"Here Daddy," Alba said, running to hug him, her stuffed wolf in her arms.

While he hugged the twins he reached for his wife's hand, tenderly rubbing his thumb over the back of it. "Everyone ready to go home?"

CHAPTER THIRTY-TWO
Another One

Aloud boom radiated in Pearl's ears. There it was again, bouncing around in her brain. She stumbled, getting off the couch. The knock came again, almost knocking her to the ground. It was more than she could take with her pounding headache.

She threw open the front door to her apartment before another crushing knock could sound.

"Hey Chief, I've been trying to get ahold of you all morning."

Without a response, Pearl went back to the couch, almost missing it when she plopped down.

"Rough night?" Weston said, spotting the empty vodka bottle on the coffee table. He pointed to it. "You should really cut that with soda when you drink it."

He discreetly sniffed in. He knew that smell. He noticed cigarette butts in a glass on the kitchen island. It took everything in him not to ask about them. Instead, he dumped them out in the trash can hoping Pearl would say something. In anticipation, he glanced at her. They locked eyes.

He was sure Pearl had surmised that as a detective he had already put her rough night together in his head.

"Why didn't you stop by last night or call me with an update?"

"Chief, you said not to. But um . . . maybe I should've. We could've had one of those ménage à trois. I'm okay with sharing."

She threw a pillow from the couch at him. It lost steam, landing a few feet from her.

Wes got his confirmation. He was passed over for Jeffrey's brother. He knew interpersonal relationships were frowned upon in the force, but he'd put in his two weeks' notice today for Pearl.

He turned away from her, a deep blush highlighting his cheeks, and rinsed out the glass with scrupulous attention to detail while he waited for his flush to die. "Cheer up Chief, last night's shit show is cleaned up and I have an update from Philly PD that I think you're gonna want to hear." He faced her with a grin that went ear to ear, his blush masked by his overzealous smile. "You're going to love this. They finally got that big safe in Bishop Baker's office open. It had the typical kind of things you expect to see in a safe: money, property deeds, etcetera. But get this, Bishop Baker keeps a second appointment book locked in his safe and guess whose name was written down on the day he died?"

"I'm listening," Pearl said, sprawled on the couch.

Weston frowned. "You're supposed to guess."

"Out with it now."

"I hate it when you get in these moods. You spoil all my fun."

"Wes!"

"None other than our very own Pastor Uriah Leeds."

She sat up. "You're kidding?!"

Wes beamed, his face lighting up again. "Nope. I'll start a pot of coffee while you go and take a cold shower. I can't wait to interrogate him after last night's stunt. I'm telling you Pearl, Christmas is coming early this year."

There was a crowd in front of the rectory when Pearl and Weston pulled up. An ambulance was in the driveway and two officers were setting up barricades to keep the neighbors back.

"What's up with the circus, Wes?" Pearl asked, looking for a place to park.

Wes pointed to the shoulder of the road a few houses down. Park here and I'll go find out. As they got out of Pearl's Crown Vic, a young officer jogged over to them. "Chief, we've been trying to get a hold of you."

"My phone died," she said quickly, realizing she never turned it back on after last night. "What's going on? And make it quick."

"A murder was called in about half an hour ago. That's all I know."

"A murder?!" Wes said, choking on his own words, his anger mounting. Soon he wouldn't be able to formulate coherent sentences. "Why, why wasn't I informed?!"

"I'm sorry Weston, I thought you were with Chief."

"And if you couldn't get a hold of her, you should have called me! It doesn't take a genius to figure that out! What's wrong with this damn town!"

Instantaneously, the officer's face turned bright red. "I'm sorry, I'm new. I didn't want to get in trouble for bothering you. When Chief didn't answer I thought you were both busy. I figured when Chief listened to her message, you'd come over here."

"Weston's the head detective. If there's a murder, you call him first, then you call me." Pearl told the new officer, making Wes feel a little bit better about being looked over.

Judging by the way Wes was cracking his knuckles, she was sure he was ready to pop the newbie's head like a pimple, and she was thinking of letting him. Pearl was tiring of police housekeeping. Her head was still pounding, and she had to stay focused. There was a murder. Her mind was spinning. *Was it Uriah, was it Trudy—did JD do it?*

"I hate newbs," Wes said to Pearl as they quickened their pace to the rectory.

Jeffrey, who was across the street at Mary Teller's house, jogged over to them. "Hey Pearl!"

Weston rolled his eyes. "Just what we need."

He caught up to them before they hit the rectory front door. No officers were willing to stop him, and risk being yelled at by Pearl. Jeffrey Lopez had become a familiar face to the police department over the last couple of years.

"Do you know what happened?" Pearl asked Jeffrey, avoiding eye contact.

"No. I just got the call from Mary about the ambulance. Uriah's not picking up, so I drove over."

"How neighborly of you Jeff," Wes, said, "but let the professionals take if from here."

"Pearl, about last night."

"I'm at work Jeffrey. It's not the time."

Weston's eyebrows corked as a grin tugged at his mouth.

"Get your mind out of the gutter Wes. It wasn't a ménage à trois," she mumbled under her breath.

Pearl knocked on the door once and let herself in. She spotted Uriah and Trudy on the couch. Uriah had his arm around Trudy's shoulder as they both sobbed.

Jeffrey sat next to Uriah. "What happened?"

"So much for letting the professionals do their job," Wes grumbled.

"It's Aiden," Trudy wept. "Someone has murdered my baby."

A thick glaze settled over Jeffrey's eyes making them look waxy in the morning light. "That's not possible."

"I'm afraid it is," JD said, coming from the kitchen wearing the same outfit he had on the night before, minus a few buttons Pearl had intentionally yanked off in her effort to undress him as quickly as possible. His normally smug manner was stiff, his eyes half hooded in grief. "I wasn't here last night. I was busy elsewhere." His eyes drifted to Pearl.

Pearl and JD locked eyes for a second before she directed her gaze to Uriah and Trudy; she couldn't deal with him right now.

"It's so horrible," Trudy cried into Uriah's chest.

Pearl watched everyone intently. She could tell Wes was ready to interrupt and throw his weight around. She put her hand up to stop him. "We can learn more from listening," she mouthed to him. She called an officer over and talked in whispers. "What did the emergency call say?"

"The mother found her son murdered in his bed this morning. He didn't come down for breakfast when he was called, and she went to check on him."

"Where's the body?"

"Room off the kitchen, Chief."

She nodded. "Check all the windows and doors and see if any were left unlocked. Pull any fingerprints on all surfaces. Once forensics is done, they can move the body. I'm going in to take my own pictures."

Pearl just stepped on Weston's toes, in fact she trampled on them, but she didn't notice. She was in the zone, her detective instincts on autopilot. It wasn't that long ago she was head detective.

She signaled for Wes to follow, and they headed to Aiden's room. A blood-soaked sheet covered the small boy where he lay in his bed. Hanging on the wall, near the bed was one of Aiden's art projects from school. It was a family tree; its leaves were made out of green construction paper cut outs of his small hands. The names of his family members were written by him in his own hand on each hand-leaf: Mom, Momma Trudy, Dad, Momma Zara, Megan, Zac, Jeffrey, Lindsey, Abby, Sammy, Alba, Maria, and Hugo. On the floor was another hand, this one read: JD.

Pearl's hand trembled as she pulled her phone from her blazer. Turning it on, she saw the missed calls. She ignored them, turning on her camera. "I don't know if I can do this, Wes."

"You can," JD said, from behind her, before Wes could offer words of motivation. "We need you to."

"Hey, do you mind waiting in the living room," Weston barked. "This is a police investigation and to my knowledge you haven't joined the force. It was bad enough when I had to worry about Jeffy Boy shadowing us, but now I have to worry about his doppelgänger too!"

"Whoever did this, knew I wasn't going to be here last night," he said, looking past Weston, who he ignored, to his brother who stood in the threshold.

Pearl glanced back at Jeffrey, careful not to lock eyes with him.

"Who knew?" Jeffrey asked.

"Only the handful of us last night knew I had plans, but not even I could've known I'd be away all night."

Weston's eyes darted to Pearl who seemed not to be listening. She was focused on the blood stain sheet. "Remove it," she said to no one in particular.

As he was closest to the bed, JD pulled back the sheet. Pearl's hands instinctively covered her mouth. No matter how many times she saw a dead body, she could never get used to it. Weston took her phone from her and took the pictures they needed. JD covered him again.

Jeffrey had turned his head when JD pulled back the sheet, catching only a glimpse before the sheet covered Aiden again. "It can't be," Jeffrey said, going to Aiden and yanking back the sheet. Jeffrey's eyes scanned over Aiden in a panic as he took in the wells of blood where his eyes used to be, the blood pouring down the sides of his face from where his ears had been sliced off, and the blood spilling over his mouth.

"What is it?" JD asked, standing alongside his brother. JD was no stranger to death and the ugliness of it. But seeing someone he cared about mangled and dead affected him more than he cared to admit. He covered the boy again.

Jeffrey put his hand to his temple before dragging his fingers through his hair compulsively. "This was in my dream. He said there was truth to them . . . I just had to be willing to see it."

"Who did?" JD asked, trying to follow him.

"The man in the cloak."

JD scrunched his eyebrows together.

This was what his father was trying to tell him. The many truths were the future. His power filled in the gaps in JD's power. He could see the future and raise the dead. The only two things JD couldn't do. Together they were unstoppable.

Jeffrey turned to Pearl shaking, his hands moving wildly as he spoke. "I saw this before it happened."

"Come on Jeff, hold it together. The last thing we need is for you to have a mental breakdown," Wes said. "We already have one loonie on the loose."

Pearl narrowed her eyes at Wes before focusing on Jeffrey. It wasn't like him to lose his cool. Jeffrey Lopez was a perfectly calculated and constructed man. He didn't deviate from that, especially not in front of the likes of Wes Weston. When he had jogged up to her before they entered the rectory, no one would've been able to tell she broke his heart last night. He had perfected his mask.

"Explain yourself," Pearl said in a calm voice, hoping to settle him down. She didn't want Weston to have ammo to use against Jeffrey. She was still blood-boiling mad at him for not trusting her with the whole truth, but she still loved him and realized she always would. It killed her to see him so agitated. But what did she expect, Aiden was family and now he was dead.

Jeffrey leaned against the bedroom wall creating distance between himself and the blood-covered sheet. "I've been having nightmares. I didn't tell anyone because I didn't know what to make of them."

"But you told him?" Pearl asked, inclining her head to JD.

"Yes, I told my brother. I thought maybe the nightmares could be more than nightmares. I've had other dreams before, but they were of the past."

Pearl's eyes flickered to JD's. An intensity burned in them that was not readable on his face. "And what's your opinion?"

"My brother has many gifts. It's not impossible to believe seeing the future is among them. I believe my nephew has a similar ability but with the past."

"Oh come off it, Pearl! I can't believe you're entertaining this!" Weston looked at Jeffrey. "Oh great and powerful Oz, tell me the winning lottery numbers and you'll never have to see my ugly mug again."

Pearl ignored Wes; she had gotten very good at that. "Jeffrey, let's say for the sake of argument you did see something happen before it did. Did you see anything else?" Did you see the killer?"

"I didn't see the killer. But I saw everyone dead."

"Everyone?" JD asked, his eyebrows elevating to his hairline.

Jeffrey pointed. "Pearl your neck. It was bruised and broken. And Wes, you got shot in the chest." He looked down at himself. "I too was shot in the chest. The twins and Lindsey were all dead. It was Sammy's neck. Aiden's eyes and mouth were bleeding and Trudy had bruises up and down her neck like she was strangled."

Jeffrey, without notice, ran out of the room.

"He's lost it Pearl," Wes said as they followed him.

Jeffrey grabbed Trudy's hand. "You need to leave now. He opened his wallet, pulling out a stack of hundred-dollar bills. "You have an aunt in Florida, don't you?"

"Yes."

"You're going to go visit her. Lindsey and the kids are going to go with you. I'll take you to the airport myself."

She looked to Uriah, "But Aiden."

"Is dead," Jeffrey said, "And you have to leave."

"What's going on?" Uriah asked, wiping his tears on the back of his hand, his eyes darting from Jeffrey to JD.

"You have to trust me on this Uriah. It's for the best," Jeffrey said.

"Of course, I trust you," he said, his body trembling. "I'll go pack her bag now." He kissed the side of Trudy's face. "I'll be right back."

Pearl and Weston followed Uriah upstairs, leaving just enough distance between them as not to invade his personal bubble.

"I'm sorry for your loss," Pearl said to Uriah as he opened a dresser drawer. He put a stack of maternity shirts on the bed. "I know this is not the best time, but I have a few questions."

Uriah broke down sobbing, taking a seat on the bed. "Right now?! My son was just murdered."

"I was coming here this morning before I knew what happened to Aiden to ask you about Bishop Baker. Your name was scribbled in his appointment book on the day he died. You may have been the last person to have seen him alive. Did you make that appointment on the seventeenth?"

"I spoke to and saw him regularly. He's in charge of the diocese. I'm not sure of the date of our last appointment, but it was early this week. You're going to have to check my calendar. It's on my desk across the hall in the new baby's room."

Wes nodded, walking across the way to get the calendar.

"Do you recall what your appointment was about?" Pearl asked.

"Yes," he said, sniffling. "We were going over the details for the opening of the new church and I was checking to see if it were possible for Pastor Joe Baker to fill in for me for the first month after the baby arrives."

Wes was back. He gave her the thumbs up, showing Pearl a picture of Uriah's calendar he'd taken on his phone. The dates matched.

Uriah wiped his tears with his shirtsleeve. Pearl noticed a blood stain on Uriah's dress shirt at his elbow. She was grateful he was wearing white, if not, she may not have noticed it.

She tugged on his shirt above the red stain. "What's this?"

Uriah stirred to life. "It's nothing—just a bug bite that got infected. Sometimes it bleeds through my shirt."

"Take your shirt off now," Pearl ordered, not giving him an inch.

Uriah glanced to Weston. "It opened back up last night with the digging," he said as he unbuttoned his dress shirt.

Pearl took his shirt and handed it to Wes. "Get this spot tested. See if it's a match for Aiden."

"I didn't do it!" Uriah sobbed, hysterical at the assumption he did. "I would never hurt Aiden."

Pearl took his hand and stretched out his arm so she could get a good look at his infected bug bite. "I didn't say you did," she said plainly, pealing back the bloody gauze wrapping to see an oozing wound. "I'm not a doctor, but you need to get this checked out before you lose your arm." She released Uriah's hand and sat down next to him. "I'm a cop. I have to follow protocol. If someone has a shirt with blood on it, the shirt gets run for DNA. It's that simple. I don't think you hurt Aiden. The reason I'm asking you questions now and not a week from now is because Bishop Baker was murdered in the same way as Aiden. I think there's a connection. Do you know anyone who would want to hurt Bishop Baker, Aiden, or any other member of your family?"

Uriah sniffled. "Bishop Baker was a bad man. He wasn't a man of God. He deserved what he got and worse." She pulled her notebook out of her back pocket, flashing Wes an intuitive look as she did. She was glad he didn't run down the staircase to forensics with Uriah's shirt but stayed with her. "He hurts children. He hurt my Lilly. I remember it all now."

"How did he hurt her?" Pearl asked, remembering meeting Lilly a few months ago in this very house.

He didn't answer. Pearl posed another question. "How do you know this? Did Baker ever hurt you?"

He went to his dresser and put on a new button-down shirt, resisting itching his bleeding arm. This one was navy blue. Pearl could see the resemblance between JD and Uriah. She still couldn't wrap her head around the idea Uriah Leeds could be JD's son, but there was no doubting a likeness. It was more in how they carried themselves than how they looked. Something in the way their footfalls were silent, the way their hair shaped their face.

"Lilly confided in me. I just recently recalled it. In the past I never did anything about it . . . " He faced Pearl and Weston. "But Aiden was good. He was such a good boy. After all that's happened to him, all he lived through, I can't believe this is how it ends for him. He was such a little angel. Please find out who did this to him and make them pay."

Pearl tossed Weston the keys to her car. "Drive, I need to think."

"You got it, Chief." He squeezed into the driver's seat, sliding it back for some much-needed leg space. He adjusted his mirror before unbuttoning his uniform shirt. He still couldn't trade in the iconic blue uniform for a detective's suit.

Pearl watched curiously. "What are you doing?"

"Putting a bullet proof vest on under my shirt."

"You believe Jeffrey?"

"I'd rather not take a chance. Dead sounds permanent. I've never seen Jeff act like that. The way he just ran out of the room . . . Well, he at least believes what he says. In my mind that can mean one of two things: He's right or he's lost his marbles, and we should escort him to Pleasant Asylum along with Tessa McCarthy when we find her."

Pearl buckled her seatbelt and leaned back in the passenger seat.

"I'm gonna keep an extra close eye on you just in case Jeffy Boy's right. I'm not in stalker mode or anything, I'm just making sure you don't get killed on my watch. Which stands to reason, I must get shot before you bite the bullet because I'd never let that happen." He struck his chest like a caveman. "Wearing a bullet proof vest should prevent you from getting your neck snapped. I feel like I'm getting smarter."

Pearl gave him a faint smile. "Or I'm the one who shoots you, and all I have to do now is aim a little higher and then I get strangled to death until my neck snaps in two like a twig."

"Always an idealist, Pearl," he said with a chuckle.

Pearl deadpanned, "I don't know about that. I just always wanted to shoot you."

Weston grinned, putting on the bulletproof vest and buttoning back up his shirt. He always wanted to *do* something to Pearl, but it wasn't shoot her. He turned the key in the ignition. The car roared to life. "I don't think he did it," Weston said, changing the conversation. He turned the Crown Vic around and headed in the direction of the police station.

"Who did what?"

"I don't think Pastor Leeds killed Aiden. I never liked him. I never like guys who look like that. It's a personal prejudice or maybe it's jealousy, but man do I feel for him. That poor guy is at the center of everything bad in this town. He's a walking shit magnet."

"It does seem that way."

"That blood on his shirt isn't going to be a match for Aiden. I noticed last night he kept itching that arm. He's had that nasty infection since the summer. I've seen it bleed through his shirt before. Trudy must be a pretty crappy nurse not to have gotten that thing cleared up already."

Pearl exhaled loudly. "I'm glad you kept that to yourself today."

He ignored her, he was thinking out loud. "Someone really sick did this. You don't think this has anything to do with those murders a couple of summers ago. Jesse Richards was never caught, maybe he's back. The hot receptionist at the Asylum seemed to think the one kid Sammy came in there with looked a lot like Jesse Richards. It could've been him."

Pearl shook her head. "It wasn't Jesse." She couldn't tell Wes that JD had confessed to those murders last night. Pearl wasn't sure if that was because she thought Wes wouldn't believe her or because she was protecting JD. Avoiding thinking about it, her mind went to the dark-haired receptionist at Pleasant Asylum. "You thought the receptionist was hot?"

"Honey, I'm forty-five this year, if she has most of her teeth and is in fact, a her, I'm in love."

Pearl laughed out loud. She needed that. "Oh Wes, I don't understand why you're still single."

"I say the same thing to myself every time I look in the mirror. I'm in great shape and have a pension. I have a nice truck, and I have lots of scars."

"Scars?"

"Yeah, chicks dig scars."

"Oh," Pearl said a smile on her lips. "I wasn't aware my species does."

"It's the job Pearl. It's why I'm single. Sure, the outside scars look cool but it's the inside ones that mess you up. Like seeing Aiden today, that left its mark. The job sucks you dry and leaves you with a nice plaque you can hang on your wall after twenty years of service. But by then there's no one there to enjoy your shiny plaque with you, 'cause the job's run them all off."

Pearl covered her ears. "Wes, please stop talking. I hate when you make sense."

"Sorry Chief."

"I was thinking Bishop Baker's murder and Aiden's does remind me of a case but it's not the Pleasant Mills Serial Killer case, but last summer's. The women last summer were all murdered in the same way," Pearl said.

"I remember," he said, running his thumb across his neck to simulate a throat being cut.

"I'm thinking we should pay our old friend Cameron Franklin a visit. He was a big help last time pinpointing the killer's next move. If it wasn't for Cam, who knows who else would've died at the church and you would have missed your photo op."

"You're right, the only good thing that came out of last summer was that nice article featuring yours truly that I was able to frame and send to my mother."

She smiled. "You really are a goofy guy."

"So, I shouldn't tell you I also sent it to my daughter."

"I'm sure she was proud."

He smiled, letting Pearl know his daughter was very proud.

"With a little luck, you'll get a nice writeup for your part in finding this sicko. We know we have two murders. Both victims eyes were cut out and ears cut off. We can assume their tongues too. We're going to have to wait until the autopsy report comes back on Aiden to be sure, but it looks that way and it feels ritualistic to me. I'd like to hear what our own occult specialist has to say about it."

CHAPTER THIRTY-THREE
Pumpkin Spice

Cam kept a vigil by his window awaiting the arrival of Chief of Police Steele. He didn't want to do anything to set her off, or more to the point, Weston. Cam was sure he heard Weston's gruff voice during his phone conversation with Pearl and had been teeming with anxiety ever since. He'd done nothing wrong, but there was a knot in his stomach twisted into an Olympic size pretzel that made it impossible for him to eat breakfast.

Cam watched as a black SUV parked in front of his apartment. Not recognizing the car, he was about to close the curtain when a woman with a familiar look alighted from it. She had on a black blazer and dress pants. Her dark hair was pulled back in a tight bun.

Cam rubbed the window with his open hand. "Is that Pearl?"

The dirt was on the outside of the window, no amount of hand polishing was going to give him a clearer view. Realizing this and not wanting to risk it, Cam went to the front door and opened it. It wasn't Pearl, but the woman in black was coming his way with two coffees in her hand.

"Hello Cameron, I'm Detective Larro," she said, walking up to his door. "Chief Steele got held up at the station. She apologizes she couldn't be here herself." Up close, Detective Larro looked very little like Pearl, but she had a familiar face. That wasn't surprising, working at the community pool he saw many faces. The woman handed Cam a coffee. "Hope you like pumpkin spice."

"I do, thank you. Nice to meet you."

Juggling her coffee, she shook his extended hand.

Detective Larro followed Cam into his living room. He took a seat on his red, velvet couch while she pulled a kitchen island stool alongside it.

"I'm happy it's you," Cam said.

She blushed; a strip of rose highlighted her blue eyes.

Noticing the pinky glow to her otherwise pale complexion, Cam's pulse raced. He was sure he said something wrong already and tried to correct himself. "Um I, um, I just meant I was glad you're not Weston." A flush of his own dabbled his cheeks as a new worry seized him. He feared Detective Larro and Detective Weston were friends and he just made things worse. They were both detectives, it seemed more than likely that would be the case.

Detective Larro attempted a smile that never reached her blue eyes. "Weston is rough. I guess you lucked out."

Gripping his coffee as a security blanket, Cam took a healthy sip. "Thanks for the coffee. I was so nervous I couldn't eat this morning, but I thought that wasn't such a bad thing. That way there would be no chance I would throw up on Weston's boots."

"Nothing to be nervous about," she said, taking out a small notebook she had tucked away in her back pants pocket as he had seen Pearl do on several occasions. "You're not being charged with anything. In fact, we owe you our gratitude for helping with this case."

"I uh, hope I can help. Um, Chief Steele had mentioned on the phone there were pictures she wanted me to look at."

"Shoot!" Detective Larro said. "I left them at the station."

Noticing tears welling in her eyes, Cam attempted to remedy the situation before they could topple over. "It's okay. Just tell me about them. I'd prefer it that way anyway. I don't have the strongest stomach."

She took a deep breath. "Thanks for being so understanding." As if to calm her nerves, she took a long sip of her coffee. "Starbucks is always good."

"It's really good. Thank you again. I always feel silly going in there. It's like everyone's speaking a foreign language."

She smiled. "Java head, it's an acquired skill."

He took another sip.

"Before we get started do you mind if I use the restroom?"

"Not at all," he said, pointing down the hall. "It's the first door to the left."

Detective Larro excused herself.

Cam relaxed, leaning back on his couch, and taking another sip of coffee. Detective Larro was nice. This was a lot different than the last time he was questioned by the police. While he waited to hear about the crime scene photographs, he checked his phone. He had missed a text message from Elsa: Can't wait for the weekend.

He texted back: Me 2. Detective's here now. I'll call u when I'm done. I love you.

Cam reread his text and smiled. He made sure he wrote out 'I love you' because he wanted her to know how much he did.

Cam went to place his phone on the coffee table. Missing it, his phone fell on the floor. He scrutinized his phone where it lay by the side of the couch, unsure how he missed the coffee table. His phone dinged; he had a new text message. He reached for his phone, his vision doubling. Before he could sit back up, he fell to the floor unconscious.

Pearl and Weston got into Weston's Black Dodge Ram pickup truck after stopping by the police station to pick up the crime scene photos from Bishop Baker's murder. Weston's truck was about to join the classics with it being just under twenty-five years old. Despite its age, it ran well, and Weston swore by it as he did most of the maintenance on it himself. Pearl felt otherwise. She thought it was a time capsule and was better left in Wes's garage with the rest of his glory day memorabilia. There was something annoying about the fuzzy dice hanging from the rearview mirror that Weston would have given a ticket for obstructing the view to anyone else.

Pearl punched the fuzzy dice, sending them swinging back and forth. "I prefer my car."

"Yeah, well since I'm driving, I prefer mine." He turned on the windshield wipers. "It's about time the damn storm gets here. I'm sick of hearing about it. What a job. Get it wrong fifty percent of the time and people still tune in to hear the weather."

"Well, if you would've stopped blabbering to Big Benny we could have been to Princeton already."

"I'm not complaining about driving in the rain. I like it. Love driving in hurricanes. Chance to use the four-wheel drive," he said, pulling on the steering wheel like a child playing with a motorized toy car. That was it—why she hated when Weston drove his truck. He transformed into a bully on the playground. "But yeah, I got a little long winded with Big Benny. I just wanted to know how many kites he had set up. Is that a crime?"

Crossing her arms over her chest, "It is when we have a *crime* to solve. And who cares about Benny's kites? He does that every storm. Really Wes, you act like a tourist."

"Yeah, but if you believe Mr. Weather Man this is going to be a whopper. Ben's been flying kites since yesterday. Kinda sad I'm going to miss the finale."

"The storm's not hitting till tonight. You'll be home."

"No I won't," he said with a sly grin.

Pearl knew he wanted her to ask why he wasn't going to be home, but she wasn't going to give him what he wanted, not when he wore a grin like that. She was pretty sure whatever it was, she didn't want to know anyway.

"I got a date," he said, not able to keep his mouth zipped.

"Do I want to know?"

"The hot receptionist from the asylum."

"When did this happen?" Pearl asked, recalling the receptionist being mentioned before their detour to the police station and finding it odd he didn't mention their date then.

"Right before Big Benny walked into the police station to pick up his permits. I gave her my card to call me if she thought of anything else after I questioned her, and she text me asking if I was free tonight."

Pearl's grin rivaled Weston's, that's why he was so chatty. He was actually in a good mood for once. She also thought it was likely Weston carried on with Big Benny just so he could play up how much he regretted he wasn't going to be around to see Benny's keys get zapped during the storm—just so he could tell Pearl he had a date.

"You could take your hot receptionist to watch the kites. I'm sure she would be really impressed if you introduced her to Big Benny. He's like a town celebrity after all, but just make sure Benny doesn't steal your date. He's tough competition."

"Ha," Weston said, his grin still plastered on his face. "You can't bring me down Pearl. I still got it." He kissed his bicep.

"Try to hold yourself together until we question Cameron Franklin." She exhaled audibly. "I could've killed you when you told Big Benny we were on our way to see Cam. You know how he gets with him. I thought for a moment Benny was going to hop in your truck with us. Thank God for the storm, otherwise I think he would've." She looked up in thought. "See, I knew it, I'm the one who shoots you."

He cracked a smile. "Yeah, that was a mistake," Weston admitted. "You said it Chief, thank God for the storm or it would have been a tight fit in the truck today and I wouldn't have worn my old boots. If Cam heaves on these boots, I'll only be slightly ticked off."

Pearl and Weston knocked on Cam's apartment door.

"This little prick better open up. He said he'd be home."

"Afraid of a little water Wes?" Pearl asked as he pulled his leather coat over his shaved head to protect it from the drizzle.

"Yeah, I melt."

It had lightly rained the whole way to Princeton. It looked like the weatherman got it right this time and a big storm was coming their way.

"Relax, he's probably in the bathroom. He knows we were on our way."

Wes knocked on the door again. "Police open up!"

Pearl grabbed his arm. "Wes really?! Are you trying to get the entire apartment complex's attention?!"

He smiled sheepishly. "I always wanted to say that."

"I swear you're regressing in front of my eyes." She pulled out her phone and dialed Cam's cell. They could hear the phone ringing in the house.

She stood akimbo. "Okay, now I'm annoyed."

"Relax, he's probably in the bathroom," Weston smirked.

"We could try the door," Weston said, turning it. "Bingo."

"How'd you know the door would be unlocked?" Pearl asked impressed.

"The kid's a bookworm. In my world that equates to a dumbass. Leave it to Cameron Franklin to live on the bad side of town and keep his door unlocked."

"Wes Weston's world, a scary place," Pearl said, letting herself into Cam's apartment. Wes followed. "Cam, it's Chief Steele and Detective Weston."

She inclined her head toward the hall. "Check the bedroom and bathroom and knock before entering Wes. If he's been in the bathroom that long, you're going to get more than you bargained for with breaking down that door."

Pearl spotted Cam's phone by the foot of the couch and picked it up. She got a strong waft of coffee. Her eyes diverted to the dark stain on his couch. It was still damp and warm. She sniffed the spot, there was no doubt it was coffee. "Pumpkin Spice."

Pearl analyzed the room with a detective's eye while she waited for Weston to find Cam. There were more coffee stains on the rug. It didn't look like much effort was put into cleaning up the coffee spill, if any. She walked around Cam's small kitchen and noticed two Starbucks cups in the trash can. One had bright red lipstick on its lip.

"He's not here," Weston said, coming from the hall.

"Well, he was here not too long ago. Coffee was spilt on the couch and rug and it's still warm. Maybe he ran out to get a fabric cleaner. Coffee stains are a real pain to remove."

"Convenient," Weston said, taking a seat on the couch, making sure to avoid the wet spot. He grabbed the remote off the coffee table and clicked on the TV.

Pearl wasn't surprised Cam didn't have a password on his phone. If he didn't lock his front door, he wouldn't think a phone password was necessary. She scrolled through his text messages. "This is strange."

With a yawn, and a few more clicks of the TV remote, "What's that?"

"About twenty minutes ago Cam text Elsa Tilton: Detective's here now. I'll call you when I'm done."

"So."

Pearl scoffed. "So?! Wes you're missing the big picture. Seriously it scares me you're a detective." She ran her hand down her face exasperated. "Oh geez, it was me who made you a detective—head detective. That's it, I'm putting in for early retirement."

"Hmm . . .," he said, finding a rerun of *Miami Vice*.

"Wes, we weren't here twenty minutes ago."

He spoke without moving his eyes from the television. "He didn't mean it literally. It's like hey, that hunky detective Weston is going to be here soon, call you later." He shut off the TV, his eyes darting to Pearl. "Wait, you said he text Elsa Tilton? Now *that's* strange."

Pearl handed him Cam's phone. "Apparently, they love each other."

"Well, I'll be damned," Weston said, running his hand over the stubble of his five o'clock shadow. "I guess our little virgin is all grown up."

"Yeah, it looks like the two of them stepped out. Our wait may be longer than a trip to Walmart."

"*Two of them*?" Wes asked.

"There's two coffee cups in the trash and one has lipstick on it. I don't imagine Cam having many friends that are girls."

"Well, I may not be the best detective—"

"Admission is the first step to recovery," Pearl playfully teased, taking a seat on the armrest of the sofa opposite to Wes.

Ignoring her, he finished his thought. "If Cam's with Elsa, call Elsa and tell Cam to get his ass home now before we arrest him."

Pearl snatched Cam's phone back from Weston, a light blush on her cheeks. "I was just going to suggest that."

"Whatever you say, Chief."

Pearl scrolled down Cam's contact list and called Elsa. She didn't want to risk calling from her own phone and Elsa not answering an unknown number.

"Hi," Elsa said, answering the call.

"Hello Elsa. This is Chief of Police Pearl Steele."

"Oh, hi. I thought you were Cam," Elsa said confusedly.

Pearl deduced Cam was not with her as they had thought. "Yes, I did call from his phone. He left it in his apartment along with a note for me saying he was stepping out. I was getting impatient and was hoping if you were with him, you could tell him we were waiting."

"Sorry, I can't help. I'm not sure where he was going. He said he was going to call me after he was done talking to you."

"No worries. I'm sure he'll be home soon. Sorry to have bothered you." Pearl hung up.

"Nice lie on the fly, Chief," Weston said, tuned back into *Miami Vice*.

"Was worth a try. I guess Cam had another girl in his apartment."

"That kid has really come out of his shell."

"Cam missed a few calls from 'Bro'," Pearl said, scrolling through Cam's phone history.

"That would be his brother Little Willy."

"I didn't know Big Benny had another son."

Wes leaned back on the couch, as if he was on his own sofa. "Yeah, poor kid, looks just like Big Benny. He's as round as a bowling ball. He ran away a few years back. Benny wanted us to drag him home. He made a big stink about it, but the kid was eighteen, so there was nothing we could do."

"I don't remember him."

"You would if you saw him."

Wes eyed Pearl. "You're thinking of calling him?"

"Should I?"

"I don't think he was the one wearing the lipstick, but then again I think I did hear Willy switched teams." Wes chuckled, turning his attention back to the TV. "Best to let it be, Chief. You don't want anything getting back to Big Benny. He'll think Cam's missing and start a search party. And remember, I have a hot date tonight."

"You're right."

"Don't I know it," Wes said with a wink.

Cam's phone rang.

"Who's calling?" Wes asked, muting the TV.

"Can you believe it—Bro. Should I answer it?"

Before Weston could say no, Pearl answered it, placing the call on speaker.

"Cam where have you been?! I need guidance."

"Hi, is this Willy?" Pearl asked, deliberately dropping the descriptor of little.

There was a momentary pause on the phone. "Maybe. Who's this?"

"Chief of Police Steele."

"What are you doing with my brother's cell phone?"

"I had an appointment to meet him this morning and he wasn't home."

"That still didn't answer my question? How did you get Cam's phone?"

Pearl's tongue stuck to the roof of her mouth. Willy would be a good detective. "He left it in his apartment. Do you know if he had other plans today?"

"No . . . he's a workaholic hermit. But uh, he has a girlfriend."

"We tried her."

"What are you saying, my brother's missing? Why are you in his apartment if he's not there?" Pearl sighed. He would make a damn good detective.

Weston shook his head.

"Your brother is not missing. There was no sign of forced entry. Like I said, I have an appointment with him. I'm sorry to have upset you."

"You did. Have Cam call me when you find him." He hung up.

"That didn't go so well," Wes said.
Pearl exhaled loudly. "You think, genius."

CHAPTER THIRTY-FOUR
Bad Blood

Stevie hung up on Pearl, throwing his cell onto the bed and plopped down next to it. He was frustrated with Issac and with Cam. He had wanted to speak to Cam and hadn't heard from him. Issac, on the other hand, had left several long messages, some apologies, some updates on Joe, another on the murder of a little boy, but all of them ending with Issac asking him to return to Pleasant Mills. He had no intention of doing that. His bags were almost packed, and he'd planned to stay with Cam until he could find his own place.

King Charles jumped on his lap. "I know," he said, stroking the Pomeranian between his ears. "We have to go back. But that doesn't mean we have to see Issac. He made his choice, and he didn't choose me, which in turn means he didn't choose us." Stevie shook his head in despair. "It's for the best, he's more of a cat guy anyway. It wouldn't have worked out." Tears blurred his vision, he pawed at them. His face hurt from all the crying he did last night. He didn't want to shed another tear over Issac Smith. He wasted two years on a man that would never love him as much as he loved his ex.

"We'll make a quick trip to my father's house and see if Cam headed home to watch the storm. If he's not at his apartment and he skipped out on the police, the only place he could possibly be is at the house."

He nibbled on his bottom lip. "King," he said looking into the dog's brown eyes, "why would Cam skip out on the police? If he'd had an emergency, he would've called me, not Dad, and he wouldn't have left his phone in his apartment . . . I have a bad feeling he's in trouble."

The dog barked as if he understood.

"Right," Stevie said, nudging King Charles off his lap. Crouching, he pulled a small metal case out from under the bed. He opened it, his hands running over his gun. "I should bring Bertha just in case."

Cam opened his eyes, wincing in pain. His brain felt like soup, the slightest movement sending it sloshing about in his skull. He took in his current predicament with dread, the sting radiating from the back of his head. Wiggling his fingers, he felt the arm rest of the wooden chair he was tied to. The rough rope was tied around his wrist and ankles. He was trapped.

Confusion set in. Cam tried to recall how he ended up tied to a chair. He was in his apartment with Detective Larro and then he woke up here. Here was dark and damp, the smell of earth, poignant. He scoured the darkness trying to ascertain where here was. His heart pounded with relief. He knew this place. He was in his father's underground workshop. Now that his eyes had adjusted to the dark, he could make out the photographs of his friends tacked to his father's back wall.

"Dad!" he yelled, his voice hoarse. "Dad, are you down here?!"

"It's okay child," he heard a voice say in a thick Spanish accent.

At the risk of perpetuating his migraine, he turned his head left to right, looking for the owner of the voice. "Who's there?!"

Walking out of the shadows of the underground bunker as if they were a shadow themselves, a slight figure emerged.

Cam sucked air. His heart thudded against his chest. He fought against the ropes that bound his arms and legs. "Please," he said in a whisper. "Don't kill me."

Anita Gomez stood before him. His mother had found him. "You look just how your father did when I killed him."

Cam's chest heaved. He struggled against the ropes, feeling them cut into his skin. "Dad help! DAD!"

She tenderly brushed his light brown hair away from his face. "Don't make this harder than it has to be."

"Oh God, please. Dad!"

"Benjamin is not home. He is flying his kites in the park."

Cam's eyes swelled with tears. He knew crying wouldn't help. To Anita Gomez, tears were a sign of weakness.

"Why are you doing this?" Cam knew the answer. Ivy and Elsa had told him Anita killed her brother for power and tried to do the same with him, and apparently had murdered his biological father for the same reason, but Cam was hoping to buy some time—hoping Big Benny would rush in and save him like he'd done in the past.

"I am not a bad mother Samuel Cameron. I had a hard decision to make, and I made it."

"Trying to kill your only son doesn't make you a bad mother, it makes you a monster."

She shook her head at him. "How little you understand Samuel Cameron. You assume I want your power for myself but that is not so."

"For whom then, if not yourself?"

Again, she brushed his hair back, her thin fingers travelling alongside his temple. "For our family. For your sisters and your nieces. I need your power to protect them from the Serrano Curse."

"Serrano?" He had heard that name before, but from where? "Curse? What are you talking about?"

When I killed my brother Enzo Serrano those many years ago, I unknowingly placed a curse on the women in our family line. I murdered my brother in cold blood. I was a stupid and jealous little girl, I thought if I had more power, his power, it would change things. It did not—and misfortune, early deaths, and sickness have plagued the women in our family since. Your poor sister Lindsey has suffered illness after illness and Francine too. And now the twins are afflicted. The only way to protect them is to drain the power from the male descendants of the Serrano line and give it to them. I had lost all hope of recovering you, resolving to have to drain my beloved Sammy in order to save my family. But things are back on track. With your death, I can spare him."

Cam held his breath; he couldn't believe this was happening.

"You were born with so much power. There has not been a warlock in the family like you for generations, since my father. You're a natural born coven leader that only the Serrano line could have produced. I had hoped to spare you by draining your father, but he was only a distant cousin, and his life force barely sustained the girls. With your power I could protect our family for generations."

"You tried to kill me to help Lindsey?"

"Yes, Samuel Cameron."

"She was already pregnant with Sammy, and I worried about her frail health. I chose to protect the next generation."

"So it's all true, you did have a brother and you murdered him. You're selfish," Cam said, scathing loathing in his tone. "Murdering one's own blood is a cardinal sin. It goes against the craft and what it stands for. Committing it will always bring about a curse. It was one of the first lessons you taught me. You knew when you murdered your brother there would be a price to pay. I know you did, don't pretend not to have known. You murdered your brother at the risk of a curse to satisfy your own ego and now you hide behind piety. You act like murdering me is for the good of the family. We both know that's not true. Why don't you give the curse the blood it really wants? —Yours!"

Silent tears rolled down Cam's face, he couldn't hold them back any longer. "Does Lindsey and Francine know what you're doing? —Do they? Are they okay with you murdering their baby brother?" He sat limp in the chair—defeated, his wrist burning from where the rope had cut into them. "No, I didn't think so. They would never allow it."

"I have thought about our last moment we shared together in your room many times over the years," Anita said in a soft voice. "The idea you died for no reason haunted me." She placed her hand on his clammy forehead. "All I ever wanted was for you to die in peace my son, knowing your death served a greater purpose. Know this, you will be the last of the male line to make this sacrifice for our family. I have at last found another way to end the curse, nonetheless it still requires your life."

Barely audible, "Mom please, I'm happy. I met this terrific girl. Don't end it like this."

"Do not beg. It begets weakness and you will find I have none."

Cam heard footsteps on the stairs. "Dad help! Come quick! She's going to kill me!" Straining his neck, he turned his head. It was his father and the detective he'd spoken to earlier. He sighed in relief.

The detective wiped away a tear. Cam's eyes shifted to his father bewildered. Big Benny's heavy footfalls fell on the damp cement floor slowly and methodically, he wasn't in a rush to help him. "Dad, what's going on?"

"It's okay Cam, this won't take long."

"What won't? Dad?!" He looked to the detective for help. "What are you waiting for?! Untie me!" He inclined his head as best he could toward Anita. "Hurry she plans to kill me!"

Detective Larro covered her face with her hand, turning away from him, a sob escaping from her covered mouth. "I'm so sorry Samuel Cameron."

Her crying made it impossible for her to suppress her Spanish accent.

"Francine? Is that you? Oh God Fran, please help me. I'm your brother. Please I don't deserve to die for something our mother did."

She wouldn't look at him. "We have to save the twins. They're just babies."

"That's not the only way Fran. If she takes my place, it will end the curse for good."

With the last of his energy, Cam rocked his chair trying to tip it over.

Benny placed his large hands on Cam's shoulders to stop him. "Easy Cam."

"Why are you helping them? You've protected me all these years. You're my dad. Don't you care about me?"

Tears stood in Benny's eyes. "When I took you in, I knew you were the means to the end."

"I don't understand, what end?!"

"You were always a bargaining chip. I'm so close now to bringing back the one person who means more to me than anyone else—more to me than you and your brother. These women are going to help me get what I want, and I, in return, will help them get what *they* want."

"That doesn't make any sense. The Serrano curse is a blood curse. It can only end with a blood sacrifice from Anita."

They heard steps above them.

"You were followed," Anita hissed at Benny.

"Not possible."

The trapped door made a grating noise as it opened. The sound was followed by soft footfalls on the stairs. "Cam, you down here?"

"RUN STEVIE!" Cam shouted. "Run and get Pearl and Weston!"

Stevie ran in the opposite direction Cam wanted him to, coming down the steps with King Charles at his heels. Benny, Anita, and Fran stepped back into the shadows.

"What twisted thing are you playing at?" Stevie asked at seeing his brother tied up.

"Stevie," Cam said as calmly as he could, "you need to leave right now and get help. Dad is nuts."

"You're just figuring that out now?" he said, pulling on the ropes. "I've been telling you that for years. That Chief of Police called looking for you. She got me freaked out. And some little kid Mike knows was just murdered the same way as Joe's grandfather. I got worried and thought about what you said about Dad's secret, creepy workshop. I was thinking Dad would make a great serial killer. Oh how I hate it when I'm right." He tugged harder on the ropes, trying to get them to come loose. "I hate it, hate it, hate it."

King Charles scented the air and barked in the direction Benny, Anita, and Fran had retreated to.

"Willy, you picked a bad time to come home for a visit."

Stevie's head jerked up to see his father. He took a step back and pulled his handgun from his coat. "No Dad, I think I picked the perfect time. And it's Stevie."

"You have a gun?!" Cam said shocked.

"I live in Philly. Everyone has a gun."

He clicked off the safety and pointed it at his father. "Now back up."

Benny didn't budge.

"I have bad news, Dad," Stevie said, glancing at his brother. "I need both hands to untie Cam so that means I'm going to have to shoot you. Pick a leg."

Ben took a step forward, his hands out in front of him with his palms up. "Willy, you're messing with things you don't understand."

"For the hundredth time it's Stevie! And I understand just fine. I understand that the birdy has finally flown the cuckoo nest. You are full-blown out of your mind if you think I'm going to let you carve Cam up like you did Joe's grandfather and that kid. Dad, you're sick and you need help. I'm going to untie Cameron and then we are going to get you the very best help."

"Willy . . . " He took another step forward.

"You can't talk your way out of this one. I know it was you. I caught you red handed," he said, kicking the chair Cam was tied to. "I don't want to shoot you but if you take one more step I will."

"You're not going to shoot me. You don't have it in you." Ben took another step closer.

"For the love of God, it's Stevie and the right leg it is." He aimed his gun at his father's right kneecap. He was just about to shoot when he noticed Anita Gomez. He jerked his gun toward her. "Who the hell are you?!"

"I'm your worst nightmare little man."

"He's not to be hurt," Ben said sternly.

"Don't worry about me, Dad. I have a full magazine. Bullets for everyone."

Anita closed her eyes, her words echoing off the bunker walls. Stevie didn't recognize the language. "Hey shut up!" He pointed his gun at his father. "Tell her to shut up!"

Stevie leaned on his brother. "Cam, I don't feel soooooo—"

Stevie collapsed on the ground in a heap, his long, brown hair covering him like a blanket, his gun skidding a cross the floor.

"Stevie!" Cam yelled, again trying to tip over his chair. He shifted his weight side to side. "What did you do to him!"

King Charles barked at Anita, dodging her as she tried to pick him up and bounded up the stairs.

"Let's begin," Anita said turning to Ben, "before we have another interruption."

"Very well."

Anita pulled out a small dagger from the purse that hung from her frail body. Cam's eyes widened. His pulse surged under his skin like his blood was made of fire. He recognized it as the same dagger she used the first time she'd tried to kill him. The zigzag pattern of the blade was unmistakable. He instinctively twisted against the ropes, disregarding the pain it caused him.

She handed the dagger to Ben. Cam's eyes followed it. With vivid clarity, he remembered the pain it caused him. He held his breath. Benny cut Cam's left hand free and turned it over, so it lay palm up. With one fluid motion, Benny cut the fat of his palm. Cam flinched in pain, a fire-like burn blooming from the gash. Without hesitation, Benny ran the blade of the knife down his left palm and gripped his son's hand, so their bloody palms met.

Cam's chest continued to heave as Benny held his hand, his eyes not leaving his father. Ben turned to Anita. "It's done. The curse has been transferred to my blood line. As it was Japhet Dean who gave my son and me immortality, the Serrano curse will never affect my line and you will never have to worry about the curse reverting back to yours. I have held up my part of the bargain, now it's time for you to do yours."

Fran touched her mother's shoulder. "Mamá, I don't know about this."

"A deal is a deal."

She took the dagger back from Benny and drove it through the joint hands of her son and Benny. Cam gritted his teeth, doing his best to hold back his scream.

> "A body for a body;
> blood for blood;
> a soul to replace a soul,

this I ask, must be done."

A spike of pain shot from Cam's hand to his brain. His vision blackened until there was nothing but darkness.

ANITA "ABBY" GOMEZ

CHAPTER THIRTY-FIVE
Under Water

Hearing Mr. Lopez pull into the driveway, Ivy made a beeline for the front door.

"They're here Grams!"

"Let him come to the door," Mary said, coming into the living room.

"Grams, I can walk to the car without being killed." Ivy eyed Danny, wanting him to intervene.

He shook his head, mouthing: "No way Jose."

Danny was nice—too nice. Ivy thought Grams bullied him. Like today, she was making him go to her senior Christmas party then to the movies to see a movie about an old person finding love in a foreign country. Ivy was positive he'd have more fun at work than eating apple pie with a bunch of cranky seniors and watching old people kiss on the big screen.

Ivy crossed her arms over her chest, narrowing her eyes to slits in her grandmother's direction. Her grandmother gave her an eye that rivaled a hawk. "Let him come to the door," she said again, this time in her all-business tone.

They waited. A few moments later, there was a knock on the door. Mary opened it.

"Hi Mary," Jeffrey said. "Hey Danny," he said, shaking his hand.

"Hey Danny," Sammy said with a handshake, mirroring his father. "Hey Grams," Sammy said, eyeing Ivy like he hadn't seen her in years.

Ivy had planned on yelling at Mr. Lopez the first chance she had for not telling them about his dreams, but after seeing him, she couldn't. He hadn't looked that haggard since Sammy went missing. His eyes were blood shot and she noticed tiny little lines by the corners of them she'd never noticed before. It was like he aged overnight. Even his demeanor seemed changed as if the day's events caused him to physically shrink.

"Drop Ivy off at Danny's when you're done, we're bringing pizza home for the kids for dinner."

"Will do," Jeffrey said.

"Ready?" he asked, glancing to Ivy.

She nodded, taking Sammy's hand that was outstretched to her.

Before she got into Mr. Lopez's SUV, she looked across the street at the rectory. Never had it looked so grim, its red door reminding her of blood. The crowd had left, and with it the barricades. Both Uriah's and Trudy's cars were in the driveway, but she knew Trudy was on her way to visit her aunt in Florida accompanied by the Lopez girls plus Hugo.

Sammy had gained his family to lose them again. She wondered if that was also wearing on Mr. Lopez. She glanced to him. He had also stopped to look across the street. She could read the guilt on his face, see it in his dark eyes. He was looking more and more like JD.

Sammy slid into the back seat next to her instead of sitting in the front. Ivy was just about to comment on how sweet that was when she heard her name from the front passenger seat.

"Hello Ivy."

Ivy jumped, hitting her head on the roof of the car. "Abby, I didn't see you there."

"You weren't looking. You were looking across the street. You have to look to the future not the past. That goes for all of you."

"I know Abby," Sammy said, buckling up. Jeffrey gave no acknowledgement.

Ivy buckled her seatbelt, fidgeting in her seat. "You didn't go to Florida with Lindsey and the kids?" Ivy felt stupid stating the obvious, but she had assumed just that and was happy Anita was far away. She needed more time to come up with how to deal with Abby moving back in with Sammy. Her boyfriend's homicidal grandmother moving back in with him was not a problem she could deal with today. Today, she was murdering her best friend.

"I am needed here," Anita said, in her usual self-important tone.

"I'm sure Lindsey needs you too."

Sammy took Ivy's hand, as if to tell her to ease off.

"I am needed here," she said again like a robot on repeat.

Ivy so badly wanted to spill the beans on Cam but felt like she needed to talk to Elsa and Cam first before she reneged on their secret pact. She had to get through today first, and tomorrow she would deal with Anita. It wasn't as much time as she would've liked, but she would make do.

Jeffrey pulled into the parking lot of Batsto State Park, parking as close to the visitor's center as he could. It was a quick walk to Batsto Lake, but Anita walked slowly, and Sammy insisted on keeping pace with her.

Approaching the lake, Ivy scanned the crowd. There was no sign of JD, but she could make out Jesse and Rosa who stood apart from everyone else. Ivy hadn't seen or spoken to Rosa after she learned what she had done to Tammy. Now when she looked at her, she didn't see her as her only friend. She had lots of friends now, and Rosa wasn't one of them.

Ivy's eyes darted to the nearby tree everyone else huddled under. Mike stood so close to Joe they might as well have been attached. Issac too was next to Joe, but not too close, well maybe too close for Stevie's liking, but she didn't see him or his cute dog. Tammy, in Tessa's body, was there with Elsa and Zac with Mona.

"Hi," Sammy said once they were in ear shot. Elsa rushed over to Ivy, giving her a big hug. "What took you guys so long?"

Ivy tilted her head in the direction of Anita. She didn't have to say more than that and didn't want to. She didn't want Rosa to know she was there, although she was sure she already knew. Elsa's voice carried on the wind like a song and who else would arrive with Sammy but her. Everyone had been waiting on them.

Ivy knew Rosa deserved what she was about to get, but part of her felt torn for the friend Rosa used to be. Ivy couldn't help but think of the first time she met Rosa. She was hired as Rosa's babysitter for a weekend after Rosa first lost her vision. She'd had a nightmare that night in which Rosa's eyes were missing. That had come to pass, but nothing did or could have prepared Ivy for Rosa's betrayal. Ivy was never the biggest fan of Tammy's, but Tammy was Tammy. Rosa had played everyone including her. Rosa wasn't her friend or anyone else's and she certainly wasn't Jesse's friend.

The Rosa she thought she knew wasn't the real Rosa. The real Rosa had murdered Tammy in cold blood. Ivy echoed Sammy's sentiment more than she cared to admit. Rosa was a murderer, but murdering Rosa made them all murderers.

If she was being honest with herself, Rosa scared her a little. The fact that Rosa could do that to someone she'd seemed to be good friends with, even if it was for Jesse's sake, was a friend she could do without. Maybe if they had more time, she could bring herself to speak to Rosa about it and get her side of the story, but they were out of time, this was happening now, and she never felt more like a coward.

Anita and Jeffrey kept their distance from everyone else. Ivy watched him scan the horizon; she wondered if he was looking for JD.

It was very quiet by the lake. The cold weather and the Nor'easter warning kept people out of the park, which was good for them, they didn't need anyone watching what they were about to do. The storm hadn't touched down yet, but the sky was dark, deeper than a purple bruise and the rain came down in scattered showers, raining one minute to stop the next.

Issac checked his phone. "Still no Stevie."

"He's trying to punish you, don't let him," Joe said, wrapping his coat around him tighter. "And you wouldn't want him to see this anyway."

"Still . . . it's not like him," Issac pouted. "He must be really mad at me this time."

"It can't hurt to try him again," Mike suggested.

A silence washed over the group as Jesse took Rosa's hand and led her to the water's edge. She relied fully on him as her eyes in the absence of her ID cane. "You promise you'll forgive me?" Rosa asked, shivering from the cold. She left her coat on the park bench to climb back into after it was all over.

"This is only a start. Every year you're going to be drowned in this lake for Joe."

"Okay," Rosa said. "I will."

"I'm going to hold you under the water until you stop breathing. Are you ready?" Jesse asked, staring into Rosa's glass eyes to see no soul.

She nodded.

"I think Stevie had the right idea," Joe said, turning around. "I can't watch. This is what happened to Wendy. My grandfather drowned her for me."

Since they'd received the letter from Bishop Baker, Mike had thought it was likely Joe's grandfather had drowned his childhood best friend but hadn't wanted to bring it up. He rubbed Joe's arm, but he couldn't help but stare.

Tammy took off her hood to get a better look. She took Mike's hand. "Are we doing the right thing?" she whispered.

"Yes, we are." You didn't deserve to die Tammy, Rosa does. I'm with Jesse on this a hundred percent. You can't stay in Tessa's body. The whole town is looking for her and even if you run away, you'll have no life without a valid ID. This is the only way to get your life back. A life Rosa stole from you in the first place."

Sammy nodded. "Mike's right."

Tammy had never heard her brother talk with unyielding conviction as he had in that moment. She needed to hear that. She squeezed his hand. Elsa took her free hand and together they watched.

Jesse and Rosa waded into the water. The water was icy, spurring gooseflesh on their extremities. Jesse took her waist deep into the water. Her hand trembled in his, he remained stony. He had killed someone he loved; this was nothing to him. Without notice, he took her by the shoulders and pushed her head underwater. She instantly struggled to get up for air, her arms flailing in the water, sending ripples across the otherwise still lake. She was no match for Jesse's strength, he held her under the water with ease.

Tammy turned around. "I can't watch Mike." Elsa did the same, turning around and rubbing her best friends back. Ivy was like Mike; she couldn't help but stare. Stare at Rosa as she struggled to live. Stare at Jesse as he killed her with his bare hands.

Mona let out a little gasping noise but remained watching. Ivy watched as Zac took her hand. She knew this must be hard for her to watch for a number of reasons. Jesse had killed her.

Ivy's vision darted to Sammy. His eyes were not on the lake, but on his own hands and she wondered if he could do what Jesse was doing for someone he loved. They locked eyes, his dark lashes holding her in place as if she was a statue. He nodded at her to say, he *would* kill for her.

After Rosa's arms stopped moving, after she stopped fighting him, Jesse continued to hold her under the water. It was over, she was dead. And he was unaffected by it all. He picked Rosa out of the water, holding her close to his chest as he took her to shore.

"Tammy!" he shouted. "You have to do it now."

Mike, with his sister's hand in his, hurried to Jesse. Sammy and Ivy followed.

"Jesse," she said, with hot tears streaming down her cheeks as she looked at Rosa's placid face, her dark hair stuck to her cheeks like seaweed, "I don't know if I can."

Jesse took her free hand, his calmness gone. His heart played ping pong in his chest. Urgency burned in his amber eyes. "Tammy, if you can't do it for yourself, do it for me. I need you. I need you with me and with Rosa's body we can be together forever. But we only have a small window."

"Okay," she said.

"Okay," he said, nodding. He knelt, thumbing Rosa's glass eyes out of her sockets.

Mike flinched.

Tammy closed her mother's eyes. Jesse and Mike waited. Everyone did, moving closer, even Jeffrey and Anita. If it worked, it wouldn't take long, a few minutes at most. Tammy just had to move her mind into the blank body, she had done it once before, she could do it again. The thing here was the timing. She had to do it at the exact moment when JD's power healed and resurrected Rosa. That was a key reason Jesse needed Sammy and Ivy there. He relied on them to sense the magic.

"Now!" Sammy and Ivy shouted at the same time.

Rosa lay on the ground, wet and still, no sign of life humming about her.

"Did it work?" Mike asked after a few moments.

As if she heard her brother, Rosa's brown eyes flashed open. She sat up, throwing her arms around Jesse's neck. "Jesse it's me!" He hugged her to him. His body was shivering from the cold, but he never felt so warm. Jesse's plan had worked. Tammy got her life back, it may not be her exact life, but she would be able to continue where she left off.

Mike hugged his sister and Jesse not breaking up their moment, then jogged to Joe where he still stood with Issac. "How do you feel? Is it over?"

"The same. I guess I won't know for sure until I'm away from you."

Mike took his hand. "Let's not test it for a while."

"Agreed," he said with a grin. "I'm moving to Pleasant Mills."

Jesse helped Tammy put on Rosa's winter coat she left on the bench near the lake. Elsa was by her side, hugging her as soon as Jesse let her go. They pulled Sammy in for a hug. Ivy kicked at the ground with her boots feeling a little left out. "Ivy, come here," Elsa said, pulling her in for a group hug.

Mike, Joe, and Issac made their way to them.

"It worked," Jesse said in a loud voice so everyone could hear. "Every year, I'll drown Tammy in the lake for Joe." His eyes found Joe. "In the beginning of the year, so you don't have to deal with the nightmares."

Tammy clung to Jesse's arm and nodded in agreement.

"Thank you," Joe said, "Both of you. All of you."

Ivy watched Jesse and Tammy with great interest. It was ironic that Rosa had always wanted to be with Jesse and in a way she was. Tammy had her body now and she would be with him forever.

"What happened to Rosa?" Zac asked, "Did she move on?"

"Rosa had no soul, she gave it to JD," Jesse told him.

"I feel a little bad," Tammy said. "We tricked her."

"Don't," Jesse said, putting his arm around her. "She sealed her fate when she killed you."

"He's right. Don't feel guilty," Ivy said, self-projecting. "Rosa's the one who tricked us. She lied to us all."

Tammy glanced at her mother who stood a few feet from them, drool already accumulating at the corners of her lips. "My poor mother."

"I'll take care of her," Mr. Lopez said. "It's why I'm here." He pulled out his phone and dialed Pearl. "You kids get back to Danny's before you freeze, I'll wait here with Tessa for Pearl to get here."

"We'll wait with you Dad," Sammy said, not wanting his father alone with Pearl. "Is that okay?" he asked Ivy.

"Yep," she said. He may have had no intention of leaving his father with Pearl, but she had no intention of leaving him alone with his grandmother.

Tammy thanked them and hugged her mother goodbye. "I promise to visit you mom," she said, kissing her cheek before letting Jesse usher her to the car.

The five of them sat in silence on a bench facing the lake for almost twenty minutes before Pearl and Weston got there. Rain came down in a faint mist, covering everything in what looked like dew. Jeffrey left the bench, going to the Crown Vic.

"Hi," he said, as she opened the car door.

"Can we talk about last night?"

Weston arched his eyebrows like they were a pair of flying seagulls but remained silent.

"Wes do me a favor, collect Tessa and get her in the car."

"On it Chief," he said with a cocky smile that Jeffrey noticed.

"Pearl—"

"You were right to go back to your wife Jeffrey. I will never forgive you for not trusting me with the truth and letting me sleep with the sociopath who killed Timothy."

"Pearl . . ."

"Don't bother trying to explain. He told me everything, well what I needed to hear. What I can't comprehend is who on Earth would stir that pot and kill Aiden Leeds."

He hung on her car door, his damp hair tucked behind his ears. He looked so much like he had when they were in high school. "Maybe whoever it was, isn't from Earth."

She scoffed. "That's what I'm afraid of."

"Pearl," he said, taking her hand, not caring if Sammy saw. His emotions from the day were heightened, he felt like he lacked self-control and didn't have enough left in the tank to reel himself in. "You know I love you."

She exhaled loudly, her heart in pain. Every inch of her was in pain when she stood that close to him. "I know Jeffrey. And I love you. We're just not meant to be together in this life."

"Maybe the next life," he said.

She gave a sad smile. "Maybe."

"I better get Tessa back to Pleasant Asylum before the town loses full confidence in the police force.

He squeezed her hand, before letting it go. It killed her to know she already forgave him for not telling her the full truth. She knew Jeffrey better than he knew himself. She knew he was trying to protect her. The reality of the situation was so crazy, she most likely wouldn't have believed him anyway. It had to be done gradually. She just had to wait. This was her fault, Jeffrey warned her about his brother, and she got impatient waiting. All she could do now is hope there was another life and somehow, they would find each other in it.

Jeffrey walked over to the bench with Pearl. She had hoped Weston would have had Tessa in the car by now, but he was too preoccupied with trying to read their lips from the bench to make a real effort.

"I thought she was a threat to herself," Pearl said, looking at the beads of drool trickling down Tessa's face.

"That's what they said Chief," Wes said. "Doctors always over exaggerate."

"She's an empty shell, her mind's somewhere else," Jeffrey said.

Ivy jumped to her feet. "Oh my God Mr. Lopez, you're right!"

He furrowed his eyebrows, looking to Sammy for a clue then back at Ivy. "Uh, right about what?"

"Teller, what are you talking about?"

"Her mind's somewhere else," she repeated. "And I know where that somewhere else is!"

"You do?!" Sammy asked.

"She's the person answering the questions in the well. She's trapped between our world and the next. Think about it—her mind's at Danny's house. Mike said his dad found Tessa staring into the mirror in the foyer, right?"

"And all the mirrors in Danny's house are broken because she got trapped in there somehow and was trying to get out," Sammy mused.

"Bingo!" Ivy said excitedly, her smile spreading across her face. "Tessa's mind is trapped behind the mirror." She tugged on Mr. Lopez's hand like a child. "Mr. Lopez, we have to go back to Danny's and try to return Tessa's mind to her body."

"Um . . ."

"Please."

"Pearl?" he said, glancing to her. "Can we try?"

"Chief this is turning into a circus," Weston groaned. "Come on, I can't believe you're entertaining this."

Ivy gave him a dirty look, scrunching her nose like he hadn't showered in a week. He ignored her. He was what her grandmother called seasoned; a dirty look wasn't going to crack him. She figured smelling bad was a rite of passage for a guy like Wes Weston and he'd take it more as a compliment than an insult, so she played it up to Pearl, folding her hands together and smiling.

"I don't see the harm it would do Wes. Look at her, she's not going anywhere," Pearl said, gesturing to Tessa sitting on the bench. "And we have to pass Danny's on the way to the asylum anyway. If it could help, we should try. It's in the job description."

"You're the Chief and I'm your faithful lacky."

Pearl smiled. "That's the smartest thing you ever said."

They stood Tessa in front of the cracked mirror in Danny's foyer, the exact place where Big Mike said he had found her. The mirror, if it weren't broken, would have been beautiful, the flower motif of dandelions being hand carved and painted.

The dandelions, however, reminded Ivy of JD. *'When a dandelion dies it leaves you a wish. Don't be afraid to make yours . . ."* Ivy tried to shake off the gnawing dread growing in the pit of her stomach. She remembered her wish all too well. *'I've made mine Japhet Dean. I wish to be with you forever.'*

Tammy took her mother's hand. "Okay what do we do?"

"I'm not sure about this part," Ivy admitted, biting the inside of her cheek. "I'm open to suggestions."

"Great," Wes said. "You know kids, some of us here have plans tonight."

Ivy rolled her eyes. "You can't be talking about yourself."

Pearl and Jeffrey suppressed a smile.

"What do we know?" Sammy asked, before Ivy got herself in trouble.

"Tessa got trapped in the mirror," Ivy said, "and couldn't find a way out."

"How would that even happen?" Mike asked. "It makes no sense."

"I'm with Mike," Issac said, "that's not logical." Joe was of the same mindset offering a shoulder shrug.

"It must have something to do with her ability to talk to ghosts," Tammy guessed. "Maybe a ghost jumped into her and when it left her, things got all jumbled and she thought the reflection was her true self."

Jesse nodded. "That seems likely."

Ivy thought about it. That seemed plausible enough, but that didn't matter right now. They just needed to figure out how to get her out of the mirror, not what had placed her behind it.

She glanced at Zac and Mona wondering if Mona had any suggestions. She seemed to have a really good handle on being a ghost.

Mona sensed her gaze and shook her head.

Ivy looked at her fractured reflection in the mirror, the way each shard came together to make up her face like a glass puzzle. The shards were slightly convex, as if something hit the mirror from the back.

"I have an idea," Ivy said. "Somehow, Tessa got herself trapped in the mirror and couldn't get out. She cracked every mirror in the house trying to make her escape, but never shattered one. Let's break the mirror completely. Maybe it will open a path for her."

"Teller, that's a great idea! I'll get a trash can."

Sammy brought the trash can from the kitchen and placed it under the mirror where it hung on the foyer wall.

"I hope this isn't seven years bad luck since it's technically already broken," Ivy said. "With the edge of a bobby pin, she pulled from her hair, Ivy lifted a shard of glass from the mirror and let it fall into the trash can. It produced a domino effect that sounded like a wind chime in the breeze, all of the shards falling one after another into the trash can. As the last shard fell, Tessa gasped.

"Mom!" Tammy said, hugging her mother.

"Hi," Mike said shocked, a hot blush traveling across the bridge of his nose.

Tessa reached for Mike to take her hand, clasping it, she pulled him to her. Hugging her two children, she looked over Tammy's shoulder at Ivy. "Thank you."

CHAPTER THIRTY-SIX
Keys

Stevie stirred. He felt a hand brush his hair away from his face. "Issac . . . I'm so sorry. I can't live without you. I love you." A pain radiated from the side of his head, behind his ear. The pain intensified as he came to.

"You really wacked yourself in the head. But you'll be okay. It's just a lump," Big Benny said, sucking on the cut on the tip of his finger. Stevie opened his eyes to find himself lying on the floor, his head in his father's lap.

Stevie pushed himself off of his father and jumped to his feet. Woozy, his hand reached for his head.

"Stevie relax."

"Finally, you learned my name." He looked around, not able to see much in the darkness. "Where's Cam? What did you do with him? Cam!" He put his hand on the metal bars enveloping them in a cage with the intention of tugging them open but pulled his hands back in pain instead. The bars were constructed of iron keys fused together, pieces of them sticking out like thorns on a rosebush.

"The bars are constructed of keys."

Stevie rubbed his hands together. "I see that . . . So, you've collected keys for all these years to make a cage for you and me? Oh wow, you're crazier than I thought. I hope you have a special key to get us out of here."

"It's me, Cam. Dad stole my body."

Stevie evaluated his father. "You're Cam? Prove it, cause you look and sound a hell of a lot like my crazy dad."

"I did call you Stevie, didn't I?" he said, folding his hands in his lap.

Stevie rested against the bars, careful not to put his full weight into it. "You did . . . but you still need to do better."

"The last time we saw each other you thought I was on drugs. I told you I wasn't. You thought I got a nose job. I told you about dad's workshop and you told me not to go home."

Stevie nibbled his bottom lip. He was almost there. "You could've ascertained all of that from what I told Cam when I came to rescue him. Which I epically failed at."

"You're the only one I told I'm dating Elsa. Dad doesn't know. No one knows."

Stevie felt the lump on the side of his head and winced. "I must have brain damage." He looked to his father sitting on the floor. "For the sake of argument, let's say I believe you and you and dad had a *Freaky Friday* moment and switched bodies. Why would he want your body? I mean, besides the obvious."

"I think he was trying to help me."

"Help you? Cam wake up. Having Dad's body is a punishment from Hell, trust me I would know. If you think Elsa is going to walk around with Big Benny Franklin on her arm, you're crazy. Which proves you're really Dad."

"The old woman you saw, that's Anita Gomez. She's my biological mother. She wanted to kill me to end a curse on our family."

"Kill you to end a curse . . ." Stevie crouched, feeling nauseous, his head burning. "Okay let me think this out. Dad took your body to save you and then he locked us up in a cage made out of keys . . . My gut and my pounding headache tells me he didn't do that to help you Cam. He did that to help himself."

"He did say he was trying to bring someone back."

"Titan?" Stevie asked, his eyes going to his father's face.

Cam shrugged. "I don't know a Titan."

"I do. I remember him . . . He was mean. Really mean to me." He looked at the puncture holes in his hands, left from the bars made of keys. "He hurt me . . . Dad looked the other way. I was happy when JD killed him. But I was scared he was going to kill Dad too. He didn't touch him, instead he turned to me and said we'll have to finish our game later."

"What are you talking about?"

Stevie rubbed his temples, trying to alleviate his searing migraine. "I think Dad wants to bring back his old lover. A real son of a bitch. But I, I don't know what that has to do with you or me. I'm certain he doesn't want to help you. If he really wanted to help, he would've let me shoot the old lady. And whatever he's up to, he's been planning it for a very long time, thus the keys, and he doesn't want us in his way—consequently we're locked in here."

Cam leaned against the bars of the cage, folding his legs against his chest to the best of his ability now that he had a large belly. "Even when I thought he was trying to help me, I didn't like the idea of him walking around in my body. Now, I'm really worried about it. What if someone thinks he's me. What if Elsa thinks so?"

Stevie rested next to his brother and put his hand on his knee. "I met Elsa. I didn't tell you before because I didn't want you to know I was in Pleasant Mills and risk you coming home. I had a bad feeling and like I said, I hate being right. But Elsa, she's awesome. I like her. Don't worry about her, she's too smart. She'd know right away if Dad tried to pull anything in your body. But I don't see why he would. Like you said, no one knows you're dating and Dad's gay ninety-five percent of the time. I was a product of alcohol. He'd be more interested in . . . I don't know, your friend Sammy Lopez. That kid is a looker."

Cam examined his bandaged hand, it burned. "You're right, but I still don't like it."

"Me either. But I'm more concerned with how we're going to get you back in your body than Dad taking it for a joyride."

"Luckily, my friend Ivy should be able to help with that."

"Good," Stevie said, with a pat to his brother's knee. "All we have to do is sit tight and wait to be rescued."

Cam exhaled sharply. "It's not like we have much of a choice in the matter. There's no door to the cage."

CHAPTER THIRTY-SEVEN
Surprise Visit

Elsa had just hung up with her mother, who was about twenty minutes from the house when she heard a knock on the front door. Elsa quickly checked her phone hoping everything was okay with Tammy. Mr. Lopez had just dropped her off at home and she was feeling guilty leaving Tammy to check on Cam, but reasoned her bestie had Jesse and Mike with her, and she was sure Tammy was itching for some alone time with Jesse. Since the call from Chief Steele on Cam's phone, she felt on edge. Not hearing from Cam all day didn't help matters. She felt a little like a neurotic girlfriend driving to Princeton to see him but figured she could play it off as a favor to Pleasant Mills PD.

Elsa swiped her phone on. There were no missed messages or calls. Feeling uneasy after the news of Aiden's murder, she looked out her bedroom window trying to get a glimpse of who knocked.

"Cam!"

Elsa ran to the front door and opened it to the soft pitter-patter of rain. The sun poked through the approaching storm clouds in streaks of yellow and gold that cast a warm glow around Cam. Elsa threw her arms around her boyfriend, almost leaping from the house. She showered him with chaste kisses. "I was so worried when Chief Steele called me looking for you. I've been waiting all day for your call. I was going to drive to your apartment as soon as my mom got home from work."

"Sorry to make you worry." He held up his bandaged hand so she could see.

She took his hand in hers, examining the bulky bandage wrapped around his left hand. "What happened?"

"Cooking accident. I went to the emergency room and left my phone in the apartment."

She pulled him into the house gently. "Come in before someone sees you. "Were you able to get in touch with Chief Steele?"

"Not yet, I came to see you first."

She smiled. "I'm glad, but I think you should call her now. You don't want it to get back to your dad you're missing. He'll go looking for you and then we'll have a problem."

"It can wait a little longer," he said, leaning in and planting a kiss on her cheek. "She just wants me to confirm the link between Bishop Baker's murder in Philly and Aiden's murder."

"Is there a link?" she asked, tarrying with Cam by the staircase.

"Yes, they're connected. Are you familiar with the saying see no evil, hear no evil, speak no evil?"

She gave him a funny look. "Yeah, the three monkeys," she said, covering her eyes, followed by her ears, then lastly her mouth. "You have them on your nightstand and gave me a pretty lengthy history about them."

"Did I tell you there's a fourth monkey?"

She looked up in thought. "No, I don't think so."

"It represents do no evil."

Her eyebrows furrowed. "How's that related to the murders?"

"Someone is getting revenge for a horrible crime committed against them."

Elsa shook her head. "That can't be right. Aiden was just a little boy. What's the worst thing he could've done?"

"Killing Aiden, permanently hurt Aiden, but it hurt someone else more.”

With eyes as large as saucers, “Pastor Leeds?”

“Maybe,” he said, drumming his fingers on her arm.

“Wow, you don’t think it was JD do you? I thought he turned a new leaf with him being related to Sammy and everything.”

“Leopards don’t change their spots my dear and JD was born from evil and is as evil as they come. He needs to be destroyed.”

Her funny look resurfaced. “You okay? You sound . . . I don’t know, stressed.”

“Yeah, sorry. I was just going into dork mode,” he said with a shoulder shrug.

She reassured him with her perfect smile. “I get it, you’re in your element.”

“Hey, how about we step out to get a bite to eat before your mother gets home? I’m starving.”

“Do you think that’s a good idea?” What if your dad spots you? And you still have to call Chief Steele.”

“I don’t think that’s going to be a problem. And I promise as soon as we get back, I’ll call Pearl.”

Elsa nibbled on the tip of her nail. “I don’t know, Ivy said to lie low. If your dad sees your face, he’ll know the spell he put on you is broken and then Sammy’s grandmother may realize who you really are. I didn’t get a chance to tell you, she’s living with him again. I don’t think we should risk going out.”

He ran his hand down the side of her face. “I really trusted you with everything, didn’t I?”

She flashed him a smile. “Of course you did. You love me.”

He leaned in and kissed her. “Did you tell anyone else about my father? —Sammy?”

“No one. I can keep a promise Cam. Only Ivy and I know.”

“Good. How about we just do drive through then?”

“Okay,” she said, “that seems like a good compromise.” She took her raincoat off a small hook by the side of the door. “Wait until I tell you about our day. Well, first things first, Tammy’s in Rosa’s body now.”

“Really?” he asked, eagerly waiting by the door, his fingers drumming on it now.

"Yeah, it was crazy. She's adjusting pretty well to it, I think. We're going to put some red highlights in her hair this weekend to help her feel more like herself and get her some new clothes."

"That sounds like fun."

Elsa's face lit up. "You have no idea how it feels to have Tammy back. I was lost without her."

"I think I do."

Elsa stepped outside, standing under the covered porch. The rain had picked up, it was pouring now. Everything was washed in a mist. The sound of the heavy rain bounced off the copper roof in thudding echoes.

"You have your dad's SUV? Where's your car?"

"It was making a strange noise on the way here, so I thought it best to play it safe. I didn't want us to break down in this weather."

"Please tell me your dad didn't see you take his car?"

"No."

She shook her head. "Cam, you're being so reckless. I'm surprised your dad's not at the field yet. He's going to be mad you took his SUV; you know he keeps his extra kites in there."

"I'm sorry," he said. "When you didn't hear from me, I knew you would be worried."

"You could've just called."

"I would have but Pearl accidently took my phone with her and besides I wanted to see you."

She touched his shoulder, tenderly. "I'm glad you're here. I just want you to be careful."

"Promise. No more unnecessary risks." He glanced to the SUV. "Let me open the door for you, so you can get right in."

She put up her hood to her raincoat, happy she had such a sweet boyfriend. "That's a good idea."

He ran to the passenger side door and opened it, before getting into the driver seat. Elsa ran to the car and hopped in laughing. "I don't know the last time it rained this hard. I must look like a drowned rat." She pulled down the sun visor mirror to check her makeup. "I think your dad's gonna strike out tonight. I think it's raining too hard for the kites to fly."

"I don't know about that he said," shutting the visor. He turned her chin to him and pressed a kiss to her lips. "You really are a beautiful flower."

Elsa giggled, pushing him away. "Cam what's wrong with you? A beautiful flower?"

"Nothing's wrong with me. I feel better than I have in a long time." He pressed his lips to hers again, not to be pushed off easily. "It didn't have to be this way. It's a shame . . ."

"What is?" she asked in between kisses.

"That my son told you everything."

Elsa slid closer to the car door, trying to create distance between them. "Cam, seriously, are you feeling alright? What are you talking about? *My son told you everything*? You don't have a son, *or do you*?"

He forced his body against hers, pressing her to the door and kissing her hard. "Cam, you're hurting me." His hands slid to her neck. He squeezed. She clawed at his hands, trying to choke out his name.

He whispered in her ear as she gasped her last breath. "I'm not Cameron."

CHAPTER THIRTY-EIGHT
The Out

Uriah answered the door. "Hello I'm Cameron Franklin. I'm not a member of Pleasant Mills Church but I was hoping to become one. Do you have time to talk tonight?"

"Of course," Uriah said, stepping to the side to let him into his home. He had expected it to be another church member at the door with a casserole dish and was happy to be wrong.

"Sorry for stopping by at a late hour. I was visiting my father and thought I'd pop in before I head home."

"No worries. Did you eat? I have plenty."

"Wow," Cam said, looking at the dishes spread out on the dining room table, "you must've had some party. What was the occasion?"

Uriah leaned against a dining room chair for support, realizing how tired he was. "It wasn't a happy one. My son passed away last night."

Cam flushed. "Oh, uh I'm so sorry. If it's not a good time, I can come back later." He turned to leave.

"No," Uriah said, straightening up, "please stay. It's a perfect time. I could use the distraction."

"Okay," Cam said.

"We can sit in the living room. It's a little more comfortable in there."

Cam followed Uriah, taking a seat in the upholstered chair across from him. The rain beaded down the large window, blurring out the Teller house across the street.

With red rimmed eyes Uriah evaluated Cam. "You look so familiar. Have we met before? Who's your father?"

"Benjamin Franklin and we've met. It was a long time ago."

"I thought so. I'm glad for the chance to get to know you better. Pleasant Mills Church is nondenominational. We accept anyone. The church's reopening is this Sunday. We have plenty of room for new members and offer Sunday service and a late Tuesday service. Other accommodations can be made if you need them."

Cam ran his finger down the plastic that covered the arm rest of the chair. "I have always admired you, Pastor Leeds."

"Please where at my home, call me Uriah."

He nodded. "I'm not surprised your little church accepts everyone. How else could you accept JD."

"Excuse me?" Uriah's mind was taking longer than usual to focus.

"I know what you really are Uriah Leeds. Like I said, I've admired you for a long time, more specifically your duplicity. Most of all I admire your face. You are such a beautiful man, it's so easy for you to hide behind that mask."

Uriah stood up. "I think you should leave."

Cam stayed put, a smile blooming across his face. "You have nothing to fear from me. I'm here to help you see the truth. After all, you didn't choose your father. What a sin it is that you embraced JD and became just as evil as him."

"I'm not evil."

"No, you kill in the name of your god, so that makes it what . . . holy work?"

"I don't know what you're talking about."

"We both know that's not true. Over the years you've killed plenty of people. One of the most recent being Bishop Baker."

"You need to leave," Uriah said in a stern voice. He didn't recognize it as his own.

"I will give it to you Uriah, killing your own son to shrug off the suspicion of murder was clever. You, as a lead suspect flew out the front door along with your son's corpse."

Uriah grabbed Cam by the collar of his raincoat. "You don't know what you're talking about!" He pushed him back, rocking the living room chair. "Now get out before I call the police!"

"I know it was you who made Bishop Baker pull the trigger. You put the idea in his head, just as you put the idea in Jeffrey Hanson's all those years ago at Batsto Lake. I was there. I saw you. I know what you did. Just as I know you told Bishop Baker to kill himself."

Uriah recalled the vivid memory of Batsto Lake: His mother dead, his son Joseph dead, and then Rupert Hanson's blood splattered across his face. Then there was his will, his burning desire for Jeffrey Hanson to turn his pistol on himself—bang. "You can't prove it," Uriah said.

Cam gripped the armrest of the chair, the plastic crunching under the weight of his fingernails. "I know Baker was a bad man and he got what he deserved. But you took it one step further, didn't you? Killing him wasn't enough. You had to disfigure him."

"No, I didn't do that. I just told him to shoot himself."

"But you did Uriah. I was there. I watched you do it."

"No," he repeated, shaking his head confusedly. "I didn't do that."

"Just like you carved up your son."

"No!" he yelled. "I would never hurt Aiden."

"But you did."

His hands balled into fists at his side. "No!"

"You kept a souvenir from your kills."

Uriah's pulse raced, the blood rushing to his head making him dizzy. "What?! No, I didn't."

"You put it where you kept the other mementos from the lives you destroyed." Cam's eyes slowly lifted to the ceiling.

"The attic . . ." Uriah bounded up the stairs.

Cam methodically got up and followed him.

Uriah threw open the attic door, falling to his knees and pulling out the jars hidden under the floorboards. He had found fetuses of his dead children under the attic floor after Ivy and Sammy had cleared the space for the community wide yard sale, along with Lilly's preserved body and his journal. He had left the jars and the journal there, unsure what else to do with them.

Uriah pulled out a jar smeared with blood, collapsing to the ground. "Oh God!" Through the blood he could make out brown eyes, a pair of ears, and a tongue. On the label, written in his own hand, read: Aiden Hanson. "No! I didn't, I wouldn't."

Cam crouched next to him, taking his hands. "You did."

The tears streaming down Uriah's face rivaled the storm outside. "No," he whimpered.

"I'm here to help you, Uriah. Repeat after me. I murdered Aiden."

"No," he said, fighting to pull his hands from Cam's grip. Hands free, he covered his face and sobbed into them.

Cam grabbed Uriah's arm, pulling up Uriah's shirt sleeve and yanking off the bandage to expose his oozing wound. "This cut was made a long time ago, by a dear friend of mine. It serves as a mirror into your soul. With each bad deed you committed it worsened. With every little lie, with every naughty thought, with every indulgence of your vanity, it festered."

Uriah looked at him through splayed fingers.

"Since I've been here, you've glanced at your reflection in objects around the house several times, evaluating your perfect face, taking pleasure in the angle of your cheek bones, the cut of your jaw. I watched you run your finger over the slight cleft in your chin, pleased with your morning shave. You have the smile of a man without nightmares because you *are* the nightmare."

"No . . . it's not true."

"It's in your blood. It's what you're destined to be. Your arm proves it. The evil has grown, and you can't control it anymore. To avenge the death of your son Joseph, you cursed the Hanson family. It made no difference to you it was Jeffrey Hanson who gave Joseph a new life, resurrecting him. You willingly enacted that curse, taking it into your own hands. You murdered and mutilated Aiden Hanson."

Uriah's words from the past rang in his head in a terrible tolling. *No mercy for you, your family, or this town. I have given enough. Leave it to the wrath of God, for it is written: 'Vengeance is mine, I will repay, says the Lord'.*

"Aiden was my son. He was a Leeds."

Cam jammed his finger into the wound in Uriah's arm. He winced in pain, pulling his arm from him. "Not by blood, he wasn't. And monsters like you always want blood. Look at the jar. Look at what you did to your son."

Uriah's sobs came in hiccups as he struggled to breathe. "It's all true . . ."

Abruptly Uriah stopped crying. He wiped his eyes with the back of his hand as the cut in his arm closed. No trace of the festering wound was evident.

"Titan is that you?" Cam beamed.

Uriah's face twisted into a wicked smile. "It's me Ben. I'm finally free."

CHAPTER THIRTY-NINE
The Garage

Weston pounded his palms against the steering wheel as he sang along to Rod Stewart's *Do You Think I'm Sexy* on the radio. He was pumped for his date, driving faster than he should in the rain, when he noticed out of the corner of his eye a Pomeranian running through the woods. "That looks like that stupid kid with the stupid hair's dog." He slammed on the brakes and pulled onto the shoulder of the road. "Ah shit," he said, sitting with his truck idling while he mulled over getting out in the rain to chase the dog. "Oh Wesley Wilham Weston, you're getting too soft." He slid on his raincoat. "I can't believe I'm going to be late picking up whatever her name is to help this dog." He zipped up his coat. "Who am I kidding, I was only going out tonight to make Pearl jealous, and she could care less."

He opened his door and whistled for the dog. The dog barked in acknowledgement and crossed the street. "Hey fleabag wrong way!" From the other side of the road the dog barked at him again. Wes looked both ways and crossed the street, determined to catch the dog even if it took all night.

Jeffrey pulled into Big Benny's driveway after dropping Elsa off at her house and Sammy, Zac, Mona, and Anita off at home. He assessed Benny's house through the sloshing windshield wipers. The lights were off, and Benny's SUV was missing. "I can't imagine he's still at the park. There's no way the kites can fly in this weather."

There was still no word from Stevie, and Issac was on edge. Danny, having come home, to only go back out with Mary to get pizza, blocked Mike's truck in. Issac couldn't wait any longer to hear from Stevie. As Stevie had taken his car, Issac had no choice but to ask Mr. Lopez, who he didn't know very well, for a ride to see if Stevie was at his father's house. Since he had to drop Elsa off, Issac didn't think he'd mind and was glad he didn't.

Issac pointed to the silver BMW in the driveway. "That's my car. Stevie may be here. Maybe they just lost electric."

"Yeah maybe," Jeffrey said. "I guess go knock on the door, if they're not home I can drive you back to Danny's."

Issac got out of the car, pulling the hood to his coat up. He was heading to the front door of the house when he noticed King Charles standing in front of the garage. He quickly changed paths jogging to the dog.

King Charles scratched at the garage door with yelping whimpers. Issac opened it. Jeffrey's curiosity coerced him out of his vehicle. He met Issac in the garage. He was drenched, thanks to his coat not having a hood. Water beaded down his hair and face. He did his best to push his wet hair behind his ears.

"What is it boy?" Jeffrey asked, knowing a thing or two about dogs thanks to his mut Hotdog. King Charles shook off and scratched at a rug in the center of the garage. "Okay boy," Jeffrey said, pulling up the rug and exposing a trapdoor in the floor.

Issac petted the dog's head. "Good boy. Is Stevie down there?" The dog barked.

"I'll take that as a yes," Jeffrey said, throwing back the trapdoor.

The dog bounded down the steps. Issac and Jeffrey followed. "Stevie," Issac yelled, "are you down here?!"

Stevie jumped to his feet, still feeling a little woozy. "Issac! I'm here. Cam and I are trapped. Call the police!"

Issac was already down the stairs and rushed to Stevie as soon as he glimpsed him. He caressed his hand through the bars. "When you didn't show up at the lake and you didn't answer your phone, I knew something happened."

Stevie wanted nothing more than to kiss Issac, but he remained focused. He had too. "Issac, I need you to listen to me very carefully. My father is mad."

Issac looked to Benny standing next to him. "It's not him," Stevie said. "He's somehow switched bodies with Cameron. I know it's crazy, I hardly believe it myself, but it's true." Stevie pulled Issac closer to the bars, pressing his lips to his, not able to resist. Issac looked so handsome when he was worried. "Issac, it's not safe for you here. I don't think my father would hurt me, but he's lost it, and I don't want you taking any chances. I need you to leave right now and bring as many cops as you can. Especially that feisty one Weston."

Reaching the bottom of the narrow stairs some moments ago, Jeffrey listened to Stevie's and Issac's conversation while continuing to evaluate the large cage surrounding Stevie and Benny. There was no door and the iron bars ran from floor to ceiling leaving less than six inches of space between each bar, making it impossible for an adult to squeeze through—even Stevie.

Jeffrey pulled out his phone, there was no cell reception.

"Let me see if we can break you out," Issac said.

"You can't, Cam and I have tried."

Stevie anxiously looked to who he thought was JD. "JD, please take him and leave now." He knelt to pet King Charles, "And take King with you."

"I'm Jeffrey."

Stevie's eyebrow corked. "Huh?"

"That's Mr. Lopez," Cam said, with Benny's husky voice.

"JD is my twin brother," Jeffrey added as an explanation.

"Oh, okay that makes sense. Please take Issac with you and get help."

Neither of them budged. Issac was too busy examining the cage. "This is strange."

"Yes, it's constructed by keys my crazy father's collected, now please go and get help!"

Jeffrey placed his hands on the bars and tugged, trying to pull a couple free. A pulse of energy coursed through Jeffrey's hands, giving off a blinding light. He struggled to pull his hands off the bars and was unable to. In the blink of an eye Jeffrey found himself inside the cage. He doubled over in pain, grabbing his stomach while his palms burned.

"What the heck just happened?!" Issac said, rubbing his eyes.

"It's the keys," they heard a voice say from the steps. Cam recognized it as his own voice and shivered.

Cam and Uriah stepped into focus. Their faces distorted by shadows cast by the series of lights in iron grates that ran down the center of the underground bunker.

"Uriah what's going on?" Jeffrey said, getting to his feet. His entire body was drenched in sweat.

Cam answered. "The keys were charged by heaven's energy. They and they alone can trap and hold a demon." Jeffrey's eyebrows furrowed. "That's right Jeffrey, we know what you really are. The cage proves it. It was built to hold someone very similar to you."

"Benny, let us out right now." Jeffrey was not quick to believe Stevie when he said Benny and Cam had switched bodies, however, now there was no doubt Stevie was right. Timid Cameron Franklin would never talk like that, and particularly not to him."

"Sorry Jeffrey, you're going to have to stay put. You're just what we need to catch the big fish."

"Sorry to break up the party," Weston said, coming down the steps like a bulldozer, "but I need to make this quick, I have a hot date waiting on me."

"As you wish," Benny said with Cam's voice, picking up Stevie's gun that had skidded across the floor when he had passed out. Before anyone could see what he'd picked up, Benny shot Weston, sending him tumbling down the rest of the stairs.

King Charles let out a fury of barks, before disappearing into the shadows of the bunker.

Benny pointed the gun at Issac. "No!" Stevie yelled. The gun fired. Issac fell to the floor by the side of the cage, his brown eyes wide open. Blood poured from the bullet hole in his neck pooling around him. He was dead.

Stevie collapsed to his knees pawing at Issac through the bars. "You killed him! Oh my God, you killed him!" With tears blinding his vision, he looked in his father's direction. "How could you do that to me?!"

"Maybe now you can understand why I would stop at nothing to bring Titan back."

Cam knelt next to Stevie, putting his father's meaty arm around him. "You didn't have to kill Issac. He was harmless."

"I'm not taking any chances this time around. I have no friends. JD taught me that. That's why I had to kill Elsa too."

"What?!" Cam choked out, tears already stinging the back of his throat.

"That's right. She's in the trunk," Uriah said with a sinister smile.

"Please tell me you're lying. Please tell me you didn't hurt her."

"I didn't hurt her, I killed her, and that's your fault Cameron. You should never have told her about me. You've left me no choice. I had to tie up loose ends. Neither of you gave me a choice. Your lovers knew too much."

Cam sat dumbstruck, silent tears welling over Big Benny's full cheeks.

Stevie ran his fingers through Issac's curls and spoke through gritted teeth. "I hate you so much. I wish Japhet Dean would have killed you that day with Titan."

Jeffrey's eyes flickered to Stevie. "What is he talking about," he mumbled under his breath. "No one calls him Japhet Dean."

Titan, in Uriah's body, crouched down on the other side of the bars to be face to face with Stevie. "Well, well, if Little Willy didn't grow up . . . Is that any way to talk about your old friend?"

"Old friend?" Stevie asked, swallowing a sob. He had never seen Uriah before and a man that looked like him would be hard to forget.

"Oh yes, your very good friend Titan Leeds. He ran his finger across Stevie's face plucking a tear from his cheek. "I look forward to getting to know you again, Willy."

Stevie pulled back from the bars, craning his neck toward his father. "You did it?!"

"I did, and Titan is just the beginning."

Benny situated the gun between the bars of the cell and pointed the gun at Jeffrey. "Sorry Jeffrey, like I said I'm not taking any chances, and we don't need you alive." The gun fired. The smell of the afterburn was all too familiar to Jeffrey. With a ringing in his ears, he collapsed to the floor as Cam and Stevie rushed to him. A bullet pierced his heart, his peacoat was soaked in blood, the smell of it filling the underground bunker. Cam checked for a pulse. Jeffrey Lopez was dead.

Benny tucked the gun into his jacket. "Let's go Titan, we have to get rid of Jeffrey's car before anyone sees it parked in the driveway." Benny stopped at Weston's slumped body by the stairs, handing his gun to Titan. He looked back toward the cage. "Behave now."

CHAPTER FORTY
Message from the Devil

Jeffrey opened his eyes to a monochromatic landscape. Everything was gray, including the sky and the rocky terrain that jutted off in different directions resembling a taxidermist's use of horns to create something new and horrifying.

In the distance sat what he assumed to be a castle. From his vantage point, he could see it reached high into the sky blurring with the horizon. The eastern wall was completely missing, due to decay or the aftermath of war, he wasn't sure. Things too large to be birds swarmed around the rocky turrets. There was no sign of the sun or a moon, however pieces of ash fell from the sky like snow.

Apart from his sense of smell, Jeffrey's senses were dulled to the point of nonexistence. He could smell the smoke laced air as if a great fire burned nearby, but that was it. His hand grazed his chest. He couldn't feel the blood that covered it. But he saw it; it too took on a gray hue along with his cadaver tinted skin. He felt nothing. The pain of the bullet tearing into him was gone.

He became aware of a traveler making their way to the castle. The traveler was bundled up in torn garments as if they were freezing.

"Hey!" Jeffrey called to the traveler, running to him.

The traveler stopped. Throwing off his hood, he smiled at Jeffrey. Jeffrey realized the traveler wasn't in torn garments, rather the garment was a quilt of human hair, mismatched and sewn together. Some of the patches were made from long hair, others short, some of the patches consisted of only human scalp, but they all took on the same gray hue.

Jeffrey took a step back. He recognized the traveler as the cloaked man in his dream, however in his dream he didn't see him in the poignant detail he now saw him in. He had not seen what made up the man's dark cloak or noticed how his alabaster skin seemed indestructible as if he was punched out from marble. The man's hair was as dark as coal and so were his eyes, which glinted like it.

"Nice to see you again Jeffrey, however you didn't have to come all the way home to say hello."

"Home?" he said, thinking of his dream and how everyone wanted to go home and blamed him for not being able to do so. Was this one of the truths hidden in his dream the cloaked man had alluded to? His father had alluded to? Did he subconsciously want to go home, but wouldn't let himself?

"I'm dead . . ." Jeffrey said, his hand once again going to the bullet hole in his chest. "I was shot. Just like in my dream."

The man approached, his cloven hooves not making a sound on the stone floor. He stuck his thumb and index finger into the bullet hole in Jeffrey's chest, plucking out the bullet. "It takes more than a bullet to kill a demon. And you're so much more than just an average run of the mill demon. Stop thinking like a man and start thinking like the god you are, my son."

Jeffrey sat up, grabbing his chest.

Cam in Benny's body left Stevie's side and ran over to him. "Mr. Lopez, you're alright! We thought you were dead."

Jeffrey got to his feet, refusing Cam's help to get up. "It takes more than a bullet to kill . . ." His voice trailed off not able to repeat his father's words. He knew he was more than human. He knew who his father really was. He just couldn't say it out loud yet.

Jeffrey opened his jacket and unbuttoned the first few buttons of his dress shirt. He wiped away the blood as best he could with his already blood drenched shirt. His bullet wound had healed. More than that, it was as if he never got shot. There wasn't even a little scar to mark the bullet's entry.

"Can you help Issac?" Stevie asked, teary eyed as he sat on the ground playing with Issac's curls through the bars that separated them.

"He's dead Stevie. He can't," Cam said, rejoining his brother by his side.

"He's JD's twin brother. I've seen stranger things."

"Maybe I can," Jeffrey said, approaching the brothers. Issac appeared how Joe did all those years ago on the shore of the lake as if he were merely sleeping. Stevie had closed his eyes and he looked oddly at peace. "There would be a cost. Similar to the cost of bringing Joe back."

"Wait, so if I believe all I've heard this week, you're the one who brought Joe Baker back after drowning?" Stevie asked.

"Yes. I'm also the one who caused all his nightmares and the need for someone to be drowned in the lake every year for him. Issac would have to pay a similar cost. The scales of life and death would be thrown off balance."

"What if you traded a life for a life?" Cam asked in a soft voice that seemed unnatural for Big Benny.

"I'm not a hundred percent sure," Jeffrey admitted, "but I think a fair trade would keep the scales balanced."

"Good," Cam said. "Take my life for Isaac's."

"But—"

Stevie interrupted Jeffrey. "And when this is all over, take my life to save Elsa."

"Stevie, you don't have to," Cam said.

"No, I do," he said, tears rolling down his cheeks. "I'm the lucky one. I get to say goodbye to Issac, you don't get that privilege with Elsa."

The brothers looked into each other's eyes and knew this was right, knew how much the people they loved meant to them. "It's settled then," Cam said, hugging his brother for the last time.

Jeffrey crouched next to Stevie. He reached through the bars and fished out the bullet lodged in Issac's neck. He thought about that day at Batsto Lake with Joseph. He recalled the injustice of it all. Joseph should never have been drowned by him and his brothers, just as Issac should never have been shot by Benny. He recalled his burning desire to change what he saw, to make Joseph live—to make Issac live.

A fire burned in Jeffrey's stomach, traveling into his chest and down his extremities. It hurt, but he didn't flinch. He remained focused on Issac, his hand still on his neck, his free hand finding Cam's knee. "A life for a life."

"It's working," Stevie gasped as the wound in Issac's neck stitched back together.

Issac bit by bit opened his eyes. His eyelashes fluttered as if he struggled to come back to the world of the living. Stevie clutched his boyfriend's hand through the bars. "It's okay Issac, I'm here."

Slowly, Issac sat up, his throat dry and his brain foggy. His hand traveled to his neck. Stevie didn't give Issac a chance to come to terms with what had happened to him. He pulled him to the bars, planting kisses all over his face, their lips locking in a long embrace.

Big Benny's lifeless body remained slouched against the bars.

"I've seen it all now," Weston said getting to his feet. "No wonder why Pearl's infatuated with you, you're the freak'n messiah."

"Wes!" Jeffrey jumped to his feet, startled at hearing Weston's voice. "I thought you were dead."

Weston opened his raincoat to show off his bullet proof vest. "I took your advice, Jeff. I thought wearing it on my date would be a conversation starter. Chicks dig a man whose being hunted by a serial killer."

Jeffrey smiled. He never thought he'd be happy to see Wes Weston alive.

"You didn't say anything about the concussion. You should've told me to wear a helmet," Weston said, rubbing the back of his head, where blood trickled down from a cut. "My head hurts more than my chest." He pulled on Issac's coat collar, "Come on Doctor Love, we don't want to be trapped down here when the crazies come back. They took my gun and I'm no good without my gun."

Stevie pulled Issac in for one last kiss. "Issac, I love you."

"I love you too. I'll be back."

"We have to leave before we can come back," Weston said. "And when we do, we'll be bringing the cavalry."

"Wes," Jeffrey yelled as they took the steps, "get my mother-in-law. Get Anita!"

CHAPTER FORTY-ONE
Transformation

JD walked through the woods, indifferent to the rain that pelted his shoulders. Usually, he enjoyed stormy weather. He saw the driving rains, the roaring thunder, the sizzle of lightning as the wrath of God and was happy he was angry. But not even this category seven storm could brighten his mood. He felt useless, a feeling he seldom felt. He had, in most scenarios, turned things around at the cost of others and coerced them to rely on him but he'd failed to protect Aiden and there was no coming back from that. He couldn't change the past or manipulate the future. Uriah was hurting and it was his fault. There was something different about causing pain when it was by your own hands, at your own design. When hurt was delt to you, it stung. And JD felt that sting with abandon, felt how very alone he was in the world.

JD was used to being alone, but the universe kept teasing him, giving him a taste of a happy life, to only pull it from him. He was accepted by Jeffrey, even sought after, then dismissed as some unwanted thing. It was the same way with Uriah. Pearl cared for him, if only for the life of a firefly. She had cared for him, to only throw him out of her life. Life was cruel.

"Some people are meant to be alone," he mumbled under his breath looking up to the dark sky and letting the rain drops strike his face. The barren branches stretched over the horizon, each branch forming the quilt work of nature. He took in the smell of the refreshing scent of the rain, wishing it could cleanse him like it did the trees.

A dog barked. JD's brown eyes locked onto the sound. A little way off he saw a white spot in the gloominess of the woods. He went to it.

"What's wrong my very wet friend?"

The Pomeranian evaluated him.

JD picked him up, bringing the dog close to his face until they were eye to eye. "Yes, as I thought, you *are* Willy's dog. And where is Willy?" The dog barked again. "Okay," JD said, placing the dog on the ground. The dog trotted a few paces away and looked back at JD. "I will follow you. Lead on." The dog bounded into the woods.

King Charles stood in the entrance of a small cave, wagging his tail. JD surveyed it. He made it a point not to come this close to Ben's property. They had an unspoken agreement not to bother each other and over the centuries, they had seen very little of each other after he had sent Titan to purgatory.

JD ran his hand over the cave entryway. He knew it was manmade. The design was too perfect. There was no signs of natural stalagmites or stalactites. He looked to the dog, his face as white as the moon peaking through the branches. "Into the cave we go."

His suspicion was correct, the cave was indeed manmade. As he walked downward into the Earth, small lights embedded in the cave wall, lit his way. Not that he needed them, he could see perfectly well in the dark. The smell of wet dirt overtook him, and he wondered how far underground they were, when he came to a wooden door. The door was old and decayed and from the looks of it had been that way for a long time. There was a small hole at the bottom of the rotten door where the rot had first seized the wooden planks. "I see," he said to King Charles. "This is how you got through."

JD took the door off the hinges; it came free easily. What was left of it, he left against the wall and continued onward. He heard the voices of

Willy, Issac, and Weston—and his brother. JD quickened his pace, King Charles trotting alongside him.

JD took in his surroundings before making himself known to his brother. He was sure Ben was behind this, which went against their silent agreement that stood for generations. He knew all too well how smart and manipulative Ben was, but yet Ben was in the cage with Jeffrey and Willy, and he was dead. He couldn't hear his heartbeat, someone had snuffed out 'his' magic that kept Ben alive for lifetimes. He knew of only one person that could have done that, and that was Jeffrey. Knowing that, JD still couldn't make sense of the situation.

Weston and Issac rushed up the stairs and he stepped out of the shadows. "Need some assistance brother?"

"JD!" Stevie said in a hushed shout, not wanting his father to hear him wherever he was. He reached through the bars for his dog. "Good boy." King Charles greedily accepted his caresses.

"Don't touch them," Jeffrey warned JD who was examining the bars of their cage with intense interest. "If you touch the bars, you end up inside the cage." He held up his hands so JD could see the burns on his palms, but they too had healed like his bullet wound. "You're going to have to trust me on this. Weston and Issac went to get help."

"How does he fit into this?" JD asked, looking at Ben's slumped corpse. "He no doubt created this," JD said, putting his hands close to the bars, sending little sparks into the air.

"Benny's not dead. He's still out there. He swapped bodies with his son Cam."

"Hmm . . .," JD said, mulling that over, his hand going into his pocket where he felt for his cigarette case. "Why would Ben do that? He loves his children. It's the one and only thing he and I have always shared and why I've left him alone."

"It's all for Titan," Stevie said, still caressing King Charles through the bars.

"Titan?"

"Yeah, he's back and I guess he's not into fat old men."

"I don't even know who this Titan guy is," Jeffrey said frustrated.

"He's a bad man," JD and Stevie said at the same time.

"JD, he's in Uriah's body," Jeffrey said.

JD's eyes flashed red, his hands going for the bars. "What?!"

Jeffrey took on an air of confidence, hoping it would calm down his brother. "We'll figure this out once Stevie and I are free. Benny built this cage to hold you not me. So let's not give him what he wants. Just wait for Weston to get back with help."

JD's face twisted in egotism. This cage cannot hold me. I will break it down and then I will rip Ben's throat out and make sure Titan stays dead."

"Don't JD," Jeffrey warned in a stern voice that he normally reserved for Sammy.

JD ignored his brother, putting his hands on the bars and pulling.

"Let go!" Jeffrey shouted as smoke came from JD's hands as they burned.

"I can't," JD said through clenched teeth. "The keys are sucking my energy. He looked to Jeffrey with scared eyes. "This isn't good."

The room shook, dust and debris shaking loose from the ceiling.

"I think he's going to bring the place down," Stevie said. King Charles barked as if in agreement.

Jeffrey tried to peel JD's hands off the bars. His brother's skin was as hot as fire, he had to pull away. "Tell me what to do," Jeffrey said urgently.

A flash of white light blinded them as an invisible energy pushed them back. The lights overhead exploded in a chain of pops that sounded like claps of thunder. Whimpering, King Charles ran back in the direction JD and he had come from.

It was dark, pitch dark for a few seconds before a series of emergency lights on the ceiling buzzed to life, casting everything in an eerie blue. JD was in the center of the cage doubled over in pain as Jeffrey had found himself.

"You alright?" Jeffrey asked, putting his hand on his shoulder.

JD's head rested on his knees. "Don't touch me," he said in a low voice that trembled with pain.

"The pain doesn't last long," Jeffrey told him. "It's something you probably don't feel often but it last only a few minutes."

"The keys drained me of my power," JD said labored. "I'm transforming. I can't stop it."

"Transforming?"

A wing punched through JD's coat compelling him to cry out in pain.

Jeffrey and Stevie took a step back, the marriage of fear and pity making them quake.

"JD tell me what to do," Jeffrey said, his tone laced with urgency.

JD's coat tore at the seams. Red skin peaked through his shredded clothing.

Another wing broke through with a ripping noise that made Stevie hug himself.

The pain shook his voice. "I can't stop it."

"There has to be something I can do," Jeffrey insisted. "How do you stop it?!"

Horns protruded from JD's dark hair twisting like vines. He bit back the pain, blood dripping from his bottom lip onto the floor. JD glanced at his brother, his eyes glowing red, his fingernails—claws that he drove into his own legs to try to regain control over his body. "I have to eat." His eyes darted to Ben's corpse.

Understanding what he meant, Stevie offered JD his father's body. "That old husk, please enjoy. My only regret is that you didn't kill him the night you killed Titan."

JD shook his head, sending his claws deeper into his calves.

"He's dead, it can't hurt him. Take what you need," Jeffrey said.

With his brother's blessing and with animal precision, JD leaped onto Benny's body. His claws tearing at his corpse.

"Don't watch," JD said in a deep voice that made Jeffrey hold his breath.

Jeffrey and Stevie turned around giving JD his privacy, not able to speak as they heard the sound of flesh ripping and ribs cracking.

Jeffrey only turned back around when he heard sobbing. The transformation had stopped, and JD was his old self once again. There were no signs of his horns, or wings, or red-tinted skin. The only hint at his transformation was his torn clothes.

JD leaned over Benny's body, tears mixing with the blood that covered his face. Jeffrey went to his brother, crouching next to him.

"I don't want this, Jeffrey. I don't want to be a monster."

Jeffrey swallowed tears, visibly effected by seeing JD vulnerable. "It's not your fault. You didn't ask to be like this." Jeffrey was in dad mode, wiping JD's face with his coat sleeve.

"I'm better now, thank you," JD said, pawing away his tears. "I haven't allowed myself to transform that fully since the first day I came into this world. I hate knowing what I really am."

"It's not what you really are."

JD held his brother in the frame of his thick lashes, lashes they both have. "It is my true face, Jeffrey. This face I wear now is yours and it's a lie. I know that now."

Jeffrey hugged his brother, the magnetic pull between them was impossible to ignore.

"This is my fault," Stevie said, his arms running up and down his arms. "I'm sorry . . . I told my father about the lightening and when you killed Titan all those years ago, I saw Titan's energy go into the baby you saved, and I told him."

"That baby was Uriah," JD said to Jeffrey.

"I guess that sort of explains why Benny was calling him Titan. He must have somehow possessed him," Jeffrey said.

JD nibbled on his lip, the metallic taste of blood blooming on his tongue. He glanced to Stevie. "What was that about you telling your father about the lightning? What do you mean?"

Stevie leaned against the bars to itch his back. "After a storm one night, one that had a lot of lightning, I saw the same energy coming off the lightning as I had seen when Titan disappeared into thin air. The difference being Titan was dark energy like a shadow and the lightning was bright white. I told my father what I saw and since then he's been flying kites with keys attached to them to collect what he calls Heaven's energy. I didn't know he was collecting the keys all of these years to trap you and make you pay for what you did to Titan, but I should've."

"He can't kill me," JD said, getting to his feet.

"No, but he can do worse," Stevie said. "He knows how much you hate to transform. I fear that's the least of his plans. I'm sorry. I owe both of you so much. You, JD, for killing Titan and you, Mr. Lopez, for bringing Isaac back. I wish there was something I could do to help."

"You already have," JD said, glancing at Ben's mutilated corpse as

Jeffrey took off his winter coat and covered it.

CHAPTER FORTY-TWO
Message From a Witch

"How long do you think until the cops realize Jeffrey Lopez never took a train?" Titan asked, pushing Uriah's wet hair out of his face.

"Days. We have days, but we should deal with Anita Gomez as soon as possible," Ben said, turning onto his street. "She's going to realize we double crossed her when the twins don't get better."

Ben's SUV swerved, changing lanes. Titan grabbed the wheel. "Hey, watch what you're doing!"

"Sorry, I just blanked out. I'm sorry."

Cam's heart pounded in his chest. It was so loud he heard it in his head. Somehow, he was back in his body. He didn't die. His mind was whirling. *My father's soul must have been attached to his body through the magic that made him immortal and when it died, his soul went with him, sending me back to my body.*

Out of the corner of his eye, he glanced at Pastor Leeds—Titan—in the passenger seat. With both hands on the steering wheel, he kept his eyes on the road, trying to act normal, but it was proving difficult. Cam was desperate to check the trunk. He played what his father said about killing Elsa on repeat in his head. *I'm not taking any chances this time around. I have no friends. JD taught me that. That's why I had to kill Elsa too.'*

Titan placed his hand on Cam's thigh. "It'd be just my luck, you finally bring me back and you kill us before we get to enjoy each other. Let's try to get to your house safely."

"Almost there. I think I can do that." Cam attempted a smile; his nerves were getting the better of him. He put his foot on the gas, they were close to the house now. He had to check the trunk before his heart exploded. The car hydroplaned. "Damn rain," he said, trying to sound like his father.

Cam pulled into the driveway and hopped out of the car, the rain coming down in sheets. He opened the trunk. A feeling like a boulder struck his heart, it felt like it was barely beating now, it thumped too slow and too low to be heard. In front of him was Elsa's corpse. Drops of rain beaded on her eyelashes, framing her open blue eyes in stillness. They were distant, cold—she was gone. He ran his hand down her lovely face and closed her eyes.

"That can wait," Titan said, running to the trunk of the car. He fought against the wind to hold his hood on. "Let's get inside." He closed the trunk, taking Cam's hand. "Come on Ben."

Cam sprinkled sugar into his tea methodically.

"Are you okay?" Titan asked, stroking his arm.

"Hmm?" He said, not looking up from his teacup.

"You couldn't keep your hands off of me at the rectory and now I can't even get you to look at me."

Cam's eyes lifted to Uriah's light blue ones. They reminded him of Elsa's. He faked a smile. "Sorry, I'm just hungry."

Titan laughed, throwing Uriah's head back. "I can tell by looking at the old you stuck in that cage, you wholly indulged yourself in my absence," he said patting Cam's stomach. "You better not spoil that body; your son is quite handsome." Titan sidled up to Cam until their thighs touched. He leaned in, pressing a kiss to his lips. "We waited a long time to be together again. I was hoping you'd find me a little more interesting than food." Titan pressed another kiss to his lips, his hands running under his T-shirt.

"Your hands are cold," Cam said, shrinking away.

Titan pulled his hands from his shirt and brought them to Cam's face. "Blow on them for me?"

Cam did as he was asked.

Titan put his warm hands to Cam's face and deepened his kiss, his hand sliding down to his fly.

A sizzling sound shot across the room before all of the lights in the house went out. Emergency flood lights turned on outside. Uriah got up, pulling Cam to his feet. "Looks like we caught the big one."

While Ivy and her friends waited for her grandmother and Danny to get back with dinner, they decided to make hot chocolate to warm themselves up. It had been a long while since Ivy had hot chocolate. It tasted better than she had remembered. It helped take her mind off the anxiety of having to part from Sammy, along with knowing Zac and Mona were with him in case Anita tried anything funny.

Ivy tossed a handful of mini marshmallows into her oversize mug of hot chocolate, grateful she was able to get any from Tammy who was hogging the bag.

"I love mini marshmallows," Tammy said, dumping more into her cup now that the first handful had melted.

It was going to take Ivy a while to get used to her talking through Rosa's body. It was strange to hear Rosa's voice and see Rosa's face but for it all to be Tammy. Rosa had been her first friend, and she'd thought her true friend and now she was gone.

"We can tell," Jesse said with his arm around Tammy as happy as he could be. He didn't seem to have any problems adjusting to the switch; if he did, he didn't show it. Tammy and Rosa couldn't have looked more different, but already Rosa seemed to be more like Tammy. Tammy ditched the braids, losing the nerdy look Rosa rocked, trading them in for confidence. The way Tammy talked, and her confidence, had always been a big part of Tammy's appeal and it was shining through Rosa.

"Mike, remember when we were little, we used to build marshmallow men out of marshmallows and toothpicks and have them fight?"

Joe smiled, brushing one of Mike's curls back. "That's really cute."

"My marshmallow man always won," she said, popping a marshmallow in her mouth.

"I'm not surprised," Jesse said, squeezing Tammy to him as if she just couldn't get close enough. Ivy was sure Jesse was going to be attached to her at the hip for a minimum of a year. Boyfriend and shield all in one.

Missing Sammy already, Ivy stirred her hot cocoa wondering how marshmallow men fought when she noticed her marshmallows rearranged themselves to form the word: Help. She glanced around the table, everyone seemed normal, no help needed. Her attention went back to her mug, the marshmallows now spelling: Benny, now: house, now: Elsa, now: is.

Ivy waited for the rest of the message, drumming her hands on the table, her pulse surging with every second the message was delayed. She knew who the message had to be from—Cam. Elsa was going to check on him after not hearing from him all day and she knew only Cam was a strong enough witch to spell things out in her hot cocoa, he was a magical prodigy after all.

Ivy couldn't take it anymore; her palm smacked the table. "Elsa is what!" she yelled into her mug.

"Um, Ivy, are you okay?" Tammy asked.

Ignoring Tammy, Ivy jumped to her feet. "We need to go now!"

"Where?!" Jesse said getting up, at her urgency.

"Elsa needs our help."

An electrical hiss engulfed the room. The pitch culminated with a pop and the lights went out.

"What's happening," Tammy said, clinging to Jesse's arm. The house was in total darkness except for the stream of light radiating from Joe's phone.

"Nothing," Jesse said kindly to Tammy, "the storm just kicked off the electric that's all. It's nothing to be afraid of."

Ivy tugged on Jesse's shirtsleeve. "Come on, we have to go. Mike give me your keys."

"This might be a bad time to remind everyone Danny blocked in my truck."

"Call Sammy," Jesse said.

Mike shook his head. "Not happening. The storm must've also messed with the cell tower. There's no service." As if on cue, they all took out their phones to check for service. Mike was right, no one was making any calls.

"We'll have to walk then," Ivy said. "Elsa's at Benny's. It's not far."

"Why would she be at Benny's?" Tammy asked. "Either way, let's go."

"Not you," Jesse told her. "You're staying here at the house with Mike and Joe."

"But Elsa," she protested.

Jesse ran his hands down her arms. "Whatever it is, Ivy and I will take care of it, right Mike?" he said with an authoritative stare that oddly resembled one of Mary Teller's infamous looks.

"Yep, she's staying here with me."

"With us," Joe corrected.

"*With us*," Mike repeated with a smile in Joe's direction.

Tammy crossed her arms over her chest. Ivy gave her credit; she was brave for someone who ended up dying the last time they were in a scrape.

Jesse turned to Ivy. "Danny has a generator in the basement. I'm going to turn it on real quick, so everyone doesn't have to sit in the dark."

Ivy nodded, gesturing for him to hurry up. She waited by the door as the lights hummed to life. Jesse emerged from the basement with two heavy duty flashlights and handed one to Ivy. "Ready?"

Tammy pulled him in for a hug. "Be safe."

"Always, I'll be back soon."

They were just about to walk out when Grams and Danny, with the Pizzas in tow, walked in. "It's raining cats and dogs out there," Danny told them shaking off like a dog.

"Better than elephants and mice," Mary said.

Danny burst into a fit of laughter.

"I'd say," Ivy said, rolling her eyes. She couldn't believe Danny laughed at her grandmother's joke. They were perfect together.

Mike took the pizzas from Danny.

"Hey kids, do you know what happened to the mirror?" Danny asked, noticing the glass was missing out of the foyer mirror as he hung his raincoat on the hook next to it.

"Sorry about that," Jesse said. "Ivy broke it. She said she'd replace it."

Ivy's eyes shot daggers at him. She wished she would've drowned *him* at the lake.

"What? You did break it," Jesse mumbled, under the weight of her stare.

"It's okay Ives, I should've replaced it a long time ago," Danny said, as if he thought Ivy was really upset and meant to console her. "It's just hard parting with things that have been in the family for so long. I gave that mirror to my son Japhet and his wife on their wedding day."

The Leeds last name was as common as Smith in South Jersey. Ivy had been trying to deny Danny's connection to the past. But there it was from his own mouth; Danny Leeds was in fact a 'Leeds'—was JD's grandfather—was Titan's father. Ivy thought she was going to be sick.

"That's a nice gift Danny, sorry it got broken," Ivy said, feeling very cold suddenly.

"Boy oh boy, did his wife love that mirror. Deborah would've combed her hair in it all day long if she could've."

Ivy's mind went to her dream of Deborah brushing her hair. She realized for the first time the mirror in Danny's foyer was the mirror she saw in her dream. The same mirror Deborah was brushing her hair in when the two cloaked men came to visit her.

Ivy shook off another chill. "Grams, I need to borrow your car."

"The heck you do! All the streetlights are out. It's a hurricane out there."

"Grams it's important," she said, trying to stress it without letting on to Danny it had to do with hocus-pocus.

"Fine," Mary said, dangling the keys in front of her granddaughter.

"Mary, I can't believe you'd let Ivy drive in this. It's dangerous."

"We'll be really safe," Ivy promised, snatching the keys and running out the door with Jesse before Danny could stop them.

CHAPTER FORTY-THREE
The Trunk

Titan pulled Cam to the front door. "Come, let's see if we caught JD." Cam hesitated. There was no way of telling if Ivy got his message, but either way he had to give her time to get there. He was in way over his head and all he could think about was getting Elsa to Mr. Lopez. He didn't know if Issac had, in fact, been saved but he had to hold out for hope. He needed Ivy to get the police before Elsa ran out of time. Titan going to the garage basement would complicate things. Help would arrive and have no idea they went underground.

Cam pulled Titan to his chest, wrapping his arms around him. "Let him wait, this is our world," he said, thinking it was something his father would've said.

Titan beamed. "There's my Benny."

Pearl was sympathetic to Tessa. She knew she had to go back to the asylum before she could be released. The best thing she could think of doing was to take Tessa to McDonalds. It had always made Pearl feel better when she was a kid and hoped it would make Tessa feel a little better now. The bottle of Vodka she finished off last night hadn't helped. It made things worse; she should've just gone out for a happy meal.

They were heading back to Pleasant Asylum when Pearl spotted Weston's truck parked on the side of the road. She pulled over, parking behind him. She knew from driving with him he would just pull over and pee, but she doubted he would do that in the pouring rain when he had a 'hot date' waiting for him.

Pearl dialed Weston; his phone went straight to voicemail. She leaned over her steering wheel, peering into the woods. It was hard to see anything in the rain. "Do you see Wes?" she asked Tessa.

Tessa wiped the condensation off her window. "No."

"I don't know," Pearl said, thinking out loud. "I don't like this."

"Maybe he got a flat," Tessa said.

"Yeah, maybe," Pearl replied, her mind still spinning, "but he would've fixed that himself in rain or snow. I bet you the dummy ran out of gas." Pearl knew Weston's affinity for waiting until he was on empty to gas up. It was something about hating other people pumping it for him, how New Jersey has it all backwards. "You don't mind a little detour, do you?"

"Not at all," Tessa said, taking a sip of her soda.

"This is probably useless," Pearl said, taking out her notebook. "I'm gonna leave him a note and take a quick drive to Benny's house to see if he's there. Benny's is the only place close to here, if he's not there, he's on his own."

Pearl scribbled: Heading to Benny's to look for you. She got out of her car, pulling up the hood to her raincoat and tucked the note under his windshield wiper.

Headlights flashed into the house. Cam sighed in relief; he didn't know how much further he could've taken the charade. He was sure Titan thought the sigh was in frustration, which worked to his advantage. "I guess we can't let whatever that is wait," Cam said, hopping to his feet and extending his hand to Titan. He took it, allowing Cam to pull him off the couch.

"You're right," Titan said, reaching for his shirt on the floor, "we should check it out. We don't want anyone spoiling our fun."

"Stay in the car," Pearl said to Tessa getting out of the Grand Vic. The rain was blinding, she strained to see. "Cam is that you?" she jogged toward him, her feet sinking into the mud. Every step sounded like a suction cup becoming detached from glass, popping and sucking.

She squinted. It was him, but he looked different from the last time she saw him. "Cameron, I've been looking for you. Did your brother and Elsa tell you?"

"Sorry Detective Steele, I've been busy."

"He's been very busy," Uriah said.

Pearl's eyebrows arched. She was surprised to see Cam with Pastor Leeds; she didn't know they were friends.

"Show her how busy you've been. Show her what's in the trunk," Uriah said.

"I don't think that's a good idea," Cam disagreed, trying to move his eyes to the side and twist his mouth as if to point at Uriah.

Pearl noticed the funny face but didn't understand what he was getting at. She, like most people, thought he was a little weird.

Pearl pushed the rain from her face. "What's in the trunk? She asked, glancing to Benny's SUV. The little hairs on the nape of her neck stood on end. Her hand moved toward her gun.

"Nothing," Cam said, continuing to make faces.

"Open the trunk," Pearl ordered. There was something about the way Uriah was smiling, how the flood lights wiped away most of his features until all she could see was his eyes and twisted mouth. "Open it now," Pearl said, her hand resting on her gun. She knew Cam had a delicate constitution, she didn't want to scare him to death, but she was ready.

Cam opened the trunk and stepped aside.

Pearl's eyes grew wide. "You killed Elsa."

Titan grabbed Pearl from behind. His hands encircled her throat and squeezed.

Pearl gasped, clawing at his hands. She attempted to shift his weight so she could throw him over her shoulder.

Cam grabbed Uriah's arm. "Stop, you're gonna kill her!"

"That's the idea." Titan released Pearl; she fell in a heap on the ground. "What's wrong with you? You strangled your son's lover in cold blood, and you have a problem getting rid of this one?"

"If she goes missing questions will be asked," Cam said, trying to calm down and act more like his father.

Titan eyed him, watching the rain drip down his blond hair and face. "We can't just let her go Ben, you open the trunk."

"That was your idea."

"With JD as our prisoner, we can make him do whatever we want. We can make all the suspicion go away. It's like you said, it's our world. Now let's go play."

Weston and Issac made it back to his truck. Weston noticed the piece of folded notepaper tucked under his wiper. He knew that paper, Pearl always carried her notepad with her. Even got him one, although he refused to use it saying he had a notebook in his head.

He pulled the note from the wiper. The paper crumpled in his hands thanks to the rain, but he could still read: Benny's house.

"Shit!" Weston yelled, jogging back in the direction of Benny's. His mind already zeroing in on what Jeffrey said about the bruises on Pearl's neck. He had been shot; Jeffrey had been right about that, he hoped he wasn't too late to save Pearl.

"What is it?!" Issac asked, following him.

Weston threw him the keys to his truck. "Get Anita and meet me back at Benny's. The Lopez house is the big one with a gate on Pleasant Mills Road, you can't miss it. And hurry!"

Weston jogged around the back of Benny's House, surveying the property. It was quiet, at least he couldn't hear anything besides the sound of rain: rain hitting the roof, rain rushing down the gutters, rain striking the top of his shaved head. Pearl's Grand Vic was in the driveway with the headlights on. He went around the back of the vehicle, crouching as not to be seen; he really wished he had his gun. The car was empty. He came around the front of the car and saw Pearl on the ground.

He rushed to her, falling to his knees. He turned her over on his lap. "I'm too late," he said, his tears mingling with the rain. His hand gently caressed her neck where a dark bruise had flowered.

"Wes, are you crying?" Pearl asked in a hoarse voice, trying to sit up.

"No," he said, blinking the tears from his eyes. "I was checking for a pulse." He helped her to her feet. "We should get you to the hospital."

"I'm fine."

"Fine, you're fine, but let's get you out of the rain before Tweedledee and Tweedledum come back."

Weston led her to the side of the house where they rested against it. The rain spilled over the soffit like a waterfall. Pearl massaged her neck. "It was Pastor Leeds."

"Yeah, from what I understand, not that I actually understand it, he's possessed by some guy named Titan. They have Jeffrey and that skinny kid with the long hair in some cage under the garage. Don't worry they're fine."

Pearl played it off that she wasn't worried, but she was. Wes, as always, was vague, and that made things worse. "*Possessed?*"

"If I'm being honest Chief, I have no clue what's going on. It's above my paygrade, but Jeffrey called for his creepy mother-in-law. Issac's getting her now, we just have to sit tight and wait."

"Tessa!"

"What about her?" Wes asked.

"I left her in the car."

"She's not there now," Wes said. "Hopefully she made a run for it when they weren't looking."

"Shit," Pearl said, feeling for her gun. "My gun's missing."

"Yeah, bastards took mine too."

Pearl exhaled, closing her eyes. "Elsa Tilton's dead. Cam killed her."

Weston shook his head. "Cam didn't do it."

Pearl arched an eyebrow. "Who did?" She held her breath, hoping he wasn't going to say JD.

"Big Benny swapped bodies with Cam. —Wow, that sounded bonkers," Weston said, shaking his head as if to reprimand himself. "I think I'm gonna beat you to that early retirement."

"Do chicks dig a man who's retired?"

"Come on Pearl, we both know I only care what one woman thinks."

She lowered her head, staring at the mud on her boots. "I like a man in uniform.”

"Yeah, I know,” he smirked, "but is it the blue uniform or the pinstriped kind?”

CHAPTER FORTY-FOUR
Family Reunion

"**D**o you really think Sammy's grandmother would hurt him?" Zac asked Mona as they watched Sammy and his grandmother talk at the kitchen table by candlelight. Anita planted a kiss on the top of Sammy's head. "She seems like she really loves him."

"The people you love can cut you the deepest," Mona said, keeping her eyes on Sammy.

Zac put his hands in his hoodie. "You're talking about Jesse?"

She nodded.

He bowed his head, letting his brown hair fall over his eyes. "Do you still love him?"

"I will always love him."

Zac knew he was dead, it was hard to forget these days with everyone getting older and him remaining the same, in the same outfit, but he still hoped to have a girlfriend one day. He really liked Mona; he would've liked her even if he was mortal and she was a ghost or vice versa. He understood why Jesse loved her, because if he was being honest with himself, he did too.

Jesse was his good friend, but a part of him would always hate him for what he did to Mona and because she still loved him.

Mona turned to Zac, as if she sensed the shift in his mood. "Because I love Jesse doesn't mean there's not room in my heart to love others." She took Zac's hand out of his hoodie. He did all he could do to make sure his chest didn't bleed like it had before he learned to control his emotions. "Why do you think I'm here Zac?"

He didn't look at her. "To make sure Sammy's grandmother doesn't try to kill him."

"I meant, why do you think I'm on this plane?"

His eyes lifted to hers. They were dark and lovely, like her hair that flowed over her shoulders in ripples. "I don't understand."

"When I chose to forgive Jesse, that choice opened the door to the next life for me. I can see my father and mother and tribe waiting for me on the other side."

"It did?" Zac asked in a panic.

"Yes, I can see it even now. I can take it when I choose to."

His eyes searched hers. "Um . . . are you going to leave?"

"No."

"But I thought you missed them," he said, thinking of his own mother and cousin who had been murdered.

"They will always be there. I have decided to stay with you."

His eyes widened, tears or what felt like tears, welled in his eyes. "Me?"

"I watch over the twins, because they remind me of myself, but I stay because of you."

He swore he could feel his cheeks reddening as they had done when he was alive.

"I will stay with you until we can cross over together."

"Mona, I know I look like a little kid, but I'm not anymore. And I just want to say . . ."

She pressed her lips to his, a spark of energy was shared between them. "I love you too, Zac."

He beamed. "You do? You love me? Dorky me?"

Her eyes smiled. "What's not to love. You're kind, thoughtful, and brave."

"Yeah, I am," he said with a grin that turned into a toothy smile. "I love you too, Mona." He pressed his own kiss to her lips, the same spark igniting between them.

A truck flew up the Lopez driveway, they could hear the roar of the engine and the exhaust.

"It's Weston's truck," Zac said, looking out the window.

"With no Weston," Mona pointed out.

"Sammy something's up!" Zac yelled.

Sammy reached the front door before Issac could knock.

"Sammy, I need your grandmother!" Issac said out of breath.

Sammy parked behind Mary Teller's station wagon which had pulled into Benny's driveway moments before them. "What's Grams doing here?" he asked Isaac, wishing he would've let Zac and Mona come. He had a bad feeling growing in the pit of his stomach, but he'd insisted they stay in the event Weston made it back to the house. With the cell tower down there was no way to get in touch with him. Weston would most likely be shocked to see Zac alive, now that Sammy had given him the sight, but Sammy thought it was the best bet.

"I don't know," Issac said with a shrug.

Ivy got out of her grandmother's station wagon and ran to Sammy's Hummer, yanking open the driver's door before Sammy could open it himself. "I'm glad you're here, hurry Elsa need's our help."

"She's dead," Pearl said in a low voice from behind Ivy.

"What?!" Ivy said, turning around to see Pearl and Weston. They were both soaked. Pearl's hair clung to her face and neck like dark tendrils, where Ivy noticed bruises.

Sammy was out of the Hummer, hugging Ivy. The rain had gone from a torrential downpour to a little pitter-patter, but it sounded so loud in Ivy's ears. She felt faint. Tears silently fell from her eyes. After so much time spent hating Elsa, she'd ended up liking her, really liking her. She was her friend and now she was dead. "Cam, is he okay?"

"He's dead too," Weston said.

Anita's eyebrows arched in surprise, lifting her tired face. "Dead," she repeated to herself, from the front passenger seat, where she twisted the loose rings around her thin fingers.

Ivy's knees buckled. Sammy supported her, letting her rest her body against his, but she could feel the tremble in his arms. "Teller, are you alright?"

Jesse stood miserable and silent.

"We're too late," Ivy said in a near whisper.

"Not to help my dad," Sammy said, tears glazing his eyes.

"Your dad?" she asked, her eyebrows furrowing. It dawned on her, that's why he was there. Sammy didn't get Cam's message, how could he? He didn't know the truth about Cam, that was a secret she shared with only him and Elsa. "What are you talking about?"

"He's trapped in the garage basement with Stevie."

"What are we waiting for," Ivy said, her strength returning to her as if by magic. She wasn't going to let anyone else die today. They ran to the garage. Ivy's mind was working on overtime as she tried to figure out what was going on and why Elsa and Cam were dead. It was time for action; she'd save Sammy's dad and then ask about the how and why.

Anita followed behind, her steps methodical, her delicate fingers continuing to twist her silver rings, clockwise, now counterclockwise, but always spinning.

"I don't know how much help we're gonna be without our guns," Weston said to Pearl. "But I want to see the guy who put those bruises on you go down and we should be there in a professional capacity as back up, or moral support, or eyewitnesses, or just because I'm curious as all hell."

Tessa ran out of the woods to Pearl. "Thank goodness you're okay! I thought they killed you."

"Tessa," Pearl said, taking her hand and looking her over with a protective eye, "are you okay?"

She nodded. "I ran and hid; they didn't see me."

Pearl normally would've told Tessa to wait in the car but since she wasn't sure where Uriah and Cam were she opted to keep her by her side. She linked arms with her. "Come with us."

Weston opened the trap door, insisting he'd be the first one down the steps. "I may not have my gun, but I have a bullet proof vest and feel legally obligated as an officer of the Pleasant Mills Police Department to go first."

Pearl shook her head, she could do without the declaration of intent. "Move it, Wes."

Weston led the way making sure to shield Pearl and Tessa just in case someone was waiting for them at the base of the stairs. Wes gave the all-clear with two thumbs up.

Anita came down the steps with Sammy, Ivy, and Jesse trailing close behind. Anita evaluated the situation with careful eyes, seeing JD standing near Jeffrey, his shirt torn to ribbons, blood on his face and hands. She also saw Benny's dead body, no coat could hide that. When Weston said Cam was dead, she thought he meant Benny in Cam's body, not the real Cam locked inside Benny—not her son.

Sammy ran to his father.

"Back up Sammy! Don't touch the bars."

"Okay," he said. "I sense their energy, it's wild."

"Me too," Ivy said, examining the odd construction of the bars.

"What happened to Benny?" Sammy asked, his eyes flickering to JD's blood covered face.

"It wasn't Benny. It was Cam, they swapped bodies," Jeffrey said.

Stevie's eyes were like slits. "Ask your grandmother Sammy. She's the one who swapped their bodies," He turned his attention to Anita. "You're lucky I'm trapped in here old lady."

"What's he talking about Abby?"

"Not now Samuel Cameron. We have to figure out how to open this cage, there is no door."

Sammy's face scrunched, transforming his eyes into blue crescents. He hated it when she called him by his full name. It had always bothered him he was named after his uncle, a magical prodigy, whose memory he could never live up to. Despite coming into his magic, he disliked being called that more than ever.

Stevie scoffed. "Oh what, you don't want your grandson to know that you murdered my brother. I guess that shatters the sweet grandmother persona."

"He was not your brother," Anita said her voice like a whip.

"He was more my brother than he was your son!"

"Your son?" Sammy asked, his face twisting in confusion.

"That's right Sammy, Cam's your long-lost uncle. My father, Big Benny, did some face voodoo on Cam to protect him from her, after the first time she tried to kill him," Stevie said, pointing at Anita through the bars as if that confirmed it.

Sammy's eyes darted to his grandmother. "Abby?"

While they talked about things he didn't understand, Weston pulled on each bar of the cage, searching for a weak point.

"That's right Sammy," Stevie said, ignoring Weston as he pulled on the bar next to him. "Cam told me all about it. She kills the males in the family to take their power to keep the women in the family healthy. When she killed her brother, she brought a curse on the family that effects the women only. She made a deal with my father. He was supposed to break the curse and she'd swap bodies for him. But the joke's on her. He didn't break the curse. Only her death can do that. He just wanted Cam's body."

Enzo's warning rang in Sammy's ears, but in his warning, he never mentioned a curse.

Anita fixated her stare on JD, who had been quiet. "I was under the impression Benny's body couldn't die. I thought he gained his immortality from you demon."

"It's true Ben's body gained his immortality from me, but he never asked for eternal youth. He aged to an old man and that's how he would've stayed for eternity, but there are other beings besides myself that have the power to break my contracts." His eyes flickered to Jeffrey.

"It matters not," JD said dismissively. "Ben's immortality could never have held a curse like the one you brought upon your family; a thing I am sure Ben knew. To think that Ben could transfer your curse to the Leeds's blood line is laughable. I thought you were a better witch than that Anita Gomez."

Anita's fingers went back to spinning her rings. "So it's true, he deceived me to get a younger body."

"Yeah," Stevie said, "for some crazy witch, you sure are stupid."

"Yes, it would appear so . . . And now Samuel Cameron is dead."

"You're just sorry it wasn't you who killed him."

Ivy's eyes flashed to Sammy. If Anita didn't drain Cam's magic that meant she would be after Sammy.

Sammy nibbled on his bottom lip, the way he did when he was in thought. He had known Cam for what felt like all his life. The idea that Cam was his uncle seemed impossible. This whole time he was hidden right in front of him, and he never knew. He directed his anger at JD. "You killed Cam!"

"No, he didn't," Jeffrey said. "I did, with his permission. I traded his life force with Isaac's to bring Issac back."

Issac sucked air, his hand running over his neck in remembrance. He did die. He had a faint impression of dying but didn't understand how that could be right. Yet it was true, he had died. Cam had given up his life for him to come back. Issac and Stevie locked eyes. Stevie mouthed, "I love you." "

"What Dad?!" Sammy said in shock.

Jeffrey combed his dark locks back, attempting to hide his shaking hands. "It appears I *can* bring back the dead."

Ivy's jaw dropped. "It all makes sense now—how Joseph was brought back and why the Midwife locked his power away. With that kind of power in the wrong hands, in JD's hands," she said in a murmur, her eyes darting to him behind the bars, "they would be unstoppable."

"Tell me he's kidding," Pearl whispered to Weston who was on his last few bars. "Nope, saw it myself, Jeffy Boy is on a whole new level, but I'm still gonna give him a hard time because he got himself trapped in a cage like a dumb dog."

Tugging on the last bar of the cage, Weston cleared his voice to get the attention of the others. "It's official, there's no weak point in the cage, that means the freaks and the geeks are up to bat. So let's do it quickly, I have a date I'd still like to make."

"You can't be serious," Pearl said. "You're soaked and covered in mud."

"I'm always serious," he said with a wink. "Chicks dig a man that just came from a crime scene."

Ivy didn't think of herself as a geek, but she was definitely a freak. "They're indestructible," she said, her eyes going to Sammy to back her up.

"That's not possible," Stevie said. "We can't be trapped in here forever!"

"Figures," Weston said with a sigh. "We have all sorts of weirdos down here and not one of them can do a thing. I have a saw at the house that I know can cut through these bars, and then we'll see how indestructible this cage is. I'll be back."

"I hate to burst your bubble Wes," Pearl said, happy to do just that, but the powers out, remember?"

"Danny has a generator we can bring over," Jesse said.

"Now we're talking," Wes grinned, as if power tools turned him on. Tessa tried to conceal her smile, Pearl didn't. "Well, there we have it. Let's go get the saw and cut our own door."

"A saw won't work," JD said.

Pearl's eyes landed on JD, she had been trying to avoid his gaze and Jeffrey's. She was worried, very worried. Looking at them only acted to perpetuate her anxiety and with her migraine that now reached epic migraine status, she didn't want to risk permanent bodily harm.

"Anita," Jeffrey said, "is there anything you can do?"

Anita, who had been staring at Benny's mutilated corpse, locked eyes with Jeffrey. "How could you Jeffrey," she said, her voice stern.

"We're back on that," Weston groaned.

"How could I?! He asked me to save Issac. He asked me to give his death purpose."

She had promised the same thing to Cam. The words stung with a new meaning.

Uriah and Cam came into focus, the emergency lights overhead painting them in a blue glow as if they were ghosts.

"Don't be too upset Anita," Titan said through Uriah, coming from the tunnel JD had taken to get into the bunker. "There's plenty of time to join him."

Sammy's eyes widened. "I must be the worst witch ever. I can't believe I couldn't see through the magic. Cam looks just like my mom." His eyes went to his grandmother as he muttered to himself. "It's all true, Enzo's murder, Cam's attempted murder as a boy, and me being in danger."

"Hi Stevie," Cam mouthed with a wink.

Stevie scrutinized him. "Hi Cam," he mouthed back with a flutter of his eyelashes.

Cam nodded, relieved to see Issac was indeed alive.

"You're a terrible shot," Titan said to Cam, seeing not only Jeffrey was standing, but Issac. "What's wrong with him?" he asked, pointing at Benny's corpse.

Stevie sat down next to his father's dead body, shielding the part Jeffrey's coat didn't cover, hoping his brother had a good plan. "He cried himself to sleep."

Uriah smiled at Ivy, drinking her in. "Hello, Ivy."

"He's not Uriah," JD said to Ivy. "It's Titan."

"You spoiled my fun JD, how rude." He captured Ivy in the frames of his lashes. "Did you miss me?"

Uriah had always been beautiful to her. Before she knew he was her son from a past life, to her mortification, she'd had the hots for him, but now he looked so different. His kind face was cruel and sharp, he looked as evil as she knew Titan was.

"Ironically," Titan said, grinning, "I have fulfilled my promise to you and to JD and have watched over Uriah these many, many years. I was always with him, the little devil sitting on his shoulder and whispering in his ear." He scoffed, "You really thought that Lenape medicine man could drive *me* out? He tried, but there was just a pinch of my essence left and with Uriah's misdeeds over the centuries I was able to grow powerful again."

"I'm only going to say this once," Ivy said, planting her feet on the ground. "Let Uriah go." Ivy swallowed hard, surprised she called him by his first name. It was as if the Midwife was standing against Titan with her.

"I like this body," he said, rolling his shoulders. "And the best part about being in it is that none of you can hurt me, not even you JD."

"If you're Titan, where's Pastor Leeds?" Sammy asked, getting up to speed as Ivy's mind raced to come up with a plan or anything at this point.

"He's in here with me."

"And that's where he's staying," Cam said, hugging Uriah from behind and planting a kiss on his cheek, keeping up the ruse he was Ben. Cam's hands slid up his chest sensually, before putting him in a full nelson. "Quick Ivy, do something!"

Everyone looked around confused, no one more so than Titan.

"I'm Cam! I'm back in my body! When Mr. Lopez brought Issac back, I was in Benny's body. It killed him and sent me back to mine. Sammy, Jesse, help me hold him!"

They rushed to help Cam. Ivy felt exulted having him restrained in front of her, like he'd done to the Midwife at the Hell's Fire Club. "You deserve to die Titan," Ivy said, her mind going back to him trying to hurt Baby Uriah.

Titan spat. "And you get to decide that Ivy Teller, do you?" Or does he get to decide," Titan said, his eyes flashing to JD. "You're not God, you don't get to choose my path for me. I hold all the power. Now let go of me before I have JD kill every last one of you. Ben and I had wanted to make this switch incognito, but it's too late for that. So you can learn to live with it or you can all join Elsa. This is a one-time offer: Leave now and live or stay and die."

"You sound scared Titan," Ivy said smugly.

The corners of Uriah's lips twisted into a malicious grin. "You should know me better than that Ivy. I always have the upper hand."

"I've been wanting to punch that face since I met Uriah Leeds and now he finally has the personality that warrants it," Weston said to Pearl cracking his knuckles.

Titan's attention was on JD. "I have something I want you to do for me."

JD sneered. "I will never do anything for you."

"I think you'll soon realize you have no choice," he said, winking at Ivy. "JD, I want you to kill someone for me."

"Pearl, we should get you out of here," Weston whispered. "I don't like where this is going.

"Jesse, quick," Ivy said, "give me your knife." She wasn't taking any chances.

"I left it at the house when I got changed out of my wet clothes."

Sammy pulled out his Swiss Army knife.

"Cut his arm below the elbow like we saw in our dream," Ivy ordered, taking to heart what Sammy said about learning from the past and doing what the Lenape boy had done all those years ago when he had tried to rid Uriah of Titan's influence.

Jesse pulled up Uriah's coat sleeve while Cam continued to hold Uriah, who wasn't putting up much of a fight, in fact, he seemed amused.

"The evil in Uriah was never JD, it was Titan," Sammy said to himself relieved, making a deep incision where hours ago an open wound had been.

Uriah laughed a high pitch, hysterical giggle that filled the room. "Don't you see, it's too late for that. I am Uriah Leeds, and he is me. We are one and the same. And now it's time for a show of my power. JD, I want you to kill Cam for me."

Startled upon hearing his death sentence, Cam loosened his grip on Uriah. Uriah wormed out of their hold, giving space between himself and everyone else. "You should never have hurt Ben. And you should never have betrayed me."

JD twitched.

"What's wrong?" Jeffrey asked.

Uriah laughed again, the angles of his face highlighted in the blue light overhead. "You and your brother will soon learn that in that cage you have no will of your own. The cage is constructed with Heaven's energy and Uriah's flesh and blood. Ben made it so I, and I only, can control whoever is in the cage.

He looked down at his bleeding arm, laughing to himself. "For generations, Ben has collected energized keys and samples of Uriah's physical body, rummaging through trash cans to get his discarded bandages, hair clippings, you name it." He smiled a cruel smile that made Ivy instinctively take a step back. Uriah had never used such a smile; it spoke a thousand words of cruelty.

Titan kept his eyes on JD, not blinking as his smile continued to distort Uriah's handsome face. "It's all been worth it to see that look in your eyes JD. It's about time you knew your master. And there's more. I was going to have Ben do the honors, but seeing that he's not with us right now, I'm sure he would understand. That night you banished me he promised you your eternity would be as lonely as his. How did he do?" Titan's smile reached Uriah's eyes, his voice seething. He glanced at Ivy, before refocusing his attention on JD. "Ben scrambled her brain, ensuring she would never remember you. You will never be able to get her back. You will never have what you took away from us. You will face eternity alone."

Ivy's eyes flickered to Cam. She knew what Benny had done to her because it was the same thing he had done to Cam. It wasn't that she didn't want to remember JD and Uriah, it was that Ben made her forget.

JD doubled over in pain much like he had when he was about to transform. He was fighting Titan's command to kill Cam, but he was losing the fight. He wrapped his arms around his legs, twisting himself into a human knot.

Titan's gaze landed on Jeffrey. "I'm impressed with your little ability. I can have a lot of fun with that. Issac looks good as new after being shot which is lucky for everyone else. If you would've cost me Ben, I would've burned this town to the ground with everyone in it. That being said, I want you to bring Ben back."

"He's dead," Jeffrey said, his neck jerking to Titan with indignation.

"Yes, and you resurrect the dead. Now bring him back!"

A sharp pain brought Jeffrey to one knee.

"Dad!" Sammy shouted.

"What are you going to do with him, you can't bring him back like that. He's hardly a corpse."

"He won't be for long because Anita is going to swap his body for me." Titan inspected everyone like he was window shopping at the mall. "Let's see," he said, "who would make the best vessel for Ben?"

"Jesse—too tall, Wes—not enough hair, Stevie—too much hair. . . ." He smiled when he came to Sammy. "Sammy's perfect. I love those eyes."

Ivy jumped in front of Sammy like a human shield, her arms and legs extended, her fingers splayed. "Over my dead body."

"That can be arranged."

"Take my body again," Cam said, his eyes flashing to Sammy before returning to Titan.

"That's very noble of you, since either way you find yourself dead, but as Ivy will tell you, I don't do favors for someone who's betrayed me. — I crush them. You never should have deceived me. For that, you will die and so will your nephew."

"I can't fight it any longer," JD said in a low voice to Jeffrey. "Uriah is my son; the pull of his command is stronger on me."

Stevie rubbed his shoulder, "JD please try."

JD bit clear through his bottom lip in one last attempt to gain control of his will. Fresh blood trickled down his chin. He outstretched his hand, flexing his fingers. "I'm sorry Stevie, I've lost control."

A ball of energy resembling a miniature tornado came hurling through the bars in Cam's direction. Anita moved in front of it, as if she had known it was coming. She, along with Cam, were knocked to the floor.

Cam rolled his mother off of him. "Mamá!" he said, his eyes going to the gushing wound in her stomach. Her hand went to his face. "This is right," she said. "Now end the curse. Do it quickly before I die and know that I am sorry Samuel Cameron."

Titan sneered with Uriah's lips, enjoying the show, knowing he could make Ivy do the body switch for him and anticipating enjoying making her submit to his will.

Pushing past Issac, Sammy rushed to his grandmother's side, taking her other hand.

"I can't do it," Cam said, tears running down his face.

Anita squeezed Sammy's hand with the little strength she had left. "I must ask this of you Sammy. This will save your sisters, do it and know that I love you all the more for your sacrifice. Take my dagger from my purse and plunge it into my heart. Do it now. You are ready for this. You are the witch I always knew you would be. I am proud of you, my Sammy."

Sammy wore a mask of grief as he took the dagger out of Anita's purse. "I love you, Abby." The dagger hovered over her heart as he readied himself. He brought the blade down hard with all his strength, stabbing his grandmother through the heart. He let his hands linger on the hilt of the knife, his heart heavy, his chest heaving. She was dead, and he had killed her.

Jesse seized the moment, ramming Uriah's body into the cage. Sparks ignited.

"Idiot, the cage answers to me," he said to Jesse who held him to the iron bars to the best of his ability.

"You're still part demon and that means it can weaken you."

"Jesse Richards, you're brilliant!" Ivy praised.

"Finally, something I can help with," Weston said, rushing to help Jesse. Weston pinned Uriah's arm to the bars. "I want to let you know that I have hair, I shave it," he said, insulted his body wasn't chosen as the best replacement for Ben.

Pearl coiled her body around Uriah's leg to stop him from moving. "Seriously Wes!"

Issac pushed Uriah's shoulders against the cage. The sound of flesh sizzling filled the bunker.

JD and Stevie, from inside the cage, helped to lock Uriah's arm to the bar. Jeffrey followed suit, latching on to Uriah's other arm, though his strength was greatly diminished, as he was still fighting Titan's order to resurrect Big Benny.

The smell of burning flesh filled the bunker snapping Sammy out of his head. His eyes traveled to Uriah pinned to the cage then back to his grandmother. Cam put his hand on his shoulder. "Thank you, Sammy."

He nodded, tears beading on his thick lashes. He pulled the dagger from his grandmother's heart and placed it over her chest. Sammy closed his grandmother's eyes and kissed her forehead. He glanced to Cam, "Let's end Titan for good."

Sammy and Cam stood by Ivy's side, careful not to get too close to the cage.

"We need to drive the spirit out, like we saw in our dream," Ivy said to Sammy. "In that, the heat of the fire weakened him, just like the cage is doing now."

"Where are we going to put him. Is it safe to let him into the world untethered and risk him finding a host?" Sammy asked. "Remember in the dream vision, the shadow escaped into the woods and the Lenape boy said the evil would die as long as it doesn't find a host. But we're all hosts!"

Tessa stepped forward. "Place his spirit in me. I can hold him with my ability. You can't let Titan's energy run wild. I have experience with ghosts and all ghosts are is energy."

"And you also got stuck behind a mirror for over a decade," Jesse said.

"I have learned since then. I'll be able to wall him off." She turned to Ivy. "Do it Ivy, I'm your only choice, he could easily possess anyone here."

Ivy knew she was right, that was why she had met Sky Wolff out in the middle of the forest when they tried to drive Titan from baby Uriah.

"Okay Tessa," she said, not able to think of a better option and wishing she had more time. Tessa did have Tammy's ability; so maybe this would work. In Tessa's body, Titan wouldn't be Titan, he would just be energy—negative energy, but still only energy. What choice did she have? Ivy was grateful Jesse made Tammy wait at the house, she would've wanted to take this on in place of her mother.

"Make an incision on Tessa's palm," Ivy ordered.

"This is going to hurt a little," Sammy said, taking Tessa's hand while everyone else kept Uriah pinned to the cage. He dragged his knife across Tessa's palm. She didn't wince.

"I wouldn't celebrate a win yet," Titan laughed. "This isn't over! It will never be over. In a few centuries we'll be doing this again! I will always be part of Uriah!"

Ivy focused her energy over the cut in Uriah's arm. Sammy and Cam joined her. Uriah's body rived in pain from the bars burning him and from Titan clawing to stay put in his body. A dark entity, like an oil spill, seeped from the cut in his arm, suspending in the air. Uriah went limp. Together, Ivy, Sammy, and Cam directed the dark spirit toward Tessa. As if the inky shadow could see the opening in her palm, it raced into it.

"It's over," Ivy said, "You can release him. Jesse helped Uriah to the ground, where he sat on his knees.

"Are you okay?" Ivy asked, crouching in front of him. His arms and back were covered in burns.

Uriah lifted his eyes to her. "I'm okay." His beautiful face was back. His kind eyes and soft smile were the same as they had always been. Ivy hugged him; he let her, despite the pain. "Benny killed Aiden, so that I would think I did it. It caused a break in my psyche, giving Titan the opportunity to seize control of my body. I'm so sorry, this is all my fault." Tears freely ran down his face. Again, Ivy thought he looked like an angel. "I killed Bishop Baker," he said, glancing to Pearl. "I killed him for abusing Lilly as a girl. I put the idea in his head to pull the trigger. Benny was the one who mutilated him to help sell the story I was losing my mind."

"Ideas in heads, that sounds like a lot of nonsense," Pearl said to Uriah. "We're a reputable police station Pastor Leeds, that's enough of that. Right Wes?"

"Right Chief."

Pearl's eyes darted to Jeffrey, who was standing tall now that he no longer felt the pull to resurrect Big Benny. His eyes said thank you and much more. Pearl's focus found JD. She knew she would always protect his family. He smiled at her, his eyes coming alive in the blue hue of the emergency lights.

Jesse noticed JD wasn't the only one smiling. Tessa wore a grin that seemed different from the smile of the meek woman he had thought her to be. It was as if this smile belonged to someone else. "Tessa," he said, "are you okay?"

"Yes Jesse Richards, I am perfect. And that wouldn't have been possible without Ivy Teller."

Ivy's dark eyes shifted to Tessa, there was something about the way she said her last name that made the hairs on her arms stand on end like she just touched one of those magnetic balls.

"It's good to be free. I've been in the well for centuries feeding information to Daniel, apart from the short time I enjoyed Lilly's body."

"Mother," JD said through clenched teeth.

"Crap," Ivy mumbled.

"Wes, we have to get the kids out of here. She's the woman who brought the church down," Pearl said in a whisper.

"What happened to Tessa?!" Jesse said, his chest tightening like his heart was in a vice.

"I happened. I had made contact with Tessa many times while she was at Daniel's house. We became so acquainted, she heard my voice even when she wasn't there. I'd whisper the future to her, just as I told Daniel many things yet to come. I told Tessa her daughter would be murdered."

"That's the message Tessa got from the voice she kept hearing. The message she never wrote down in her journal: Tammy would be murdered," Jesse said to Ivy.

"One day Tessa was alone in Daniel's home, standing in front of the mirror in the foyer. I told her I could save her daughter if she let me out of the mirror." Tessa's mouth twisted into a wicked grin. "She silenced her own mind rather than help me."

"Tessa was brave. Tammy got that from her," Jesse said.

Ivy shook her head vehemently, denial running strong through her veins. "This isn't possible. JD and Jeffrey destroyed your heart. I was there, I saw it turn to dust."

"As you know Ivy, we are tied to each other in blood. As long as you exist, I exist, and I had fetters to my heart, and to my beloved mirror that saw everything. I believe you knew this. It's twice now that you brought me back. I hope this time you will stand by my side and help me destroy my sons. My side is the side of the just. I was manipulated into conceiving them by a demon. They are evil and need to perish. I know you feel the same. It's why you subconsciously helped me again. We are linked, you and I. We are sisters. Stand with me."

"No way," Ivy said. "I'm not excusing JD's behavior, but you're way worse because you think you're righteous and there's nothing worse than a righteous witch."

"By my side or as my enemy, my resolve will come to pass. Just as I predicted Tammy's murder, I have predicted the outcome of today and I shall stand victorious." Her eyes narrowed in on JD and Jeffrey in the cage. "I will end what I begot today."

She put her hands through the bars. "Japhet Dean hold my hands."

JD's body twitched like an electric current ran through it. His open hands gravitated toward Deborah.

"What are you doing?! Jeffrey said. He went to stop him, but he was no match for JD's strength.

"I can't help it," he said. "She's compelling me somehow."

Tessa's grin spread. "I took Titan into myself for a purpose, now it is I who control Japhet Dean and Jeffrey."

"What?! It's Uriah who controls who's in the cage not Titan," Ivy said.

"It's like Titan said, Uriah and he will always be linked."

"Oh fudge," Ivy grumbled.

"I can fix this one," Weston said, yanking his gun from Uriah's coat. "Lower your hands lady, whoever the hell you are."

She turned to Weston and grinned, looking oddly a lot like Tammy. "Here's another gift from Uriah Leeds. Wes, turn the gun on yourself and fire."

Without delay Weston pointed the gun at his head. "No!" Pearl shouted, pushing his arm as the gun went off. Weston hit the ground like a ton of bricks.

Issac ran to help. He took off his coat to use as a tourniquet. Pearl had managed to redirect the bullet, but it pierced his shoulder going through his bullet proof vest due to the close range it was fired from. "It's a good thing you had this bullet proof vest on, or you'd be dead."

"So much for bullet proof," Wes huffed. "I shot myself. I'm the worst cop ever." Aching, he glanced to Pearl who was at his side, "This does not leave this room."

"I will refrain from commenting until I know you're going to be okay," Pearl said, her voice laced with anxiety. "Well?" she asked, her eyes burning holes in Issac.

"He's going to be alright, but we need to get him to a hospital."

"No one is going anywhere," Deborah said. "I want you to watch as I set the world right. I want you to remember today and that it was Deborah Smith Leeds who saved Pleasant Mills from The Leeds Devil."

A bang overhead boomed as the trapdoor to the basement slammed shut. Deborah returned her attention to JD. He held both of her hands through the bars now.

"You can't end me mother. You of all people should know that."

"I can't, but *you* can."

He smirked knowingly. "Well mother, I suppose it's come to this."

"It's overdue my son. I will destroy you, then your brother."

JD's eyes darted to Jeffrey, his body stiffening. "He's done nothing.

He's never killed anyone. Leave him and his family alone."

"I can't do that Japhet Dean, there's no assurance he won't. He is evil and all evil must be cleansed from this world. He, along with his family, will join you in oblivion."

The muscle in JD's jaw jumped. "I will not let you hurt him or his family."

"It is my will that will win today, not yours."

He set his jaw.

"Japhet Dean, I order you to curse yourself. A curse of expulsion. A curse to exile. A curse to oblivion. A curse on you."

Air sucked from the room, filling the cage with a howling wind. It whipped around tousling their hair. Stevie stepped back.

"Uriah," Jeffrey said urgently, "Try to counter the curse, the cage should still answer to you."

"Yes of course," Uriah said, getting to his feet. "He reached his hand through the bars gripping his father's arm, not sure if that would strengthen his will. "JD, do not curse yourself."

"It's too late Uriah, I'm sorry. This is goodbye. I'm sorry for the pain I've caused you. The pain I've caused everyone," he said, his eyes darting around the room to Jesse, to Sammy, to Pearl. Pearl bowed her head, unsure of what she was feeling. JD glanced at Jeffrey. "I want to say so much but can say nothing."

"It can't be," Ivy mumbled to herself. "Uriah," she said, squeezing his free hand, "say it again and again, until it works!"

"JD, do not curse yourself. Do not listen to this woman. She holds no control over you or your will. You answer to me. To your son," Uriah said, tears glazing his eyes. Uriah had spent so many years of his life grateful to his guardian angel who had saved Lilly and restored his health and so many years hating his father for killing Lilly. To know this was the end to their story filled him with a sadness beyond words. After losing Aiden, he didn't think he could take this blow. Something in him needed his father and knew he always would.

"A curse to eternal darkness. A curse to nothingness," Deborah went on.

The wind in the room continued to build momentum like a storm on the open sea. Uriah stumbled back.

"STOP!" Ivy shouted from the top of her lungs. She had wanted to destroy JD herself for a long time, but the idea of him actually being gone frightened her as if in destroying him a piece of her would also be lost.

"JD," Ivy said, her voice cracking, "there has to be something you can do to stop this."

"Ms. Teller is right mother, there is something I can do. I may not be able to stop the curse you set in motion, but I can take you with me." He dug his claw-like nails into her hands. She flinched in pain. "You're on this plane mother because you're tethered to this body. Without this body, you don't exist. And I fully plan on taking you with me into obscurity where you will not be able to hurt the people I love."

"Release my hands," Deborah said.

"No mother," JD said, sinking his claws in deeper, before her will could make him let her go. "I came into this world with you, and I will leave it with you."

JD glanced to Ivy, tears in his eyes. Ivy saw the same soulful brown eyes the Midwife had first fallen in love with. She saw the good in him, the part of him that was an angel. "*When a dandelion dies it leaves you a wish. I know when you make yours Ms. Teller, it's going to be something beautiful.*"

JD and Deborah burst into flames.

"NO!" Ivy screamed. Sammy, Uriah, and Jesse held her back, afraid of what she would do. "Do something!" she shouted at Jeffrey. "You can't let it end like this for him, he deserves better. He deserves a chance to be what he wants to be."

Stevie took ahold of Jeffrey's arm and pulled him away, the heat becoming intolerable. "Mr. Lopez, there's nothing you can do," he said in a soft voice. "They're not in their bodies anymore. They're gone. I'm sorry."

Jeffrey's hand went to his cheek, he was crying. "He was my brother."

Pearl watched JD burn. "Do something," she whispered under her breath as his skin flaked away to ash.

Ivy also whispered under her breath.

An explosion of light and force pushed everyone back. They fought to their feet, disoriented as their ears rang. JD and Deborah were gone, in their place were two piles of ashes.

Jesse stared at JD's ashes. His eyes wide in disbelief. "I can't believe he's really gone."

Ivy, on her knees, sobbed into her hands as so many emotions ravaged her body. Uriah held her.

"It's over," Sammy said, hugging Ivy from behind. Sammy held back his good riddance speech for Ivy and his father's sake, and Wes did too.

Issac took Stevie's hand through the bars and kissed them. "How are we going to get you out of here?"

Uriah released Ivy, handing her off to Sammy. "I know how to open the door. I know everything Titan knew. It's Benny's blood. His blood's the key. Place it on any of the bars and you'll be able to bend them."

"That makes sense," Cam said. "When I was in my father's body, I noticed a cut on my finger that was bleeding."

"Big Benny's blood's the door to the cage and Uriah's blood controlled it," Sammy said.

"Yeah, that's my father's twisted idea of romance," Stevie said, disgusted.

"Speaking of blood, can we get me to the hospital before I bleed out," Weston grumbled.

With the inside of his elbow, Jeffrey dried his tears. He went over to Benny's corpse, letting Benny's blood paint his fingertips red before going over to the bars.

The rain had stopped. The smell of damp earth clung to the air, like it was a spring day, and from all of the rain would come flowers, not death. The clouds had parted from the moon, leaving Benny's yard in streamers of silver and dark blue.

Sammy and Ivy carried Anita's body. Ivy was amazed by how light she was. Sammy had been strong this entire time but now that it was over, Ivy could tell the weight of what he'd done was sinking in. They placed Anita in the front passenger seat like she was alive. Sammy buckled her seat belt; his eyes were like frost on a frozen lake.

Ivy took his hand. "What you did in there was brave."

He enveloped her in a hug. "I ended a curse," he said, speaking into Ivy's hair, "but killing one's own family member comes with a price."

She glanced up at him, knowing she was making one of her funny faces. "What price?"

"I don't know, but it's nothing we can't handle together."

He leaned into her, pressing a kiss to her lips. They never felt so soft. "I'm nothing without you Ivy Teller."

Pearl and Jesse helped get Wes into Mary's old station wagon, her eyes darting from Wes complaining to Jeffrey who hurried to the back of Benny's SUV with Cam, Stevie, and Issac.

King Charles trotted up to Stevie. He picked him up, bringing him to his face for a kiss. "I was hoping to get a chance to say goodbye to you."

"Goodbye?" Issac said.

"I have a promise to keep to my brother."

"No Stevie," Cam said. "I can't have you do that for me. I'll do it. I just hope Mr. Lopez can still help Elsa."

Cam opened the trunk to his father's SUV. Stevie sucked air seeing Elsa like that. Her pale skin appeared hard and cold like stone. He shielded King Charles's view; so he didn't have to see her like that. "I can't believe our father did that to her."

"Can you, Mr. Lopez? Can you still help her?" Cam asked, his body a bundle of nerves.

Jeffrey nodded. He knew he could, just like he knew he could've brought Big Benny back as Titan had ordered.

"Good," Cam said overcome with emotion, trying not to cry. "Use me to bring her back."

"No," Stevie said. "This was our agreement. I'm glad you didn't die Cam, very glad. Freaking ecstatic. I got to say my goodbyes to Issac and King. You should get to see Elsa again and see your sister again. We just have to say goodbye to each other now."

Issac's body pulsated with fear at the thought of losing Stevie. "I could never say goodbye to you," he said, taking Stevie's hand.

"Or I could . . ," Jeffrey pondered, the cloaked man's words ringing in his ears, the words of his father: '*She would have been yours . . . Next time, don't be afraid to use the gifts Ezekiel has given you. Never before has a demon possessed such power. Do not waste your gifts my son.*' He wondered if that meant Elsa would be indebted to him like Jesse was to JD. That wouldn't be so bad, he'd never ask anything of her. He couldn't see ending Stevie's or Cam's life even to save Elsa, there had been enough death today. He would do it this new way and deal with the consequences if and when they came

"Could what Dad?" Sammy asked, coming to stand next to his father with Ivy. Sammy diverted his eyes to the ground; he couldn't bear the sight of Elsa like that. Ivy, on the other hand, stared at her friend, not able to blink or turn away.

"I'm gonna try something else, and hopefully no one dies."

He looked to Ivy as if for approval. "Yeah, try it. We'll deal with the consequences when they come," she said as if she had just read his thoughts.

Touching Elsa's arm, Jeffrey closed his eyes. At first all he saw was darkness, then bright lights like the twinkling of fireflies, bled from the edges of his vision. The lights came into focus, they were souls, all he had to do was find Elsa. He called out to her with his mind, focusing on the girl he'd known. He saw her; he reached his hand out for hers, she took it. A coldness, so bitter cold it burned, traveled up Jeffrey's hand, but he didn't let Elsa go. "Go home," he whispered to her.

Elsa came to life, her blue eyes flashing open as she gasped for breath. Seeing Cam, she pushed him away from her. He hugged her close to his chest. "It's me. It's the real me. You're okay."

CHAPTER FORTY-FIVE
Dreams Do Come True

The crowds came out for the grand reopening of Pleasant Mills Church. Ivy was pretty sure the entire town was there. Standing at the threshold, a chill like a winter breeze ran down her spine covering her in gooseflesh. The new church looked exactly like the old one that had burned down. There had been no modifications to the original design, not one improvement, not one architectural festoon—not one change. It was if all the horrible things that happened there never occurred. Like the new building washed away the old memories and with it the old stains. She knew last summer was not the first time Pleasant Mills Church had burned and she had an awful feeling it wouldn't be the last.

"Admit it's creepy how the church looks exactly the same," Ivy said to Sammy as he ushered her in.

He gave her his classic side grin. "I'll give you this Teller, it's a little strange. You think they would've made the place bigger, but my dad said something about the township dictating they use the original foundation."

"Ah," Ivy said, "so, it's the town's fault there's no seating."

"I saved you, Grams, and Danny, seats with us up front."

Ivy took her seat with the Lopez clan next to Sammy taking Anita's old spot and signaled for Grams and Danny to follow. Never before had he asked her to sit with him at church. The wasps in her stomach danced in harmony until they transformed back into butterflies. The bitter sting was gone, in its place was trust. The past was in the past and they weren't going to let it repeat itself.

Ivy looked around the small church at the faces she had come to know. Somehow, they had made it through. Behind her sat the Handovers. Mike next to Joe and Jesse next to Tammy, who was looking a lot more like her old self these days. Red highlights and a perm, in addition to a stylish wardrobe, had turned Rosa's girl-next-door look into a head turner. She was currently known to her parents as Mike's good friend. In time, Tammy hoped to tell them the truth. Zac and Mona were there too. Ivy noticed they held hands. With Elsa and her mother, sat Cam, Stevie, and Issac. King Charles waited outside, but he didn't mind. There were rumors Cam was already shopping around for an engagement ring but promised Issac not to propose until he popped the big question to Stevie on their vacation. Pearl and Weston stood in the back as sentinels and members, Pearl in her black suit and Weston in his iconic blue uniform.

Trudy sat next to Lindsey and Jeffrey, the twins sat on their lap, while Hugo napped in his car seat. Tears welled in Trudy's eyes as Uriah made it to the pulpit. Not everyone had survived. Anita had passed and Aiden. Uriah and Trudy's beloved son had been murdered and his killer, Big Benny, had also died along with Titan Leeds, for good this time, they hoped, despite Titan and Deborah attesting Titan would always be linked to Uriah. Ivy felt guilty that she was so happy when Uriah and Trudy were so sad. Baby Lilly would be there in a few months, and she hoped she could help them find happiness again.

And then there was Japhet Dean Leeds, after centuries of living as the Leeds Devil, finding local fame as the notorious Jersey Devil, JD too had perished.

After church, they congregated at the back of the cemetery. The stones here were old and dated back to the founders of the town. You could hear the sound of the river as it snaked its way over rocks and fallen trees disappearing into the forest. It was here that Uriah had a headstone placed for his father that simply read: JD.

"I know most of you know JD as a plight, but under it all he had a good heart and in the end he saved us all. And I will miss him," Uriah said.

"I will too," Jeffrey said unabashed.

"I won't," Sammy whispered to Ivy, making sure his father couldn't hear him.

Ivy's stomach did a somersault. She had wanted to make him pay so badly for all the rotten things he had put Sammy and her through, but yet there was a part of her that *would* miss him. Ivy glanced to her friends. She was sure most of them shared Sammy's sentiment. She knew Zac did, how couldn't he. JD had murdered him after all. She wondered if Jesse would miss him. He was hard to read as always. He held Tammy's hand staring at the headstone as if it said more than just JD.

Ivy noticed something peculiar. Pearl seemed off; tears stood in her eyes, on the brink of spilling over. Ivy thought she'd be happy the town's problems were over. Weston looked happy enough, well for Weston. Ivy watched Pearl deliberately place her hand over her stomach. It happened so fast she didn't have a chance to call Sammy's attention to it. Maybe she was seeing things, or maybe she wasn't.

Weston wrapped his arm around Pearl. "Come on Pearl, we don't want to miss snacks at Jeff's house. Lindsey said they're going to have those little hotdogs."

Just like that, one by one, everyone left. It was just her and Sammy standing in front of JD's headstone—a marker with no body. A memorial to commemorate a monster she brought into the world when she carelessly asked heaven and hell for help.

"You ready?" Sammy asked, with a squeeze to her hand, happy to see she was again wearing the bracelet he'd gotten her for her birthday and the matching heart earrings.

The wind picked up, the sound of branches scraping together like the legs of a cricket against tin. Ivy looked into the forest behind the river. She thought she heard something more, a sound that made her think of spring.

"Yeah, let's go Sammy."

With one last look into the dark woods that had first served as a warning to her when she came to Pleasant Mills, she followed Sammy back to the church.

PLEASANT MILLS CEMETERY: JAPHET DEAN LEEDS'S HEADSTONE

Leaves crunched under foot while the rustling of the thicket against clothing sounded over the babbling river. From the woods, stepped out two men. The one man put his cigarette out on top of the headstone. "Another son, what a pleasant thing."

The other man glanced in the direction Ivy and Sammy had gone. "There's a price she has to pay for summoning an angel even if the summons was to save my only son." Ezekiel turned to JD. "Her cost is your choice Japhet Dean," he said, brushing JD's dark hair away from his face. He smiled, seeing his likeness in his son. "What shall it be?"

A smirk tugged on the corners of JD's lips until he wore a devilish grin. He pulled out the dried dandelion the Midwife had given him long ago, her words buzzing through his head. *'When a dandelion dies it leaves you a wish. Don't be afraid to make yours'.* He looked to his father, each of Ezekiel's many eyes on his wings twinkling with mischief. "It appears dreams are not dead. Just as my old friend, Ben, punished Ivy by taking away her memories, I shall punish her by giving them back to her. I wish for Ivy to remember everything."

The End . . .

Want more?

CHECK OUT MY OTHER BOOKS!

Thanks for reading!

If this book helped you escape, if only for a moment, please consider taking the time to leave a review or star rating on Amazon or whatever platform you use. It would warm the cockles of my little, black heart to hear from you.

Looking for something else to read? Don't forget to check out my other books on Amazon.

Follow me on social media (I'm on all platforms under Holly Knightley). Sign up for my newsletter for the latest news, glimpse into my wacky process, and occasional freebie. Stay spooky and happy reading!

9 781958 761588